The Tom Swift Omnibus #7

The Tom Swift Omnibus #7
by Victor Appleton

Tom Swift and His Big Tunnel
(Or the Hidden City of the Andes)

Tom Swift in the Land of Wonders
(Or the Underground Search for the Idol of Gold)

Tom Swift and His War Tank
(Or Doing His Bit for Uncle Sam)

TOM SWIFT AND HIS BIG TUNNEL
Or The Hidden City of the Andes

TABLE OF CONTENTS:

AN APPEAL FOR AID

Tom Swift, seated in his laboratory engaged in trying to solve a puzzling question that had arisen over one of his inventions, was startled by a loud knock on the door. So emphatic, in fact, was the summons that the door trembled, and Tom started to his feet in some alarm.

"Hello there!" he cried. "Don't break the door, Koku!" and then he laughed. "No one but my giant would knock like that," he said to himself. "He never does seem able to do things gently. But I wonder why he is knocking. I told him to get the engine out of the airship, and Eradicate said he'd be around to answer the telephone and bell. I wonder if anything has happened?"

Tom shoved back his chair, pushed aside the mass of papers over which he had been puzzling, and strode to the door. Flinging it open he confronted a veritable giant of a man, nearly eight feet tall, and big in proportion. The giant, Koku, for that was his name, smiled in a good-natured way, reminding one of an overgrown boy.

"Master hear my knock?" the giant asked cheerfully.

"Hear you, Koku? Say, I couldn't hear anything else!" exclaimed Tom. "Did you think you had to arouse the whole neighborhood just to let me know you were at the door? Jove! I thought you'd have it off the hinges."

"If me break, me fix," said Koku, who, from his appearance and from his imperfect command of English, was evidently a foreigner.

"Yes, I know you can fix lots of things, Koku," Tom went on, kindly enough. "But you musn't forget what enormous strength you have. That's the reason I sent you to take the engine out of the airship. You can lift it without using the chain hoist, and I can't get the chain hoist fast unless I remove all the superstructure. I don't want to do that. Did you get the engine out?"

"Not quite. Almost, Master."

"Then why are you here? Has anything gone wrong?"

"No, everything all right, Master. But man come to machine shop and say he must have talk with you. I no let him come past the gate, but I say I come and call you."

"That's right, Koku. Don't let any strangers past the gate. But why didn't Eradicate come and call me. He isn't doing anything, is he? Unless, indeed, he has gone to feed his mule, Boomerang."

"Eradicate, he come to call you, but that black man no good!" and Koku chuckled so heartily that he shook the floor of the office.

"What's the matter with Eradicate?" asked Tom, somewhat anxiously. "I hope you and he haven't had another row?" Eradicate had served Tom and his father long before Koku, the giant, had been brought back from one of the young inventor's many strange trips, and ever since then there had been a jealous rivalry between the twain as to who should best serve Tom.

"No trouble, Master," said Koku. "Eradicate he start to come and tell you strange man want to have talk, but Eradicate he no come fast enough. So I pick him up, and I set him down by gate to stand on guard, and I come to tell you. Koku come quick!"

"Oh, I knew it must be something like that!" exclaimed Tom in some vexation. "Now I'll have Eradicate complaining to me that you mauled him. Picked him up and set him down again;

"Sure. One hand!" boasted the giant. "Eradicate him not be heavy. More as a sack of flour now."

"No, poor Eradicate is getting pretty old and thin," commented Tom. "He can't move very quickly. But you should have let him come, Koku. It makes him feel badly when he thinks he can't be of service to me any more."

"Man say he in hurry." The giant spoke softly, as though he felt the gentle rebuke Tom administered. "Koku run quick tell you—bang on door."

"Yes, you banged all right, Koku. Well, it can't be helped, I reckon. Where is this strange man? Who is he? Did you ever see him before?"

"Me no can tell, Master. Not sure. But him now be at the outer gate. Eradicate watch."

"All right. I'll go and see who it is. I don't want any strangers poking around here, especially With the plans of my new gyroscope lying in plain view."

Before he left the laboratory Tom swept into a desk drawer the mass of papers and blue prints, and locked the receptacle.

"No use taking any chances," he remarked. "I've had too much trouble with people trying to get inside information about dad's and my patents. Now, Koku, I'll go and see this man."

The buildings composing the plant of Tom Swift and his father at Shopton were enclosed by a high, board fence, and at one of the entrances was a sort of gate-house, where some one was always on guard. Only those who could give a good account of themselves, workmen in the plant, or those known to the sentinel were admitted.

It happened that the colored man, Eradicate, was on guard at the gates this day when the stranger asked to see Tom. Koku, working on the airship engine not far away, saw the stranger. Hearing the man say he was in a hurry and noting the slow progress of the aged Eradicate, who was troubled with rheumatism, the giant took matters into his own hands.

Tom Swift entered the gate-house and saw, seated in a chair, a man who was impatiently tapping the floor with his thick-soled shoe.

"Looks like a detective or a policeman in disguise," thought Tom, for, almost invariably, members of this profession wear very thick-soled shoes. Opposite the stranger sat Eradicate, a much-injured look on his honest, black face.

"Oh, Massa Tom!" exclaimed Eradicate, as soon as the young inventor entered. "Dat Koku he—he—he done gone and cotch me by de collar ob mah coat, an' den he lif' me up, an' he sot me down so hard—so hard—dat he jar loose all mah back teef!" and Eradicate opened his mouth wide to display his gleaming ivories.

"Eradicate, he no can come quick. He walk like so fashion!" and Koku, who had followed the young inventor, imitated the limping gait of the colored man with such a queer effect that Tom could not help laughing, and the stranger smiled.

"Ef I gits holt on yo'—ef I does, yo' great, big, overgrown lummox, Ah'll—Ah'll—" began the colored man, stammeringly.

"There. That will do now!" interrupted Tom. "Don't quarrel in here. Koku, get back to that engine and lift out the motor. Eradicate, didn't father tell you to whitewash the chicken coops today?"

"Dat's what he done, Massa Tom.

"Well, go and see about that. I'll stay here for a while, and when I leave I'll call one of you, or some one else, to be on guard. Skip now!"

Having thus disposed of the warring factions, Tom turned to the stranger and after apologizing for the little interruption, asked:

"You wished to see me?"

"If you're Tom Swift; yes."

"Well, I'm Tom Swift," and the young owner of the name smiled.

"I hope you will pardon a stranger for calling on you," resumed the man, "but I'm in a lot of trouble, and I think you are the only one who can help me out."

"What sort of trouble?" Tom inquired.

"Contracting trouble—tunnel blasting, to be exact. But if you have a few minutes to spare perhaps you will listen to my story. You will then be better able to understand my difficulty."

Tom Swift considered a moment. He was used to having appeals for help made to him, and usually they were of a begging nature. He was often asked for money to help some struggling inventor complete his machine.

In many cases the machines would have been of absolutely no use if perfected. In other cases the inventions were of the utterly hopeless class, incapable of perfection, like some perpetual motion apparatus. In these cases Tom turned a deaf ear, though if the inventor were in want our hero relieved him.

But this case did not seem to be like anything Tom had ever met with before.

"Contracting trouble—blasting," repeated the youth, as he mused over what he had heard.

"That's it," the man went on. "Permit me to introduce myself" and he held out a card, on which was the name

Mr. Job Titus

Down in the lower left-hand corner was a line:

"Titus Brothers, Contractors."

"I am glad to meet you, "Mr. Titus," Tom said warmly, offering his hand. "I don't know anything about the contracting business, but if you do blasting I suppose you use explosives, and I know a little about them."

"So I have heard, and that's why I came to you," the contractor went on. "Now if you'll give me a few minutes of your time—"

"You had better come up to the house," interrupted Tom. "We can talk more quietly there."

Calling a young fellow who was at work near by to occupy the gate-house, Tom led Mr. Titus toward the Swift homestead, and, a little later, ushered him into the library.

"Now I'll listen to you," the youth said, "though I can't promise to aid you."

"I realize that," returned Mr. Titus. "This is a sort of last chance I'm taking. My brother and I have heard a lot about you, and when he wrote to me that he was unable to proceed with his contract of tunneling the Andes Mountains for the Peruvian government, I made up my mind you were the one who could help us if you would."

"Tunneling the Andes Mountains!" exclaimed Tom.

"Yes. The firm represented by my brother and myself have a contract to build a railroad for the Peruvian government. At a point some distance back in the district east of Lima, Peru, we are making a tunnel under the mountain. That is, we have it started, but now we can't advance any further."

"Why not?"

"Because of the peculiar character of the rock, which seems to defy the strongest explosive we can get. Now I understand you used a powder in your giant cannon that—"

Mr. Titus paused in his explanation, for at that moment there arose such a clatter out on the front piazza as effectually to drown conversation. There was a noise of the hoofs of a horse, the fall of a heavy body, a tattoo on the porch floor and then came an excited shout:

"Whoa there! Whoa! Stop! Look out where you're kicking! Bless my saddle blanket! Ouch! There I go!"

EXPLANATIONS

"What in the world is that?" cried Mr. Job Titus, in alarm.

Tom Swift did not answer. Instead he jumped up from his chair and ran toward the front door. Mr. Titus followed. They both saw a strange sight.

Standing on the front porch, which he seemed to occupy completely, was a large horse, with a saddle twisted underneath him. The animal was looking about him as calmly as though he always made it a practice to come up on the front piazza when stopping at a house.

Off to one side, with a crushed hat on the back of his head, with a coat split up the back, with a broken riding crop in one hand and a handkerchief in the other, sat a dignified, elderly gentleman.

That is, he would have been dignified had it not been for his position and condition. No gentleman can look dignified with a split coat and a crushed hat on, sitting under the nose of a horse on a front piazza, with his raiment otherwise much disheveled, while he wipes his scratched and bleeding face with a handkerchief.

"Bless my—bless my—" began the elderly gentleman, and he seemed at a loss what particular portion of his anatomy or that of the horse, to bless, or what portion of the universe to appeal to, for he ended up with: "Bless everything, Tom Swift!"

"I heartily agree with you, Mr. Damon!" cried Tom. "But what in the world happened?"

"That!" exclaimed Mr. Damon, pointing with his broken crop at the horse on the piazza. "I was riding him when he ran away—just as my motorcycle tried to climb a tree. No more horses for me! I'll stick to airships," and slamming his riding crop down on the porch floor with such force that the horse started back, Mr. Damon arose, painfully enough if the contortions on his face and his grunts of pain went for anything.

"Let me help you!" begged Tom, striding forward. "Mr. Titus, perhaps you will kindly lead the horse down off the piazza?"

"Certainly!" answered the tunnel contractor. "Whoa now!" he called soothingly, as the steed evinced a disposition to sit down on the side railing. "Steady now!"

The horse finally allowed himself to be led down the broad front steps, sadly marking them, as well as the floor of the piazza, with his sharp shoes.

"Ouch! Oh, my back!" exclaimed Mr. Damon, as Tom helped him to stand up.

"Is it hurt?" asked Tom, anxiously.

"No, I've just got what old-fashioned folks call a 'crick' in it," explained the elderly horseman. "But it feels more like a river than a 'crick.' I'll be all right presently."

"How did it happen?" asked Tom, as he led his guest toward the hall. Meanwhile Mr. Titus, wondering what it was all about, had tied the horse to a post out near the street curb, and had re-entered the library.

"I was riding over to see you, Tom, to ask you if you wouldn't go to South America with me," began Mr. Damon, rubbing his leg tenderly.

"South America?" cried Tom, with a sudden look at Mr. Titus.

"Yes, South America. Why, there isn't anything strange in that, is there? You've been to wilder countries, and farther away than that."

"Yes, I know—it's just a coincidence. Go on."

"Let me get where I can sit down," begged Mr. Damon. "I think that crick in my back is running down into my legs, Tom. I feel a bit weak. Let me sit down, and get me a glass of water. I shall be all right presently."

Between them Tom and Mr. Titus assisted the horseman into an easy chair, and there, under the influence of a cup of hot tea, which Mrs. Baggert, the housekeeper, insisted on making for him, he said he felt much better, and would explain the reason for his call which had culminated in such a sensational manner.

And while Mr. Damon is preparing his explanation I will take just a few moments to acquaint my new readers with some facts about Tom Swift, and the previous volumes of this series in which he has played such prominent parts.

Tom Swift was the son of an inventor, and not only inherited his father's talents, but had greatly added to them, so that now Tom had a wonderful reputation.

Mr. Swift was a widower, and he and Tom lived in a big house in Shopton, New York State, with Mrs. Baggert for a housekeeper. About the house, from time to time, shops and laboratories had been erected, until now there was a large and valuable establishment belonging to Tom and his father.

The first volume of this series is entitled, "Tom Swift and His Motor Cycle." It was through a motor cycle that Tom became acquainted with Mr. Wakefield Damon, who lived in a neighboring town. Mr. Damon had bought the motor cycle for himself, but, as he said, one day in riding it the machine tried to climb a tree near the Swift house.

The young inventor (for even then he was working on several patents) ministered to Mr. Damon, who, disgusted with the motor cycle, and wishing to reward Tom, let the young fellow have the machine.

Tom's career began from that hour. For he learned to ride the motor cycle, after making some improvements in it, and from then on the youth had led a busy life. Soon afterward he secured a motor boat and from that it was but a step to an airship.

The medium of the air having been conquered, Tom again turned his attention to the water, or rather, under the water, and he and his father made a submarine. Then he built an electric runabout, the speediest car on the road.

It was when Ton Swift had occasion to send his wireless message from a lonely island where he had been shipwrecked that he was able to do Mr. and

Mrs. Nestor a valuable service, and this increased the regard which Miss Mary Nestor felt for the young inventor, a regard that bid fair, some day, to ripen into something stronger.

Tom Swift might have made a fortune when he set out to discover the secret of the diamond makers. But Fate intervened, and soon after that quest he went to the caves of ice, where he and his friends met with disaster. In his sky racer Tom broke all records for speed, and when he went to Africa to rescue a missionary, had it not been for his electric rifle the tide of battle would have gone against him and his party.

Marvelous, indeed, were the adventures underground, which came to Tom when he went to look for the city of gold, but the treasure there was not more valuable than the platinum which Tom sought in dreary Siberia by means of his air glider.

Tom thought his end had come when he fell into captivity among the giants; but even that turned out well, and he brought two of the giants away with him. Koku, one of the two giants, became devotedly attached to the lad, much to the disgust of Eradicate Sampson, the old negro who had worked for the Swifts for a generation, and who, with his mule Boomerang, "eradicated" from the place as much dirt as possible.

With his wizard camera Tom did much to advance the cause of science. His great searchlight was of great help to the United States government in putting a stop to the Canadian smugglers, while his giant cannon was a distinct advance in ordnance, not excepting the great German guns used in the European war.

When Tom perfected his photo telephone the last objection to rendering telephonic conversation admissible evidence in a law court was done away with, for by this invention a person was able to see, as well as to hear, over the telephone wire. One practically stood face to face with the person, miles away, to whom one was talking.

The volume immediately preceding this present one is called: "Tom Swift and His Aerial Warship." The young inventor perfected a marvelous aircraft that was the naval terror of the seas, and many governments, recognizing what an important part aircraft were going to play in all future conflicts, were anxious to secure Tom's machine. But he was true to his own country, though his rivals were nearly successful in their plots against him.

The Mars, which was the name of Tom's latest craft, proved to be a great success, and the United States government purchased it. It was not long after the completion of this transaction that the events narrated in the first chapter of this book took place.

Mr. Damon and Tom had been firm friends ever since the episode of the motor cycle, and the eccentric gentleman (who blessed so many things) often went with Tom on his trips. Besides Mary Nestor, Tom had other friends. The one, after Miss Nestor, for whom he cared most (if we except Mr. Damon) was Ned Newton, who was employed in a Shopton bank. Ned also had often gone with Tom, though lately, having a better position, he had less time to spare.

"Well, do you feel better, Mr. Damon?" asked Tom, after a bit.

"Yes, very much, thank you. Bless my pen wiper! but I thought I was done for when I saw my horse bolt for your front stoop. He rushed up it, fell down, but, fortunately, I managed to get out of his way, though the saddle girth slipped. And all I could think of was that my wife would say: 'I told you so!' for she warned me not to ride this animal.

"But he never ran away with me before, and I was in a hurry to get over to see you, Tom. Now then, let's get down to business. Will you go to South America with me?"

"Whereabout in South America are you going, Mr. Damon, and why?" Tom asked.

"To Peru, Tom."

"What a coincidence!" exclaimed Mr. Titus.

"I beg your pardon?" said Mr. Damon, interrogatively.

"I said what a coincidence. I am going there myself."

"Excuse me," interposed Tom, "I don't believe, in the excitement of the moment, I introduced you gentlemen. Allow me—Mr. Damon—Mr. Titus."

The presentation over, Mr. Damon went on:

"You see, Tom, I have lately invested considerable money in a wholesale drug concern. We deal largely in Peruvian remedies, principally the bark of the cinchona tree, from which quinine is made. Of late there has been some trouble over our concession from the Peruvian government, and the company has decided to send me down there to investigate.

"Of course, as soon as I made up my mind to go I thought of you. So I came over to see if you would not accompany me. All went well until I reached your front gate. Then my horse became frightened by a yellow toy balloon some boy was blowing up in the street and bolted with me. I suppose if it had been a red or green balloon the effect would have been the same. However, here I am, somewhat the worse for wear. Now Tom, what do you say? Will you go to South America—to Peru—with me, and help look up this Quinine business?"

Once more Mr. Titus and Tom looked at each other.

A FACE AT THE WINDOW

"What is the matter?" asked Mr. Damon, catching the glance between Tom and the contractor. "Is there anything wrong with South America—Peru? I know they have lots of revolutions in those countries, but I don't believe Peru is what they call a 'banana republic'; is it?"

"No," and Mr. Titus shook his head. "It isn't a question of revolutions."

"But it's something!" insisted Mr. Damon. "Bless my ink bottle! but it's something. As soon as I mention Peru, Tom, you and Mr. Titus eye each other as if I'd said something dreadful. Out with it! What is it?"

"It's just—just a coincidence," Tom said. "But go on, Mr. Damon. Finish what you have to say and then we'll explain."

"Well, I guess I've told you all you need to know for the present. I went into this wholesale drug concern, hoping to make some money, but now, on account of the trouble down in Peru, we stand to lose considerable unless I can get back the cinchona concession."

"What does that mean?" Tom asked.

"Well, it means that our concern secured from the Peruvian government the right to take this quinine-producing bark from the trees in a certain tropical section. But there has been a change in the government in the district where our men were working, and now the privilege, or concession, has been withdrawn. I'm going down to see if I can't get it back. And I want you to go with me."

"And I came here for very nearly the same thing," went on Mr. Titus. "That is where the coincidence comes in. It is strange that we should both appeal to Mr. Swift at the same time."

"Well, Tom's a valuable helper!" exclaimed Mr. Damon. "I know him of old, for I've been on many a trip with him."

"This is the first time I have had the pleasure of meeting him," resumed the tunnel contractor, "but I have heard of him. I did not ask him to go to South America for us. I only wanted to get some superior explosive for my brother, who is in charge of driving the railroad tunnel through a spur of the Andes. I look after matters up North here, but I may have to go to Peru myself.

"As I told Mr. Swift, I had read of his invention of the giant cannon and the special powder he used in it to send a projectile such a distance. The cannon is now mounted as one of the pieces of ordnance for the defense of the Panama Canal, is it not?" he asked Tom.

The young inventor nodded in assent.

"Having heard of you, and the wonderful explosive used in your big cannon," the contractor went on, "I wrote to my brother that I would try and get some for him.

"You see," he resumed, "this is the situation. Back in the Andes Mountains, a couple of hundred miles east of Lima, the government is building a short railroad line to connect two others. If this is done it will mean that the products of Peru—quinine bark, coffee, cocoa, sugar, rubber, incense and gold can more easily be transported. But to connect the two railroad lines a big tunnel must be constructed.

"My brother and I make a specialty of such work, and when we saw bids advertised for, our firm put in an estimate. There was some trouble with a rival firm, which also bid, but we secured the contract, and bound ourselves to have the tunnel finished within a certain time, or forfeit a large sum.

"That was over a year ago. Since then our men, aided by the native Indians of Peru, have been tunneling the mountain, until, about a month back, we struck a snag."

"What sort of snag?" Tom asked.

"A snag in the shape of extra hard rock," replied the tunnel contractor. "Briefly, Paleozoic rocks make up the eastern part of the Andean Mountains in Peru, while the western range is formed of Mesozoic beds, volcanic ashes and lava of comparatively recent date. Near the coast the lower hills are composed of crystalline rocks, syenite and granite, with, here and there, a strata of sandstone or limestone. These are, undoubtedly, relics of the lower Cretaceous age, and we, or rather, my brother, states that he has found them covered with marine Tertiary deposits.

"Now this Mesozoic band varies greatly. Porphyritic tuffs and massive limestone compose the western chain of the Andes above Lima, while in the Oroya Valley we find carbonaceous sandstones. Some of the tuffs may be of the Jurassic age, though the Cretaceous period is also largely represented.

"Now while these different masses of rock formation offer hard enough problems to the tunnel digger, still we are more or less prepared to meet them, and we figured on a certain percentage of them. Up to the present time we have met with just about what we expected, but what we did not expect was something we came upon when the tunnel had been driven three miles into the mountain."

"What did you find?" asked Tom, who knew enough about geology to understand the terms used. Mr. Damon did not, however, and when Mr. Titus rolled off some of the technical words, the drug investor softly murmured such expressions as

"Bless my thermometer! Bless my porous plaster!"

"We found," resumed Mr. Titus, "after we bad bored for a considerable distance into the mountain, a mass of volcanic rock which is so hard that our best diamond drills are dulled in a short time, and the explosives we use merely shatter the face of the cutting, and give us hardly any progress at all.

"It was after several trials, and when my brother found that he was making scarcely any progress, compared to the energy of his men and the blasting, that he wrote to me, explaining matters. I at once thought of you, Tom Swift, and your powerful explosive, for I had read about it.

"Now then, will you sell us some of your powder—explosive or whatever you call it—Mr. Swift, or tell us where we can get it? We need it soon, for we are losing valuable time."

Mr. Titus paused to draw on a piece of paper a rough map of Peru, and the district where the tunnel was being constructed. He showed where the two railroad lines were, and where the new route would bring them together, the tunnel eliminating a big grade up which it would have been impossible to haul trains of any weight.

"What do you say, Mr. Swift?" the contractor concluded. "Will you let us have some of your powder? Or, better still, will you come to Peru yourself? That would suit us immensely, for you could be right on the ground. And you could carry out your plan of going with your friend here," and Mr. Titus nodded toward Mr. Damon. "That is, if you were thinking of going."

"Well, I was thinking of it," Tom admitted. "Mr. Damon and I have been on so many trips together that it seems sort of natural for us to 'team it.' I have never been to Peru, and I should like to see the country. There is only one matter though, that bothers me."

"What is it?" asked Mr. Titus quickly. "If it is a question of money dismiss it from your mind. The Peruvian government is paying a large sum for this tunnel, and we stand to make considerable, even if we were the lowest bidders. We can afford to pay you well—that is, we shall be able to if we can complete the bore on time. That is what is bothering me now—the unexpected strata of hard rock we have met with, which seems impossible to blast. But I feel sure we can do it with the explosive used in your giant cannon."

"That is just the point!" Tom exclaimed. "I am not so sure my explosive would do."

"Why not?" the tunnel contractor asked. "It's powerful enough; isn't it?"

"Yes, it is powerful enough, but whether it will have the right effect on volcanic rock is hard to say. I should like to see a rock sample."

"I can telegraph to have some sent here to you," said Mr. Titus eagerly. "Meantime, here is a description of it. I can read you that"; and, taking a letter from his pocket, he read to Tom a geological description of the hard rock.

"Hum! Yes," mused Tom, as he listened. "It seems to be of the nature of obsidian."

"Bless my watch chain!" cried Mr. Damon. "What's that?"

"Obsidian is a volcanic rock—a sort of combination of glass and flint for hardness," Tom explained. "It is brittle, black in color, and the natives of the Admiralty Islands use it for tipping their spears with which they slay victims for their cannibalistic feasts."

"Bless my—bless my ear-drums!" gasped Mr. Damon. "Cannibals!"

"Obsidian was also used by the ancient Mexicans to make knives and daggers," Tom went on. "When Cortez conquered Mexico he found the priests cutting the hearts from their living victims with knives made from this volcanic glass-like rock, known as obsidian. It may be that your brother has met with a vein of that in the tunnel," Tom said to the contractor.

"Possibly," admitted Mr. Titus.

"In that case," Tom stated, "I may have to use a new kind of explosive. That used for my giant cannon would merely crumble the hard rock for a short distance."

"Then will you accept the contract, and help us out?" asked Mr. Titus eagerly. "We will pay you well. Will you come to Peru and look over the ground?"

"And kill two birds with one stone, and come with me also?" put in Mr. Damon.

Tom pondered for a moment. He was about to answer when the tunnel contractor, who was looking from the library window, suddenly jumped from his chair crying:

"There he is again! Once more dogging me!"

As he rushed from the room, Tom and Mr. Damon had a glimpse of a face at one of the low library windows—a face that had an evil look. It disappeared as Mr. Titus ran from the room.

Tom's Experiments

"Bless my looking glass, Tom, what does that mean?" exclaimed Mr. Damon. "That face!"

"I don't know," answered the young inventor. "But the sight of some one looking in here seemed to disturb Mr. Titus. We must follow him."

"Perhaps he saw your giant Koku looking in," suggested the odd, little man who blessed everything he could think of. "The sight of his face, to any one not knowing him, Tom, would be enough to cause fright."

"It wasn't Koku who looked in the window," said Tom, decidedly. "It was some stranger. Come on."

The young inventor and Mr. Damon hurried out after the tunnel contractor, who was running down the road that led in front of the Swift homestead.

"He's chasing some one, Tom," called Mr. Damon.

"Yes, I see he is. But who?"

"I can't see any one," reported Mr. Damon, who had run down to the gate, at which his horse was still standing. Mr. Damon had washed the dirt from his hands and face, and was wearing one of Mr. Swift's coats in place of his own split one.

Tom joined the eccentric man and together they looked down the road after the running Mr. Titus. They were in half a mind to join him, when they saw him pull up short, raise his hands as though he had given over the pursuit, and turn back.

"I guess he got away, whoever he was," remarked Tom. "We'll walk down and meet Mr. Titus, and ask him what it all means."

Shortly afterward they came up to the contractor, who was breathing heavily after his run, for he was evidently not used to such exercise.

"I beg your pardon, Tom Swift, for leaving you and Mr. Damon in such a fashion," said Mr. Titus, "but I had to act quickly or lose the chance of catching that rascal. As it was, he got away, but I think I gave him a scare, and h~e knows that I saw him. It will make him more cautious in the future."

"Who was it?" asked Tom.

"Well, I didn't have as close a look as I could have wished for," the contractor said, as he walked back toward the house with Tom and Mr. Damon, "but I'm pretty sure the face that peered in at us through the library window was that of Isaac Waddington."

"And who is he, if it isn't asking information that ought not be given out?" inquired Mr. Damon.

"Oh, no, certainly. I can tell you," said the contractor. "Only perhaps we had better wait until we get back to the house.

"Since one of their men was seen lurking around here there may be others," went on Mr. Titus, when the three were once more seated in the Swift library. "It is best to be on the safe side. The face I saw, I'm sure, was that of

Waddington, who is a tool of Blakeson & Grinder, rival tunnel contractors. They put in a bid on this Andes tunnel, but we were lower in our figures by several thousand dollars, and the contract was awarded to us.

"Blakeson & Grinder tried, by every means in their power, to get the job away from us. They even invoked the aid of some Peruvian revolutionists and politicians, but we held our ground and began the work. Since then they have had spies and emissaries on our trail, trying their best to make us fail in our work, so the Peruvian officials might abrogate the contract and give it to them.

"But, so far, we've managed to come out ahead. This Waddington is a sort of spy, and I've found him dodging me several times of late. I suppose he wants to find out my plans so as to be ready to jump in the breach in case we fail."

"Do you think your rivals had anything to do with the difficulties you are now meeting with in digging the tunnel?" asked Mr. Damon. Mr. Titus shook his head.

"The present difficulties are all of Nature's doing," he said. "It's just the abnormally hard rock that is bothering us. Only for that we'd be all right, though we might have petty difficulties because of the mean acts of Blakeson & Grinder. But I don't fear them."

"How do you think this Waddington, if it was he, knew you were coming here?" asked Tom.

"I can only guess. My brother and I have had some correspondence regarding you, Tom Swift. That is, I announced my intention of coming to see you, and my brother wrote me to use my discretion. I wrote back that I would consult you

"Our main office is in New York, where we employ a large clerical and expert force. There is nothing to prevent one of our stenographers, for instance, turning traitor and giving copies of the letters of my brother and myself to our rivals.

"Mind you, I don't say this was done, and I don't suspect any of our employees, but it would be an easy matter for any one to know my plans. I never thought of making a secret of them, or of my trip here. In some way Waddington found out about the last, and he must have followed me here. Then he sneaked up under the window, and tried to hear what we said."

"Do you think he did?" asked Tom.

"I wouldn't be surprised. We took no pains to lower our voices. But, after all, he hasn't learned much that he didn't know before, if he knew I was coming here. He didn't learn the secret of the explosive that must be used, and that is the vital thing. For I defy him, or any other contractor, to blast that hard rock with any known explosive. We've tried every kind on the market and we've failed. We'll have to depend on you, Tom Swift, to help us out with some of your giant cannon powder."

"And I'm not sure that will work," said the young inventor. "I think I'll have to experiment and make a new explosive, if I conclude to go to Peru."

"Oh, you'll go all right!" declared Mr. Titus with a smile. "I can see that you are eager for the adventures I am sure you'll find there, and, besides, your friend here, Mr. Damon, needs you."

"That's what I do, Tom!" exclaimed the odd man. "Bless my excursion ticket, but you must come!"

"I'll have to invent the new powder first," Tom said.

"That's what I like to hear!" exclaimed Mr. Titus. "It shows you are thinking of coming with us."

Tom only smiled.

"I am so anxious to get the proper explosive," went on Mr. Titus, "that I would even purchase it from our rivals, Blakeson & Grinder, if I thought they had it. But I'm sure they have not, though they may think they can get it.

"That may be the reason they are following me so closely. They may want to know just when we will fail, and have to give up the contract, and they may think they can step in and finish the work. But I don't believe, without your help, Tom Swift, that they can blast that hard rock, and—"

"Well, I'll say this," interrupted Tom, "first come, first served with me, other things being equal. You have applied to me and, like a lawyer, I won't go over to the other side now. I consider myself retained by your firm, Mr. Titus, to invent some sort of explosive, and if I am successful I shall expect to be paid."

"Oh, of course!" cried the contractor eagerly.

"Very good," Tom went on. "You needn't fear that I'll help the other fellows. Now to get down to business. I must see some samples of this rock in order to know what kind of explosive force is needed to rend it."

"I have some in New York," went on the contractor. "I'll have it sent to you at once. I would have brought it, only it is too heavy to carry easily, and I was not sure I could engage you."

"Did that fellow—Waddington, I believe you called him— get away from you?" asked Mr. Damon.

"Clean away," the contractor answered. "He was a better runner than I."

"It doesn't matter much," Tom said. "He didn't hear anything that would benefit him, and I'll give my men orders to be on the lookout for him. What sort of fellow is he, Mr. Titus?"

The contractor described the eavesdropper, and Mr. Damon exclaimed:

"Bless my turkey wish-bone! I'm sure I passed that chap when I was riding over to see you a while ago, Tom."

"You did?"

"Yes, on the highway. He inquired the way to your place. But there was nothing strange in that, since you employ a number of men, and I thought this one was coming to look for work. I can't say I liked his appearance, though."

"No, he isn't a very prepossessing individual," commented Mr. Titus. "Well, now what's the first thing to be done, Tom Swift?"

"Get me some samples of the rock, so I can begin my experiments."

"I'll do that. And now let us consider about going to Peru. For I'm sure you will be successful in your experiments, and will find for us just the powder or explosive we need."

"We can go together." said Mr. Damon. "I shall certainly feel more at home in that wild country if I know Tom Swift is with me, and I will appreciate the help of you and your friends, Mr. Titus, in straightening out the tangles of our drug business."

"I'll do all I can for you, Mr. Damon."

The three then talked at some length regarding possible plans. Tom sent out word to one of his men to keep a sharp watch around the house and grounds, against the possible return of Waddington, but nothing more was seen of him, at least for the time being.

Mr. Titus drew up a sort of tentative agreement with Tom, binding his firm to pay a large sum in case the young inventor was successful, and then the contractor left, promising to have the rock samples come on later by express.

Mr. Damon, after blessing a few dozen more or less impersonal objects, took his departure, his fractious horse having quieted down in the meanwhile, and Tom was left to himself.

"I wonder what I've let myself in for now," the youth mused, as he went back to his laboratory. "It's a new field for me—tunnel blasting. Well, perhaps something may come of it."

But of the strange adventure that was to follow his agreement to help Mr. Titus, our hero, Tom Swift, had not the least inkling.

Tom went back to his labors over the gyroscope problem, but he could arrive at no satisfactory conclusion, and, tossing aside the papers, covered with intricate figures, he exclaimed:

"Oh, I'm going for a walk! This thing is getting on my nerves."

He strolled through the Shopton streets, and as he reached the outskirts of the town, he saw just ahead of him the figure of a girl. Tom quickened his pace, and presently was beside her.

"Where are you going, Mary?" he asked.

"Oh, Tom! How you startled me!" she exclaimed, turning around. "I was just thinking of you."

"Thanks! Something nice?"

"I shan't tell you!" and she blushed. "But where are you going?"

"Walking with you!"

Tom was nothing if not bold.

"Hadn't you better wait until you're asked?" she retorted, mischievously.

"If I did I might not get an invitation. So I'm going to invite myself, and then I'm going to invite you in here to have an ice cream soda," and he and Miss Nestor were soon seated at a table in a candy shop.

Tom had nearly finished his ice cream when he glanced toward the door, and started at the sight of a man who was entering the place.

"What's the matter?" asked Mary. "Did you drop some ice cream, Tom?"

"No, Mary. But that man—"

Mary turned in time to see an excited man hurry out of the candy shop after a hasty glance at Tom Swift.

"Who was he?" the girl asked.

"I—er—oh, some one I thought I knew, but I guess I don't," said Tom, quickly. "Have some more cream, Mary?"

"No, thank you. Not now."

Tom was glad she did not care for any, as he was anxious to get outside, and have a look at the man, for he thought he had recognized the face as the same that had peered in his window. But when he and Miss Nestor reached the front of the shop the strange man was not in sight.

"I guess he came in to cool off after his run," mused Tom, "but when he saw me he didn't care about it. I wonder if that was Waddington? He's a persistent individual if it was he."

"Are you undertaking any new adventures, Tom?" asked Mary.

"Well, I'm thinking of going to Peru."

"Peru!" she cried. "Oh, what a long way to go! And when you get there will you write to me? I'm collecting stamps, and I haven't any from Peru."

"Is that—er—the only reason you want me to write?" asked Tom.

"No," said Mary softly, as she ran up the walk.

Tom smiled as he turned away.

Three days later he received a box from New York. It contained the samples from the Andes tunnel, and Tom at once began his experiments to discover a suitable explosive for rending the hard stone.

"It is compressed molten lava," said Mr. Swift. "You'll never get an explosive that will successfully blast that, Tom."

"We'll see," declared the young inventor.

MARY'S PRESENT

Outside a rudely-constructed shack, in the middle of a large field, about a mile away from the nearest of the buildings owned by Tom Swift and his father, were gathered a group of figures one morning. From the shack, trailing over the ground, were two insulated wires, which led to a pile of rocks and earth some distance off. Out of the temporary building came Koku, the giant, bearing in his arms a big rock, of peculiar formation.

"That's it, Koku!" exclaimed Tom Swift. "Now don't drop it on your toes."

"No, Master, me no drop," the giant said, as he strode off with the heavy load as easily as a boy might carry a stone for his sling-shot.

Koku placed the big rock on top of the pile of dirt and stones and came back to the hut, just as Eradicate, the colored man-of-all-work, emerged. Koku was not looking ahead, and ran into Eradicate with such force that the latter would have fallen had not the giant clasped his big arms about him.

"Heah now! Whut yo' all doin' t' me?" angrily demanded Eradicate. "Yo' done gone an' knocked de breff outen me, dat's whut yo' all done! I'll bash yo' wif a rock, dat's what I'll do!"

Koku, laughing, tried to explain that it was all an accident, but Eradicate would not listen. He looked about for a stone to throw at the giant, though it was doubtful, with his feeble strength, and considering the great frame of the big man, if any damage would have been done. But Eradicate saw no rocks nearer than the pile in which ended the two insulated wires, and, with mutterings, the negro set off in that direction, shuffling along on his rheumatic legs.

From the shack Tom Swift hailed:

"Hi there, Rad! Come back! Where are you going?"

"I'se gwine t' git a rock, Massa Tom, an' bash de haid ob dat big lummox ob a giant! He done knocked de breff outen me, so he did."

"You come back from that stone pile!" Tom ordered. "I'm going to blow it up in a minute, and if you get too near you'll have the breath knocked out of you worse than Koku did it. Come back, I say!"

But Eradicate was obstinate and kept on. Tom, who was adjusting a firing battery in the shack, laughed, and then in exasperation cried:

"Koku, go and get him and bring him back. Carry him if he won't come any other way. I don't want the dear old chump to get the fright of his life, and he sure will if he goes too close. Bring him back!"

"Koku bring, Master," was the giant's answer.

He ran toward Eradicate, who, seeing his tormentor approaching, redoubled his shuffling pace toward the stone pile. But he was no match for the giant, who, ignoring his struggles, picked up Eradicate, and, flinging him over his shoulder like a sack of meal, brought him to the shack.

"There him be, Master!" said the giant.

"So I see," laughed Torn. "Now you stay here, Rad."

"No, sah! No, sah, Massa Tom! I—I'se gwine t' git a rock an'—an' bash his haid—dat's what I'se gwine t' do!" and the colored man tried to struggle to his feet.

"Look out now!" cried Tom, suddenly. "If things go right there won't be a rock left for you to 'bash' anybody's head with, Rad. Look out!"

The three cowered inside the shack, which, though it was rudely made, was built of heavy logs and planks, with a fronting of sod and bags of sand.

Tom turned a switch. There was a loud report, and where the stone pile had been there was a big hole in the ground, while the air was filled with fragments of rock and dirt. These came down in a shower on the roof of the shack, and Eradicate covered his ears with his trembling hands.

"Am—am de world comin' to de end, Massa Tom?" he asked. "Am dat Gabriel's trump I done heah?"

"No, you dear old goose!" laughed the young inventor. "That was just a charge of my new explosive—a small charge, too. But it seems to have done the work."

He ran from the shack to the place where the rock pile had been, and picked up several small fragments.

"Busted all to pieces!" exulted Tom Swift. "Not a piece left as big as a hickory nut. That's going some! I've got the right mixture at last. If an ounce did that, a few hundred pounds ought to knock that Andes tunnel through the mountain in no time. I'll telegraph to Mr. Titus."

Leaving Koku and Rad to collect the wires and firing apparatus, there being no danger now, as no explosive was left in the shack, Tom made his way back to the house. His father met him.

"Well, Tom," he asked, "another failure?"

"No, Dad! Success! This time I turned the trick. I seem to have gotten just the right mixture. Look, these are some of the pieces left from the big rock—one of the samples Mr. Titus sent me. It was all cracked up as small as this," and he held out the fragments he had picked up in the field.

Mr. Swift regarded them for a few moments.

"That's better, Tom," he said. "I didn't think you could get an explosive that would successfully shatter that hard rock, but you seem to have done it. Have you the formula all worked out?"

"All worked out, Dad. I only made a small quantity, but the same proportions will hold good for the larger amounts. I'm going to start in and make it now. And then—Ho! for Peru!"

Tom struck an attitude, such as some old discoverer might have assumed, and then he hurried into the house to telephone a telegram to the Shop' ton office. The message was to Mr. Titus, and read:

"Explosive success. Start making it at once. Ready for Peru in month's time."

"Thirteen words," repeated Tom, as the operator called them back to him. "I hope that doesn't mean bad luck."

The experiment which Tom Swift had just brought to a successful conclusion was one of many he had conducted, extending over several wearying weeks.

As soon as Tom had received the samples of the rock he had begun to experiment. First he tried some of the explosive that was so successful in the giant cannon, As he had feared, it was not what was needed. It cracked the rock, but did not disintegrate it, and that was what was needed. The hard rock must be broken up into fragments that could be easily handled. Merely to crack it necessitated further explosions, which would only serve to split it more and perhaps wedge it fast in the tunnel.

So Tom tried different mixtures, using various chemicals, but none seemed to be just right. The trials were not without danger, either. Once, in mixing some ingredients, there was an explosion that injured one man, and blew Tom some distance away. Fortunately for him, there was an open window in the direction in which he was propelled, and he went through that, escaping with only some cuts and bruises.

Another time there was a hang-fire, and the explosive burned instead of detonating, so that one of the shops caught, and there was no little work in subduing the flames.

But Tom would not give up, and finally, after many trials, he hit on what he felt to be the right mixture. This he took out to the big lot, and having made a miniature tunnel with some of the sample rock, and having put some of the explosive in a hole bored in the big chunk Koku carried, Tom fired the charge. The result we have seen, It was a success.

A day after receiving Tom's message Mr. Titus came on and a demonstration was given of the powerful explosive.

"Tom, that's great!" cried the tunnel contractor. "Our troubles are at an end now."

But, had he known it, new ones were only just beginning.

Tom at once began preparations for making the explosive on a large scale, as much of it would be needed in the Andes tunnel. Then, having turned the manufacturing end of it over to his men, Tom began his preparations for going to Peru.

Mr. Damon was also getting ready, and it was arranged that he, with Tom and Mr. Titus, should take a vessel from San Francisco, crossing the continent by train. The supply of explosive would follow them by special freight.

"We might have gone by Panama except for the slide in the canal," Tom said. "And I suppose I could take you across the continent in my airship, Mr. Titus, if you object to railroad travel."

"No, thank you, Tom. If it's just the same to you, I'd rather stay on the ground," the contractor said. "I'm more used to it."

A day or so before the start for San Francisco was to be made, Tom, passing a store in Shopton, saw something in the window he thought Mary Nestor would like. It was a mahogany work-box, of unique design, beautifully decorated, and Tom purchased it.

"Shall I have it sent?" asked the clerk.

"No, thank you," Tom answered.

He knew the young lady who had waited on him, and, for reasons of his own, he did not want her to know that Mary was to get the box.

Carrying the present to his laboratory, Tom prepared to wrap it up suitably to send to Mary, with a note. Just, however, as he was looking for a box suitable to contain the gift, he received a summons to the telephone. Mr. Titus, in New York, wanted to speak to him.

"Here, Rad!" Tom called. "Just box this up for me, like a good fellow, and then take it to Miss Nestor at this address; will you?" and Tom handed his man the addressed letter he had written to Mary. "Be careful of it," Tom cautioned.

"Oh, I'll be careful, Massa Tom," was the reply. "I'll shore be careful."

And Eradicate was—all too careful.

MR. NESTOR'S LETTER

"Got t' git a good strong box fo' dish yeah," murmured Eradicate, as he looked at the beautiful mahogany present Tom had turned over to him to take to Mary. "Mah Landy! Dat suttinly am nice; Ah! Um! Jest laik some ob de old mahogany furniture dat was in our fambily down Souf." Eradicate did not mean his family, exactly, but the one in which he had been a slave.

"Yassum, dat shore am nice!" he went on, talking to himself as he admired the present. "I shore got t' put dat in a good box! An' dish year note, too. Let's see what it done say on de outside."

Eradicate held the envelope carefully upside down, and read—or rather pretended to read—the name and address. Eradicate knew well enough where Mary lived, for this was not the first time he had gone there with messages from his young master.

"Massa Tom shore am a fine writer," mused the negro, as he slowly turned the envelope around. "I cain't read nobody's writin' but hisen, nohow."

Had Eradicate been strictly honest with himself, he would have confessed that he could not read any writing, or printing either. His education had been very limited, but one could show him, say, a printed sign and tell him it read "Danger" or "Five miles to Branchville," or anything like that, and the next time he saw it, Eradicate would know what that sign said. He seemed to fix a picture of it in his mind, though the letters and figures by themselves meant nothing to him. So when Tom told him the envelope contained the name and address of Miss Nestor, Eradicate needed nothing more.

He rummaged about in some odds and ends in the corner of the laboratory, and brought out a strong, wooden box, which had a cover that screwed down.

"Dat'll be de ticket!" Eradicate exclaimed. De mahogany present will jest fit." Eradicate took some excelsior to pad the box, and then, dropping inside it the gift, already wrapped in tissue paper, he proceeded to screw on the cover.

There was something printed in red letters on the outside box, but Eradicate could not read, so it did not trouble him.

"Dat Miss Nestor shore will laik her present," he murmured. "An' I'll be mighty keerful ob it' laik Massa Tom tole me. He wouldn't trust dat big lummox Koku wif anyt'ing laik dis."

Screwing on the cover, and putting a piece of wrapping paper outside the rough, wooden box. with the letter in his hand, Eradicate, full of his own importance, set off for Miss Nestor's house. Tom had not returned from the telephone, over which he was talking to Mr. Titus.

The message was an important one. The contractor said he had received word from his brother in Peru that his presence was urgently needed there.

"Could you arrange to get off sooner than we planned, Tom?" asked Mr. Titus. "I am afraid something has happened down there. Have you sent the first shipment of explosive?"

"Yes, that went three days ago. It ought to arrive at Lima soon after we do. Why yes, I can start tonight if we have to. I'll find out if Mr. Damon can be with us on such short notice."

"I wish you would," came from Mr. Titus. "And say, Tom, do you think you could take that giant Koku with you?"

"Why?"

"Well, I think he'd come in handy. There are some pretty rough characters in those Andes Mountains, and your big friend might be useful."

"All right. I was thinking of it, anyhow. Glad you mentioned it. Now I'll call up Mr. Damon, and I'll let you know, in an hour or so, if he can make it."

"Bless my hair brush, yes, Tom!" exclaimed the eccentric man, when told of the change in plans. "I can leave tonight as well as not."

Word to this effect was sent on to Mr. Titus, and then began some hurrying on the part of Tom Swift. He told Koku to get ready to leave for New York at once, where he and the giant would join Mr. Titus and Mr. Damon, and start across the continent to take for steamer for Lima, Peru.

"Rad, did you send that present to Miss Nestor?" asked Tom, later, as he finished packing his grip.

"Yas, sah. I done did it. Took it mase'f!"

"That's good! I guess I'll have to say good-bye to Mary over the telephone. I won't have time to call. I'm glad I thought of the present."

Tom got the Nestor house on the wire. But Mary was not in.

"There's a package here for her," said the girl's mother. "Did you—?"

"Yes, I sent that," Tom said. "Sorry I won't he able to call and say good-bye, but I'm in a terrible rush. I'll see her as soon as I get back, and I'll write as soon as I arrive."

"Do," urged Mrs. Nestor. "We'll all be glad to hear from you," for Tom and Mary were tentatively engaged to be married.

Tom and Koku went on with their hurried preparations to leave for New York. Eradicate begged to be taken along, but Tom gently told the faithful old servant that it was out of the question.

"Besides, Rad," he said, "it's dangerous in those Andes Mountains. Why, they have birds there, as big as cows, and they can swoop down and carry off a man your size."

"Am dat shorely so, Massa Tom?"

"Of course it is! You get the dictionary and read about the condors of the Andes Mountains."

"Dat's what I'll do, Massa Tom. Birds as big as cows what kin pick up a man in dere beaks, an' carry him off! Oh, my! No, sah, Massa Tom! I don't want t' go. I'll stay right yeah!"

Shortly before Tom and Koku departed for the railroad station, where they were to take a train for New York, Mary Nestor returned home.

"Tom called you on the telephone to say good-bye," her mother informed her, "and said he was sorry he could not see you. But he sent some sort of gift."

"Oh, how sweet of him!" Mary exclaimed. "Where is it?"

"On the dining room table. Eradicate brought it with a note."

Mary read the note first.

In it Tom begged Mary to accept the little token, and to think of him when she used it.

"Oh! I wonder what it can be," she cried in delight.

"Better open it and see," advised Mr. Nestor, who had come in at that moment.

Mary cut the string of the outside paper, and folded back the wrapper. A wooden box was exposed to view, a solid, oblong, wooden box, and on the top, in bold, red letters Mary, her father and her mother read:

Dynamite! Handle with Care!

"Oh! Oh!" murmured Mrs. Nestor.

"Dynamite! Handle with care!" repeated Mr. Nestor, in a sort of dazed voice. "Quick! Get a pail of water! Dump it in the bathtub! Soak it good, and then telephone for the police. Dynamite! What does this mean?"

He rushed toward the kitchen, evidently with the intention of getting a pail of water, but Mary clasped him by the arm.

"Father!" she exclaimed. "Don't get so excited!"

"Excited!" he cried. "Who's excited? Dynamite! We'll all be blown up! This is some plot! I don't believe Tom sent this at all! Look out! Call the police! Excited! Who's getting excited?"

"You are, Daddy dear!" said Mary calmly. "This is some mistake. Tom did send this—I know his writing. And wasn't it Eradicate who brought this package, Mother?"

"Yes, my dear. But your father is right. Let him put it in water, then it will be safe. Oh, we'll all be blown up. Get the water!"

"No!" cried Mary. "There is some mistake. Tom wouldn't send me dynamite, There must be a present for me in there. Tom must have put it in the wrong box by mistake. I'm going to open it."

Mary's calmness had its effect on her parents. Mr. Nestor cooled down, as did his wife, and a closer examination of the outer box did not seem to show that it was an infernal machine of any kind.

"It's all a mistake, Daddy," Mary said. "I'll show you. Get me a screw driver."

After some delay one was found, and Mr. Nestor himself opened the box. When the tissue paper wrappings of the mahogany gift were revealed he gave a sigh of relief, and when Mary undid the wrappings, and saw what Tom had sent her, she cried:

"Oh, how perfectly dear! Just what I wanted! I wonder how he knew? Oh, I just love it!" and she hugged the beautiful box in her arms.

"Humph!" exclaimed Mr. Nestor, a slowly gathering light of anger showing in his eyes. "It is a nice present, but that is a very poor sort of joke to play, in my estimation."

"Joke! What joke?" asked Mary.

"Putting a present in a box labeled Dynamite, and giving us such a scare," went on her father.

"Oh, Father, I'm sure he didn't mean to do it!" Mary said, earnestly.

"Well, maybe he didn't! He may have thought it a joke, and he may not have! But, at any rate, it was a piece of gross carelessness on his part, and I don't care to consider for a son-in-law a young man as careless as that!"

"Oh, Daddy!" expostulated Mary.

"Now, now! Tut, tut!" exclaimed Mr. Nestor. "It isn't your fault, Mary, but this Tom Swift must be taught a lesson. He was careless, if nothing worse, and, for all he knew, there might have been some stray bits of dynamite in that packing box. It won't do! It won't do! I'll write him a letter, and give him a piece of my mind!"

And in spite of all his wife and his daughter could say, Mr. Nestor did write Tom a scathing letter. He accused him of either perpetrating a joke, or of being careless, or both, and he intimated that the less he saw of Tom at the Nestor home hereafter the better pleased he would be.

"There! I guess that will make him wish he hadn't done it!" exclaimed Mr. Nestor, as he called a messenger and sent the letter to Tom's house.

Mary and her mother did not know the contents of the note, but Mary tried to get Tom on the wire and explain. However, she was unable to reach him, as Tom was on the point of leaving.

The messenger, with Mr. Nestor's letter, arrived just as our hero was receiving the late afternoon mail from the postman, and just as Tom and Koku were getting in an automobile to leave for the depot.

"Good-bye, Dad!" Tom called. "Good-bye, Mrs. Baggert!" He thrust Mr. Nestor's letter, unopened, together with some other mail matter, which he took to be merely circulars, into an inner pocket, and jumped into the car.

Tom and Koku were off on the first stage of their journey.

OFF FOR PERU

"Well, Tom Swift, you're on time I see," was Mr. Job Titus' greeting, when our hero, and Koku, the giant, alighted from a taxicab in New York, in front of the hotel the contractor had appointed as a meeting place.

"Yes, I'm here."

"Did you have a good trip?"

"Oh, all right, yes. Nothing happened to speak of, though we were delayed by a freight wreck. Has Mr. Damon got here yet?"

"Not yet, Tom. But I had a message saying he was on his way. "Come on up to the rooms I have engaged. Hello, what's all the crowd here for?" asked the contractor in some surprise, for a throng had gathered at the hotel entrance.

"I expect it's Koku they're staring at," announced Tom, and the giant it was who had attracted the attention. He was carrying his own big valise, and a small steamer trunk belonging to Tom, as easily as though they weighed nothing, the trunk being under one arm.

"I guess they don't see men of his size outside of circuses," commented the contractor. "We can pretty nearly, though not quite match him, down in Peru though, Tom. Some of the Indians are big fellows."

"We'll get up a wrestling match between one of them and Koku," suggested Tom. "Come on!" he called to the giant, who was surrounded by a crowd.

Koku pushed his way through as easily as a bull might make his way through a throng of puppies about his heels, and as Tom, Mr. Titus and the giant were entering the hotel corridor, the chauffeur of the taxicab called out with a laugh:

"I say, boss, don't you think you ought to pay double rates on that chap," and he nodded in the direction of the giant.

"That's right!" added some one in the crowd with a laugh. "He might have broken the springs."

"All right," assented Tom, good-naturedly, tossing the chauffeur a coin. "Here you are, have a cigar on the giant."

There was more laughter, and even Koku grinned, though it is doubtful if he knew what about, for he could not understand much unless Tom spoke to him in a sort of code they had arranged between them.

"Sorry to have hastened your departure," began Mr. Titus when he and Tom sat in the comfortable hotel rooms, while Koku stood at a window, looking out at what to him were the marvelous wonders of the New York streets.

"It didn't make any difference," replied the young inventor. "I was about ready to come anyhow. I just had to hustle a little," and he thought of how he had had to send Mary's present to her instead of taking it himself. As yet he was all unaware of the commotion it had caused.

"Did you get the powder shipment off all right?"

"Yes, and it will be there almost as soon as we. Other shipments will follow as we need them. My father will see to that."

"I'm glad you hit on the right kind of powder," went on the contractor. "I guess I didn't make any mistake in coming to you, Tom."

"Well, I hope not. Of course the explosive worked all right in experimental charges with samples of the tunnel rock. It remains to be seen what it will do under actual conditions, and in big service charges."

"Oh, I've no doubt it will work all right."

"What time do we leave here?" Tom asked.

"At two-thirty this afternoon. We have just time to get a good dinner and have our baggage transferred to the Chicago limited. In less than a week we ought to be in San Francisco and aboard the steamer. I hope Mr. Damon arrives on time."

"Oh, you can generally depend on him," said Tom. "I telephoned him, just before I started from Shopton, and he said—"

"Bless my carpet slippers!" cried a voice outside the hotel apartment. "But I can find my way all right. I know the number of the room. No! you needn't take my bag. I can carry it my self!"

"There he is!" laughed Tom, opening the door to disclose the eccentric gentleman himself, struggling to keep possession of his valise against the importunities of a bellboy.

"Ah, Tom—Mr. Titus! Glad to see you!" exclaimed Mr. Damon. "I—I am a little late, I fear—had an accident—wait until I get my breath," and he sank, panting, into a chair.

"Accident?" cried Tom. "Are you—?"

"Yes—my taxicab ran into another. Nobody hurt though."

"But you're all out of breath," said Mr. Titus. "Did you run?"

"No, but I walked upstairs."

"What! Seven flights?" exclaimed Tom. "Weren't the hotel elevators running?"

Yes, but I don't like them. I'd rather walk. And I did— carried my valise—bellboy tried to take it away from me every step—here you are, son—it wasn't the tip I was trying to get out of," and he tossed the waiting and grinning lad a quarter.

"There, I'm better now," went on Mr. Damon, when Tom had given him a glass of water. "Bless my paper weight! The drug concern will have to vote me an extra dividend for what I've gone through. "Well, I'm here, anyhow. How is everything?"

"Fine!" cried Tom. "We'll soon be off for Peru!"

They talked over plans and made sure nothing had been forgotten. Their railroad tickets had been secured by Mr. Titus so there was nothing more to do save wait for train-time.

"I've never been to Peru," Tom remarked shortly before lunch. "What sort of country is it?"

"Quite a wonderful country," Mr. Titus answered. "I have been very much interested in it since my brother and I accepted this tunnel contract. Peru seems to have taken its name from Peru, a small river on the west coast of Colombia, where Pizarro landed. The country, geographically, may be divided into three sections longitudinally. The coast region is a sandy desert, with here and there rivers flowing through fertile valleys. The sierra region is the Andes division, about two hundred and fifty miles in width."

"Is that where we're going?" asked Tom.

"Yes. And beyond the Andes (which in Peru consist of great chains of mountains, some very high, interspersed with table lands, rich plains and valleys) there is the montana region of tropical forests, running down to the valley of the Amazon.

"That sounds interesting," commented Mr. Damon.

"It is interesting," declared Mr. Titus. "For it is from this tropical region that your quinine comes, Mr. Damon, though you may not have to go there to straighten out your affairs. I think you can do better bargaining with the officials in Lima, or near there."

"Are there any wild animals in Peru?" Tom inquired.

"Well, not many. Of course there are the llamas and alpacas, which are the beasts of burden—almost like little camels you might say, though much more gentle. Then there is the wild vicuna, the fleece of which is made into a sort of wool, after which a certain kind of cloth is named.

"Then there is the taruco, a kind of deer, the viscacha, which is a big rat, the otoc, a sort of wild dog, or fox, and the ucumari, a black bear with a white nose. This bear is often found on lofty mountain tops, but only when driven there in search of food.

"The condors, of course, are big birds of prey in the Andes. You must have read about them; how they seem to lie in the upper regions of the air, motionless, until suddenly they catch sight of some dead animal far down below when they sweep toward it with the swiftness of the wink. There is another bird of the vulture variety, with wings of black and white feathers. The ancient Incas used to decorate their head dresses with these wing feathers."

"Well, I'm glad I'm going to Peru," said Tom. "I never knew it was such an interesting country. But I don't suppose we'll have time to see much of it."

"Oh, I think you will," commented Mr. Titus. "We don't always have to work on the tunnel. There are numerous holidays, or holy-days, which our Indian workers take off, and we can do nothing without them. I'll see that you have a chance to do some exploring if you wish."

"Good!" exclaimed Tom. "I brought my electric rifle with me, and I may get a chance to pop over one of those bears with a white nose. Are they good to eat?"

"The Indians eat them, I believe, when they can get them, but I wouldn't fancy the meat," said the contractor.

Luncheon over, the three travelers departed with their baggage for the Chicago Limited, which left from the Pennsylvania Station at Twenty-third Street. As usual, Koku attracted much attention because of his size.

The trip to San Francisco was without incident worth narrating and in due time our friends reached the Golden Gate where they were to go aboard their steamer. They had to wait a day, during which time Tom and Mr. Titus made inquiries regarding the first powder shipment. They had had unexpected good luck, for the explosive, having been sent on ahead by fast freight, was awaiting them.

"So we can take it with us on the Bellaconda," said, Tom, naming the vessel on which they were to sail.

The powder was safely stowed away, and our friends having brought their baggage aboard, putting what was wanted on the voyage in their staterooms, went out on deck to watch the lines being cast off.

A bell clanged and an officer cried:

"All ashore that's going ashore!"

There were hasty good-byes, a scramble on the part of those who had come to bid friends farewell, and preparations were made to haul in the gangplank.

Just as the tugs were slowly pushing against the Bellaconda to get her in motion to move her away from the wharf, there was a shout down the pier and a taxicab, driven at reckless speed, dashed up.

"Wait a minute! Hold that gangway. I have a passenger for you!" cried the chauffeur.

He pulled up with a screeching of brakes, and a man with a heavy black beard fairly leaped from the vehicle, running toward the plank which was all but cast off.

"My fare! My fare!" yelled the tax~cab driver.

"Take it out of that! Keep the change!" cried the bearded man over his shoulder, tossing a crumpled bill to the chauffeur. And then, clutching his valise in a firm hand, the belated passenger rushed up the gangplank just in time to board the steamer which was moving away from the dock.

"Close shave—that," observed Tom.

"That's right," assented Mr. Titus.

"Well, we're off for Peru!" exclaimed Mr. Damon, as the vessel moved down the bay.

The Bearded Man

Travel to Tom and Mr. Damon presented no novelties. They had been on too many voyages over the sea, under the sea and even in the air above the sea to find anything unusual in merely taking a trip on a steamer.

Mr. Titus, though he admitted he had never been in a submarine or airship, had done considerable traveling about the world in his time, and had visited many countries, either for business or pleasure, so he was an old hand at it.

But to Koku, who, since he had been brought from the land where Tom Swift had been made captive, had gone about but little, everything was novel, and he did not know at what to look first.

The giant was interested in the ship, in the water, in the passengers, in the crew and in the sights to be seen as they progressed down the harbor.

And the big man himself was a source of wonder to all save his own party. Everywhere he went about the decks, or below, he was followed by a staring but respectful crowd. Koku took it all good-naturedly, however, and even consented to show his great strength by lifting heavy weights. Once when several sailors were shifting one of the smaller anchors (a sufficiently heavy one for all that) Koku pushed them aside with a sweep of his big arm, and, picking up the big "hook," turned to the second mate and asked:

"Where you want him?"

"Good land, man!" cried the astonished officer. "You'll kill yourself!"

But Koku carried the anchor where it ought to go, and from then on he was looked up to with awe and admiration by the sailors.

From San Francisco to Callao, Peru (the latter city being the seaport of Lima, which is situated inland), is approximately nine hundred miles. But as the Bellaconda was a coasting steamer, and would make several stops on her trip, it would be more than a week before our friends would land at Callao, then to proceed to Lima, where they expected to remain a day or so before striking into the interior to where the tunnel was being bored through the mountain.

The first day was spent in getting settled, becoming used to their new surroundings, finding their places and neighbors at table, and in making acquaintances. There were some interesting men and women aboard the Bellaconda, and Tom Swift, Mr. Damon and Mr. Titus soon made friends with them. This usually came about through the medium of Koku, the giant. Persons seeing him would inquire about him, and when they learned he was Tom Swift's helper it was an easy topic with which to open conversation.

Tom told, modestly enough, how he had come to get Koku in his escape from captivity, but Mr. Damon was not so simple in describing Tom's feats, so that before many days had passed our hero found himself regarded as a personage of considerable importance, which was not at all to his liking.

"But bless my fountain pen!" cried Mr. Damon, When Tom objected to so much notoriety. "You did it all; didn't you?"

"Yes, I know. But these people won't believe it."

"Oh, yes they will!" said the odd man. "I'll take good care that they believe it."

"If any one say it not so, you tell me!" broke Koku, shaking his huge fist.

"No, I guess I'd better keep still," said Tom, with a laugh.

The weather was pleasant, if we except a shower or two, and as the vessel proceeded south, tropical clothing became the order of the day, while all who could, spent most of their time on deck under the shade of awnings.

"Did you ever hear anything more of that fellow, Waddington?" asked Tom of Mr. Titus one day.

"Not a thing. He seems to have dropped out of sight."

"And are your rivals, Blakeson & Grinder, making any trouble?"

"Not that I've heard of. Though just what the situation may be down in Peru I don't know. I fancy everything isn't going just right or my brother would not be so anxious for me to come on in such a hurry."

"Do you anticipate any real trouble?"

Mr. Titus paused a moment before answering.

"Well, yes," he said, finally, "I do!"

"What sort?" asked Tom.

"That I can't say. I'll be perfectly frank with you, Tom. You know I told you at the time that we were in for difficulties. I didn't want you to go into this thing blindly."

"Oh, I'm not afraid of trouble," Tom hastened to assure his friend. "I've had more or less of it in my life, and I'm willing to meet it again. Only I like to know what kind it is."

"Well, I can't tell you—exactly," went an the tunnel contractor. "Those rivals of ours, Blakeson & Grinder, are unscrupulous fellows. They feel very bitter about not getting the contract, I hear. And they would be only too glad to have us fail in the work. That would mean that they, as the next lowest bidders, would be given the job. And we would have to make up the difference out of our pockets, as well as lose all the work we have, so far, put on the tunnel."

"And you don't want that to happen!"

"I guess not, my boy! Well, it won't happen if we get there in time with this new explosive of yours. That will do the business I'm sure."

"I hope so," murmured Tom. "Well, we'll soon see. And now I think I'll go and write a few letters. We are going to put in at Panama, and I can mail them there."

Tom started for his stateroom, and rapidly put his hand in the inner pocket of his coat. He drew out a bundle of letters and papers, and, as he looked at them, a cry of astonishment came from his lips.

"What's the matter?" asked Mr. Titus.

"Matter!" cried Tom. "Why here's a letter from Mary—from Mr. Nestor," he went on, as he scanned the familiar handwriting. "I never opened it! Let's see—when did I get that?"

His memory went back to the day of his departure from Shopton when he had sent Mary the gift, and he recalled that the letter had arrived just as he was getting into the automobile.

"I stuck it in my pocket with some other mail," he mused, "and I never thought of it again until just now. But this is the first time I've worn this coat since that day. A letter from Mr. Nestor! Probably Mary wrote, thanking me for the box, and her father addressed the envelope for her. Well, let's see what it says."

Tom retired to the privacy of his stateroom to read the note, but he had not glanced over more than the first half of it before he cried out:

"Dynamite! Great Scott! What does this mean? 'Gross carelessness! Poor idea of a joke! No person with your idea of responsibility will ever be my son-in-law!' Box labeled 'open with care!' Why—why—what does it all mean?"

Tom read the letter over again, and his murmurs of astonishment were so loud that Mr. Damon, in the next room, called out:

"What's the matter, Tom?" Get bad news?"

"Bad news? I should say so! Mary—her father—he forbids me to see her again. Says I tried to dynamite them all—or at least scare them into believing I was going to. I can't understand it!"

"Tell me about it, Tom," suggested Mr. Damon, coming into Tom's stateroom. "Bless my gunpowder keg! what does it mean?"

Thereupon Tom told of having purchased the gift for Mary, and of having, at the last minute, told Eradicate to put it in a box and deliver it at the Nestor home.

"Which he evidently did," Tom went on, "but when it got there Mary's present was in a box labeled 'Dynamite. Handle with care.' I never sent that."

Mr. Damon read over Mr. Nestor's letter which had lain so long in Tom's pocket unopened.

"I think I see how it happened," said the old man. "Eradicate can't read; can he, Tom?"

"No, but he pretends he can."

"And did you have any empty boxes marked dynamite in your laboratory?"

"Why yes, I believe I did. I used dynamite as one of the ingredients of my new explosive."

"Well then, it's as clear as daylight. Eradicate, being unable to read, took one of the empty dynamite boxes in which to pack Mary's present. That's how it happened."

Tom thought for a moment. Then he burst into a laugh.

"That's it," he said, a bit ruefully. "That's the explanation. No wonder Mr. Nestor was roiled. He thought I was playing a joke. I'll have to explain. But how?"

"By letter," said Mr. Damon.

"Too slow. I'll send a wireless," decided Tom, and he began the composition of a message that cost him considerable in tolls before he had hit on the explanation that suited him.

"That ought to clear the atmosphere," he said when the wireless had shot his message into the ether. "Whew! And to think, all this while, Mary and her folks have believed that I tried to play a miserable joke on them! My! My! I wonder if they'll ever forgive me. When I get hold of Eradicate—"

"Better teach him to read if he's going to do up love packages," interrupted Mr. Damon, dryly.

"I will," decided the young inventor.

The Bellaconda stopped at Panama and then kept on her way south. Soon after that she ran into a severe tropical storm, and for a time there was some excitement among the passengers. The more timid of them put on life preservers, though the captain and his officers assured them there was no danger.

Tom and Mr. Titus, descending from the deck, whence they had been warned by one of the mates, were on their way to their stateroom, walking with some difficulty owing to the roll of the ship.

As they approached their quarters the door of a stateroom farther up the passage opened, and a head was thrust out.

"Will you send a steward to me?" a man requested. "I am feeling very ill, and need assistance."

"Certainly," Tom answered, and at that moment he heard Mr. Titus utter an exclamation.

"What is it?" asked Tom, for the man who had appealed for help, had withdrawn his head.

"That—that man!" exclaimed the contractor. "That was Waddington, the tool of our rivals."

"Waddington!" repeated Tom, with a look at the now closed door. "Why, the bearded man has that stateroom—the bearded man who so nearly lost the steamer. He isn't Waddington!"

"And I tell you Waddington is in that room!" insisted the contractor. "I only saw the upper part of his face, but I'd know his eyes anywhere. Waddington is spying on us!"

THE BOMB

Tom Swift and Mr. Titus withdrew a little way down the corridor, around a bulkhead and out of sight of any one who might look out from the stateroom whence had come the appeal for help. But, at the same time, they could keep watch over it.

"I tell you Waddington is in there!" insisted Mr. Titus, hoarsely whispering.

"Well, perhaps he may be," admitted Tom. "But several times I have seen the bearded man going in there, and it's only a single stateroom, for it's so marked on the deck plan."

"Waddington might be disguised with a false beard, Tom."

"Yes, he might. But did the man who just now looked out have a beard?"

"I couldn't tell, as I saw only the upper part of his face. But those were Waddington's shifty eyes, I'm positive."

"If Waddington were on board don't you suppose you would have seen him before this?"

"Not positively, no. If he and the bearded man are one and the same that would account for it. But I haven't noticed the bearded man once since he came aboard in such a hurry."

"Nor have I, now that I come to think of it," Tom admitted. "However, there is an easy way to prove who is in there."

"How?"

"We'll knock on the door and go in."

"Perhaps he won't let us."

"He'll think it's the steward he called for. Come, you know Waddington better than I do. You knock and go in."

"I don't know Waddington very well," admitted the contractor. "I have only seen him a few times, but I am sure that was he. But what shall I do when he sees I'm not the steward?"

"Tell him you have sent for one. I'll go with the message, so it will be true enough. Even if you have only a momentary glance at him in close quarters you ought to be able to tell whether or not he has on a false beard, and whether or not it is Waddington."

Mr. Titus considered for a moment, and then he said:

"Yes, I guess that is a good plan. You go for the steward, Tom, and I'll see if I can get in that stateroom. But I'm sure I'm not mistaken. I'll find Waddington in there, perhaps in the person of the bearded man, disguised. Or else they are using a single stateroom as a double one." And while Tom went off down the pitching and rolling corridor to find a steward, Mr. Titus, not without some apprehension, advanced to knock on the door of the suspect.

"If it is Waddington he'll know me at once, of course," thought the contractor, "and there may be a row. Well, I can't help it. The success of my brother and myself depends on finishing that tunnel, and we can't have Waddington, and those whose tool he is, interfering. Here goes!"

He tapped on the door, and a faint voice called:

"Come in!"

The contractor entered, and saw the bearded man lying in his berth.

"Is there anything I can do for you?" asked the contractor, bending close over the man. He wanted to see if the beard were false. Somewhat to his surprise the contractor saw that undoubtedly it was real.

"Steward, will you kindly get me—Oh, you're not the steward!" the bearded man exclaimed.

"No, my friend and I heard you call," replied the contractor. "He has gone for the steward, who will be here soon. Can I do anything for you in the meanwhile?"

"No—not a thing!" was the rather snappish answer, and the man turned his face away. "I beg your pardon," he went on, as if conscious that he had acted rudely, "but I am suffering very much. The steward knows just what I want. I have had these attacks before. I am a poor sailor. If you will send the steward to me I will be obliged to you. He can fix me up."

"Very well," assented Mr. Titus. "But if there is anything I can do —"

At that moment footsteps and voices were heard in the corridor, and as the door of the bearded man's stateroom was opened, Mr. Titus had a glimpse of Tom and one of the stewards.

"Yes, I'll look after him," the steward said "He's been this way before. Thank you, sir, for calling me."

"I guess the steward has been well tipped," thought Tom. As Mr. Titus came out and the door was shut, the young inventor asked in a whisper

"Well, was it be?"

The contractor shook his head.

"No," he answered. "I never was more surprised in my life. I felt sure it was Waddington in there, but it wasn't. That man's beard is real, and while he has a look like Waddington about the eyes and upper part of his face, the man is a stranger to me. That is I think so, but in spite of all that, I have a queer feeling that I have met him before."

"Where?" Tom inquired.

"That I can't say," and the tunnel contractor shook his head. "Whew! That was a bad one!" he exclaimed, as the steamer pitched and tossed in an alarming manner.

"Yes, the storm seems to be getting worse instead of better," agreed Tom. "I hope none of the cargo shifts and comes banging up against my new explosive. If it does, there'll be no more tunnel digging for any of us."

"Better not mention the fact of the explosives on board," suggested Mr. Titus.

"I won't," promised Tom. "The passengers are frightened enough as it is. But I watched the powder being stored away. I guess it is safe."

The storm raged for two days before it began to die away. Meanwhile, nothing was seen, on deck or in the dining cabins, of the bearded man.

Tom and Mr. Titus made some guarded inquiries of the steward who had attended the sick man, and from him learned that he was down on the passenger list as Senor Pinto, from Rio de Janeiro, Brazil. He was traveling in the interests of a large firm of coffee importers of the United States, and was going to Lima.

"And there's no trace of Waddington?" asked Tom of Mr. Titus, as they were discussing matters in their stateroom one day.

"Not a trace. He seems to have dropped out of sight, and I'm glad of it."

"Perhaps Blakeson & Grinder have given up the fight against you."

"I wish they had, though I don't look for any such good luck. But I'm willing to fight them, now that we have an even chance, thanks to your explosive."

The storm blew itself out. The Bellaconda "crossed the line," and there was the usual horseplay among the sailors when Father Neptune came aboard to hold court. Those who had never before been below the equator were made to undergo more or less of an initiation, being lathered and shaved, and then pushed backward into a canvas tank of water on deck.

While Tom enjoyed the voyage, with the possible exception of the storm, he was anxious, and so was Mr. Titus, for the time to come when they should get to the tunnel and try the effect of the new explosive. Mr. Damon found an elderly gentleman as fond of playing chess as was the eccentric man himself, and his days were fully occupied with castles, pawns, knights, kings, queens and so on. As for Koku he was taken in charge by the sailors and found life forward very agreeable.

Senor Pinto had recovered from his seasickness, the steward told Tom and Mr. Titus, but still he kept to his stateroom.

It was when the Bellaconda was within a day or two of Callao that a wireless message was received for Mr. Titus. It was from his brother. The message read:

"Have information from New York office that rivals are after you. Look out for explosive."

"What does that mean?" asked Tom.

"Well, I presume it means our rival contractors know we have a supply of your new powder on board, and they may try to get it away from us."

"Why?" Tom demanded.

"To prevent our using it to complete the tunnel. In that case they'll get the secret of it to use for themselves, when the contract goes to them by default. Can we do anything to protect the powder, Tom?"

"Well, I don't know that we'll need to while it's stowed away in the cargo. They can't get at it any more than we can, until the ship unloads. I guess it's safe enough. We'll just have to keep our eyes open when it's taken out of the hold, though."

Tom and Mr. Titus, both of whom were fond of fresh air and exercise, had made it a practice to get up an hour before breakfast and take a constitutional about the steamer deck. They did this as usual the morning after the wireless warning was received, and they were standing near the port rail, talking about this, when they heard a thud on the deck behind them. Both turned quickly, and saw a round black object rolling toward them. From the object projected what seemed to be a black cord, and the end of this cord was glowing and smoking.

For a moment neither Tom nor Mr. Titus spoke. Then, as a slow motion of the ship rolled the round black thing toward Tom, he cried:

"It a bomb!"

He darted toward it, but Mr. Titus pulled him back.

"Run!" yelled the contractor.

Before either of them could do anything, a queer figure of an elderly gentleman stepped partly from behind a deck-house, and stooped over the smoking object.

"Look out!" yelled Mr. Titus, crouching low. "That's an explosive bomb! Toss it overboard!"

PROFESSOR BUMPER

Fairly fascinated by the spluttering fuse, neither Tom nor Mr. Titus moved for a second, while the deadly fire crept on through the black string-like affair, nearer and nearer to the bomb itself.

Then, just as Tom, holding back his natural fear, was about to thrust the thing overboard with his foot, hardly realizing that it might be even more deadly to the ship in the water than it was on the deck, the foot of the newcomer was suddenly thrust out from behind the deck-house, and the sizzling fuse was trodden upon.

It went out in a puff of smoke, but the owner of the foot was not satisfied with that for a hand reached down, lifted the bomb, the fuse of which still showed a smouldering spark of fire, and calmly pulled out the "tail" of the explosive. It was harmless then, for the fuse, with a trail of smoke following, was tossed into the sea, and the little man came out from behind the deck-house, holding the unexploded bomb.

For a moment neither Tom nor Mr. Titus could speak. They felt an inexpressible sense of relief. Then Tom managed to gasp out:

"You—you saved our lives!"

The little man who had stepped on the fuse, and had then torn it from the bomb, looked at the object in his hand as though it were the most natural thing in the world to pick explosives up off the deck of passenger steamers, as he remarked:

"Well, perhaps I did. Yes, I think it would have gone off in another second or two. Rather curious; isn't it?"

"Curious? Curious!" asked and exclaimed Mr. Titus.

"Why, yes," went on the little man, in the most matter of fact tone. "You see, most explosive bombs are round, made that way so the force will be equal in all directions. But this one, you notice, has a bulge, or protuberance, on one side, so to speak. Very curious!

"It might have been made that way to prevent its rolling overboard, or the bomb's walls might be weaker near that bulge to make sure that the force of the explosion would be in that direction. And the bulge was pointed toward you gentlemen, if you noticed."

"I should say I did!" cried Mr. Titus. "My dear sir, you have put us under a heavy debt to you! You saved our lives! I—I am in no frame of mind to thank you now, but—"

He strode over to the little man, holding out his hand.

"No, no, I'd better keep it," went on the person who had rendered the bomb ineffective. "You might drop it you know. You are nervous—your hand shakes."

"I want to shake hands with you!" exclaimed Mr. Titus— "to thank you!"

"Oh, that's it. I thought you wanted the bomb. Shake hands? Certainly!"

And while this ceremony was being gone through with, Tom had a moment to study the appearance of the man who had saved their lives. He had seen the passenger once or twice before, but had taken no special notice of him. Now he had good reason to observe him.

Tom beheld a little, thin man, little in the sense of being of the "bean pole" construction. His head was as bald as a billiard ball, as the young inventor could notice when the stranger took off his hat to bow formally in response to the greeting of some ladies who passed, while Mr. Titus was shaking hands with him.

The bald head was sunk down between two high shoulders, and when the owner wished to observe anything closely, as he was now observing the bomb, the head was thrust forward somewhat as an eagle might do. And Tom noticed that the eyes of the little man were as bright as those of an eagle. Nothing seemed to escape them.

"I want to add my thanks to those of Mr. Titus for saving our lives," said Tom, as he advanced. "We don't know what to make of it all, but you certainly stopped that bomb from going off."

"Yes, perhaps I did," admitted the little man coolly and calmly, as though preventing bomb explosions was his daily exercise before breakfast.

Tom and Mr. Titus introduced themselves by name.

"I am Professor Swyington Bumper," said the bomb-holder, with a bow, removing his hat, and again disclosing his shiny bald head. "I am very glad to have met you indeed."

"And we are more than glad," said Tom, fervently, as he glanced at the explosive.

"Now that the danger is over," went on Mr. Titus, "suppose we make an investigation, and find out how this bomb came to be here."

"Just what I was about to suggest," remarked Professor Bumper. "Bombs, such as this, do not sprout of themselves on bare decks. And I take it this one is explosive."

"Let me look at it," suggested Tom. "I know something of explosives."

It needed but a casual examination on the part of one who had done considerable experimenting with explosives to disclose the fact that it had every characteristic of a dangerous bomb. Only the pulling out of the fuse had rendered it harmless.

"If it had gone off," said Tom, "we would both have been killed, or. at least, badly injured, Mr. Titus."

"I believe you, Tom. And we owe our lives to Professor Bumper."

"I'm glad I could be of service, gentlemen," the scientist remarked, in an easy tone. "Explosives are out of my line, but I guessed it was rather dangerous to let this go off. Have you any idea how it got here?"

"Not in the least," said Tom. "But some one must have placed it here, or dropped it behind us."

"Would any one have an object in doing such a thing?" the professor asked.

Tom and Mr. Titus looked at one another.

"Waddington!" murmured the contractor. "If he were on board I should say he might have done it to get us out of the way, though I would not go so far as to say he meant to kill us. It may be this bomb has only a light charge in it, and he only meant to cripple us."

"We'll find out about that," said Tom. "I'll open it."

"Better be careful," urged Mr. Titus.

"I will," the young inventor promised. "I beg your pardon," he went on to Professor Bumper. "We have been talking about something of which you know nothing. Briefly, there is a certain man who is trying to interfere in some work in which Mr. Titus and I are interested, and we think, if he were on board, he might have placed this bomb where it would injure us."

"Is he here?" asked the professor.

"No. And that is what makes it all the more strange," said Mr. Titus. "At one time I thought he was here, but I was mistaken."

Tom took the now harmless bomb to his stateroom, and there, after taking the infernal machine apart, he discovered that it was not as dangerous as he had at first believed.

The bomb contained no missiles, and though it held a quantity of explosive, it was of a slow burning kind. Had it gone off it would have sent out a sheet of flame that would have severely burned him and Mr. Titus, but unless complications had set in death would not have resulted.

"They just wanted to disable us," said the contractor. "That was their game. Tom, who did it?"

"I don't know. Did you ever see this Professor Bumper before?"

"I never did."

"And did it strike you as curious that he should happen to be so near at hand when the bomb fell behind us?"

"I hadn't thought of that," admitted the contractor. "Do you mean that he might have dropped it himself?"

"Well, I wouldn't go so far as to say that," replied Tom, slowly. "But I think it would be a good idea to find out all we can of Professor Swyington Bumper."

"I agree with you, Tom. We'll investigate him."

IN THE ANDES

Professor Swyington Bumper seemed to live in a region all by himself. Though he was on board the Bellaconda, he might just as well have been in an airship, or riding along on the back of a donkey, as far as his knowledge, or recognition, of his surroundings went. He seemed to be thinking thoughts far, far away, and he was never without a book—either a bound volume or a note-book. In the former he buried his hawk-like nose, and Tom, looking over his shoulder once, saw that the book was printed in curious characters, which, later, he learned were Sanskrit. If he had a note-book the bald-headed professor was continually jotting down memoranda in it.

"I can hardly think of him as a conspirator against us," said Tom to Mr. Titus.

"After you have been in the contracting business as long as I have you'll distrust every one," was the answer. "Waddington isn't on board, or I'd distrust him. That Spaniard, Senor Pinto. seems to be out of consideration, and there only remains the professor. We must watch him."

But Professor Bumper proved to be above suspicion. Carefully guarded inquiries made of the captain, the purser and other ships' officers, brought out the fact that he was well known to all of them, having traveled on the line before.

"He is making a search for something, but he won't say what it is," the captain said. "At first we thought it was gold or jewels, for he goes away off into the Andes Mountains, where both gold and jewels have been found. He never looks for treasure, though, for though some of his party have made rather rich discoveries, he takes no interest in them."

"What is he after then?" asked Mr. Titus.

"No one knows, and he won't tell. But whatever it is he has never found it yet. Always, when he comes back, unsuccessful, from a trip to the interior and goes back North with us, he will remark that he has not the right directions. That he must seek again.

"Back he comes next season, as full of hope as before, but only to be disappointed. Each time he goes to a new place in the mountains where he digs and delves, so members of the parties he hires tell me, but with no success. He carries with him something in a small iron box, and, whatever this is, he consults it from time to time. It may be directions for finding whatever he is after. But there seems to be something wrong."

"This is quite a mystery," remarked Tom.

"It certainly is. But Professor Bumper is a fine man. I have known him for years."

"This seems to dispose of the theory that he planted the bomb, and that he is one of the plotters in the pay of Blakeson & Grinder," said Mr. Titus, when he and Tom were alone.

"Yes, I guess it does. But who can have done it?"

That was a question neither could answer.

Tom had a theory, which he did not disclose to Mr. Titus, that, after all, the somewhat mysterious Senor Pinto might, in some way, be mixed up in the bomb attempt. But a close questioning of the steward on duty near the foreigner's cabin at the time disclosed the fact that Pinto had been ill in his berth all that day.

"Well, unless the bomb fell from some passing airship, I don't see how it got on deck," said Tom with a shake of his head. "And I'm sure no airship passed over us."

They had kept the matter secret, not telling even Mr. Damon, for they feared the eccentric man would make a fuss and alarm the whole vessel. So Mr. Damon, occasionally blessing his necktie or his shoe laces, played chess with his elderly gentleman friend and was perfectly happy.

That Professor Bumper not only had kept his promise about not mentioning the bomb, but that he had forgotten all about it, was evident a day or two after the happening. Tom and Mr. Titus passed him on deck, and bowed cordially. The professor returned the salutation, but looked at the two in a puzzled sort of fashion.

"I beg your pardon," he remarked, "but your faces are familiar, though I cannot recall your names. Haven't I seen you before?"

"You have," said Tom, with a smile. "You saved our lives from a bomb the other day."

"Oh, yes! So I did! So I did!" exclaimed Professor Bumper. "I felt sure I had seen you before. Are you all right?"

"Yes. There haven't been any more bombs thrown at us," the contractor said. "By the way, Professor Bumper, I understand you are quite a traveler in the Andes, in the vicinity of Lima."

"Yes, I have been there," admitted the bald-headed scientist in guarded tones.

"Well, I am digging a tunnel in that vicinity," went on Mr. Titus, "and if you ever get near Rimac, where the first cutting is made, I wish you would come and see me—Tom too, as he is associated with me."

"Rimac-Rimac," murmured the professor, looking sharply at the contractor. "Digging a tunnel there? Why are you doing that?" and he seemed to resent the idea.

"Why, the Peruvian government engaged me to do it to connect the two railroad lines," was the answer. "Do you know anything about the place?"

"Not so much as I hope to later on," was the unexpected answer. "As it happens I am going to Rimac, and I may visit your tunnel."

"I wish you would," returned Mr. Titus.

Later on, in their stateroom, the contractor remarked to the young inventor:

"Sort of queer; isn't it?"

"What?" asked Tom. "His not remembering us?"

"No, though that was odd. But I suppose he is forgetful, or pretends to be. I mean it's queer he is going to Rimac."

"What do you mean?" asked Tom.

"Well, I don't know exactly what I mean," went on the tunnel contractor, "but our tunnel happens to start at Rimac, which is a small town at the base of the mountains."

"Maybe the professor is a geologist," suggested Tom, "and he may want to get some samples of that hard rock."

"Maybe," admitted Mr. Titus. "But I shall keep my eyes on him all the same. I'm not going to have any strangers, who happen to be around when bombs drop near us, get into my tunnel."

"I think you're wrong to doubt Professor Bumper," Tom said.

A few days after this, when Tom and Mr. Titus were casually discussing the weather on deck and wondering how much longer it would be before they reached Callao, Mr. Damon, who had been playing numberless games of chess, came up for a breath of air.

"Mr. Damon," called Tom, "come over here and meet a friend of ours, Professor Bumper," and he was about to introduce them, for the two, as far as Tom knew, had not yet met. But no sooner had the professor and Mr. Damon caught sight of each other than there was a look of mutual recognition.

"Bless my fountain pen!" cried the eccentric man. "If it isn't my old friend!"

"Mr. Damon!" cried the professor. "I am delighted to see you again. I did not know you were on board!"

"Nor I you. Bless my apple dumpling! Are you still after those Peruvian antiquities?"

"I am, Mr. Damon. But I did not know you were acquainted with Mr. Swift."

"Oh, Tom and I are old friends."

"Professor Bumper saved the lives of Mr. Titus and myself," said Tom, "or at least he saved us from severe injury by a bomb."

"Pray do not mention it, my friends," put in the professor, casually. "It was nothing."

Of course he did not mean it just that way.

Then, naturally, Mr. Damon had to be told all about the bomb for the first time, and his wonder was great. He blessed everything he could think of.

"And to think it should be my old friend, Professor Bumper, who saved you," said the odd man to Tom and Mr. Titus later that day.

"Do you know him well?" asked Mr. Titus.

"Very well indeed. Our drug concern sells him many chemicals for his experiments."

"Well, if you know him I guess he can't be what I thought he was," the contractor went on. "I'm glad to know it. Why is he going to the Andes?"

"Oh, for many years he has been interested in collecting Peruvian antiquities. He has a certain theory in regard to something or other about their ancient civilization, but just what it is I have, at this moment, forgotten.

Only I know you can thoroughly trust Professor Bumper, for a finer man never lived, though he is a bit absent-minded at times. But you will like him very much."

Thus the last lingering doubt of Professor Bumper was removed. Mr. Damon told something of how the scientist had been honored by degrees from many colleges and was regarded as an authority on Peruvian matters.

But who had placed the bomb on deck remained a mystery.

In due time Callao, the seaport of Lima, was reached and our friends disembarked. Tom saw to the unloading of the explosive, which was to be sent direct to the tunnel at Rimac. Mr. Titus, Tom and Mr. Damon would remain in Lima a day or so.

Professor Bumper disembarked with our friends, and stopped at the same hotel. Tom kept a lookout for Senor Pinto, but did not see him, and concluded that the Spaniard was ill, and would be carried ashore on a stretcher, perhaps.

Lima, the principal city and capital of Peru, proved an interesting place. It was about eight miles inland and was built on an arid plain about five hundred feet above sea level. Yet, though it was on what might be termed a desert, the place, by means of irrigation, had been made into a beauty spot.

Tom found the older part of the city was laid out with mathematical regularity, each street crossing the other at right angles. But in the new portions there was not this adherence to straightness.

"Bless my transfer! Why, they have electric cars here!" exclaimed Mr. Damon, catching sight of one on the line between Callao and the capital.

"What did you think they'd have?" asked Mr. Titus, "elephants or camels?"

"I—I didn't just know," was the answer.

"Oh, you'll find a deal of civilization here," the contractor said. "Of course much of the population is negro or Indian, but they are often rich and able to buy what they want. There is a population of over 150,000, and there are two steam railroads between Callao and Lima, while there is one running into the interior for 130 miles, crossing the Andes at an elevation of over three miles. It is a branch of that road, together with a branch of the one running to Ancon, that I am to connect with a tunnel."

Tom found some beautiful churches and cathedrals in Lima, and spent some time visiting them. He and Mr. Damon also visited, in the outskirts, the tobacco, cocoa and other factories.

Three days after reaching the capital, Mr. Titus having attended to some necessary business while Mr. Damon set on foot matters connected with his affairs, it was decided to strike inland to Rimac, and to try the effect of Tom Swift's explosive on the tunnel.

The journey was to be made in part by rail, though the last stages of it were over a rough mountain trail, with llamas for beasts of burden, while our friends rode mules.

As Tom, Mr. Damon, Koku, and Mr. Titus were going to the railroad station they saw Professor Bumper also leaving the hotel.

"I believe our roads lie together for a time," said the bald-headed scientist, "and, if you have no objections, I will accompany you."

"Come, and welcome!" exclaimed Mr. Titus, all his suspicions now gone.

"And it may be that you will be able to help me," the scientist went on.

"Help you—how?" asked Tom.

"I will tell you when we reach the Andes," was the mysterious answer.

It was a day later when they left the train at a small station, and struck off into the foothills of the great Andes Mountains, where the tunnel was started, that the professor again mentioned his object.

"Friends," he said, as he gazed up at the towering cliffs and crags, "I am searching for the lost city of Pelone, located somewhere in these mountains. Will you help me to find it?"

THE TUNNEL

Mr. Damon, of the three who heard Professor Bumper make this statement, showed the least sign of astonishment. It would have been more correct to say that he showed none at all. But Tom could not restrain himself.

"The lost city of Pelone!" he exclaimed.

"Is it here—in these mountains?" asked Mr. Titus.

"I have reason to hope that it is," went on the professor. "The golden tablets are very vague, but I have tried many locations, and now I am about to try here. I hope I shall succeed. At any rate, I shall have agreeable company, which has not always been my luck on my previous expeditions seeking to find the lost city."

"Oh, Professor, are you still on that quest?" asked Mr. Damon, in a matter-of-fact tone.

"Yes, Mr. Damon, I am. And now that I look about me, and see the shape of these mountains, I feel that they conform more to the description on the golden plates than any location I have yet tried. Somehow I feel that I shall be successful here."

"Did you know Professor Bumper was searching for a lost city of the Andes?" asked Tom, of his eccentric friend.

"Why yes," answered Mr. Damon. "He has been searching for years to locate it."

"Why didn't you tell us?" inquired Mr. Titus.

"Why, I never thought of it. Bless my memorandum book! it never occurred to me. I did not think you would be interested. Tell them your story, Professor Bumper."

"I will soon. Just now I must see to my equipment. The story will keep."

And though Tom and Mr. Titus were both anxious to hear about the lost city, they, too, had much to do to get ready for the trip into the interior.

The beginning of the tunnel under one of the smaller of the ranges of the Andes lay two days journey from the end of the railroad line. And the trip must be made on mules, with llamas as beasts of burden, transporting the powder and other supplies.

"We'll only need to take enough food with us for the two days," said Mr. Titus. "We have a regular camp at the tunnel mouth, and my brother has supplies of grub and other things constantly coming in. We also have shacks to live in; but on this trip we will use tents, as the weather at this season is fine."

It was quite a little expedition that set off up the mountain trail that afternoon, for they had arrived at the end of the railroad line shortly before dinner, and had eaten at a rather poor restaurant.

Professor Bumper had made up his own exploring party, consisting of himself and three native Indian diggers with their picks and shovels. They were to do whatever excavating he decided was necessary to locate the hidden city.

Several mules and llamas, laden with the new explosive, and burdened with camp equipment and food, and a few Indian servants made up the cavalcade of Tom, the contractor, Mr. Damon and Koku. The giant was almost as much a source of wonder to the Peruvians as he had been on board the ship. And he was a great help, too. For some of the Indians were under-sized, and could not lift the heavy boxes and packages to the backs of the beasts of burden.

But Koku, thrusting the little men aside, grasped with one hand what two of them had tried in vain to lift, and set it on the back of mule or llama.

The way was rough but they took their time to it, for the trail was an ascending one. Above and beyond them towered the great Andes, and Tom, gazing up into the sky, which in places seemed almost pierced by the snow-covered peaks, saw some small black specks moving about.

"Condors," said Mr. Titus, when his attention was called to them. "Some of them are powerful birds, and they sometimes pick up a sheep and make off with it, though usually their food consists of carrion."

They went into camp before the sun went down, for it grew dark soon after sunset, and they wanted to be prepared. Supper was made ready by the Indian helpers, and when this was over, and they sat about a camp fire, Tom said:

"Now, Professor Bumper, perhaps you'll explain about the lost city."

"I wish I could explain about it," began the scientist. "For years I have dreamed of finding it, but always I have been disappointed. Now, perhaps, my luck may change."

"Do you think it may be near here?" asked Mr. Titus, motioning toward the dark and frowning peaks all about them.

"It may be. The signs are most encouraging. In brief, the story of the lost city of Pelone is this. Thousands of years ago—in fact I do not know how many—there existed somewhere in Peru an ancient city that was the centre of civilization for this region. Older it was than the civilization of the Mexicans—the Montezumas—older and more cultured.

"It is many years since I became interested in Peruvian antiquities, and then I had no idea of the lost city. But some of the antiques I picked up contained in their inscriptions references to Pelone. At first I conceived this to be a sort of god, a deity, or perhaps a powerful ruler. But as I went on in my work of gathering ancient things from Peru, I saw that the name Pelone referred to a city—a seat of government, whence everything had its origin.

"Then I got on the track more closely. I examined ancient documents. I found traces of an ancient language and writings, different from anything else in the world. I managed to construct an alphabet and to read some of the documents. From them I learned that Pelone was a city situated in some fertile valley of the Andes. It had existed for thousands of years; it was the seat of learning and culture. Much light would be thrown on the lives of the people who lived in Peru before the present races inhabited it, if I could but locate Pelone.

"Then I came across two golden tablets on which were graven the information that Pelone had utterly vanished."

"How?" asked Tom.

"The golden tablets did not say. They simply stated the fact that Pelone was lost, and one sentence read: 'He who shall find it again shall be richly rewarded.' But it is not for that that I seek. It is that I may give to the world the treasures it must contain—the treasures of an ancient civilization."

"And how do you think the city disappeared?" asked Mr. Titus.

"I do not know. Whether it was destroyed by enemies, whether it was buried under the ashes of a volcano, whether it still exists, deserted and solitary in some valley amid the mountain fastnesses of the Andes, I do not know. But I am certain the city once existed, and it may exist yet, though it may be in dust-covered ruins. That is what I seek to find. See! Here are the tablets telling about it. I got them from an old Peruvian grave."

He took from a box two thin sheets of yellow metal. They were covered with curious marks, but Tom and the others could make nothing of them. Only Professor Bumper was able to decipher them.

"And that is the story of the lost city of Pelone —as much as I know," he said. "For years I have sought it. If I can find it I shall be famous, for I shall have added to human knowledge."

"If the people of that city wrote on golden tablets, the yellow metal must have been plentiful," commented Mr. Titus. "You might strike a rich mine."

"I have no use for riches," said the professor.

"Well, I have," the contractor said, with a laugh. "That's why I'm putting through this tunnel. And if my brother and I don't do it we'll be in a bad way financially. We have struck traces of gold, but not in paying quantities. I should like to see this lost city of yours, Professor Bumper. It may contain gold."

"You may have all the gold, if I am allowed to keep the antiquities we find," stipulated the scientist. "Then you will help me in my search?"

"As much as we can spare time for from the tunnel work," promised Mr. Titus. "I'll instruct my men to keep their eyes open for any sign of ancient writings on the rocks we blast out."

"Thank you," said the professor.

The night passed uneventfully enough, if one excepts the mosquitoes which seemed to get through the nets, making life miserable for all. And once Tom thought he heard gruntings in the bush back of the tent, which noises might, he imagined, have been caused by a bear. Toward morning he heard an unearthly screech in the woods, and one of the Indians, tending the fire, grunted out a word which meant pumas.

"I can see it isn't going to be dull here," Tom mused, as he turned over and tried to sleep.

Breakfast made them all feel better, and they set off on the final stage of their journey.

"If all goes well we'll be at the tunnel entrance and camp tonight," said the contractor. "This second half of the trip is the roughest."

There was no need of saying that, for it was perfectly evident. The trail was a most precarious one, and only a mule or llama could have traveled it. The mules were most sure-footed, but, as it was, one slipped, and came near falling over a cliff.

But no real accident occurred, and finally, about an hour before sunset, the cavalcade turned down the slope and emerged on a level plain, which ended against the face of a great cliff.

As Tom rode nearer the cliff he could make out around it groups of rude buildings, covered with corrugated iron. There was quite a settlement it seemed.

Then, in the face of the cliff there showed something black—like a blot of ink, though more regular in outline.

"The mouth of the tunnel," said Mr. Titus to Tom. "Come on over to the office and I'll introduce you to my brother. I guess he will be glad we've arrived."

Tom dismounted from his mule, an example followed by the others. Professor Bumper gazed up at the great mountains and murmured:

"I wonder if the lost city of Pelone lies among them?"

Suddenly the silence of the evening was broken by a dull, rumbling sound.

"Bless my court plaster!" cried Mr. Damon. "What's that?"

"A blast," answered Mr. Titus. "But I never knew them to set off one so late before. I hope nothing is wrong!"

And, as he spoke, panic-stricken men began running out of the mouth of the tunnel, while those outside hastened toward them, shouting and calling.

TOM'S EXPLOSIVE

"Something has happened!" cried Mr. Titus as he ran forward, followed by Tom, Mr. Damon and Koku. Professor Bumper started with them, but on the way he saw a curious bit of rock which he stopped to pick up and examine.

At the entrance of the tunnel, from which came rushing dirt-stained and powder-blackened men, Mr. Titus was met by a man who seemed to be in authority.

"Hello, Job!" he cried. "Glad you're back. We're in trouble!"

"What's the matter?" was the question. "This is my brother Walter," he said. "This is Tom Swift and Mr. Damon," thus hurriedly he introduced them. "What happened, Walter?"

"Premature blast. Third one this week. Somebody is working against us!"

"Never mind that now," cried Job Titus. "We must see to the poor fellows who are hurt." "I guess there aren't many," his brother said. "They were on their way out when the charge went off. Some more of Blakeson & Grinder's work, I'll wager!"

They were rushing in to the smoke-filled tunnel now, followed by Tom, Mr. Damon and Koku, who would follow his young master anywhere. Tom saw that the tunnel was lighted with incandescent lamps, suspended here and there from the rocky roof or sides. The electric lights were supplied with current from a dynamo run by a gasoline engine.

"Where is it, Serato? Where was the blast?" asked Walter Titus, of a tall Indian, who seemed to be in some authority.

"Back at second turn," was the answer, in fairly good English. "I go get beds."

"He means stretchers," translated Job. "That's our Peruvian foreman. A good fellow, but easily scared."

They ran on into the tunnel, Tom and Mr. Damon noticing that a small narrow-gage railroad was laid on the floor, mules being the motive power to bring out the small dump cars loaded with rock and dirt, excavated from the big hole.

"Mind the turn!" called Job Titus, who was ahead of Tom and Mr. Damon. "It's rough here."

Tom found it so, for he slipped over some pieces of rock, and would have fallen had not Koku held him up.

"Thanks," gasped Tom, as on he ran.

A little later he came to a place where a cluster of electric lights gave better illumination, and he could see it was there that the damage had been done.

A number of men were lying on the dirt and rock floor of the tunnel, and some of them were bleeding. Others were staggering about as though shocked or stunned.

"We must get the injured ones out of here!" cried Walter Titus. "Where are the men with stretchers?"

"I sint that Spalapeen Serato for thim!" broke in a voice, rich in Irish brogue. "But he's thot stupid he might think I was after sindin' him fer wather!"

"No, Tim. Serato is after the stretchers all right," said Walter. "We passed him on the way."

"That's Tim Sullivan, our Irish foreman, though he has only a few of his own kind to boss," explained Job Titus in a whisper.

Some of the workmen (all of whom save the few Irish referred to were Peruvian Indians) had now recovered from their shock, or fright, and began to help the Titus brothers, Tom, Mr. Damon and Koku in looking after the injured. Of these there were five, only two of whom were, seemingly, seriously hurt.

"Me take them out," said Koku, and placing one gently over his left shoulder, and the other over his right, out of the tunnel he stalked with them, not waiting for the stretchers.

And it was well he did so, for one man was in need of an immediate operation, which was performed at the rude hospital the contractors maintained at the tunnel mouth. The other man died as Koku was carrying him out, but the giant had saved one life.

Serato, the Indian foreman, with some of his men now came in, and the other injured were carried out on stretchers, being attended to by the two doctors who formed part of the tunnel force. Among a large body of men some were always falling ill or getting hurt, and in that wild country a doctor had to be kept near at hand.

When the excitement had died down, and it was found that one death would be the total toll of the accident and that the premature blast had done no damage to the tunnel, the two Titus brothers began to consider matters.

Tom, Mr. Damon and the two contractors sat in the main office and talked things over. Koku was eating supper, though the others had finished. but, naturally, it took Koku twice as long as any one else. Professor Bumper was busy transcribing material in his note-book.

"Well, I'm glad you've come back, Job," said his brother. "Things have been going at sixes and sevens here since you went to get some new kind of blasting powder. By the way, I hope you got it, for we are practically at a standstill."

"Oh, I got it all right—some of Tom Swift's best— specially made for us. And, better still, I've brought Tom back with me."

"So I see. Well, I'm glad he's here."

"Now what about this accident today?" went on Job.

"Well, as I said, it's the third this week. All of them seemed to be premature blasts. But I've sent for some of the fuses used. I'm going to get at the bottom of this. Here is Sullivan with them now. Come in, Tim," he called, as the Irishman knocked at the door.

"Are they the fuses used in the blasts?" Walter asked.

"They are, sor. An' they mostly burn five minutes, which is plenty of time fer all th' min t' git out of danger. Only this time th' fuse didn't seem to burn more than a minute, an' I lit it meself."

"Let's see how long they burn now," suggested Job.

One of the longer fuses was lighted. It spluttered and smoked, while the contractors timed it with their watches.

"Four minutes!" exclaimed Job. "That's queer, and they're the regular ten minute length. I wonder what this means.

He took up another fuse, and examined it closely.

"Why!" he cried. "These aren't our fuses at all. They're another make, and much more rapid in burning. No wonder you've been having premature blasts. They go off in about half the time they should."

"I can't understhand thot!" said Tim, thoughtfully. "I keep all the fuses locked up, and only take thim out when I need thim."

"Then somebody has been at your box, Tim, and they took out our regular fuses and put in these quicker ones. It's a game to make trouble for us among our men, and to damage the tunnel."

"Bless my rubber boots!" cried Mr. Damon. "Who would do a thing like that?"

"Our rivals, perhaps, though I do not like to accuse any man on such small evidence," said Walter. "But we must adopt new measures."

"And be very careful of the fuses," said Job.

"Thot's what I will!" declared Tim. "I'll put th' supply in a new place. No wonder there was blasts before th' min could git out th' way! Bad cess t' th' imps thot did this!" and he banged his big fist down on the table.

Since the trouble began a guard had been always posted around the tunnel entrance and surrounding buildings, and this night the patrol was doubled. Tom, Mr. Damon and the two Titus brothers sat up quite late, talking over plans and ideas.

Professor Bumper went to bed early, as he said he was going to set off before sunrise to make a search for the lost city.

"I regard him as more or less of a visionary," said Mr. Job Titus; "but he seems a harmless gentleman, and we'll do all we can to help him."

"Surely," agreed his brother.

The night was not marked by any disturbance, and after breakfast, Tom, under the guidance of the Titus brothers, looked over the tunnel with a view to making his first experiment with the new explosive.

The tunnel was being driven straight into the face of one of the smaller ranges of the Andes Mountains. It was to be four miles in length, and when it emerged on the other side it would enable trains to make connections between the two railroads, thus tapping a rich and fertile country.

On the site of the tunnel, which was two days' mule travel east from Rimac, the Titus brothers had assembled their heavy machinery. They had brought some of their own men, including Tim Sullivan, with them, but the other labor was that of Peruvian Indians, with a native foreman, Serato, over them.

There were engines, boilers, dynamos, motors, diamond drills, steam shovels and a miniature railway, with mules as the motive power. A small village had sprung up at the tunnel mouth, and there was a general store, besides many buildings for the sleeping and eating quarters of the laborers, as well as places where the white men could live. Their quarters were some distance from the native section.

Powder, supplies, in fact everything save what game could be obtained in the forest, or what grains or fruits were brought in by natives living near by, had to be brought over the rough trail. But Titus Brothers had a large experience in engineering matters in wild and desolate countries, and they knew how to be as comfortable as possible.

Mr. Damon learned that one of the districts whence his company had been in the habit of getting quinine was distant a day's journey over the mountain, so he decided to make the trip, with a native guide, and see if he could get at the bottom of the difficulty in forwarding shipments.

This was a few days after the arrival of our friends. Meanwhile, Tom had been shown all through the tunnel by the Titus Brothers and had had his first sight of the hard cliff of rock which seemed to be a veritable stone wall in the way of progress—or at least such progress as was satisfactory to the contractors.

"Well, we'll try what some of my explosive will do," said Tom, when he had finished the examination. "I don't claim it will be as successful as the sample blast we set off at Shopton, but we'll do our best."

Holes were drilled in the face of the rock, and several charges of the new explosive tamped in. Wires were attached to the fuses, which were of a new kind, and warning was given to clear the tunnel. The wires ran out to the mouth of the horizontal shaft and Tom, holding the switch in his hand made ready to set off the blast.

"Are they all out?" he asked Tim Sullivan, who had emerged, herding the Indian laborers before him. Tim insisted on being the last man to seek safety when an explosion was to take place.

"All ready, sor," answered the foreman.

"Here she goes!" cried Tom, as his fingers closed the circuit.

Mysterious Disappearances

There was a dull, muffled report, a sort of rumbling that seemed to extend away down under the earth and then echo back again until the ground near the mouth of the tunnel, where the party was standing, appeared to rock and heave. There followed a cloud of yellow, heavy smoke which made one choke and gasp, and Tom, seeing it, cried:

"Down! Down, everybody! There's a back draft, and if you breathe any of that powder vapor you'll have a fearful headache! Get down, until the smoke rises!"

The tunnel contractors and their men understood the danger, for they had handled explosives before. It is a well-known fact that the fumes of dynamite and other giant powders will often produce severe headaches, and even illness. Tom's explosive contained a certain percentage of dynamite, and he knew its ill effects. Stretched prone, or crouching on the ground, there was little danger, as the fumes, being lighter than air, rose. The yellow haze soon drifted away, and it was safe to rise.

"Well, I wonder how much rock your explosive tore loose for us, Tom," observed Job Titus, as he looked at the thin, yellowish cloud of smoke that was still lazily drifting from the tunnel.

"Can't tell until we go in and take a look," replied the young inventor. "It won't be safe to go in for a while yet, though. That smoke will hang in there a long time. I didn't think there'd be a back draft."

"There is, for we've often had the same trouble with our shots," Walter Titus said. "I can't account for it unless there is some opening in the shaft, connecting with the outer air, which admits a wind that drives the smoke out of the mouth, instead of forward into the blast hole. It's a queer thing and we haven't been able to get at the bottom of it."

"That's right," agreed his brother. "We've looked for some opening, or natural shaft, but haven't been able to find it. Sometimes we shoot off a charge and everything goes well, the smoke disappears in a few minutes. Again it will all blow out this way and we lose half a day waiting for the air to clear. There's a hidden shaft, or natural chimney, I'm sure, but we can't find it."

"Thot blast didn't make much racket," commented Tim Sullivan. "I doubt thot much rock come down. An' thot's not sayin' anythin' ag'in yer powder, lad," he went on to Tom.

"Oh, that's all right," Tom Swift replied, with a laugh. "My explosive doesn't work by sound. It has lots of power, but it doesn't produce much concussion."

"We've often made more noise with our blasts," confirmed Job Titus, "but I can't say much for our results."

They were all anxious, Tom included, to hurry into the tunnel to see how much rock had been loosened by the blast, but it was not safe to venture in until the fumes had been allowed to disperse. In about an hour, however, Tim Sullivan, venturing part way in, sniffed the air and called:

"It's all right, byes! Air's clear. Now come on!"

They all hurried eagerly into the shaft, Mr. Damon stumbling along at Tom's side, as anxious as the lad himself. Before they reached the face of the cliff against which the bore had been driven, and which was as a solid wall of rock to further progress, they began to tread on fragments of stone.

"Well, it blew some as far back as here," said Walter Titus. "That's a good sign."

"I hope so," Tom remarked.

There were still some fumes noticeable in the tunnel, and Mr. Damon complained of a slight feeling of illness, while Koku, who kept at Tom's side, murmured that it made his eyes smart. But the sensations soon passed.

They came to a stop as the face of the cliff loomed into view in the glare of a searchlight which Job Titus switched on. Then a murmur of wonder came from every one, save from Tom Swift. He, modestly, kept silent.

"Bless my breakfast orange!" cried Mr. Damon. "What a big hole!"

There was a great gash blown in the hard rock which had acted as a bar to the further progress of the tunnel. A great heap of rock, broken into small fragments, was on the floor of the shaft, and there was a big hole filled with debris which would have to be removed before the extent of the blast could be seen.

"That's doing the work!" cried Job Titus.

"It beats any two blasts we ever set off," declared his brother.

"Much fine!" muttered the Peruvian foreman, Serato.

"It's a lalapaloosa, lad! Thot's what it is!" enthusiastically exclaimed Tim Sullivan. "Now the black beggars will have some rock to shovel! Come on there, Serato, git yer lazy imps t' work cartin' this stuff away. We've got a man on th' job now in this new powder of Tom Swift's. Git busy!"

"Um!" grunted the Indian, and he called to his men who were soon busy with picks and shovels, loading the loosened rock and earth into the mule-hauled dump cars which took it to the mouth of the tunnel, whence it was shunted off on another small railroad to fill in a big gulch to save bridging it.

Tom's first blast was very successful, and enough rock was loosed to keep the laborers busy for a week. The contractors were more than satisfied.

"At this rate we'll finish ahead of time, and earn a premium," said Job to his brother.

"That's right. You didn't make any mistake in appealing to Tom Swift. But I wonder if Blakeson & Grinder have given up trying to get the job away from us?"

"I don't know. I'd never trust them. We must watch out for Waddington. That bomb on the vessel had a funny look, even if it was not meant to kill Tom or me. I won't relax any."

"No, I guess it wouldn't be safe."

But a week went by without any manifestation having been made by the rival tunnel contractors. During that week more of Tom's explosive arrived, and he busied himself getting ready another blast which could be set off as soon as the debris from the first should have been cleared away.

Meanwhile, Professor Bumper, with his Indian guides and helpers, had made several trips into the mountain regions about Rimac, but each time that he returned to the tunnel camp to renew his supplies, he had only a story of failure to recite.

"But I am positive that somewhere in this vicinity is the lost Peruvian city of Pelone," he said. "Every indication points to this as the region, and the more I study the plates of gold, and read their message, the more I am convinced that this is the place spoken of.

"But we have been over many mountains, and in more valleys, without finding a trace of the ancient civilization I feel sure once flourished here. There are no relics of a lost race—not so much as an arrow or spear head. But, somehow or other, I feel that I shall find the lost city. And when I do I shall be famous!"

"Mr. Damon and I will help you all we can, Tom said. "As soon as I get ready the next blast I'll have a little time to myself, and we will go with you on a trip or two."

"I shall be very glad to have you," the bald-headed scientist remarked.

Tom's second blast was even more successful than the first, and enough of the hard rock was loosed and pulverized to give the Indian laborers ten days' work in removing it from the tunnel.

Then, as the services of the young inventor would not be needed for a week or more, he decided to go on a little trip with Professor Bumper.

"I'll come too," said Mr. Damon. "One of the sub-contractors whose men are gathering the cinchona bark for our firm has his headquarters in the region where you are going, and I can go over there and see why he isn't up to the mark."

Accordingly, preparations having been made to spend a week in camp in the forests of the Andes, Tom and his party set off one morning. Professor Bumper's Indian helpers would do the hard work, and, of course, Koku, who went wherever Tom went, would be on hand in case some feat of strength were needed.

It was a blind search, this hunt for a lost city, and as much luck might be expected going in one direction as in another; so the party had no fixed point toward which to travel. Only Mr. Damon stipulated that he wanted to reach a certain village, and they planned to include that on their route.

Tom Swift took his electric rifle with him, and with it he was able to bring down a couple of deer which formed a welcome addition to the camp fare.

The rifle was a source of great wonder to the Peruvians. They were familiar with ordinary firearms, and some of them possessed old-fashioned guns. But Tom's electric weapon, which made not a sound, but killed with the swiftness of light, was awesome to them. The interpreter accompanying Professor

Bumper confided privately to Tom that the other Indians regarded the young inventor as a devil who could, if he wished, slay by the mere winking of an eye.

Mr. Damon located the quinine-gathering force he was anxious to see, and, through the interpreter, told the chief that more bark must be brought in to keep up to the terms of the contract.

But something seemed to be the matter. The Indian chief was indifferent to the interpreted demands of Mr. Damon, and that gentleman, though he blessed any number of animate and inanimate objects, seemed to make no impression.

"No got men to gather bark, him say," translated the interpreter.

"Hasn't got any men!" exclaimed Mr. Damon. "Why, look at all the lazy beggars around the village."

This was true enough, for there were any number of able-bodied Indians lolling in the shade.

"Him say him no got," repeated the translator, doggedly.

At that moment screams arose back of one the grass huts, and a child ran out into the open, followed by a savage dog which was snapping at the little one's bare legs.

"Bless my rat trap!" gasped Mr. Damon. "A mad dog!"

Shouts and cries arose from among the Indians. Women screamed, and those who had children gathered them up in their arms to run to shelter. The men threw all sorts of missiles at the infuriated animal, but seemed afraid to approach it to knock it over with a club, or to go to the relief of the frightened child which was now only a few feet ahead of the animal, running in a circle.

"Me git him!" cried Koku, jumping forward.

"No, Wait!" exclaimed Tom Swift. "You can kill the dog all right, Koku," he said, "but a scratch from his tooth might be fatal. I'll fix him!"

Snatching his electric rifle from the Indian bearer who carried it, Tom took quick aim. There was no flash, no report and no puff of smoke, but the dog suddenly crumpled up in a heap, and, with a dying yelp, rolled to one side. The child was saved.

The little one, aware that something had happened, turned and saw the stretched out form of its enemy. Then, sobbing and crying, it ran toward its mother who had just heard the news.

While the mothers gathered about the child, and while the older boys and girls made a ring at a respectful distance from the dog, there was activity noticed among the men of the village. They began hurrying out along the forest paths.

"Where are they going?" asked Tom. "Is there some trouble? Was that a sacred dog, and did I get in bad by killing it?"

The interpreter and the native chief conversed rapidly for a moment and then the former, turning to Tom, said:

"Men go git cinchona bark now. Plenty get for him," and he pointed to Mr. Damon. "They no like stay in village. T'ink yo' got lightning in yo' pocket," and he pointed to the electric rifle.

"Oh, I see!" laughed Tom. "They think I'm a sort of wizard. Well, so I am. Tell them if they don't get lots of quinine bark I'll have to stay here until all the mad dogs are shot."

The interpreter translated, and when the chief had ceased replying, Tom and the others were told:

"Plenty bark git. Plenty much. Yo' go away with yo' lightning. All right now."

"Well, it's a good thing I keeled over that dog," Tom said. "It was the best object lesson I could give them."

And from then on there was no more trouble in this district about getting a supply of the medicinal bark.

A week passed and Professor Bumper was no nearer finding the lost city than he had been at first. Reluctantly, he returned to the tunnel camp to get more provisions.

"And then I'll start out again," he said.

"We'll go with you some other time," promised Tom. "But now I expect I'll have to get another blast ready."

He found the debris brought down by the second one all removed, and in a few days, preparations for exploding more of the powder were under way.

Many holes had been drilled in the face of the cliff of hard rock, and the charges tamped in. Electric wires connected them, and they were run out to the tunnel mouth where the switch was located.

This was done late one afternoon, and it was planned to set off the blast at the close of the working day, to allow all night for the fumes to be blown away by the current of air in the tunnel.

"Get the men out, Tim," said Tom, when all was ready.

"All right, sor," was the answer, and the Irish foreman went back toward the far end of the bore to tell the last shift of laborers to come out so the blast could be set off.

But in a little while Tim came running back with a queer look on his face.

"What's the matter?" asked Tom. "Why didn't you bring the men with you?"

"Because, sor, they're not there!"

"Not in the tunnel? Why, they were working there a little while ago, when I made the last connection!"

"I know they were, but they've disappeared."

"Disappeared?"

"Yis sir. There's no way out except at this end an' you didn't see thim come out: did you?"

"Then they've disappeared! That's all there is to it! Bad goin's on, thot's what it is, sor! Bad!" and Tim shook his head mournfully.

FRIGHTENED INDIANS

"There must be some mistake," said Tom, wondering if the Irish foreman were given to joking. Yet he did not seem that kind of man.

"Mistake? How can there be a mistake, sor? I wint in there to tell th' black imps t' come out, but they're not there to tell!"

"What's the trouble?" asked Job Titus, coming out of the office near the tunnel mouth. "What's wrong, Tom?"

"Why, I sent Tim in to tell the men to come out, as I was going to set off a blast, but he says the men aren't in there. And I'm sure the last shift hasn't come out."

By this time Koku, Mr. Damon and Walter Titus had come up to find out what the trouble was.

"The min have disappeared—that's all there is to it!" Tim said.

"Perhaps they have missed their way—the lights may have gone out, and they might have wandered into some abandoned cutting," suggested Tom.

"There aren't any abandoned cuttin's," declared Tim. "It's a straight bore, not a shaft of any kind. I've looked everywhere, and th' min aren't there I tell ye!"

"Are the lights going?" asked Job. "You might have missed them in the dark, Tim."

"The lights are going all right, Mr. Titus," said the young man in charge of the electrical arrangements. "The dynamo hasn't been stopped today."

"Come on, we'll have a look," proposed Walter Titus. "There must be some mistake. Hold back the blast, Tom."

"All right," and the young inventor disconnected the electrical detonating switch. "I'll come along and have a look too," he added. "Don't let anybody meddle with the wires, Jack," he said to the young Englishman who was in charge of the dynamo.

Into the dimly-lit tunnel advanced the party of investigators, with Tim Sullivan in the lead.

"Not a man could I find!" he said, murmuring to himself. "Not a man! An' I mind th' time in Oireland whin th' little people made vanish a whole village like this, jist bekase ould Mike Maguire uprooted a bed of shamrocks."

"That's enough of your superstitions, Tim," warned Job Titus. "If some of the other Indians hear you go on this way they'll desert as they did once before."

"Did they do that?" asked Tom.

"Yes, we had trouble that way when we first began the work. The place here was a howling wilderness then, and there were lots of pumas around.

"A puma is a small sized lion, you know, not specially dangerous unless cornered. Well, some of the men had their families here with them, and a couple of children disappeared. The story got started that there was a big puma—the king of them all—carrying off the little ones, and my brother and I awoke one morning to find every laborer missing. They departed bag and baggage. Afraid of the pumas."

"What did you do?"

"Well, we organized ourselves and our white helpers into a hunting party and killed a lot of the beasts. There wasn't any big one though."

"And what had become of the children?"

"They weren't eaten at all. They had wandered off into the woods, and some natives found them and took care of them. Eventually, they got back home. But it was a long while before we could persuade the Indians to come back. Since then we haven't had any trouble, and I don't want Tim, with his superstitious fancies, to start any."

"But the min are gone!" insisted the Irish foreman, who had listened to this story as he and the others walked along.

"We'll find them," declared Mr. Titus.

But though they looked all along the big shaft, and though the place was well lighted by extra lamps that were turned on when the investigation started, no trace could be found of the workmen, who had been left in the tunnel to finish tamping the blast charges. The party reached the rocky heading, in the face of which the powerful explosive had been placed, and not an Indian was in sight. Nor, as far as could be told, was there any side niche, or blind shaft, in which they could be hiding.

Sometimes, when small blasts were set off, the men would go behind a projecting shoulder of rock to wait until the charge had been fired, but now none was in such a refuge.

"It is queer," admitted Walter Titus. "Where can the men have gone?"

"That's what I want to know!" exclaimed Tim.

"Are you sure they didn't come out the mouth of the tunnel?" asked Job Titus.

"Positive," asserted Tom. I was there all the while, rigging up the fires."

"We'll call the roll, and check up," decided Job Titus. "Get Serato to help."

The Indian foreman had not been in the tunnel with the last shift of men, having left them to Tim Sullivan to get out in time. The Indian foreman was called from his supper in the shack where he had his headquarters, and the roll of workmen was called.

Ten men were missing, and when this fact became known there were uneasy looks among the others.

"Well," said Mr. Titus, after a pause. "The men are either in the tunnel or out of it. If they're in we don't dare set off the blast, and if they're out they'll show up, sooner or later, for supper. I never knew any of 'em to miss a meal."

"If such a thing were possible," said Walter Titus, "I would say that our rivals had a hand in this, and had induced our men to bolt in order to cripple our force. But we haven't seen any of Blakeson & Grinder's emissaries about, and, if they were, how could they get the ten men out of the tunnel without our Seeing them? It's impossible!"

"Well, what did happen then?" asked Tom.

"I'm inclined to think that the men came out and neither you, nor any one else, saw them. They ran away for reasons of their own. We'll take another look in the morning, and then set off the blast."

And this was done. There being no trace of the men in the tunnel it was deemed safe to explode the charges. This was done, a great amount of rock being loosened.

The laborers hung back when the orders were given to go in and clean up. There were mutterings among them.

"What's the matter?" asked Job Titus.

"Them afraid," answered Serato. "Them say devil in tunnel eat um up! No go in."

"They won't go in, eh?" cried Tim Sullivan. "Well, they will thot! If there's a divil inside there's a worse one outside, an' thot's me! Git in there now, ye black-livered spalapeens!" and catching up a big club the Irishman made a rush for the hesitating laborers. With a howl they rushed into the tunnel, and were soon loading rock into the dump cars.

ON THE WATCH

The mystery of the disappearance of the ten men—for mystery it was—remained, and as no side opening or passage could be found within the tunnel, it came to be the generally accepted explanation that the laborers had come out unobserved, and, for reasons of their own, had run away.

This habit on the part of the Peruvian workers was not unusual. In fact, the Titus brothers had to maintain a sort of permanent employment agency in Lima to replace the deserters. But they were used to this. The difference was that the Indians used to vanish from camp at night, and invariably after pay-day.

"And that's the only reason I have a slight doubt that they walked out of the tunnel," said Job Titus. "There was money due em."

"They never came out of the front entrance of the tunnel," said Tom. "Of that I'm positive."

But there was no way of proving his assertion.

The third blast, while not as successful as the second in the amount of rock loosened, was better than the first, and made a big advance in the tunnel progress. Tom was beginning to understand the nature of the mountain into which the big shaft was being driven and he learned how better to apply the force of his explosive.

That was the work which he had charge of—the placing of the giant powder so it would do the most effective work. Then, when the fumes from the blast had cleared away, in would surge the workmen to clear away the debris.

Under the direction of Mr. Swift, left at Shopton to oversee the manufacture of the explosive, new shipments came on promptly to Lima, and were brought out to the tunnel on the backs of mules, or in the case of small quantities, on the llamas. But the latter brutes will not carry a heavy load, lying down and refusing to get up if they are overburdened, whereas one has yet to find a mule's limit.

After his first success in getting the natives to take a more active interest in the gathering of the cinchona bark, Mr. Damon found it rather easy, for the story of Tom's electric rifle and how it had killed the mad dog spread among the tribes, and Mr. Damon had but to announce that the "lightning shooter," as Tom was called, was a friend of the drug concern to bring about the desired results. Mr. Damon, by paying a sort of bribe, disguised under the name "tax," secured the help of Peruvian officials so he had no trouble on that score.

Koku was in his element. He liked a wild life and Peru was much more like the country of giants where Tom had found him, than any place the big man had since visited. Koku had great strength and wanted to use it, and after a week or so of idleness he persuaded Tom to let him go in the tunnel to work.

The giant was made a sort of foreman under Tim, and the two became great friends. The only trouble with Koku was that he would do a thing himself instead of letting his men do it, as, of course, all proper foremen should do. If the giant saw two or three of the Indians trying to lift a big rock into the little dump cars, and failing because of its great weight, he would good-naturedly thrust them aside, pick up the big stone in his mighty arms, and deposit it in its place.

And once when an unusually big load had been put in a car, and the mule attached found it impossible to pull it out to the tunnel mouth, Koku unhitched the creature and, slipping the harness around his waist, walked out, dragging the load as easily as if pulling a child on a sled.

Professor Bumper kept on with his search for the lost city of Pelone. Back and forth he wandered among the wild Andes Mountains, now hopeful that he was on the right trail, and again in despair. Tom and Mr. Damon went with him once more for a week, and though they enjoyed the trip, for the professor was a delightful companion, there were no results. But the scientist would not give up.

Tom Swift was kept busy looking after the shipments of the explosive, and arranging for the blasts. He had letters from Ned Newton in which news of Shopton was given, and Mr. Swift wrote occasionally. But the mails in the wilderness of the Andes were few and far between.

Tom wrote a letter of explanation to Mr. Nestor, in addition to the wireless he had sent regarding the box labeled dynamite, but he got no answer. Nor were his letters to Mary answered.

"I wonder what's wrong?" Tom mused. "It can't be that they think I did that on purpose. And even if Mr. Nestor is angry at me for something that wasn't my fault, Mary ought to write."

But she did not, and Tom grew a bit despondent as the days went by and no word came.

"I suppose they might be offended because I left Rad to do up that package instead of attending to it myself," thought Tom. "Well, I did make a mistake there, but I didn't mean to. I never thought about Eradicate's not reading. I'll make him go to night school as soon as I get back. But maybe I'll never get another chance to send Mary anything. If I do, I'll not let Rad deliver it—that's sure."

The feeling of alarm engendered among the Indians by the disappearance of their ten fellow-workers seemed to have disappeared. There were rumors that some of the mysterious ten had been seen in distant villages and settlements, but the Titus brothers could not confirm this.

"I don't think anything serious happened to them, anyhow," said Job Titus one day. "And I should hate to think our work was responsible for harm to any one."

"Your rivals don't seem to be doing much to hamper you," observed Tom. "I guess Waddington gave up."

"I won't be too sure of that," said Mr. Titus.

"Why, what has happened?" Tom asked.

"Well, nothing down here—that is, directly—but we are meeting with trouble on the financial end. The Peruvian government is holding back payments."

"Why is that?"

"They claim we are not as far advanced as we ought to be."

"Aren't you?"

"Practically, yes. There was no set limit of work to be done for the intermediate payments. We bonded ourselves to have the tunnel done at a certain date.

"If we fail, we lose a large sum, and if we get it done ahead of time we get a big premium. There was no question as to completing a certain amount of footage before we received certain payments. But Senor Belasdo, the government representative, claims that we will not be done in time, and therefore he is holding back money due us. I'm sure the rival contractors have set him up to this, because he was always decent to us before.

"Another matter, too, makes me suspicious. We have tried to raise money in New York to tide us over while the government is holding up our funds here. But our New York office is meeting with difficulties. They report there is a story current to the effect that we are going to fail, and while that isn't so, you know how hard it is to borrow money in the face of such rumors. We are doing all we can to fight them, of course, and maybe we'll beat out our rivals yet.

"But that isn't all. I'm sure some one is on the ground here trying to make trouble among our workers. I never knew so many men to leave, one after another. It's keeping the employment agency in Lima busy supplying us with new workers. And so many of them are unskilled. They aren't able to do half the work of the old men, and poor Tim Sullivan is in despair."

"You think some one here is causing dissensions and desertions among your men?"

"I'm sure of it! I've tried to ferret out who it is, but the spy, for such he must be, keeps his identity well hidden."

Tom thought for a moment. Then he said:

"Mr. Titus, with your permission, I'll see if I can find out about this for you."

"Find out what, Tom?"

"What is causing the men to leave. I don't believe it's the scare about the ten missing ones."

"Nor do I. That's past and gone. But how are you going to get at the bottom of it?"

"By keeping watch. I've got nothing to do now for the next week. "We've just set off a big blast, and I've got the powder for the following one all ready. The men will be busy for some time getting out the broken rock. Now what I propose to do is to go in the tunnel and work among them until I can learn something.

"I can understand the language pretty well now, though I can't speak much of it. I'll go in the tunnel every day and find out what's going on."

"But you'll be known, and if one of our men, or one who we suppose is one, turns out to be a spy, he'll be very cautious while you're in there."

"He won't know me," Tom said. "This is how I'll work it. I'll go off with Professor Bumper the next time he starts on one of his weekly expeditions into the woods. But I won't go far until I turn around and come back. I'll adopt some sort of disguise, and I'll apply to you for work. You can tell Tim to put me on. You might let him into the secret, but no one else."

A few days later Tom was seen departing with Professor Bumper into the interior, presumably to help look for the lost city. Mr. Damon was away from camp on business connected with the drug concern, and Koku, to his delight, had been given charge of a stationary hoisting engine outside the tunnel, so he would not come in contact with Tom. It was not thought wise to take the giant into the secret.

Then one day, shortly after Professor Bumper and Tom had disappeared into the forest, a ragged and unkempt white man applied at the tunnel camp for work. There was just the barest wink as he accosted Mr. Titus, who winked in turn, and then the new man was handed over to Tim Sullivan, as a sort of helper.

And so Tom Swift began his watch.

THE CONDOR

Left to himself, with only the rather silent gang of Peruvian Indians as company, Tom Swift looked about him. There was not much active work to be done, only to see that the Indians filled the dump cars evenly full, so none of the broken rock would spill over the side and litter the tramway. Then, too, he had to keep the Indians up to the mark working, for these men were no different from any other, and they were just as inclined to "loaf on the job" when the eye of the "boss" was turned away.

They did not talk much, murmuring among themselves now and then, and little of what they said was intelligible to Tom. But he knew enough of the language to give them orders, the main one of which was:

"Hurry up!"

Now, having seen to it that the gang of which he was in temporary charge was busily engaged, Tom had a chance to look about him. The tunnel was not new to him. Much of his time in the past month had been spent in its black depths, illuminated, more or less, by the string of incandescent lights.

"What I want to find," mused Tom, as he walked to and fro, "is the place where those Indians disappeared. For I'm positive they got away through some hole in this tunnel. They never came out the main entrance."

Tom held to this view in spite of the fact that nearly every one else believed the contrary—that the men had left by the tunnel mouth, near which Tom happened to be alone at the time.

Now, left to himself, with merely nominal duties, and so disguised that none of the workmen would know him for the trim young inventor who oversaw the preparing of the blast charges, Tom Swift walked to and fro, looking for some carefully hidden passage or shaft by means of which the men had got away.

"For it must be well hidden to have escaped observation so long," Tom decided. "And it must be a natural shaft, or hole, for we are boring into native rock, and it isn't likely that these Indians ever tried to make a tunnel here. There must be some natural fissure communicating with the outside of the mountain, in a place where no one would see the men coming out."

But though Tom believed this it was another matter to demonstrate his belief. In the intervals of seeing that the natives properly loaded the dump cars, and removed as much of the debris as possible, Tom looked carefully along the walls and roof of the tunnel thus far excavated.

There were cracks and fissures, it is true, but they were all superficial ones, as Tom ascertained by poking a long pole up into them.

"No getting out that way," he said, as he met with failure after failure.

Once, while thus engaged, he saw Serato, the Indian foreman looking narrowly at him, and Serato said something in his own language which Tom could not understand. But just then along came Tim Sullivan, who, grasping the situation, exclaimed:

"Thot's all roight, now, Serri, me lad!" for thus he contracted the Indian's name. "Thot's a new helper I have, a broth of a bye, an' yez kin kape yer hands off him. He's takin' orders from me!"

"Um!" grunted the Indian. "Wha for he fish in tunnel roof?" for Tom's pole was one like those the Indians used when, on off days, they emulated Izaak Walton.

"Fishin' is it!" exclaimed Tim. "Begorra 'tis flyin' fish he's after I'm thinkin'. Lave him alone though, Serri! I'm his boss!"

"Um!" grunted the Indian again, as he moved off into the farther darkness.

"Be careful, Tom," whispered the Irishman, when the native had gone. "These black imps is mighty suspicious. Maybe thot fellah had a hand in th' disappearances hisself."

"Maybe," admitted Tom. "He may get a percentage on all new hands that are hired."

Tom kept on with his search, always hoping he might find some hidden means of getting out of the tunnel. But as the days went by, and he discovered nothing, he began to despair.

"The queer thing about it," mused Tom, "is what has become of the ten men. Even if they did find some secret means of leaving, what has become of them? They couldn't completely disappear, and they have families and relatives that would make some sort of fuss if they were out of sight completely this long. I wonder if any inquiries have been made about them?"

When Tom came off duty he asked the Titus brothers whether or not any of the relatives of the missing men had come to seek news about them. None had.

"Then," said Tom, "you can depend on it the men are all right, and their relatives know it. I wonder how it would do to make inquiries at that end? Question some of the relatives."

"Bless my hat hand!" exclaimed Mr. Damon, who was at the conference. "I never thought of that. I'll do it for you."

The odd man had gotten his quinine gathering business well under way now, and he had some spare time. So, with an interpreter who could be trusted, he went to the native village whence had come nearly all of the ten missing men. But though Mr. Damon found some of their relatives, the latter, with shrugs of their shoulders, declared they had seen nothing of the ones sought.

"And they didn't seem to worry much, either," reported Mr. Damon.

"Then we can depend on it," remarked Tom, "that the men are all right and their relatives know it. There's some conspiracy here."

So it seemed. But who was at the bottom of it?

"I can't figure out where Blakeson & Grinder come in," said Job Titus. "They would have an object in crippling us, but they seem to be working from the financial end, trying to make us fail there. I haven't seen any of their sneaking agents around here lately, and as for Waddington he seems to have stayed up North."

Tom resumed his vigil in the tunnel, poking here and there, but with little success. His week was about up, and he would soon have to resume his character as powder expert, for the debris was nearly all cleaned up, and another blast would have to be fired shortly.

"Well, I'm stumped!" Tom admitted, the day when he was to come on duty for the last time as a pretended foreman. "I've hunted all over, and I can't find any secret passage."

It was warm in the tunnel, and Tom, having seen one train of the dump cars loaded, sat down to rest on an elevated ledge of rock, where he had made a sort of easy chair for himself, with empty cement bags for cushions.

The heat, his weariness and the monotonous clank-clank of a water pump near by, and the equally monotonous thump of the lumps of rocks in the cars made Tom drowsy. Almost before he knew it he was asleep.

What suddenly awakened him he could not tell. Perhaps it was some influence on the brain cells, as when a vivid dream causes us to start up from slumber, or it may have been a voice. For certainly Tom heard a voice, he declared afterward.

As he roused up he found himself staring at the rocky wall of the tunnel. And yet the wall seemed to have an opening in it and in the opening, as if it were in the frame of a picture, appeared the face Tom had seen at his library the day Job Titus called on him—the face of Waddington!

Tom sat up so quickly that he hit his head sharply on a projecting rock spur, and, for the moment he "saw stars." And with the appearance of these twinkling points of light the face of Waddington seemed to fade away, as might a vision in a dream.

"Bless my salt mackerel, as Mr. Damon would say!" cried Tom. "What have I discovered?"

He rubbed his head where he had struck it, and then passed his hand before his eyes, to make sure he was awake. But the vision, if vision it was, had vanished, and he saw only the bare rock wall. However, the echo of the voice remained in his ears, and, looking down toward the tunnel floor Tom saw Serato, the Indian foreman.

"Were you speaking to me?" asked Tom, for the man understood and spoke English fairly well.

"No, sar. I not know you there!" and the fore man seemed startled at seeing Tom. Clearly he was in a fright.

"You were speaking!" insisted Tom.

"No, sar!" The man shook his head.

"To some one up there!" went on the young inventor, waving his hand toward the spot where he had seen the face in the rock.

"Me speak to roof? No, sar!" Serato laughed.

Tom did not know what to believe.

"You hear me tell um lazy man to much hurry," the Indian went on. "Me not know you sleep there, sar!"

"Oh, all right," Tom said, recollecting that he must keep up his disguise. "Maybe I was dreaming."

"Yes, sar," and the foreman hurried on, with a backward glance over his shoulder.

"Now was I dreaming or not?" thought Tom. "I'm going to have a look at that place though, where I saw Waddington's face. Or did I imagine it?"

He got a long pole and a powerful flash lamp, and when he had a chance, unobserved, he poked around in the vicinity where he had seen the face.

But there was only solid rock.

"It must have been a dream," Tom concluded. "I've been thinking too much about this business. I'll have to give up. I can't solve the mystery of the missing men."

The next day, much disappointed, he resumed his own character as explosive expert, and prepared for another blast. The net result of his watch was that he became suspicious of Serato, and so informed the Titus Brothers.

"Oh, but you're mistaken," said Job "We have had him for years, on other contracts in Peru, and we trust him."

"Well, I don't," Tom said, but he had to let it go at that.

Another blast was set off, but it was not very successful.

"The rock seems to be getting harder the farther in we go," commented Walter Titus. "We're not up to where we ought to be."

"I'll have to look into it," answered Tom. "I may have to change the powder mixture. Guess I'll go up the mountain a way, and see if there are any outcroppings of rock there that would give me an idea of what lies underneath."

Accordingly, while the men in the tunnel were clearing away the rock loosened by the blast, Tom, one day, taking his electric rifle with him, went up the mountain under which the big bore ran.

He located, by computation, the spot beneath which the end of the tunnel then was, and began collecting samples of the outcropping ledge. He wanted to analyze these pieces of stone later. Koku was with him, and, giving the giant a bag of stones to carry, Tom walked on rather idly.

It was a wild and desolate region in which he found himself on the side of the mountain. Beyond him stretched towering and snow-clad peaks, and high in the air were small specks, which he knew to be condors, watching with their eager eyes for their offal food.

As Tom and Koku made their way along the mountain trail they came unexpectedly upon an Indian workman who was gathering herbs and bark, an industry by which many of the natives added to their scanty livelihood. The woman was familiar with the appearance of the white men, and nodded in friendly fashion.

Tom passed on, thinking of many things, when he was suddenly startled by a scream from the woman. It was a scream of such terror and agony that, for the moment, Tom was stunned into inactivity. Then, as he turned, he saw a great condor sweeping down out of the air, the wind fairly whistling through the big, outstretched wings.

"Jove!" ejaculated Tom. "Can the bird be going to attack the woman?"

But this was not the object of the condor. It was aiming to strike, with its fierce talons, at a point some paces distant from where the woman stood, and in the intervals between her screams Tom heard her cry, in her native tongue:

"My baby! My baby! The beast-bird will carry off my baby!"

Then Tom understood. The woman herb-gatherer had brought her infant with her on her quest, and had laid it down on a bed of soft grass while she worked. And it was this infant, wrapped as Tom afterward saw in a piece of deer-skin, at which the condor was aiming.

"Master shoot!" cried Koku, pointing to the down-sweeping bird.

"You bet I'll shoot!" cried Tom.

Throwing his electric rifle to his shoulder, Tom pressed the switch trigger. The unseen but powerful force shot straight at the condor.

The outstretched wings fell limp, the great body seemed to shrivel up, and, with a crash, the bird fell into the underbrush, breaking the twigs and branches with its weight. The electric rifle, a full account of which was given in the volume entitled "Tom Swift and His Electric Rifle," had done its work well.

With a scream, in which was mingled a cry of thanks, the woman threw himself on the sleeping child. The condor bad fallen dead not three paces from it.

Tom Swift had shot just in time.

THE INDIAN STRIKE

Snatching up in her arms the now awakened child, the woman gazed for a moment into its face, which she covered with kisses. Then the herb-gatherer looked over to the dead, limp body of the great condor, and from thence to Tom.

In another moment the woman had rushed forward, and knelt at the feet of the young inventor. Holding the baby in one arm, in her other hand the woman seized Toms and kissed it fervently, at the same time pouring forth a torrent of impassioned language, of which Tom could only make out a word now and then. But he gathered that the woman was thanking him for having saved the child.

"Oh, that's all right," Tom said, rather embarrassed by the hand-kissing. "It was an easy shot."

An Indian came bursting through the bushes, evidently the woman's husband by the manner in which she greeted him, and Tom recognized the newcomer as one of the tunnel workers. There was some quick conversation between the husband and wife, in which the latter made all sorts of motions, including in their scope Tom, his rifle, the dead condor and the now smiling baby.

The man took off his hat and approached Tom, genuflecting as he might have done in church.

"She say you save baby from condor," the man said in his halting English. "She t'ank you—me, I t'ank you. Bird see babe in deer skin—t'ink um dead animal. Maybe so bird carry baby off, drop um on sharp stone, baby smile no more. You have our lives, senor! We do anyt'ing we can for you."

"Thanks," said Tom, easily. "I'm glad I happened to be around. I supposed condors only went for things dead, but I reckon, as you say, it mistook the baby in the deer skin for a dead animal. And I guess it might have carried your little one off, or at least lifted it up, and then it might have dropped it far enough to have killed it. It sure is a big bird," and Tom strolled over to look at what he had bagged.

The condor of the Andes is the largest bird of prey in existence. One in the Bronx Zoo, in New York, with his wings spread out, measured a little short of ten feet from tip to tip. Measure ten feet out on the ground and then imagine a bird with that wing stretch.

This same condor in the park was made angry by a boy throwing a feather boa up into the air outside the cage. The condor raised himself from the ground, and hurled himself against the heavy wire netting so that the whole, big cage shook. And the breeze caused by the flapping wings blew off the hats of several spectators. So powerful was the air force from the condor's wings that it reminded one of the current caused when standing behind the propellers of an aeroplane in motion. The condor rarely attacks living persons or animals, though it has been known to carry off big sheep when driven by hunger.

It was one of these animals Tom Swift had shot with his electric rifle.

"We do anyt'ing you want," the man gratefully repeated.

"Well, I've got about all I want," Tom said. "But if you could tell me where those ten missing men are, and how they got out of the tunnel, I'd be obliged to you."

The woman did not seem to comprehend Tom's talk, but the man did. He started, and fear seemed to come over him.

"Me—I—I can not tell," he murmured.

"No, I don't suppose you can," said Tom, musingly. "Well," it doesn't matter, I guess I'll have to cross it off my books. I'll never find out."

Again the Indian and his wife expressed their gratitude, and Tom, after letting the little brown baby cling to his finger, and patting its chubby cheek, went on his way with Koku.

"Well, that was some excitement," mused Tom, who made little of the shot itself, for the condor was such a mark that he would have had to aim very badly indeed to miss it. And perhaps only the electric rifle could have killed quickly enough to prevent the baby's being injured in some way by the big bird, even though it was dying.

"Master heap good shot!" exclaimed Koku, admiringly.

The tunnel work went on, though not so well as when Tom's explosive was first used. The rock was indeed getting harder and was not so easily shattered. Tom made tests of the pieces he had obtained from the outcropping ledge on the mountain where he had shot the condor, and decided to make a change in the powder.

Shipments were regularly received from Shop ton, Mr. Swift keeping things in progress there. Mr. Damon's business was going on satisfactorily, and he lent what aid he could to Tom. As for Professor Bumper he kept on with his search for the lost city of Pelone, but with no success.

The scientist wanted Tom and Mr. Damon to go on another trip with him, this time to a distant sierra, or fertile valley, where it was reported a race of Indians lived, different from others in that region.

"It may be that they are descendants from the Pelonians," suggested the professor. Tom was too busy to go, but Mr. Damon went. The expedition had all sorts of trouble, losing its way and getting into a swamp from which escape was not easy. Then, too, the strange Indians proved hostile, and the professor and his party could not get nearer than the boundaries of the valley.

"But the difficulties and the hostile attitude of these natives only makes me surer that I am on the right track," said Mr. Bumper. "I shall try again."

Tom was busy over a problem in explosives one day when he saw Tim Sullivan hurrying into the office of the two brothers. The Irishman seemed excited.

"I hope there hasn't been another premature blast," mused Tom. "But if there had been I think I'd have heard it."

He hastened out to see Job and Walter Titus in excited conversation with Tim.

"They didn't come out, an' thot's all there is to it," the foreman was saying. "I sint thim in mesilf, and they worked until it was time t' set off th' blast. I wint t' get th' fuse, an' I was goin' t' send th' black imps out of danger, whin—whist—they was gone whin I got back—fifteen of 'ern this time!"

"Do you mean that fifteen more of our men have vanished as the first ten did?" asked Job Titus.

"That's what I mean," asserted the Irishman.

"It can't be!" declared Walter.

"Look for yersilf!" returned Tim. "They're not in th' tunnel!"

"And they didn't come out?"

"Ask th' time-keeper," and Tim motioned to a young Englishman who, since the other disappearance, had been stationed at the mouth of the tunnel to keep a record of who went in and came out.

"No, sir! Nobody kime hout, sir!" the Englishman declared. "Hi 'aven't been away frim 'ere, sir, not since hi wint on duty, sir. An' no one kime out, no, sir!"

"We've got to stop this!" declared Job Titus.

"I should say so!" agreed his brother.

With Tom and Tim the Titus brothers went into the tunnel. It was deserted, and not a trace of the men could be found. Their tools were where they had been dropped, but of the men not a sign.

"There must be some secret way out," declared Tom.

"Then we'll find it," asserted the brothers.

Work on the tunnel was stopped for a day, and, keeping out all natives, the contractors, with Tom and such white men as they had in their employ, went over every foot of roof, sides and floor in the big shaft. But not a crack or fissure, large enough to permit the passage of a child, much less a man, could be found.

"Well, I give up!" cried Walter Titus in despair. "There must be witchcraft at work here!"

"Nonsense!" exclaimed his brother. "It's more likely the craft of Blakeson & Grinder, with Waddington helping them."

"Well, if a human agency made these twenty-five men disappear, prove it!" insisted Walter.

His brother did not know what to say.

"Well, go on with the work," was Job's final conclusion. "We'll have one of the white men constantly in the tunnel after this whenever a gang is working. We won't leave the natives alone even long enough to go to get a fuse. They'll be under constant supervision."

The tunnel was opened for work, but there were no workers. The morning after the investigation, when the starting whistle blew there was no line of Indians ready to file into the big, black hole. The huts where they slept were deserted. A strange silence brooded over the tunnel camp.

"Where are the men, Serato?" asked Tom of the Indian foreman.

"Men um gone. No work any more. What you call a hit."

"You mean a strike?" asked Tom.

"Sure—strike—hit—all um same. No more work—um 'fraid!"

A Woman Tells

"Well, if this isn't the limit!" cried Torn Swift. "As if we didn't have trouble enough without a strike on our hands!"

"I should say yes!" chimed in Job Titus.

"Do you mean that the men won't work any more?" asked his brother of the native foreman.

"Sure, no more work—um much 'fraid big devil in tunnel carry um off an' eat um."

"Well, I don't know that I blame 'em for being a bit frightened," commented Job. "It is a queer proceeding how twenty-five men can disappear like that. Where have the men gone, Serato?"

"Gone home. No more work. Go on hit—strike—same like white men."

"They waited until pay day to go on strike," commented the bookkeeper, a youth about Tom's age.

This was true. The men had been paid off the day before, and usually on such occasions many of them remained away, celebrating in the nearest village. But this time all had left, and evidently did not intend to come back.

"We'll have to get a new gang," said Job. "And it's going to delay us just at the wrong time. Well, there's no help for it. Get busy, Serato. You and Tim go and see how many men you can gather. Tell them we'll give them a sol a week more if they do good work. (A sol is the standard silver coin of Peru, and is worth in United States gold about fifty cents.)

"Half a dollar a day more will look mighty big to them," went on the contractor. "Get the men, Serato, and we'll raise your wages two sols a week."

The eyes of the Indian gleamed, and he went off, saying.

"Um try, but men much 'fraid.'

Whether Serato used his best arguments could not, of course, be learned, but he came back at the close of the day, unaccompanied by any workers, and he shook his head despondently.

"Indians no come for one sol, mebby not for two," he said. "I no can git."

"Then I'll try!" cried Job. "I'll get the workers. I'll make our old ones come back, for they'll be the best."

Accompanied by his brother and Tom he went to the various Indian villages, including the one whence most of the men now on strike had come. The fifteen missing ones were not found, though, as before, their relatives, and, in some cases, their families, did not seem alarmed. But the men who had gone on strike were found lolling about their cabins and huts, smoking and taking their ease, and no amount of persuasion could induce them to return.

Some of them said they had worked long enough and were tired, needing a rest. Others declared they had money enough and did not want more. Even two more sols a week would not induce them to return.

And many were frankly afraid. They said so, declaring that if they went back to the tunnel some unknown devil might carry them off under the earth.

Job Titus and his brother, who could speak the language fairly well, tried to argue against this. They declared the tunnel was perfectly safe. But one native worker, who had been the best in the gang, asked:

"Where um men go?"

The contractors could not answer.

"It's a trick," declared Walter. "Our rivals have induced the men to go on strike in order to hamper us with the work so they'll get the job."

But the closest inquiry failed to prove this statement. If Blakeson & Grinder, or any of their agents, had a hand in the strike they covered their operations well. Though diligent inquiry was made, no trace of Waddington, or any other tool, could be found.

Tom, who had some sort of suspicion of the bearded man on the steamer, tried to find him, even taking a trip in to Lima, but without avail.

The tunnel work was at a standstill, for there was little use in setting off blasts if there were no men to remove the resulting piles of debris. So, though Tom was ready with some specially powerful explosive, he could not use it.

Efforts were made to get laborers from another section of the country, but without effect. The contractors heard of a big force of Italians who had finished work on a railroad about a hundred miles away, and they were offered places in the tunnel. But they would not come.

"Well, we may as well give up," said Walter, despondently, to his brother one day. "We'll never get the tunnel done on time now."

"We still have a margin of safety," declared job. "If we could get the men inside of a couple of weeks, and if Tom's new powder rips out more rock, we'll finish in time."

"Yes, but there are too many ifs. We may as well admit we've failed."

"I'll never do that!"

"What will you do?"

But Job did not know.

"If we could git a gang of min from the ould sod—th' kind I used t' work wit in N'Yark," said Tim Sullivan, "I'd show yez whot could be done! We'd make th' rock fly!"

But that efficient labor was out of the question now. The tunnel camp was a deserted place.

"Come on, Koku, we'll go hunting," said Tom one day. "There's no use hanging around here, and some venison wouldn't go bad on the table."

"I'll come, too," said Mr. Damon. "I haven't anything to do."

The Titus brothers had gone to a distant village, on the forlorn hope of getting laborers, so Tom was left to his own devices, and he decided to go hunting with his electric rifle.

The taruco, or native deer, had been plentiful in the vicinity of the tunnel until the presence of so many men and the frequent blasts had driven them farther off, and it was not until after a tramp of several miles that Tom saw one. Then, after stalking it a little way, he managed to kill it with the electric rifle.

Koku hoisted the animal to his big shoulders, and, as this would provide meat enough for some time, Tom started back for camp.

As he and Mr. Damon, with Koku in the rear, passed through a little clearing, they saw, on the far side, a native hut. And from it rushed a woman, who approached Tom, casting herself on her knees, while she pressed his free hand to her head.

"Bless my scarf pin!" exclaimed Mr. Damon. "What does this mean, Tom?"

"Oh, this is the mother of the child I saved from the condor," said Tom. "Every time she sees me she thanks me all over again. How is the baby?" he asked in the Indian tongue, for he was a fair master of it by now.

"The baby is well. Will the mighty hunter permit himself to enter my miserable hovel and partake of some milk and cakes?"

"What do you say, Mr. Damon?" Tom asked. "She's clean and neat, and she makes a drink of goat's milk that isn't bad. She bakes some kind of meal cakes that are good, too. I'm hungry."

"All right, Tom, I'll do as you say."

A little later they were partaking of a rude, but none the less welcome, lunch in the woman's hut, while the baby whose life Tom had saved cooed in the rough log cradle.

"Say, Masni," asked Tom, addressing the woman by name, "don't you know where we can get some men to work the tunnel?" Of course Tom spoke the Indian language, and he had to adapt himself to the comprehension of Masni.

"Men no work tunnel?" she inquired.

"No, they've all skipped out—vamoosed. Afraid of some spirit."

The woman looked around, as though in fear. Then she approached Tom closely and whispered:

"No spirit in tunnel—bad man!"

"What!" cried Tom, almost jumping off his stool. "What do you mean, Masni?"

"Me tell mighty hunter," she went on, lowering her voice still more. "My man he no want to tell, he 'fraid, but I tell. Mighty hunter save Vashni," and she looked toward the baby. "Me help friends of mighty hunter. Bad man in tunnel— no spirit!

"Men go. Spirit no take um—bad man take um."

"Where are they now?" asked Tom. "Jove, if I could find them the secret would be solved!"

The woman looked fearfully around the hut and then whispered:

"You come—me show!"

"Bless my toothbrush!" cried Mr. Damon. "What is going to happen, Tom Swift?"

"I don't know," was the answer, "but something sure is in the wind. I guess I shot better than I knew when I killed that condor."

Despair

Calling to a girl of about thirteen years to look after her baby, Masni slipped along up a rough mountain trail, motioning to Tom, Mr. Damon and Koku to follow. Or rather, the woman gave the sign to Tom, ignoring the others, who, naturally, would not be left behind. Masni seemed to have eyes for no one but the young inventor, and the manner in which she looked at him showed the deep gratitude she felt toward him for having saved her baby from the great condor.

"Come," she said, in her strange Indian tongue, which Tom could interpret well enough for himself now.

"But where are we going, Masni?" he asked. "This isn't the way to the tunnel."

"Me know. Not go to tunnel now," was her answer. "Me show you men."

"But which men do you mean, Masni?" inquired Tom. "The lost men, or the bad ones, who are making trouble for us? Which men do you mean?"

Masni only shook her head, and murmured: "Me show."

Probably Tom's attempt to talk her language was not sufficiently clear to her.

"My man—he good man," she said, coming to a pause on the rough trail after a climb which was not easy.

"Yes, I know he is," Tom said. "But he went on a strike with the others, Masni. He no work. He go on a 'hit,' as Serato calls it," and Tom laughed.

"My man he good man—but he 'fraid," said the wife. "He want to tell you of bad mans, but he 'fraid. You save my baby, I no 'fraid. I tell."

"Oh, I see," said Tom. "Your husband would have given away the secret, only he's afraid of the bad men. He likes me, too?"

"Sure!" Masni exclaimed. "He want tell, but 'fraid. He go 'way, I tell."

Tom was not quite sure what it all meant, but it seemed that after his slaying of the condor both parents were so filled with gratitude that they wanted to reveal some secret about the tunnel, only Masni's husband was afraid. She, however, had been braver.

"Something is going to happen," said Tom Swift. "I feel it in my bones!"

"Bless my porous plaster!" cried Mr. Damon. "I hope it isn't anything serious."

"We'll see," Tom went on.

They resumed their journey up the mountain trail. It wound in and out in a region none of them had before visited. Though it could not be far from the tunnel, it was almost a strange country to Tom.

Suddenly Masni stopped in a narrow gorge where the walls of rock rose high on either hand. She seemed looking for something. Her sharp, black eyes scanned the cliff and then with an exclamation of satisfaction she approached a certain place. With a quick motion she pulled aside a mass of tangled vines, and disclosed a path leading down through a V shaped crack in the cliff.

"Mans down there," she said. "You go look."

For a moment Tom hesitated. Was this a trap? If he and his friends entered this narrow and dark opening might not the Indian woman roll down some rock back of them, cutting off forever the way of escape?

Tom turned and looked at Masni. Then he was ashamed of his suspicion, for the honest black face, smiling at him, showed no trace of guile.

"You go—you see lost men," the woman urged.

"Come on!" cried Tom. "I believe we're on the track of the mystery!"

He led the way, followed by Mr. Damon, while Koku came next and then Masni. It could be no trap since she entered it herself.

The path widened, but not much. There was only room for one to walk at a time. The trail twisted and turned, and Tom was wondering how far it led, when, from behind him, came the cry of the woman:

"Watch now—no fall down."

Tom halted around a sharp turn, and stood transfixed at the sight which met his gaze. He found himself looking out through a crack in the face of a sheer stone cliff that went straight down for a hundred feet or more to a green-carpeted valley.

Tom was standing in a narrow cleft of rock—the same rock through which they had made their way. And at the foot of the cliff was a little encampment of Indians. There were a dozen huts, and wandering about them, or sitting in the shade, were a score or more of Indians.

"There men from tunnel," said Masni, and, as he looked, wondering, Tom saw some of the workers he knew. One especially, was a laborer who walked with a peculiar limp.

"The missing men!" gasped the young inventor.

"Bless my almanac!" cried Mr. Damon. "Where?"

"Here," answered Tom. "If you squeeze past me you can see them."

Mr. Damon did so.

"How did they get here?" asked the odd man, as he looked down in the little valley where the missing ones were sequestered.

"That's what we've got to find out," Tom said. "At any rate here they are, and they seem to be enjoying life while we've been worrying as to what had become of them. How did they get here, Masni?"

"Me show you. Come."

"Wait until I take another look," said Tom.

"Be careful they don't see you," cautioned Mr, Damon.

"They can't very well. The cleft is screened by bushes."

Tom looked down once more on the group of men who had so mysteriously disappeared. The little valley stretched out away from the face of the cliff, through which, by means of the crack, or cleft in it, Tom and the others had come. Tom looked down the wall of rock. It was as smooth as the side of a building, and offered no means of getting down or up. Doubtless there was an easier entrance to the valley on the other side. It was like looking down into some vast hall through an upper window or from a balcony.

"And those men have been in hiding, or been hidden here, ever since they disappeared from the tunnel," said Mr. Damon.

"It doesn't look as though they were detained by force," Tom remarked. "I think they are being paid to stay away. How did they get here, Masni?"

"Me show you. Come!"

They went back along the trail that led through the split in the rock, until they had come to the place where the natural curtain of vines concealed the entrance. Tom took particular notice of this place so he would know it again.

Then Masni led them over the mountain, and this time Tom saw that they were approaching the tunnel. He recognized some places where he had taken samples of rock from the outcropping to test the strength of his explosive.

Reaching a certain wild and desolate place, Masni made a signal of caution. She seemed to be listening intently. Then, as if satisfied there was no danger, she parted some bushes and glided in, motioning the others to follow.

"Now I wonder what's up," Tom mused.

He and the others were soon informed.

Masni stopped in front of a pile of brush. With a few vigorous motions of her arms she swept it aside and revealed a smooth slab of rock. In the centre was what seemed to be a block of metal Masni placed her foot on this and pressed heavily.

And those watching saw a strange thing.

The slab of rock tilted to one side, as if on a pivot, revealing a square opening which seemed to lead through solid stone. And at the far end of the opening Tom Swift saw a glimmer of light

Stooping down, he looked through the hole thus strangely opened and what he saw caused him to cry out in wonder.

"It's the tunnel!" he cried. "I can look right clown into the tunnel. It's the incandescent lights I see. I can look right at the ledge of rock where I kept watch that day, and where I saw—where I saw the face of Waddington!" he cried. "It wasn't a dream after all. This is a shaft connecting with the tunnel. We didn't discover it because this rock fits right in the opening in the roof. It must have been there all the while, and some blast brought it to light. Is this how the men got out, or were taken out of the tunnel, Masni?" Tom asked.

"This how," said the Indian woman. "See, here rope!"

She pawed aside a mound of earth, and disclosed a rope buried there, a rope knotted at intervals. This, let down through the hole in the roof of the tunnel, provided a means of escape, and in such a manner that the disappearance of the men was most mysterious.

"I see how it is!" cried Tom. "Some one interested, Waddington probably, who knew about this old secret shaft going down into the earth, used it as soon as our blasting was opened that far. They got the men out this way, and hid them in the secret valley."

"But what for?" cried Mr. Damon.

"To cripple us! To cause the strike by making our other workers afraid of some evil spirit! The men were taken away secretly, and, doubtless, have been kept in idleness ever since—paid to stay away so the mystery would be all the deeper. Our rivals finding they couldn't stop us in any other way have taken our laborers away from us."

"Bless my meal ticket! It does look like that!" cried Mr. Damon.

"Of course that's the secret!" cried Tom. "Blakeson & Grinder, or some of their tools—probably the bearded man or Waddington—found out about this shaft which led down into our tunnel. They induced the first ten men to quit, and when Tim went to get the fuse the rope was let down, and the men climbed up here, one after the other. Those Indians can climb like cats. Once the ten were out the shaft was closed with the rock, and the ten men taken off to the valley to be secreted there.

"The same was done with the next fifteen, and, I suppose, if the strike hadn't come, more of our workers would have been induced to leave in this way. They're probably being better paid than when earning their wages; and their relatives must know where they are, and also be given a bonus to keep still. No wonder they didn't make a fuss.

"And no wonder we couldn't find any opening in the tunnel roof. This rock must fit in as smoothly as a secret drawer in the kind of old desk where missing wills are found in stories."

"You say you saw Waddington, or the bearded man?" asked Mr. Damon.

"At the time," replied Tom, "I thought it was a dream. Now I know it wasn't. He must have opened the shaft just as I awakened from a doze. He saw me and closed it again. He may have been getting ready then to take off more of our men, so as to scare the others. Well, we've found out the trick."

"And what are you going to do next?" asked Mr. Dam~n.

"Get those missing men back. That will break the hoodoo, and the others will come back to work. Then we'll get on the trail of Wadding ton, or Blakeson & Grinder, and put a stop to this business. We know their secret now."

"You mean to get the men out of the secret valley, Tom?"

"Yes. There must be some other way into it than down the rock where we were. How about it, Masni?" and he inquired as to the valley. The Indian woman gave Tom to understand that there was another entrance.

"Well, close up this shaft now before some one sees us at it—the bearded man, for example," Tom suggested. He took another look down into the tunnel, which was now deserted on account of the strike, and then Masni pressed on the mechanism that worked the stone. She showed Tom how to do it.

"Just a counter-balanced rock operating on the same principle as does a window," Tom explained, after a brief examination. "Probably some of the old Indian tribes made this shaft for ceremonial purposes. They never dreamed we would drive a tunnel along at the bottom of it. The shaft probably opened into a cave, and one of our blasts made it part of the tunnel. Well, this is part of the secret, anyhow. Much obliged to you, Masni!"

The Indian woman had indeed revealed valuable information. They covered the secret rock with brush, as it had been, hid the rope and came away. But Tom knew how to find the place again.

Events moved rapidly from then on. The Titus brothers were more than astonished when Tom told them what he had learned. Masni had told him how to get into the secret valley by a round about, but easy trail, and thither Tom, the contractors, Mr. Damon and some of the white tunnel workers went the next day.

The sequestered men, taken completely by surprise, tried to bolt when they saw that they were discovered, and then, shamefacedly enough, admitted their part in the trick.

They would not, however, reveal who had helped them escape from the tunnel. Threats and promises of rewards were alike unavailing, but Tom and his employers knew well enough who it was. The tunnel workers seemed rather tired of living in comparative luxury and idleness, and agreed to come back to their labors.

They packed up their few belongings, mostly cooking pots and pans, and marched out of the valley to the village at Rimac.

And so the strike was broken.

The reappearance of the missing men, in better health and spirits than when they went away, acted like magic. The other men, who had missed their wages, crowded back into the shaft, and the sounds of picks and shovels were heard again in the tunnel.

Whether the missing ones told the real story, or whether they made up some tale to account for their absence, Tom and his friends could not learn. Nor did the bearded man (if he it were who had helped in the plot), nor any representative of Blakeson & Grinder appear. The work on the tunnel was resumed as if nothing had happened. But Tom arranged a bright light so it would reflect on the spot in the roof where the moving rock was, so that if the evil face of the bearded man, or of Waddington, appeared there again, it would quickly be seen. A search of the neighborhood, and diligent inquiries, failed to disclose the presence of any of the plotters.

And then, as if Fate was not making it hard enough for the tunnel contractors, they encountered more trouble. It was after Tom had set off a big blast that Tim Sullivan, after inspecting what had happened, came out to ask.

"I soy, Mr. Swift, why didn't yez use more powder?"

"More powder!" cried Tom. "Why, this is the most I have ever set off."

"Then somethin's wrong, sor. Fer there's only a little rock down. Come an' see fer yersilf."

Tom hastened in. As the foreman had said, the effect of the blast was small indeed. Only a little rock had been shaled off. Tom picked up some of this and took it outside for examination.

"Why, it's harder than the hardest flint we've found yet," he said. "The powder didn't make any impression on it at all. I'll have to use terrific charges."

This was done, but with little better effect. The explosive, powerful as it was, ate only a little way into the rock. Blast after blast had the same poor effect.

"This won't do," said Job Titus, despairingly, one day. "We aren't making any progress at all. There's a half mile of this rock, according to my calculations, and at this rate we'll be six months getting through it. By that time our limit will be up, and we'll be forced to give up the contract What can we do, Tom Swift?"

A New Explosive

The young inventor was idly handling some pieces of the very hard rock that had cropped out in the tunnel cut Tom had tested it, he had pulverized it (as well as he was able), he had examined it under the microscope, and he had taken great slabs of it and set off under it, or on top of it, charges of explosive of various power to note the effect. But the results had not been at all what he had hoped for.

"What's to be done, Tom?" repeated the contractor.

"Well, Mr. Titus," was the answer, "the only thing I see to do is to make a new explosive."

"Can you do it, Tom?"

The reply was characteristic.

"I can try."

And in the days that followed, Tom began work on a new line. He had brought from Shopton with him much of the needful apparatus, and he found he could obtain in Lima what he lacked.

A message to his father brought the reply that the new ingredients Tom needed would be shipped.

"The kind of explosive we need to rend that very hard rock," the young inventor explained to the Titus brothers, "is one that works slowly."

"I thought all explosions had to be as quick as a flash," said Walter.

"Well, in a sense, they do. Yet we have quick burning and slow-burning powders, the same as we have fuses. A quick-burning explosive is all right in soft rock, or in soil with rock and earth mingled. But in rock that is harder than flint if you use a quick explosive, only the outer surface of the rock will be scaled off.

"If you take a hammer and bring it down with all your force on a hard rock you may chip off a lot of little pieces, or you may crack the rock, but you won't, under ordinary circumstances, pulverize it as we want to do in the tunnel.

"On the other hand, if you take a smaller hammer, and keep tapping the rock with comparatively gentle blows, you will set up a series of vibrations, that, in time, will cause the hard rock to break up into any number of small pieces.

"Now that is the kind of explosive I want one that will deal a succession of constant blows at the hard rock instead of one great big blast."

"Can you make it, Tom?"

"Well, I don't know. I'll do the best I can."

From then on Tom was busy with his experiments.

Work on the tunnel did not cease while he was searching for a new explosive. There was plenty of the old explosive left and charges of this were set off as fast as holes could be drilled to receive it. But comparatively little was accomplished. Sometimes more rock would be loosed than at others, and the native laborers, now seemingly perfectly contented, would be kept busy. Again, when a heavy blast would be set off hardly a dozen dump cars could be filled.

But the work must go on. Already the time limit was getting perilously close, and the contractors did not doubt that their rivals were only waiting for a chance to step in and take their places.

Nothing more had been seen or heard of the bearded man, Waddington, or Blakeson & Grinder. But that the rival firm had not given up was evidenced by the efforts made in New York to cripple, financially, the firm in which Tom was interested. In fact, at one time the Titus brothers were so tied up that they could not get money enough to pay their men. But Tom cabled his father, who was quite wealthy, and Mr. Swift loaned the contractors enough to proceed with until they could dispose of some securities.

It might be mentioned that Tom was to get a large sum if the tunnel were completed on time, so it was to his interest and his father's, to bring this about if he could.

Tom kept on with his powder experiments. Mr. Damon helped him, for that gentleman had succeeded in putting the affairs of the wholesale drug business on a firm foundation, and there was no more trouble about getting the supplies of cinchona bark to market. The natives seemed to have taken kindly to the eccentric man, or perhaps it was the reputation of Tom Swift and his electric rifle that induced them to work hard.

It must not be supposed that Professor Bumper was idle all this while.

He came and went at odd times, accompanied by his little retinue of Indians, a guide and a native cook. He would come back to the tunnel camp, where he made his headquarters, travel stained, worn and weary, with disappointment showing on his face.

"No luck," he would report. "The hidden city of Pelone is still lost."

Then he would retire to his tent, to pour over his note-books, and make a new translation of the inscription on the golden plates. In a day or so, refreshed and rested, he would prepare for another start.

"I'll find it this time, surely!" he would exclaim, as he marched off up the mountain trail. "I have heard of a new valley, never before visited by a white man, in which there are some old ruins. I'm sure they must be those of Pelone."

But in a week or so he would come back, worn out and discouraged again.

"The ruins were only those of a native village," he would say. "No trace of an ancient civilization there."

The professor took little or no interest in the tunnel, though he expressed the hope that Tom and his friends would be successful. But industrial pursuits had no charm for the scientist. He only lived to find the hidden city which was to make him famous.

He heard the story of the queer shaft leading down into the bore under the mountain, and, for a time, hoped that might be some clue to the lost Pelone. But, after an examination, he decided it was but the shaft to some ancient mine which had not panned out, and so had been abandoned after having been fitted with a balanced rocky door, perhaps for some heathen religious rite.

There seemed to be no further trouble among the Indian tunnel workers. Those who had disappeared—who had, seemingly, gone willingly up the knotted rope to hide themselves in the valley—kept on with their work. If they told their fellows why and where they had gone, the others gave no sign. The evil spirits of the tunnel had been exorcised, and there was now peace, save for the blasts that were set off every so often.

Tom tried combination after combination, testing them inside and outside the tunnel, always seeking for an explosive that would give a slow, rending effect instead of a quick blow, the power of which was soon lost. And at last he announced:

"I think I have it!"

"Have you? Good!" cried Job Titus.

"Yes," Tom went on, "I've got a mixture here that seems to give just the effect I want. I tried it on some small pieces of rock, and now I want to test it on some large chunks. Have you brought any down lately?"

"Yes, we have some big slabs in there."

Some large pieces of the hard rock, which had been brought down in a recent blast, were taken outside the tunnel, and in them one afternoon Tom placed, in holes drilled to receive it, some of his new explosive. The rocks were set some distance away from the tunnel camp, and Tom attached the electric wires that were to detonate the charge

"Well, I guess we're ready," announced the young inventor, as he looked about him.

The tunnel workers had been allowed to go for the day, and in a log shack, where they would be safe from flying pieces of rock, were Tom, Mr. Damon and the two Titus brothers.

Tom held the electric switch in his hand, and was about to press it.

"This explosive works differently from any other," he explained. "When the charge is fired there is not instantly a detonation and a bursting. The powder burns slowly and generates an immense amount of gas. It is this gas, accumulating in the cracks and crevices of the rock, that I hope will burst and disintegrate it. Of course, an explosion eventually follows, as you will see. Here she goes!"

Tom pressed the switch and, as he did so, there was a cry of alarm from Mr. Damon.

"Bless my safety match, Tom!" cried the old man. "Look! Koku!"

For, as the charge was fired, the giant emerged from the woods and calmly took a seat on the rock that was about to be broken up into fragments by Tom's new explosive.

The Fight

"Get off there, Koku!"

"Stand up!"

"Run!"

"Get out uf the way! That's going up!"

Thus cried Tom and his friends to the big, good-natured, but somewhat stupid, giant who had sat down in the dangerous spot. Koku looked toward the hut, in front of which the young inventor and the others stood, waving their hands to him and shouting.

"Get up! Get up!" cried Tom, frantically. The powder is going off, Koku!"

"Can't you stop it?" asked Job Titus.

"No!" answered Tom. "The electric current has already ignited the charge. Only that it's slow-burning it would have been fired long ago. Get up, Koku!"

But the giant did not seem to understand. He waved his hand in friendly greeting to Tom and the others, who dared not approach closer to warn him, for the explosion would occur any second now.

Then Mr. Damon had an inspiration.

"Call him to come to you, Tom!" shouted the odd man. "He always comes to you in a hurry, you know. Call him!"

Tom acted on the suggestion at once.

"Here, Koku!" he cried. "Come here, I want you! Kelos!"

This last was a word in the giant's own language, meaning "hurry." And Koku knew when Tom used that word that there was need of haste. So, though he had sat down, evidently to take his ease after a long tramp through the woods, Koku sprang up to obey his master's bidding.

And, as he did so, something happened. The first spark from the fuse, ignited by the electric current, had reached the slow-burning powder. There was a crackle of flame, and a dull rumble. Koku sprang up from the big stone as though shot. What he saw and heard must have alarmed him, for he gave a mighty jump and started to run, at the same time shouting:

"Me come, Master!"

"You'd better!" cried the young inventor.

Koku got away only just in time, for when he was half way between the group of his friends and the big rock, the utmost force of the explosion was felt. It was not so very loud, but the power of it made the earth tremble.

The rock seemed to heave itself into the air, and when it settled back it was seen to be broken up into many pieces. Koku looked back over his shoulder and gave another tremendous leap, which carried him out of the way of the flying fragments, some of which rattled on the roof of the log hut.

"There!" cried Tom. "I guess something happened that time! The rock is broken up finer than any like it we tried to shatter before. I think I've got the mixture just right!"

"Bless my handkerchief!" cried Mr. Damon. "Think of what might have happened to Koku if he had been sitting there."

"Well," said Tom, "he might not have been killed, for he would probably have been tossed well out of the way at the first slow explosion, but afterward—well, he might have been pretty well shaken up. He got away just in time."

The giant looked thoughtfully back toward the place of the experimental blast.

"Master, him do that?" he asked.

"I did," Tom replied. "But I didn't think you'd walk out of the woods, just at the wrong time, and sit down on that rock."

"Um," murmured the giant. "Koku—he—he—Oh, by golly!" he yelled. And then, as if realizing what he had escaped, and being incapable of expressing it, the giant with a yell ran into the tunnel and stayed there for some time.

The experiment was pronounced a great success and, now that Tom had discovered the right kind of explosive to rend the very hard rock, he proceeded to have it made in sufficiently large quantities to be used in the tunnel.

"We'll have to hustle," said Job Titus. "We haven't much of our contract time left, and I have reason to believe the Peruvian government will not give any extension. It is to their interest to have us fail, for they will profit by all the work we have done, even if they have to pay our rivals a higher price than we contracted for. It is our firm that will pocket the loss."

"Well, we'll try not to have that happen," said Tom, with a smile.

"If you're going to use bigger charges of this new explosive, Tom, won't more rock be brought down?" asked Walter Titus.

"That's what I hope."

"Then we'll need more laborers to bring it out of the tunnel."

"Yes, we could use more I guess. The faster the blasted rock is removed, the quicker I can put in new charges."

"I'll get more men," decided the contractor. "There won't be any trouble now that the hoodoo of the missing workers is solved. I'll tell Serato to scare up all his dusky brethren he can find, and we'll offer a bonus for good work."

The Indian foreman readily agreed to get more laborers.

"And get some big ones, Serato," urged Job Titus. "Get some fellows like Koku," for the giant did the work of three men in the tunnel, not because he was obliged to, but because his enormous strength must find an outlet in action.

"Um want mans like him?" asked the Indian, nodding toward the giant. He and Koku were not on good terms, for once, when Koku was a hurry, he had picked up the Indian (no mean sized man himself) and had calmly set him to one side. Serato never forgave that.

"Sure, get all the giants you can," Tom said. "But I guess there aren't any in Peru."

Where Serato found his man, no one knew, and the foreman would not tell; but a day or so later he appeared at the tunnel camp with an Indian so large in size that he made the others look like pygmies, and many of them were above the average in height, too.

"Say, he's a whopper all right!" exclaimed Tom. "But he isn't as big or as strong as Koku."

"He comes pretty near it," said Job Titus. "With a dozen like him we'd finish the tunnel on time, thanks to your explosive."

Lamos, the Indian giant, was not quite as large as Koku. That is, he was not as tall, but he was broader of shoulder. And as to the strength of the two, well, it was destined to be tried out in a startling fashion.

In about a week Tom was ready with his first charges of the new explosive. The extra Indians were on hand, including Lamos, and great hopes of fast progress were held by the contractors.

The charge was fired and a great mass of broken rock brought down inside the tunnel.

"That's tearing it up!" cried Job Titus, when the fumes had blown away, the secret shaft having been opened to facilitate this. "A few more shots like that and we'll be through the strata of hard rock."

The Indians, Koku and Lamos doing their share of the work, were rushed in to clear away the debris, so another charge might be fired as soon as possible. This would be in a day or so. The contract time was getting uncomfortably close.

Blast after blast was set off, and good progress was made. But instead of half a mile of the extra hard rock the contractors found it would be nearer three quarters.

"It's going to be touch and go, whether or not we finish on time," said Mr. Job Titus one afternoon, when a clearance had been made and the men had filed out to give the drillers a chance to make holes for a new blast.

Tom was about to make a remark when Tim Sullivan came running out of the tunnel, his face showing fright and wonder.

"What's up now, I wonder," said Mr. Titus. "More men missing?"

"Quick! Come quick!" cried the Irishman. "Thim two giants is fightin' in there, an' they'll tear th' tunnel apart if we don't stop 'em. It's an awful fight! Awful!"

A GREAT BLAST

Hardly comprehending what the Irish foreman had said, Tom Swift, the Titus brothers and Mr. Damon followed Tim Sullivan back into the tunnel. They had not gone far before they heard the murmur of many voices, and mingled with that were roarings like those of wild beasts.

"That's thim!" cried Tim. "They're chawin' each other up!"

"Koku and that Indian giant fighting!" cried Tom. "What's it all about?"

"Don't ask me!" shouted Tim. "They've been on bad terms iver since they met." This was true enough, for one giant was jealous of the other's power, and they were continually trying feats of strength against one another. Probably this had culminated in a fight, Tom concluded.

"And it will be some fight!" mused the young inventor.

Hurrying on, Tom and his companions came upon a strange and not altogether pleasant sight. In an open place in the tunnel, where the lights were brightest, and in front of the rocky wall which offered a bar to further progress and which was soon to be blasted away, struggled the two giants.

With their arms locked about one another, they swayed this way and that—a struggle between two Titans. Of nearly the same height and bigness, it was a wrestling match such as had never been seen before. Had it been merely a friendly test of strength it would have been good to look upon. But it needed only a glance into the faces of either giant to show that it was a struggle in deadly earnest.

Back and forth they reeled over the rocky floor of the tunnel, bones and sinews cracking. One sought to throw the other, and first, as Koku would gain a slight advantage, his friends would call encouragement, while, when Lamos seemed about to triumph, the Indians favoring him would let out a yell of triumph.

For a few minutes Tom and his friends watched, fascinated. Then they saw Koku slip, while Lamos bent him farther toward the earth. The Indian giant raised his big fist, and Tom saw in it a rock, which the big man was about to bring down on Koku's head.

"Look out, Koku!" yelled Tom.

Tom's giant slid to one side only just in time, for the blow descended, catching him on his muscular shoulder where it only raised a bruise. And then Koku gathered himself for a mighty effort. His face flamed with rage at the unfair trick.

"Bless my bath sponge!" cried Mr. Damon. "This is awful!"

"They must stop!" said Job Titus. "We can't have them fighting like this. It is bad for the others. If it were in fun it would be all right, but they are in deadly earnest. They must stop!"

"Koku, stop!" called Tom. "You must not fight any more!"

"No fight more!" gasped the giant, through his clenched teeth. "This end fight!"

With a mighty effort he broke the hold of Lamos' arms. Then stooping suddenly he seized his rival about the middle, and with a tremendous heave, in which his muscles stood out in great bunches while his very bones seemed to crack, Koku raised Lamos high in the air. Up over his head he raised that mass of muscle, bone and flesh, squirming and wriggling, trying in vain to save itself.

Up and up Koku raised Lamos as the murmur of those watching grew to a shout of amazement and terror. Never had the like been seen in that land for generations. Up and up one giant raised the other. Then calling out something in his native tongue Koku hurled the other from him, clear across the tunnel and up against the opposite rocky wall. The murmuring died to frightened whispers as Lamos fell in a shapeless heap on the floor.

"Ah!" breathed Koku, stretching himself, and extending his brawny arms. "Fight all over, Master."

"Yes, so it seems, Koku," said Tom, solemnly, "but you have killed him. Shame on you!" and he spoke bitterly.

Job Titus had hurried over to the fallen giant.

"He isn't dead," he called, "but I guess he won't wrestle or fight any more. He's badly crippled."

"And him no more try to blow up tunnel, either," said Koku in his hoarse voice. "Me fix: him! No more him take powder, and make tunnel all bust."

"What do you mean, Koku?" asked Tom. "Is that why you fought him? Did he try to wreck the tunnel?"

"So him done, Master. But Koku see—Koku stop. Then um fight."

"Be jabbers an' I wouldn't wonder but what he was right!" cried Tim Sullivan, excitedly. "I did see that beggar." and he pointed to Lamos, who was slowly crawling away, "at the chist where I kape th' powder, but I thought nothin' of it at th' time. What did he try t' do, Koku?"

Then the giant explained in his own language, Tom Swift translating, for Koku spoke English but indifferently well.

"Koku says," rendered Torn, "that he saw Lamos trying to put a big charge of powder up in the place where the balanced rock fits in the secret opening of the tunnel roof. The charge was all ready to fire, and if the giant had set it off he might have brought down the roof of the tunnel and so choked it up that we'd have been months cleaning it out. Koku saw him and stopped him, and then the fight began. We only saw the end."

"Bless my shoe string!" gasped Mr. Damon. "And a terrible end it was. Will Lamos die?"

"I don't think so," answered Job Titus. "But he will be a cripple for life. Not only would he have wrecked the tunnel, but he would have killed many of our men had he set off that blast. Koku saved them, though it seems too bad he had to fight to do it."

An investigation showed that Koku spoke truly. The charge, all ready to set off, was found where he had knocked it from the hand of Lamos. And so Tom's giant saved the day. Lamos was sent back to his own village, a broken and humbled giant. And to this day, in that part of Peru, the great struggle between Koku and Lamos is spoken of with awe where Indians gather about their council fires, and they tell their children of the Titanic fight.

"It was part of the plot," said Job Titus when the usual blast had been set off that day, with not very good results. "This giant was sent to us by our rivals. They wanted him to hamper our work, for they see we have a chance to finish on time. I think that foreman, Serato, is in the plot. He brought Lamos here. We'll fire him!"

This was done, though the Indian protested his innocence. But he could not be trusted.

"We can't take any chances," said Job Titus. "Our time is too nearly up. In fact I'm afraid we won't finish on time as it is. There is too much of that hard rock to cut through."

"There's only one thing to do," said Tom, after an investigation. "As you say, there is more of that hard rock than we calculated on. To try to blast and take it out in the ordinary way will be useless. We must try desperate means."

"What is that?" asked Walter Titus.

"We must set off the biggest blast we can with safety. We'll bore a lot of extra holes, and put in double charges of the explosive. I'll add some ingredients to it that will make it stronger. It's our last chance. Either we'll blow the tunnel all to pieces, or we'll loosen enough rock to make sufficient progress so we can finish on time. What do you say? Shall we take the chance?"

The Titus brothers looked at one another. Failure stared them in the face. Unless they completed the tunnel very soon they would lose all the money they had sunk in it.

"Take the chance!" exclaimed Job. "It's sink or swim anyhow. Set off the big blast, Tom."

"All right. We'll get ready for it as soon as we can."

That day preparations were made for setting off a great charge of the powerful explosive. The work was hurried as fast as was consistent with safety, but even then progress was rather slow. Precautions had to be taken, and the guards about the tunnel were doubled. For it was feared that some word of what was about to be done would reach the rival firm, who might try desperate means to prevent the completion of the work.

There was plenty of the explosive on hand, for Mr. Swift had sent Tom a large shipment. All this while no word had come from Mr. Nestor, and Tom was beginning to think that his prospective father-in-law was very angry with him. Nor had Mary written.

Professor Bumper came and went as he pleased, but his quest was regarded as hopeless now. Tom and his friends had little time for the bald-headed scientist, for they were too much interested in the success of the big blast.

"Well, we'll set her off to-morrow," Tom said one night, after a hard day's work. "The rocky wall is honeycombed with explosive. If all goes well we ought to bring down enough rock to keep the gangs busy night and day."

Everything was in readiness. What would the morrow bring— success or failure?

THE HIDDEN CITY

Gathered beyond the mouth of the tunnel, far enough away so that the wind of the great blast would not bowl them over like ten pins, stood Tom Swift and his friends. In his hand Tom held the battery box, the setting of the switch in which would complete the electrical circuit and set off the hundreds of pounds of explosive buried deep in the hard rock.

"Are all the men out?" asked the young inventor of Tim Sullivan, who had charge of this important matter. Tim was in sole charge as foreman now, having picked up enough of the Indian language to get along without an interpreter.

"All out, sor," Tim responded. "Yez kin fire whin ready, Mr. Swift."

It was a portentous moment. No wonder Tom Swift hesitated. In a sense he and his friends, the contractors, had staked their all on a single throw. If this blast failed it was not likely that another would succeed, even if ther should be time to prepare one.

The time limit had almost expired, and there was still a half mile of hard rock between the last heading and the farther end of the big tunnel. If the blast succeeded enough rock might be brought down to enable the work to go on, by using a night and day shift of men. Then, too, there was the chance that the hard strata of rock would come to an end and softer stone, or easily-dug dirt, be encountered.

"Well, we may as well have it over with," said Tom in a low voice. Every one was very quiet—tensely quiet.

The young inventor looked up to see Professor Bumper observing him.

"Why, Professor!" Tom exclaimed, "I thought you had gone off to the mountains again, looking for the lost city."

"I am going, Tom, very soon. I thought I would stop and see the effect of your big blast. This is my last trip. If I do not find the hidden city of Pelone this time, I am going to give up."

"Give up!" cried Mr. Damon. "Bless my fountain pen!"

"Oh, not altogether," went on the bald-headed scientist. "I mean I will give up searching in this part of Peru, and go elsewhere. But I will never completely give up the search, for I am sure the hidden city exists somewhere under these mountains," and he looked off toward the snow-covered peaks of the Andes.

Tom looked at the battery box. He drew a long breath, and said:

"Here she goes!"

There was a contraction of his hand as he pressed the switch over, and then, for perhaps a half second, nothing happened. Just for an instant Tom feared something had gone wrong that the electric current had failed, or that the wires had become disconnected—perhaps through some action of the plotting rivals.

And then, gently at first, but with increasing intensity, the solid ground on which they were all standing seemed to rock and sway, to heave itself up, and then sink down.

"Bless my—" began Mr. Damon, but he got no further, for a mighty gust of wind swept out of the tunnel, and blew off his hat. That gust was but a gentle breeze, though, compared to what followed. For there came such a rush of air that it almost blew over those standing near the opening of the great shaft driven under the mountain. There was a roar as of Niagara, a howling as in the Cave of the Winds, and they all bent to the blast.

Then followed a dull, rumbling roar, not as loud as might have been expected, but awful in its intensity. Deep down under the very foundations of the earth it seemed to rumble.

"Run! Run back!" cried Tom Swift. "There's a back-draft and the powder gas is poisonous. Stoop down and run back!"

They understood what he meant. The vapor from the powder was deadly if breathed in a confined space. Even in the open it gave one a terrible headache. And Tom could see floating out of the tunnel the first wisps of smoke from the fired explosive. It was lighter than air, and would rise. Hence the necessity, as in a smoke-filled room, of keeping low down where the air is purer.

They all rushed back, stooping low. Mr. Damon stumbled and fell, but Koku picked him up and, tucking him under one arm, as he might have done a child, the giant followed Tom to a place of safety.

"Well, Tom, it went off all right," said Mr. Job Titus, as they stood among the shacks of the workmen and watched the smoke pouring out of the tunnel mouth.

"Yes, it went off. But did it do the work? That's what we've got to find out."

They waited impatiently for the deadly vapor to clear out of the tunnel. It was more than an hour before they dared venture in, and then it was with smarting eyes and puckered throats. But the atmosphere was quickly clearing.

"Switch on the lights," cried Tom to Tim, for the illuminating current had been cut off when the blast was fired. "Let's see what we've brought down."

Following the eager young inventor came the contractors, some of the white workers, Mr. Damon and Professor Bumper. The little scientist said he would like to see the effect of the big blast.

Along they stumbled over pieces of rock, large and small.

"Some force to it," observed Job Titus, as he observed pieces of rock close to the mouth of the tunnel. "If it only exerted the force the other way, against the face of the rock, as well as back this way, we'll be all right."

"The greater force was in the opposite direction," Tom said.

A big search-light had been got ready to flash on the place where the blast had been set off. This was to enable them to see how much rock had been torn away. And, as they reached the place where the flint-like wall had been, they saw a strange sight.

"Bless my strawberry short-cake!" gasped Mr. Damon. "What a hole!"

"It is a bole," admitted Tom, in a low voice. "A bigger hole than I dared hope for."

For a great cave, seemingly, had been blown in the face of the rock wall that had hindered the progress of the tunnel. A great black void confronted them.

"Shift the light over this way," called Tom to Walter Titus, who was operating it. "I can't see anything."

The great beam of light flashed into the void, and then a murmur of awe came from every throat.

For there, revealed in the powerful electrical rays, was what seemed to be a long tunnel, high and wide, as smooth as a paved street. And on either side of it were what appeared to be buildings, some low, others taller. And, branching off from the main tunnel, or street, were other passages, also lined with buildings, some of which had crumbled to ruins.

"Bless my dictionary!" cried Mr. Damon. "What is it?"

Professor Bumper had crawled forward over the mass of broken rock. He gazed as if fascinated at what the searchlight showed, and then he cried:

"I have found it! I have found it! The hidden city of Pelone!"

SUCCESS

Had it not been for Tom Swift, the excited professor would have rushed pellmell over the jagged pile of rocks into the great cave which had been opened by the blast, the cave in which the scientist declared was the lost city for which he had been searching. But the young inventor grasped Mr. Bumper by the arm.

"Better wait a bit," Tom suggested. "There may be powder gas in there. Some of it must have blown forward."

"I don't care!" excitedly cried the professor. "That is the hidden city! I'm sure of it! I have found it at last! I must go in and examine it!"

"There'll be plenty of time," said Tom. "It isn't going to run away. Wait until I make a test Tim, hand me one of those torches."

Some torches of a very inflammable wood were used to test for the presence of the deadly smoke-gas. Lighting one of these, Tom tossed it into the big excavation.

It fell to the stone floor—to the stone street to be more exact—and, flaring up brightly, further revealed the rows of houses as they stood, silent and uninhabited.

"It's all right," Tom announced. "There's no danger so long as the torch burns. You can go on, Professor."

And Professor Bumper rushed forward, scrambling over the pile of blasted rock, followed by Tom and the others. Some of the debris from the explosion had fallen into the cave, and was scattered for some distance along the main street of what had been Pelone. But beyond that the way was clear.

"Yes, it is Pelone," cried Professor Bumper. "See!"

He pointed to inscriptions in queer characters over the doorway of some of the houses, but he alone could read them.

"I have found Pelone!" he kept repeating over and over again.

And that is just what had happened. That last great blast Tom Swift had set off had broken down the rock wall that hid the lost city from view. There it was, buried deep down under the mountain, where it had been covered from sight ages ago by some mighty earthquake or landslide; perhaps both. And the earth and rocks had fallen over the main portion of the city of Pelone in such a way—in such an arch formation—that the greater part of it was preserved from the pressure of the mountain above it.

The outlying portions were crushed into dust by the awful pressure of the mountain—millions of tons of stone—but where the natural arch had formed the weight was kept off the buildings, most of which were as perfect as they had been before the cataclysm came.

The buildings were of stone block construction, mostly only one story in height, though some were two. They were simply made, somewhat after the fashion of the Aztecs. A look into some of them by the light of portable electric lamps showed that the houses were furnished with some degree of taste and luxury. There were traces of an ancient civilization.

But of the inhabitants, there was not a trace. either they had fled before the earthquake or the volcanic eruption had engulfed the city, or the countless centuries had turned their very bones to dust.

"Oh, what a find! What a find!" murmured Professor Bumper. "I shall be famous! And so will you, Tom Swift. For it was your blast that revealed the lost city of Pelone. Your name will be honored by every archeological society in the world, and all will be eager to make you an honorary member."

"That's all very nice," said Tom, "but what pleases me better is that this tunnel is a success."

"Success!" cried Mr. Damon. "I should call it a failure, Tom Swift. Why, you've run smack into an old city, and you'll have either to curve the tunnel to one side, or start a new one."

"Nothing of the sort!" laughed Tom. "Don't you see? The tunnel comes right up to the main street of Pelone. And the street is as straight as a die, and just the width and height of the tunnel. All we will have to do will be to keep on blasting away, where the main street comes to an end, and our tunnel will be finished. The street is over half a mile long, I should judge, and we'll save all that blasting. The tunnel will be finished in time!"

"So it will!" cried Job Titus. "We can use the main street of the hidden city as part of the tunnel."

"Use the street all you like," said Mr. Bumper. "but leave the houses to me. They are a perfect mine of ancient lore and information. At last I have found it! The ancient, hidden city of Pelone, spoken of on the Peruvian tablets, of gold."

The story of the discoveries the scientist made in Pelone is an enthralling one. But this is a story of Tom Swift and his big tunnel, and no place for telling of the archeological discoveries.

Suffice it to say that Professor Bumper, though be found no gold, for which the contractors hoped, made many curious finds in the ancient houses. He came upon traces of a strange civilization, though he could find no record of what had caused the burial of Pelone beneath the mountains. He wrote many books about his discovery, giving Tom Swift due credit for uncovering the place with the mighty blast. Other scientists came in flocks, and for a time Pelone was almost as busy a place as it had been originally.

Even when the tunnel was completed and trains ran through it, the scientists kept on with their work of classifying what they found. An underground station was built on the main street of the old city, and visitors often wandered through the ancient houses, wherein was the bone-dust of the dead and gone people.

But to go back to the story of Tom Swift. Tom's surmise was right. He and the contractors were able to use the main street of Pelone as part of their tunnel, and a good half mile of blasting through solid rock was saved. The flint came to an end at the extremity of Pelone, and the last part of the tunnel had only to be dug through sand-stone and soft dirt, an easy undertaking.

So the big bore was finished on time—ahead of time in fact, and Titus Brothers received from Senor Belasdo, the Peruvian representative, a large bonus of money, in which Tom Swift shared.

"So our rivals didn't balk us after all," said Walter Titus, "though they tried mighty hard."

The big tunnel was finished—at least Tom Swift's work on it. All that remained to do was to clear away the debris and lay the connecting rails. Tom and Mr. Damon prepared to go back home. The latter's work was done. As for Professor Bumper, nothing could take him from Pelone. He said he was going to live there, and, practically, he did.

Tom, Koku and Mr. Damon returned to Lima, thence to go to Callao to take the steamer for San Francisco. One day the manager of the hotel spoke to them.

"You are Americans, are you not?" he asked.

"Yes," answered Tom. "Why?"

"Because there is another American here. He is friendless and alone, and he is dying. He has no friends, he says. Perhaps—"

"Of course we'll do what we can for him," said Tom, impulsively. "Where is he?"

With Mr. Damon he entered the room where the dying man lay. He had caught a fever, the hotel manager said, and could not recover. Tom, catching sight of the sufferer, cried:

"The bearded man! Waddington!"

He had recognized the mysterious person who had been on the Bellaconda, and the man whose face had stared at him through the secret shaft of the tunnel.

"Yes, the 'bearded man' now," said the sufferer in a hoarse voice, "and some one else too. You are right. I am Waddington!"

And so it proved. He had grown a beard to disguise himself so he might better follow Tom Swift and Mr. Titus. And he had followed them, seeking to prevent the completion of the tunnel. But he had not been successful.

Waddington it was who had thrown the bomb, though he declared he only hoped to disable Tom and Mr. Titus, and not to injure them. He was fighting for delay. And it was Waddington, working in conjunction with the rascally foreman Serato, who had induced the tunnel workers to desert so mysteriously, hoping to scare the other Indians away. He nearly succeeded too, had it not been for the gratitude of the woman whose baby Tom had saved from the condor.

Waddington had been an actor before he became involved with the rival contractors. He was smooth shaven when first he went to Shopton, to spy on Mr. Titus, whose movements he had been commanded to follow by Blakeson & Grinder. Then he disappeared after Mr. Titus chased him, only to reappear, in disguise, on board the Bellaconda, as Senor Pinto.

Waddington, meanwhile, had grown a beard and this, with his knowledge of theatrical makeup, enabled him to deceive even Mr. Titus. Of course it was comparatively easy to deceive Tom, who had not known him. Waddington had really been ill when he called for help on the ship, and he had not noticed that it was Tom and Mr. Titus who came into his stateroom to his aid. When he did recognize them, he relied on his disguise to screen him from recognition, and he was successful. He had only pretended to be ill, though, the time he slipped out and threw the bomb.

Reaching Peru he at once began his plotting. Serato told him about the secret shaft leading into the tunnel, and with the knotted rope, and with the aid of the faithless foreman, the men were got out of the tunnel and paid to hide away. Waddington was planning further disappearances when Tom saw him, but thought it a dream.

Masni, the Indian woman, out herb-hunting one day, had seen Waddington, 'the bearded man' as he then was—working the secret stone. Hidden, she observed him and told her husband, who was afraid to reveal what he knew. But when Tom saved the baby the woman rewarded him in the only way possible. And it was Serato, who, at Waddington's suggestion, caused the "hit" among the men by working on their superstitious fears.

Waddington, knowing that he was dying, confessed everything, and begged forgiveness from Tom and his friends, which was granted, in as much as no real harm had been done. Waddington was but a tool in the hands of the rival contractors, who deserted him in his hour of need. His last hours, however, were made as comfortable as possible by the generosity of Tom and Mr. Damon.

No effort was made to bring Blakeson & Grinder to justice, as there was no evidence against them after Waddington died. And, as the tunnel was finished, the Titus brothers had no further cause for worry.

"But if it had not been for Tom's big blast, and the discovery of the hidden city of Pelone just in the right place, we might be digging at that tunnel yet," said Job Titus.

The day before the steamer was to sail, Tom Swift received a cable message. Its receipt seemed to fill him with delight, so that Mr. Damon asked:

"Is it from your father, Tom?"

"No it's from Mary Nestor. She says her father has forgiven me. They have been away, and Mary has been ill, which accounts for no letters up to now. But everything is all right now, and they feel that the dynamite trick wasn't my fault. But, all the same, I'm going to teach Eradicate to read," concluded Tom.

"I think it would be a good idea," agreed Mr. Damon.

Tom, Mr. Damon and Koku, bidding farewell to the friends they had made in Peru, went. aboard the steamer, Job Titus and his brother coming to see them off.

"Give us an option on all that explosive you make, Tom Swift!" begged Walter Titus. "We were so successful with this tunnel, thanks to you, that the government is going to have us dig another. Will you come down and help?"

"Maybe," said Tom, with a smile. "But I'm going home first," and once more he read the message from Mary Nestor.

And as Tom, on the deck of the steamer, waved his hands to Professor Bumper and his other friends whom he was leaving in Peru, we also, will say farewell.

Tom Swift in the Land of Wonders
Or the Underground Search for the Idol of Gold

TABLE OF CONTENTS:

A WONDERFUL STORY

Tom Swift, who had been slowly looking through the pages of a magazine, in the contents of which he seemed to be deeply interested, turned the final folio, ruffled the sheets back again to look at a certain map and drawing, and then, slapping the book down on a table before him, with a noise not unlike that of a shot, exclaimed:

"Well, that is certainly one wonderful story!"

"What's it about, Tom?" asked his chum, Ned Newton. "Something about inside baseball, or a new submarine that can be converted into an airship on short notice?"

"Neither one, you—you unscientific heathen," answered Tom, with a laugh at Ned. "Though that isn't saying such a machine couldn't be invented."

"I believe you—that is if you got on its trail," returned Ned, and there was warm admiration in his voice.

"As for inside baseball, or outside, for that matter, I hardly believe I'd be able to tell third base from the second base, it's so long since I went to a game," proceeded Tom. "I've been too busy on that new airship stabilizer dad gave me an idea for. I've been working too hard, that's a fact. I need a vacation, and maybe a good baseball game——"

He stopped and looked at the magazine he had so hastily slapped down. Something he had read in it seemed to fascinate him.

"I wonder if it can possibly be true," he went on. "It sounds like the wildest dream of a professional sleep-walker; and yet, when I stop to think, it isn't much worse than some of the things we've gone through with, Ned."

"Say, for the love of rice-pudding! will you get down to brass tacks and strike a trial balance? What are you talking of, anyhow? Is it a joke?"

"A joke?"

"Yes. What you just read in that magazine which seems to cause you so much excitement."

"Well, it may be a joke; and yet the professor seems very much in earnest about it," replied Tom. "It certainly is one wonderful story!"

"So you said before. Come on—the 'fillium' is busted. Splice it, or else put in a new reel and on with the show. I'd like to know what's doing. What professor are you talking of?"

"Professor Swyington Bumper."

"Swyington Bumper?" and Ned's voice showed that his memory was a bit hazy.

"Yes. You ought to remember him. He was on the steamer when I went down to Peru to help the Titus Brothers dig the big tunnel. That plotter Waddington, or some of his tools, dropped a bomb where it might have done us some injury, but Professor Bumper, who was a fellow passenger, on his way to South America to look for the lost city of Pelone, calmly picked up the bomb, plucked out the fuse, and saved us from bad injuries, if not death. And he was as cool about it as an ice-cream cone. Surely you remember!"

"Swyington Bumper! Oh, yes, now I remember him," said Ned Newton. "But what has he got to do with a wonderful story? Has he written more about the lost city of Pelone? If he has I don't see anything so very wonderful in that."

"There isn't," agreed Tom. "But this isn't that," and Tom picked up the magazine and leafed it to find the article he had been reading.

"Let's have a look at it," suggested Ned. "You act as though you might be vitally interested in it. Maybe you're thinking of joining forces with the professor again, as you did when you dug the big tunnel."

"Oh, no. I haven't any such idea," Tom said. "I've got enough work laid out now to keep me in Shopton for the next year. I have no notion of going anywhere with Professor Bumper. Yet I can't help being impressed by this," and, having found the article in the magazine to which he referred, he handed it to his chum.

"Why, it's by Bumper himself!" exclaimed Ned.

"Yes. Though there's nothing remarkable in that, seeing that he is constantly contributing articles to various publications or writing books. It's the story itself that's so wonderful. To save you the trouble of wading through a lot of scientific detail, which I know you don't care about, I'll tell you that the story is about a queer idol of solid gold, weighing many pounds, and, in consequence, of great value."

"Of solid gold you say?" asked Ned eagerly.

"That's it. Got on your banking air already," Tom laughed. "To sum it up for you—notice I use the word 'sum,' which is very appropriate for a bank—the professor has got on the track of another lost or hidden city. This one, the name of which doesn't appear, is in the Copan valley of Honduras, and—"

"Copan," interrupted Ned. "It sounds like the name of some new floor varnish."

"Well, it isn't, though it might be," laughed Tom. "Copan is a city, in the Department of Copan, near the boundary between Honduras and Guatemala. A fact I learned from the article and not because I remembered my geography."

"I was going to say," remarked Ned with a smile, "that you were coming it rather strong on the school-book stuff."

"Oh, it's all plainly written down there," and Tom waved toward the magazine at which Ned was looking. "As you'll see, if you take the trouble to go through it, as I did, Copan is, or maybe was, for all I know, one of the most important centers of the Mayan civilization."

"What's Mayan?" asked Ned. "You see I'm going to imbibe my information by the deductive rather than the excavative process," he added with a laugh.

"I see," laughed Tom. "Well, Mayan refers to the Mayas, an aboriginal people of Yucatan. The Mayas had a peculiar civilization of their own, thousands of years ago, and their calendar system was so involved—"

"Never mind about dates," again interrupted Ned. "Get down to brass tacks. I'm willing to take your word for it that there's a Copan valley in Honduras. But what has your friend Professor Bumper to do with it?"

"This. He has come across some old manuscripts, or ancient document records, referring to this valley, and they state, according to this article he has written for the magazine, that somewhere in the valley is a wonderful city, traces of which have been found twenty to forty feet below the surface, on which great trees are growing, showing that the city was covered hundreds, if not thousands, of years ago."

"But where does the idol of gold come in?"

"I'm coming to that," said Tom. "Though, if Professor Bumper has his way, the idol will be coming out instead of coming in."

"You mean he wants to get it and take it away from the Copan valley, Tom?"

"That's it, Ned. It has great value not only from the amount of pure gold that is in it, but as an antique. I fancy the professor is more interested in that aspect of it. But he's written a wonderful story, telling how he happened to come across the ancient manuscripts in the tomb of some old Indian whose mummy he unearthed on a trip to Central America.

"Then he tells of the trouble he had in discovering how to solve the key to the translation code; but when he did, he found a great story unfolded to him.

"This story has to do with the hidden city, and tells of the ancient civilization of those who lived in the Copan valley thousands of years ago. The people held this idol of gold to be their greatest treasure, and they put to death many of other tribes who sought to steal it."

"Whew!" whistled Ned. "That IS some yarn. But what is Professor Bumper going to do about it?"

"I don't know. The article seems to be written with an idea of interesting scientists and research societies, so that they will raise money to conduct a searching expedition.

"Perhaps by this time the party may be organized—this magazine is several months old. I have been so busy on my stabilizer patent that I haven't kept up with current literature. Take it home and read it! Ned. That is if you're through telling me about my affairs," for Ned, who had formerly worked in the Shopton bank, had recently been made general financial manager of the interests of Tom and his father. The two were inventors and proverbially poor business men, though they had amassed a fortune.

"Your financial affairs are all right, Tom," said Ned. "I have just been going over the books, and I'll submit a detailed report later."

The telephone bell rang and Tom picked up the instrument from the desk. As he answered in the usual way and then listened a moment, a strange look came over his face.

"Well, this certainly is wonderful!" he exclaimed, in much the same manner as when he had finished reading the article about the idol. "It certainly is a strange coincidence," he added, speaking in an aside to Ned while he himself still listened to what was being told to him over the telephone wire.

Professor Bumper Arrives

"What's the matter, Tom? What is it?" asked Ned Newton, attracted by the strange manner of his chum at the telephone. "Has anything happened?"

But the young inventor was too busy listening to the unseen speaker to answer his chum, even if he heard what Ned remarked, which is doubtful.

"Well, I might as well wait until he is through," mused Ned, as he started to leave the room. Then as Tom motioned to him to remain, he murmured: "He may have something to say to me later. But I wonder who is talking to him."

There was no way of finding out, however, until Tom had a chance to talk to Ned, and at present the young scientist was eagerly listening to what came over the wire. Occasionally Ned could hear him say:

"You don't tell me! That is surprising! Yes —yes! Of course if it's true it means a big thing, I can understand that. What's that? No, I couldn't make a promise like that. I'm sorry, but—"

Then the person at the other end of the wire must have plunged into something very interesting and absorbing, for Tom did not again interrupt by interjected remarks.

Tom. Swift, as has been said, was an inventor, as was his father. Mr. Swift was now rather old and feeble, taking only a nominal part in the activities of the firm made up of himself and his son. But his inventions were still used, many of them being vital to the business and trade of this country.

Tom and his father lived in the village of Shopton, New York, and their factories covered many acres of ground. Those who wish to read of the earliest activities of Tom in the inventive line are referred to the initial volume, "Tom Swift and His Motor Cycle." From then on he and his father had many and exciting adventures. In a motor boat, an airship, and a submarine respectively the young inventor had gone through many perils. On some of the trips his chum, Ned Newton, accompanied him, and very often in the party was a Mr. Wakefield Damon, who had a curious habit of "blessing" everything that happened to strike his fancy.

Besides Tom and his father, the Swift household was made up of Eradicate Sampson, a colored man-of-all-work, who, with his mule Boomerang, did what he could to keep the grounds around the house in order. There was also Mrs. Baggert, the housekeeper, Tom's mother being dead. Mr. Damon, living in a neighboring town, was a frequent visitor in the Swift home.

Mary Nestor, a girl of Shopton, might also be mentioned. She and Tom were more than just good friends. Tom had an idea that some day——. But there, I promised not to tell that part, at least until the young people themselves were ready to have a certain fact announced.

From one activity to another had Tom Swift gone, now constructing some important invention for himself, as among others, when he made the photo-telephone, or developed a great searchlight which he presented to the Government for use in detecting smugglers on the border.

The book immediately preceding this is called "Tom Swift and His Bit, Tunnel," and deals with the efforts of the young inventor to help a firm of contractors penetrate a mountain in Peru. How this was done and how, incidental-ly, the lost city of Pelone was discovered, bringing joy to the heart of Professor Swyington Bumper, will be found fully set forth in the book.

Tom had been back from the Peru trip for some months, when we again find him interested in some of the work of Professor Bumper, as set forth in the magazine mentioned.

"Well, he certainly is having some conversation," reflected Ned, as, after more than five minutes, Tom's ear was still at the receiver of the instrument, into the transmitter of which he had said only a few words.

"All right," Tom finally answered, as he hung the receiver up, "I'll be here," and then he turned to Ned, whose curiosity had been growing with the telephone talk, and remarked:

"That certainly was wonderful!"

"What was?" asked Ned. "Do you think I'm a mind reader to be able to guess?"

"No, indeed! I beg your pardon. I'll tell you at once. But I couldn't break away. It was too important. To whom do you think I was talking just then?"

"I can imagine almost any one, seeing I know something of what you have done. It might be almost anybody from some person you met up in the caves of ice to a red pygmy from the wilds of Africa."

"I'm afraid neither of them would be quite up to telephone talk yet," laughed Tom. "No, this was the gentleman who wrote that interesting article about the idol of gold," and he motioned to the magazine Ned held in his hand.

"You don't mean Professor Bumper!"

"That's just whom I do mean."

"What did he want? Where did he call from?"

"He wants me to help organize an expedition to go to Central America—to the Copan valley, to be exact—to look for this somewhat mythical idol of gold. Incidentally the professor will gather in any other antiques of more or less value, if he can find any, and he hopes, even if he doesn't find the idol, to get enough historical material for half a dozen books, to say nothing of magazine articles."

"Where did he call from; did you say?"

"I didn't say. But it was a long-distance call from New York. The Professor stopped off there on his way from Boston, where he has been lecturing before some society. And now he's coming here to see me," finished Tom.

"What! Is he going to lecture here?" cried Ned. "If he is, and spouts a whole lot of that bone-dry stuff about the ancient Mayan civilization and their antiquities, with side lights on how the old-time Indians used to scalp their enemies, I'm going to the moving pictures! I'm willing to be your financial manager, Tom Swift, but please don't ask me to be a high-brow. I wasn't built for that."

"Nor I, Ned. The professor isn't going to lecture. He's only going to talk, he says."

"What about?"

"He's going to try to induce me to join his expedition to the Copan valley."

"Do you feel inclined to go?"

"No, Ned, I do not. I've got too many other irons in the fire. I shall have to give the professor a polite but firm refusal."

"Well, maybe you're right, Tom; and yet that idol of gold—*gold*—weighing how many pounds did you say?"

"Oh, you're thinking of its money value, Ned, old man!"

"Yes, I'd like to see what a big chunk of gold like that would bring. It must be quite a nugget. But I'm not likely to get a glimpse of it if you don't go with the professor."

"I don't see how I can go, Ned. But come over and meet the delightful gentleman when he arrives. I expect him day after to-morrow."

"I'll be here," promised Ned; and then he went downtown to attend to some matters con-nected with his new duties, which were much less irksome than those he had had when he had been in the bank.

"Well, Tom, have you heard any more about your friend?" asked Ned, two days later, as he came to the Swift home with some papers needing the signature of the young inventor and his father.

"You mean——?"

"Professor Bumper."

"No, I haven't heard from him since he telephoned. But I guess he'll be here all right. He's very punctual. Did you see anything of my giant Koku as you came in?"

"Yes, he and Eradicate were having an argument about who should move a heavy casting from one of the shops. Rad wanted to do it all alone, but Koku said he was like a baby now."

"Poor Rad is getting old," said Tom with a sigh. "But he has been very faithful. He and Koku never seem to get along well together."

Koku was an immense man, a veritable giant, one of two whom Tom had brought back with him after an exciting trip to a strange land. The giant's strength was very useful to the young inventor.

"Now Tom, about this business of leasing to the English Government the right to manufac-ture that new explosive of yours," began Ned, plunging into the business at hand. "I think if you stick out a little you can get a better royalty price."

"But I don't want to gouge 'em, Ned. I'm satisfied with a fair profit. The trouble with you is you think too much of money. Now—"

At that moment a voice was heard in the hall of the house saying:

"Now, my dear lady, don't trouble yourself. I can find my way in to Tom Swift perfectly well by myself, and while I appreciate your courtesy I do not want to trouble you."

"No, don't come, Mrs. Baggert," added another voice. "Bless my hat band, I think I know my way about the house by this time!"

"Mr. Damon!" ejaculated Ned.

"And Professor Bumper is with him," added Tom. "Come in!" he cried, opening the hall door, to confront a bald-headed man who stood peering at our hero with bright snapping eyes, like those of some big bird spying out the land from afar. "Come in, Professor Bumper; and you too, Mr. Damon!"

Blessings and Enthusiasm

Greetings and inquiries as to health having been passed, not without numerous blessings on the part of Mr. Damon, the little party gathered in the library of the home of Tom Swift sat down and looked at one another.

On Professor Bumper's face there was, plainly to be seen, a look of expectation, and it seemed to be shared by Mr. Damon, who seemed eager to burst into enthusiastic talk. On the other hand Tom Swift appeared a bit indifferent.

Ned himself admitted that he was frankly curious. The story of the big idol of gold had occupied his thoughts for many hours.

"Well, I'm glad to see you both," said Tom again. "You got here all right, I see, Professor Bumper. But I didn't expect you to meet and bring Mr. Damon with you."

"I met him on the train," explained the author of the book on the lost city of Pelone, as well as books on other antiquities. "I had no expectation of seeing him, and we were both surprised when we met on the express."

"It stopped at Waterfield, Tom," explained Mr. Damon, "which it doesn't usually do, being an aristocratic sort of train, not given even to hesitating at our humble little town. There were some passengers to get off, which caused the flier to stop, I suppose. And, as I wanted to come over to see you, I got aboard."

"Glad you did," voiced Tom.

"Then I happened to see Professor Bumper a few seats ahead of me," went on Mr. Damon, "and, bless my scarfpin! he was coming to see you also."

"Well, I'm doubly glad," answered Tom.

"So here we are," went on Mr. Damon, "and you've simply got to come, Tom Swift. You must go with us!" and Mr. Damon, in his enthusiasm, banged his fist down on the table with such force that he knocked some books to the floor.

Koku, the giant, who was in the hall, opened the door and in his imperfect English asked:

"Master Tom knock for him bigs man?"

"No," answered Tom with a smile, "I didn't knock or call you, Koku. Some books fell, that is all."

"Massa Tom done called fo' me, dat's what he done!" broke in the petulant voice of Eradicate.

"No, Rad, I don't need anything," Tom said. "Though you might make a pitcher of lemonade. It's rather warm."

"Right away, Massa Tom! Right away!" cried the old colored man, eager to be of service.

"Me help, too!" rumbled Koku, in his deep voice. "Me punch de lemons!" and away he hurried after Eradicate, fearful lest the old servant do all the honors.

"Same old Rad and Koku," observed Mr. Damon with a smile. "But now, Tom, while they're making the lemonade, let's get down to business. You're going with us, of course!"

"Where?" asked Tom, more from habit than because he did not know.

"Where? Why to Honduras, of course! After the idol of gold! Why, bless my fountain pen, it's the most wonderful story I ever heard of! You've read Professor Bumper's article, of course. He told me you had. I read it on the train coming over. He also told me about it, and—— Well, I'm going with him, Tom Swift.

"And think of all the adventures that may befall us! We'll get lost in buried cities, ride down raging torrents on a raft, fall over a cliff maybe and be rescued. Why, it makes me feel quite young again!" and Mr. Damon arose, to pace excitedly up and down the room.

Up to this time Professor Bumper had said very little. He had sat still in his chair listening to Mr. Damon. But now that the latter had ceased, at least for a time, Tom and Ned looked toward the scientist.

"I understand, Tom," he said, "that you read my article in the magazine, about the possibility of locating some of the lost and buried cities of Honduras?"

"Yes, Ned and I each read it. It was quite wonderful."

"And yet there are more wonders to tell," went on the professor. "I did not give all the details in that article. I will tell you some of them. I have brought copies of the documents with me," and he opened a small valise and took out several bundles tied with pink tape.

"As Mr. Damon said," he went on while arranging his papers, "he met me on the train, and he was so taken by the story of the idol of gold that he agreed to accompany me to Central America."

"On one condition!" put in the eccentric man.

"What's that? You didn't make any conditions while we were talking," said the scientist.

"Yes, I said I'd go if Tom Swift did."

"Oh, yes. You did say that. But I don't call that a condition, for of course Tom Swift will go. Now let me tell you something more than I could impart over the telephone.

"Soon after I called you up, Tom—and it was quite a coincidence that it should have been at a time when you had just finished my magazine article. Soon after that, as I was saying, I arranged to come on to Shopton. And now I'm glad we're all here together.

"But how comes it, Ned Newton, that you are not in the bank?"

"I've left there," explained Ned.

"He's now general financial man for the Swift Company," Tom explained. "My father and I found that we could not look after the inventing and experimental end, and money matters, too, and as Ned had had considerable experience this way we made him take over those worries," and Tom laughed genially.

"No worries at all, as far as the Swift Company is concerned," returned Ned.

"Well, I guess you earn your salary," laughed Tom. "But now, Professor Bumper, let's hear from you. Is there anything more about this idol of gold that you can tell us?"

"Plenty, Tom, plenty. I could talk all day, and not get to the end of the story. But a lot of it would be scientific detail that might be too dry for you in spite of this excellent lemonade,"

Between them Koku and Eradicate had managed to make a pitcher of the beverage, though Mrs. Baggert, the housekeeper, told Tom afterward that the two had a quarrel in the kitchen as to who should squeeze the lemons, the giant insisting that he had the better right to "punch" them.

"So, not to go into too many details," went on the professor, "I'll just give you a brief outline of this story of the idol of gold.

"Honduras, as you of course know, is a republic of Central America, and it gets its name from something that happened on the fourth voyage of Columbus. He and his men had had days of weary sailing and had sought in vain for shallow water in which they might come to an anchorage. Finally they reached the point now known as Cape Gracias-a-Dios, and when they let the anchor go, and found that in a short time it came to rest on the floor of the ocean, some one of the sailors—perhaps Columbus himself— is said to have remarked:

"'Thank the Lord, we have left the deep waters (honduras)' that being the Spanish word for unfathomable depths. So Honduras it was called, and has been to this day.

"It is a queer land with many traces of an ancient civilization, a civilization which I believe dates back farther than some in the far East. On the sculptured stones in the Copan valley there are characters which seem to resemble very ancient writing, but this pictographic writing is largely untranslatable.

"Honduras, I might add, is about the size of our state of Ohio. It is rather an elevated table-land, though there are stretches of tropical forest, but it is not so tropical a country as many suppose it to be. There is much gold scattered throughout Honduras, though of late it has not been found in large quantities.

"In the old days, however, before the Spaniards came, it was plentiful, so much, so that the natives made idols of it. And it is one of the largest of these idols—by name Quitzel—that I am going to seek."

"Do you know where it is?" asked Ned.

"Well, it isn't locked up in a safe deposit box, of that I'm sure," laughed the professor. "No, I don't know exactly where it is, except that it is somewhere in an ancient and buried city known as Kurzon. If I knew exactly where it was there wouldn't be much fun in going after it. And if it was known to others it would have been taken away long ago.

"No, we've got to hunt for the idol of gold in this land of wonders where I hope soon to be. Later on I'll show you the documents that put me on the track of this idol. Enough now to show you an old map I found, or, rather, a copy of it, and some of the papers that tell of the idol," and he spread out his packet of papers on the table in front of him, his eyes shining with excitement and pleasure. Mr. Damon, too, leaned eagerly forward.

"So, Tom Swift," went on the professor, "I come to you for help in this matter. I want you to aid me in organizing an expedition to go to Honduras after the idol of gold. Will you?"

"I'll help you, of course," said Tom. "You may use any of my inventions you choose—my airships, my motor boats and submarines, even my giant cannon if you think you can take it with you. And as for the money part, Ned will arrange that for you. But as for going with you myself, it is out of the question. I can't. No Honduras for me!"

FENIMORE BEECHER

Had Tom Swift's giant cannon been discharged somewhere in the vicinity of his home it could have caused but little more astonishment to Mr. Damon and Professor Bumper than did the simple announcement of the young inventor. The professor seemed to shrink back in his chair, collapsing like an automobile tire when the air is let out. As for Mr. Damon he jumped up and cried:

"Bless my——!"

But that is as far as he got—at least just then. He did not seem to know what to bless, but he looked as though he would have liked to include most of the universe.

"Surely you don't mean it, Tom Swift," gasped Professor Bumper at length. "Won't you come with us?"

"No," said Tom, slowly. "Really I can't go. I'm working on an invention of a new aeroplane stabilizer, and if I go now it will be just at a time when I am within striking distance of success. And the stabilizer is very much needed."

"If it's a question of making a profit on it, Tom," began Mr. Damon, "I can let you have some money until—"

"Oh, no! It isn't the money!" cried Tom. "Don't think that for a moment. You see the European war has called for the use of a large number of aeroplanes, and as the pilots of them frequently have to fight, and so can not give their whole attention to the machines, some form of automatic stabilizer is needed to prevent them turning turtle, or going off at a wrong tangent.

"So I have been working out a sort of modified gyroscope, and it seems to answer the purpose. I have already received advance orders for a number of my devices from abroad, and as they are destined to save lives I feel that I ought to keep on with my work.

"I'd like to go, don't misunderstand me, but I can't go at this time. It is out of the question. If you wait a year, or maybe six months—"

"No, it is impossible to wait, Tom," declared Professor Bumper.

"Is it so important then to hurry?" asked Mr. Damon. "You did not mention that to me, Professor Bumper."

"No, I did not have time. There are so many ends to my concerns. But, Tom Swift, you simply must go!"

"I can't, my dear professor, much as I should like to."

"But, Tom, think of it!" cried Mr. Damon, who was as much excited as was the little bald-headed scientist. "You never saw such an idol of gold as this. What's its name?" and he looked questioningly at the professor.

"Quitzel the idol is called," supplied Professor Bumper. "And it is supposed to be in a buried city named Kurzon, somewhere in the Sierra de Merendon range of mountains, in the vicinity of the Copan valley. Copan is a city, or maybe we'll find it only a town when we get there, and it is not far from the borders of Guatemala.

"Tom, if I could show you the translations I have made of the ancient documents, referring to this idol and the wonderful city over which it kept guard, I'm sure you'd come with us."

"Please don't tempt me," Tom said with a laugh. "I'm only too anxious to go, and if it wasn't for the stabilizer I'd be with you in a minute. But—— Well, you'll have to get along without me. Maybe I can join you later."

"What's this about the idol keeping guard over the ancient city?" asked Ned, for he was interested in strange stories.

"It seems," explained the professor, "that in the early days there was a strange race of people, inhabiting Central America, with a somewhat high civilization, only traces of which remained when the Spaniards came.

"But these traces, and such hieroglyphics, or, to be more exact pictographs, as I have been able to decipher from the old documents, tell of one country, or perhaps it was only a city, over which this great golden idol of Quitzel presided.

"There is in some of these papers a description of the idol, which is not exactly a beauty, judged from modern standards. But the main fact is that it is made of solid gold, and may weigh anywhere from one to two tons."

"Two tons of gold!" cried New Newton. "Why, if that's the case it would be worth—" and he fell to doing a sum in mental arithmetic.

"I am not so concerned about the monetary value of the statue as I am about its antiquity," went on Professor Bumper. "There are other statues in this buried city of Kurzon, and though they may not be so valuable they will give me a wealth of material for my research work."

"How do you know there are other statues?" asked Mr. Damon.

"Because my documents tell me so. It was because the people made other idols, in opposition, as it were, to Quitzel, that their city or country was destroyed. At least that is the legend. Quitzel, so the story goes, wanted to be the chief god, and when the image of a rival was set up in the temple near him, he toppled over in anger, and part of the temple went with him, the whole place being buried in ruins. All the inhabitants were killed, and trace of the ancient city was lost forever. No, I hope not forever, for I expect to find it."

"If all the people were killed, and the city buried, how did the story of Quitzel become known?" asked Mr. Damon.

"One only of the priests in the temple of Quitzel escaped and set down part of the tale," said the professor. "It is his narrative, or one based on it, that I have given you."

"And now, what I want to do, is to go and make a search for this buried city. I have fairly good directions as to how it may be reached. We will have little difficulty in getting to Honduras, as there are fruit steamers frequently sailing. Of course going into the interior—to the Copan valley—is going to be harder. But an expedition from a large college was recently there and succeeded, after much labor, in ex-cavating part of a buried city. Whether or not it was Kurzon I am unable to say.

"But if there was one ancient city there must be more. So I want to make an attempt. And I counted on you, Tom. You have had considerable experience in strange quarters of the earth, and you're just the one to help me. I don't need money, for I have interested a certain millionaire, and my own college will put up part of the funds."

"Oh, it isn't a question of money," said Tom. "It's time."

"That's just what it is with me!" exclaimed Professor Bumper. "I haven't any time to lose. My rivals may, even now, be on their way to Honduras!"

"Your rivals!" cried Tom. "You didn't say anything about them!"

"No, I believe I didn't There were so many other things to talk about. But there is a rival archaeologist who would ask nothing better than to get ahead of me in this matter. He is younger than I am, and youth is a big asset nowadays."

"Pooh! You're not old!" cried Mr. Damon. "You're no older than I am, and I'm still young. I'm a lot younger than some of these boys who are afraid to tackle a trip through a tropical wilderness," and he playfully nudged Tom in the ribs.

"I'm not a bit afraid!" retorted the young inventor.

"No, I know you're not," laughed Mr. Damon. "But I've got to say something, Tom, to stir you up. Ned, how about you? Would you go?"

"I can't, unless Tom does. You see I'm his financial man now."

"There you are, Tom Swift!" cried Mr. Damon. "You see you are holding back a number of persons just because you don't want to go."

"I certainly wouldn't like to go without Tom," said the professor slowly. "I really need his help. You know, Tom, we would never have found the city of Pelone if it had not been for you and your marvelous powder. The conditions in the Copan valley are likely to be still more difficult to overcome, and I feel that I risk failure without your young energy and your inventive mind to aid in the work and to suggest possible means of attaining our object. Come, Tom, reconsider, and decide to make the trip."

"And my promise to go was dependent on Tom's agreement to accompany us," said Mr. Damon

"Come on!" urged the professor, much as one boy might urge another to take part in a ball game. "Don't let my rival get ahead of me."

"I wouldn't like to see that," Tom said slowly. "Who is he—any one I know?"

"I don't believe so, Tom. He's connected with a large, new college that has plenty of money to spend on explorations and research work. Beecher is his name—Fenimore Beecher."

"Beecher!" exclaimed Tom, and there was such a change in his manner that his friends could not help noticing it. He jumped to his feet, his eyes snapping, and he looked eagerly and anxiously at Professor Bumper.

"Did you say his name was Fenimore Beecher?" Tom asked in a tense voice.

"That's what it is—Professor Fenimore Beecher. He is really a learned young man, and thoroughly in earnest, though I do not like his manner. But he is trying to get ahead of me, which may account for my feeling."

Tom Swift did not answer. Instead he hurried from the room with a murmured apology.

"I'll be back in about five minutes," he said, as he went out.

"Well, what's up now?" asked Mr. Damon of Ned, as the young inventor departed. "What set him off that way?"

"The mention of Beecher's name, evidently. Though I never heard him mention such a person before."

"Nor did I ever hear Professor Beecher speak of Tom," said the bald-headed scientist. "Well, we'll just have to wait until—"

At that moment Tom came back into the room.

"Gentlemen," he said, "I have reconsidered my refusal to go to the Copan valley after the idol of gold. I'm going with you!"

"Good!" cried Professor Bumper.

"Fine!" ejaculated Mr. Damon. "Bless my time-table! I thought you'd come around, Tom Swift."

"But what about your stabilizer?" asked Ned.

"I was just talking to my father about it,' the young inventor replied. "He will be able to put the finishing touches on it. So I'll leave it with him. As soon as I can get ready I'll go, since you say haste is necessary, Professor Bumper."

"It is, if we are to get ahead of Beecher."

"Then we'll get ahead of him!" cried Tom. "I'm with you now from the start to the finish. I'll show him what I can do!" he added, while Ned and the others wondered at the sudden change in their friend's manner.

The Little Green God

"Tom how soon can we go?" asked Professor Bumper, as he began arranging his papers, maps and documents ready to place them back in the valise.

"Within a week, if you want to start that soon."

"The sooner the better. A week will suit me. I don't know just what Beecher's plans are, but, he may try to get on the ground first. Though, without boasting, I may say that he has not had as much experience as I have had, thanks to you, Tom, when you helped me find the lost city of Pelone."

"Well, I hope we'll be as successful this time," murmured Tom. "I don't want to see Beecher beat you."

"I didn't know you knew him, Tom," said the professor.

"Oh, yes, I have met him. once," and there was something in Tom's manner, though he tried to speak indifferently, that made Ned believe there was more behind his chum's sudden change of determination than had yet appeared.

"He never mentioned you," went on Professor Bumper; "yet the last time I saw him I said I was coming to see you, though I did not tell him why."

"No, he wouldn't be likely to speak of me," said Tom significantly.

"Well, if that's all settled, I guess I'll go back home and pack up," said Mr. Damon, making a move to depart.

"There's no special rush," Tom said. "We won't leave for a week. I can't get ready in much less time than that."

"Bless my socks! I know that," ejaculated Mr. Damon. "But if I get my things packed I can go to a hotel to stay while my wife is away. She might take a notion to come home unexpectedly, and, though she is a dear, good soul, she doesn't altogether approve of my going off on these wild trips with you, Tom Swift. But if I get all packed, and clear out, she can't find me and she can't hold me back. She is visiting her mother now. I can send her a wire from Kurzon after I get there."

"I don't believe the telegraph there is work-ing," laughed Professor Bumper. "But suit yourself. I must go back to New York to arrange for the goods we'll have to take with us. In a week, Tom, we'll start."

"You must stay to dinner," Tom said. "You can't get a train now anyhow, and father wants to meet you again. He's pretty well, considering his age. And he's much better I verily believe since I said I'd turn over to him the task of finishing the stabilizer. He likes to work."

"We'll stay and take the night train back," agreed Mr. Damon. "It will be like old times, Tom," he went on, "traveling off together into the wilds. Central America is pretty wild, isn't it?" he asked, as if in fear of being disappointed! on that score.

"Oh, it's wild enough to suit any one," answered Professor Bumper.

"Well, now to settle a few details," observed Tom. "Ned, what is the situation as regards the financial affairs of my father and myself? Nothing will come to grief if we go away, will there?"

"I guess not, Tom. But are you going to take your father with you?"

"No, of course not."

"But you spoke of 'we.' "

"I meant you and I are going."

"Me, Tom?"

"Sure, you! I wouldn't think of leaving you behind. You want Ned along, don't you, Professor?"

"Of course. It will be an ideal party—we four. We'll have to take natives when we get to Honduras, and make up a mule pack-train for the interior. I had some thoughts of asking you to take an airship along, but it might frighten the Indians, and I shall have to depend on them for guides, as well as for porters. So it will be an old-fashioned expedition, in a way."

Mr. Swift came in at this point to meet his old friends.

"The boy needs a little excitement," he said. "He's been puttering over that stabilizer invention too long. I can finish the model for him in a very short time."

Professor Bumper told Mr. Swift something about the proposed trip, while Mr. Damon went out with Tom and Ned to one of the shops to look at a new model aeroplane the young inventor had designed.

There was a merry party around the table at dinner, though now and then Ned noticed that Tom had an abstracted and preoccupied air.

"Thinking about the idol of gold?" asked Ned in a whisper to his chum, when they were about to leave the table.

"The idol of gold? Oh, yes! Of course! It will be great if we can bring that back with us." But the manner in which he said this made Ned feel sure that Tom had had other thoughts, and that he had used a little subterfuge in his answer.

Ned was right, as he proved for himself a little later, when, Mr. Damon and the professor having gone home, the young financial secretary took his friend to a quiet corner and asked:

"What's the matter, Tom?"

"Matter? What do you mean?"

"I mean what made you make up your mind so quickly to go on this expedition when you heard Beecher was going?"

"Oh—er—well, you wouldn't want to see our old friend Professor Bumper left, would you, after he had worked out the secret of the idol of gold? You wouldn't want some young whipper-snapper to beat him in the race, would you, Ned?"

"No, of course not."

"Neither would I. That's why I changed my mind. This Beecher isn't going to get that idol if I can stop him!"

"You seem rather bitter against him."

"Bitter? Oh, not at all. I simply don't want to see my friends disappointed."

"Then Beecher isn't a friend of yours?"

"Oh, I've met him, that is all," and Tom tried to speak indifferently.

"Humph!" mused Ned, "there's more here than I dreamed of. I'm going to get at the bottom of it."

But though Ned tried to pump Tom, he was not successful. The young inventor admitted knowing the youthful scientist, but that was all, Tom reiterating his determination not to let Professor Bumper be beaten in the race for the idol of gold.

"Let me see," mused Ned, as he went home that evening. "Tom did not change his mind until he heard Beecher's name mentioned. Now this shows that Beecher had something to do with it. The only reason Tom doesn't want Beecher to get this idol or find the buried city is because Professor Bumper is after it. And yet the professor is not an old or close friend of Tom's. They met only when Tom went to dig his big tunnel. There must be some other reason."

Ned did some more thinking. Then he clapped his hands together, and a smile spread over his face.

"I believe I have it!" he cried. "The little green god as compared to the idol of gold! That's it. I'm going to make a call on my way home."

This he did, stopping at the home of Mary Nestor, a pretty girl, who, rumor had it, was tacitly engaged to Tom. Mary was not at home, but Mr. Nestor was, and for Ned's purpose this answered.

"Well, well, glad to see you!" exclaimed Mary's father. "Isn't Tom with you?" he asked a moment later, seeing that Ned was alone.

"No, Tom isn't with me this evening," Ned answered. "The fact is, he's getting ready to go off on another expedition, and I'm going with him."

"You young men are always going somewhere," remarked Mrs. Nestor. "Where is it to this time?"

"Some place in Central America," Ned answered, not wishing to be too particular. He was wondering how he could find out what he wanted to know, when Mary's mother unexpectedly gave him just the information he was after.

"Central America!" she exclaimed. "Why, Father," and she looked at her husband, "that's where Professor Beecher is going, isn't it?"

"Yes, I believe he did mention something about that."

"Professor Beecher, the man who is an author-ity on Aztec ruins?" asked Ned, taking a shot in the dark.

"Yes," said Mr. Nestor. "And a mighty fine young man he is, too. I knew his father well. He was here on a visit not long ago, young Beecher was, and he talked most entertainingly about his discoveries. You remember how interested Mary was, Mother?"

"Yes, she seemed to be," said Mrs. Nestor. "Tom Swift dropped in during the course of the evening," she added to Ned, "and Mary introduced him to Professor Beecher. But I can't say that Tom was much interested in the professor's talk."

"No?" questioned Ned.

"No, not at all. But Tom did not stay long. He left just as Mary and the professor were drawing a map so the professor could indicate where he had once made a big discovery."

"I see," murmured Ned. "Well, I suppose Tom must have been thinking of something else at the time."

"Very likely," agreed Mr. Nestor. "But Tom missed a very profitable talk. I was very much interested myself in what the professor told us, and so was Mary. She invited Mr. Beecher to come again. He takes after his father in being very thorough in what he does.

"Sometimes I think," went on Mr. Nestor, "that Tom isn't quite steady enough. He's thinking of so many things, perhaps, that he can't get his mind down to the commonplace. I remember he once sent something here in a box labeled 'dynamite.' Though there was no explosive in it, it gave us a great fright. But Tom is a boy, in spite of his years. Professor Beecher seems much older. We all like him very much."

"That's nice," said Ned, as he took his departure. He had found out what he had come to learn.

"I knew it!" Ned exclaimed as he walked home. "I knew something was in the wind. The little green god of jealousy has Tom in his clutches. That's why my inventive friend was so anxious to go on this expedition when he learned Beecher was to go. He wants to beat him. I guess the professor has plainly shown that he wouldn't like anything better than to cut Tom out with Mary. Whew! that's something to think about!"

Unpleasant News

Ned Newton decided to keep to himself what he had heard at the Nestor home. Not for the world would he let Tom Swift know of the situation.

"That is, I won't let him know that I know," said Ned to himself, "though he is probably as well aware of the situation as I am. But it sure is queer that this Professor Beecher should have taken such a fancy to Mary, and that her father should regard him so well. That is natural, I suppose. But I wonder how Mary herself feels about it. That is the part Tom would be most interested in.

"No wonder Tom wants to get ahead of this young college chap, who probably thinks he's the whole show. If he can find the buried city, and get the idol of gold, it would be a big feather in his cap.

"He'd have no end of honors heaped on him, and I suppose his hat wouldn't come within three sizes of fitting him. Then he'd stand in better than ever with Mr. Nestor. And, maybe, with Mary, too, though I think she is loyal to Tom. But one never can tell.

"However, I'm glad I know about it. I'll do all I can to help Tom, without letting him know that I know. And if I can do anything to help in finding that idol of gold for Professor Bumper, and, incidentally, Tom, I'll do it," and he spoke aloud in his enthusiasm.

Ned, who was walking along in the darkness, clapped his open hand down on Tom's magazine he was carrying home to read again, and the resultant noise was a sharp crack. As it sounded a figure jumped from behind a tree and called tensely:

"Hold on there!"

Ned stopped short, thinking he was to be the victim of a holdup, but his fears were allayed when he beheld one of the police force of Shopton confronting him.

"I heard what you said about gettin' the gold," went on the officer. "I was walkin' along and I heard you talkin'. Where's your pal?"

"I haven't any, Mr. Newbold," answered Ned with a laugh, as he recognized the man.

"Oh, pshaw! It's Ned Newton!" exclaimed the disappointed officer. "I thought you was talkin' to a confederate about gold, and figured maybe you was goin' to rob the bank."

"No, nothing like that," answered Ned, still much amused. "I was talking to myself about a trip Tom Swift and I are going to take and—"

"Oh, that's all right," responded the policeman. "I can understand it, if it had anything to do with Tom. He's a great boy."

"Indeed he is," agreed Ned, making a mental resolve not to be so public with his thoughts in the future. He chatted for a moment with the officer, and then, bidding him good-night, walked on to his home, his mind in a whirl with conglomerate visions of buried cities, great grinning idols of gold, and rival professors seeking to be first at the goal.

The next few days were busy ones for Tom, Ned and, in fact, the whole Swift household. Tom and his father had several consultations and conducted several experiments in regard to the new stabilizer, the completion of which was so earnestly desired. Mr. Swift was sure he could carry the invention to a successful conclusion.

Ned was engaged in putting the financial affairs of the Swift Company in shape, so they would practically run themselves during his ab-sence. Then, too, there was the packing of their baggage which must be seen to.

Of course, the main details of the trip were left to Professor Bumper, who knew just what to do. He had told Tom and Ned that all they and Mr. Damon would have to do would be to meet him at the pier in New York, where they would find all arrangements made.

One day, near the end of the week (the beginning of the next being set for the start) Eradicate came shuffling into the room where Tom was sorting out the possessions he desired to take with him, Ned assisting him in the task.

"Well, Rad, what is it?" asked Tom, with businesslike energy.

"I done heah, Massa Tom, dat yo' all's gwine off on a long trip once mo'. Am dat so?"

"Yes, that's so, Rad."

"Well, den, I'se come to ast yo' whut I'd bettah take wif me. Shall I took warm clothes or cool clothes?"

"Well, if you were going, Rad," answered Tom with a smile, "you'd need cool clothes, for we're going to a sort of jungle-land. But I'm sorry to say you're not going this trip."

"I—— I ain't gwine? Does yo' mean dat yo' all ain't gwine to take me, Massa Tom?"

"That's it, Rad. It isn't any trip for you."

"In certain not!" broke in the voice of Koku, the giant, who entered with a big trunk Tom had sent him for. "Master want strong man like a bull. He take Koku!"

"Look heah!" spluttered Eradicate, and his eyes flashed. "Yo'—yo' giant yo'—yo' may be strong laik a bull, but ya' ain't got as much sense as mah mule, Boomerang! Massa Tom don't want no sich pusson wif him. He's gwine to take me."

"He take me!" cried Koku, and his voice was a roar while he beat on his mighty chest with his huge fists.

Tom, seeing that the dispute was likely to be bothersome, winked at Ned and began to speak.

"I don't believe you'd like it there, Rad—not where we're going. It's a bad country. Why the mosquitoes there bite holes in you—raise bumps on you as big as eggs."

"Oh, good land!" ejaculated the old colored man. "Am dat so Massa Tom?"

"It sure is. Then there's another kind of bug that burrows under your fingernails, and if you don't get 'em out, your fingers drop off."

"Oh, good land, Massa Tom! Am dat a fact?"

"It sure is. I don't want to see those things happen to you, Rad."

Slowly the old colored man shook his head.

"I don't mahse'f," he said. "I—— I guess I won't go."

Eradicate did not stop to ask how Tom and Ned proposed to combat these two species of insects.

But there remained Koku to dispose of, and he stood smiling broadly as Eradicate shuffled of.

"Me no 'fraid bugs," said the giant.

"No," said Tom, with a look at Ned, for he did not want to take the big man on the trip for various reasons. "No, maybe not, Koku. Your skin is pretty tough. But I understand there are deep pools of water in the land where we are going, and in them lives a fish that has a hide like an alligator and a jaw like a shark. If you fall in it's all up with you."

"Dat true, Master Tom?" and Koku's voice trembled.

"Well, I've never seen such a fish, I'm sure, but the natives tell about it."

Koku seemed to be considering the matter. Strange as it may seem, the giant, though afraid of nothing human and brave when it came to a hand-to-claw argument with a wild animal, had a very great fear of the water and the unseen life within it. Even a little fresh-water crab in a brook was enough to send him shrieking to shore. So when Tom told of this curious fish, which many natives of Central America firmly believe in, the giant took thought with himself. Finally, he gave a sigh and said:

"Me stay home and keep bad mans out of master's shop."

"Yes, I guess that's the best thing for you," assented Tom with an air of relief. He and Ned had talked the matter over, and they had agreed that the presence of such a big man as Koku, in an expedition going on a more or less secret mission, would attract too much attention.

"Well, I guess that clears matters up," said Tom, as he looked over a collection of rifles and small arms, to decide which to take. "We won't have them to worry about."

"No, only Professor Beecher," remarked Ned, with a sharp look at his chum.

"Oh, we'll dispose of him all right!" asserted Tom boldly. "He hasn't had any experience in business of this sort, and with that you and Professor Bumper and Mr. Damon know we ought to have little trouble in getting ahead of the young man."

"Not to speak of your own aid," added Ned.

"Oh, I'll do what I can, of course," said Tom, with an air of indifference. But Ned knew his chum would work ceaselessly to help get the idol of gold.

Tom gave no sign that there was any complication in his affair with Mary Nestor, and of course Ned did not tell anything of what he knew about it.

That night saw the preparations of Ned and Tom about completed. There were one or two matters yet to finish on Tom's part in relation to his business, but these offered no difficulties.

The two chums were in the Swift home, talking over the prospective trip, when Mrs. Baggert, answering a ring at the front door, announced that Mr. Damon was outside.

"Tell him to come in," ordered Tom.

"Bless my baggage check!" exclaimed the excitable man, as he shook hands with Tom and Ned and noted the packing evidences all about. "You're ready to go to the land of wonders."

"The land of wonders?" repeated Ned.

"Yes, that's what Professor Bumper calls the part of Honduras we're going to. And it must be wonderful, Tom. Think of whole cities, some of them containing idols and temples of gold, buried thirty and forty feet under the surface! Wonderful is hardly the name for it!"

"It'll be great!" cried Ned. "I suppose you're ready, Mr. Damon—you and the professor?"

"Yes. But, Tom, I have a bit of unpleasant news for you."

"Unpleasant news?"

"Yes. You know Professor Bumper spoke of a rival—a man named Beecher who is a member of the faculty of a new and wealthy college."

"I heard him speak of him—yes," and the way Tom said it no one would have suspected that he had any personal interest in the matter.

"He isn't going to give his secret away," thought Ned.

"Well, this Professor Beecher, you know," went on Mr. Damon, "also knows about the idol of gold, and is trying to get ahead of Professor Bumper in the search."

"He did say something of it, but nothing was certain," remarked Tom.

"But it is certain!" exclaimed Mr. Damon. "Bless my toothpick, it's altogether too certain!"

"How is that?" asked Tom. "Is Beecher certainly going to Honduras?"

"Yes, of course. But what is worse, he and his party will leave New York on the same steamer with us!"

Tom Hears Something

On hearing Mr. Damon's rather startling announcement, Tom and Ned looked at one another. There seemed to be something back of the simple statement—an ominous and portending "something."

"On the same steamer with us, is he?" mused Tom.

"How did you learn this?" asked Ned.

"Just got a wire from Professor Bumper telling me. He asked me to telephone to you about it, as he was too busy to call up on the long distance from New York. But instead of 'phoning I decided to come over myself."

"Glad you did," said Tom, heartily. "Did Professor Bumper want us to do anything special, now that it is certain his rival will be so close on his trail?"

"Yes, he asked me to warn you to be careful what you did and said in reference to the expedition."

"Then does he fear something?" asked Ned.

"Yes, in a way. I think he is very much afraid this young Beecher will not only be first on the site of the underground city, but that he may be the first to discover the idol of gold. It would be a great thing for a young archaeologist like Beecher to accomplish a mission of this sort, and beat Professor Bumper in the race."

"Do you think that's why Beecher decided to go on the same steamer we are to take?" asked Ned.

"Yes, I do," said Mr. Damon. "Though from what Professor Bumper said I know he regards Professor Beecher as a perfectly honorable man, as well as a brilliant student. I do not believe Beecher or his party would stoop to anything dishonorable or underhand, though they would not hesitate, nor would we, to take advantage of every fair chance to win in the race."

"No, I suppose that's right," observed Tom; but there was a queer gleam in his eye, and his chum wondered if Tom did not have in mind the prospective race between himself and Fenimore Beecher for the regard of Mary Nestor. "We'll do our best to win, and any one is at liberty to travel on the same steamer we are to take," added the young inventor, and his tone became more incisive.

"It will be all the livelier with two expeditions after the same golden idol," remarked Ned.

"Yes, I think we're in for some excitement," observed Tom grimly. But even he did not realize all that lay before them ere they would reach Kurzon.

Mr. Damon, having delivered his message, and remarking that his preparations for leaving were nearly completed, went back to Waterfield, from there to proceed to New York in a few days with Tom and Ned, to meet Professor Bumper.

"Well, I guess we have everything in pretty good shape," remarked Tom to his chum a day or so after the visit of Mr. Damon. "Everything is packed, and as I have a few personal matters to attend to I think I'll take the afternoon off."

"Go to it!" laughed Ned, guessing a thing of two. "I've got a raft of stuff myself to look after, but don't let that keep you."

"If there is anything I can do," began Tom, "don't hesitate to—"

"Nonsense!" exclaimed Ned. "I can do it all alone. It's some of the company's business, anyhow, and I'm paid for looking after that."

"All right, then I'll cut along," Tom said, and he wore a relieved air.

"He's going to see Mary," observed Ned with a grin, as he observed Tom hop into his trim little roadster, which under his orders, Koku had polished and cleaned until it looked as though it had just come from the factory.

A little later the trim and speedy car drew up in front of the Nestor home, and Tom bounded up on the front porch, his heart not altogether as light as his feet.

"No, I'm sorry, but Mary isn't in," said Mrs. Nestor, answering his inquiry after greeting him.

"Not at home?"

"No, she went on a little visit to her cousin's at Fayetteville. She said something about letting you know she was going."

"She did drop me a card," answered Tom, and, somehow he did not feel at all cheerful. "But I thought it wasn't until next week she was going."

"That was her plan, Tom. But she changed it. Her cousin wired, asking her to advance the date, and this Mary did. There was something about a former school chum who was also to be at Myra's house—Myra is Mary's cousin you know."

"Yes, I know," assented the young inventor. "And so Mary is gone. How long is she going to stay?"

"Oh, about two weeks. She wasn't quite certain. It depends on the kind of a time she has, I suppose."

"Yes, I suppose so," agreed Tom. "Well, if you write before I do you might say I called, Mrs. Nestor."

"I will, Tom. And I know Mary will be sorry she wasn't here to take a ride with you; it's such a nice day," and the lady smiled as she looked at the speedy roadster.

"Maybe—maybe you'd like to come for a spin?" asked Tom, half desperately.

"No, thank you. I'm too old to be jounced around in one of those small cars."

"Nonsense! She rides as easily as a Pullman sleeper."

"Well, I have to go to a Red Cross meeting, anyhow, so I can't come, Tom. Thank you, just the same."

Tom did not drive back immediately to his home. He wanted to do a bit of thinking, and he believed he could do it best by himself. So it was late afternoon when he again greeted Ned, who, meanwhile, had been kept very busy.

"Well?" called Tom's chum.

"Um!" was the only answer, and Tom called Koku to put the car away in the garage.

"Something wrong," mused Ned.

The next three days were crowded with events and with work. Mr. Damon came over frequently to consult with Tom and Ned, and finally the last of their baggage had been packed, certain of Tom's inventions and implements sent on by express to New York to be taken to Honduras, and then our friends themselves followed to the metropolis.

"Good-bye, Tom," said his father. "Good-bye, and good luck! If you don't get the idol of gold I'm sure you'll have experiences that will be valuable to you."

"We're going to get the idol of gold!" said Tom determinedly.

"Look out for the bad bugs," suggested Eradicate.

"We will," promised Ned.

Tom's last act was to send a message to Mary Nestor, and then he, with Ned and Mr. Damon, who blessed everything in sight from the gasoline in the automobile to the blue sky overhead, started for the station.

New York was reached without incident. The trio put up at the hotel where Professor Bumper was to meet them.

"He hasn't arrived yet," said Tom, after glancing over the names on the hotel register and not seeing Professor Bumper's among them.

"Oh, he'll be here all right," asserted Mr. Damon. "Bless my galvanic battery! he sent me a telegram at one o'clock this morning saying he'd be sure to meet us in New York. No fear of him not starting for the land of wonders."

"There are some other professors registered, though," observed Ned, as he glanced at the book, noting the names of several scientists of whom he and Tom had read.

"Yes. I wonder what they're doing in New York," replied Tom. "They are from New England. Maybe there's a convention going on. Well, we'll have to wait, that's all, until Professor Bumper comes."

And during that wait Tom heard something that surprised him and caused him no little worry. It was when Ned came back to his room, which adjoined Tom's, that the young treasurer gave his chum the news.

"I say, Tom!" Ned exclaimed. "Who do you think those professors are, whose names we saw on the register?"

"I haven't the least idea."

"Why, they're of Beecher's party!"

"You don't mean it!"

"I surely do."

"How do you know?"

"I happened to overhear two of them talking down in the lobby a while ago. They didn't make any secret of it. They spoke freely of going with Beecher to some ancient city in Honduras, to look for an idol of gold."

"They did? But where is Beecher?"

"He hasn't joined them yet. Their plans have been changed. Instead of leaving on the same steamer we are to take in the morning they are to come on a later one. The professors here are waiting for Beecher to come."

"Why isn't he here now?"

"Well, I heard one of the other scientists say that he had gone to a place called Fayetteville, and will come on from there."

"Fayetteville!" ejaculated Tom. "Yes. That isn't far from Shopton."

"I know," assented Tom. "I wonder—I wonder why he is going there?"

"I can tell you that, too."

"You can? You're a regular detective."

"No, I just happened to overhear it. Beecher is going to call on Mary Nestor in Fayetteville, so his friends here said he told them, and his call has to do with an important matter—to him!" and Ned gazed curiously at his chum.

Off for Honduras

Just what Tom's thoughts were, Ned, of course, could not guess. But by the flush that showed under the tan of his chum's cheeks the young financial secretary felt pretty certain that Tom was a bit apprehensive of the outcome of Professor Beecher's call on Mary Nestor.

"So he is going to see her about `something important,' Ned?"

"That's what some members of his party called it."

"And they're waiting here for him to join them?"

"Yes. And it means waiting a week for another steamer. It must be something pretty important, don't you think, to cause Beecher to risk that delay in starting after the idol of gold?"

"Important? Yes, I suppose so," assented Tom. "And yet even if he waits for the next steamer he will get to Honduras nearly as soon as we do."

"How is that?"

"The next boat is a faster one."

"Then why don't we take that? I hate dawdling along on a slow freighter."

"Well, for one thing it would hardly do to change now, when all our goods are on board. And besides, the captain of the *Relstab*, on which we are going to sail, is a friend of Professor Bumper's."

"Well, I'm just as glad Beecher and his party aren't going with us," resumed Ned, after a pause. "It might make trouble."

"Oh, I'm ready for any trouble HE might make!" quickly exclaimed Tom.

He meant trouble that might be developed in going to Honduras, and starting the search for the lost city and the idol of gold. This kind of trouble Tom and his friends had experienced before, on other trips where rivals had sought to frustrate their ends.

But, in his heart, though he said nothing to Ned about it, Tom was worried. Much as he disliked to admit it to himself, he feared the visit of Professor Beecher to Mary Nestor in Fayetteville had but one meaning.

"I wonder if he's going to propose to her," thought Tom. "He has the field all to himself now, and her father likes him. That's in his favor. I guess Mr. Nestor has never quite forgiven me for that mistake about the dynamite box, and that wasn't my fault. Then, too, the Beecher and Nestor families have been friends for years. Yes, he surely has the inside edge on me, and if he gets her to throw me over—— Well, I won't give up without a fight!" and Tom mentally girded himself for a battle of wits.

"He's relying on the prestige he'll get out of this idol of gold if his party finds it," thought on the young inventor. "But I'll help find it first. I'm glad to have a little start of him, anyhow, even if it isn't more than two days. Though if our vessel is held back much by storms he may get on the ground first. However, that can't be helped. I'll do the best I can."

These thoughts shot through Tom's mind even as Ned was asking his questions and making comments. Then the young inventor, shaking his shoulders as though to rid them of some weight, remarked:

"Well, come on out and see the sights. It will be long before we look on Broadway again."

When the chums returned from their sightseeing excursion, they found that Professor Bumper had arrived.

"Where's Professor Bumper?" asked Ned, the next day.

"In his room, going over books, papers and maps to make sure he has everything."

"And Mr. Damon?"

Tom did not have to answer that last question. Into the apartment came bursting the excited individual himself.

"Bless my overshoes!" he cried, "I've been looking everywhere for you! Come on, there's no time to lose!"

"What's the matter now?" asked Ned. "Is the hotel on fire?"

"Has anything happened to Professor Bumper?" Tom demanded, a wild idea forming in his head that perhaps some one of the Beecher party had tried to kidnap the discoverer of the lost city of Pelone.

"Oh, everything is all right," answered Mr. Damon. "But it's nearly time for the show to start, and we don't want to be late. I have tickets."

"For what?" asked Tom and Ned together.

"The movies," was the laughing reply. "Bless my loose ribs! but I wouldn't miss him for anything. He's in a new play called 'Up in a Balloon Boys.' It's great!" and Mr. Damon named a certain comic moving picture star in whose horse-play Mr. Damon took a curious interest. Tom and Ned were glad enough to go, Tom that he might have a chance to do a certain amount of thinking, and Ned because he was still boy enough to like moving pictures.

"I wonder, Tom," said Mr. Damon, as they came out of the theater two hours later, all three chuckling at the remembrance of what they had seen, "I wonder you never turned your inventive mind to the movies."

"Maybe I will, some day," said Tom.

He spoke rather uncertainly. The truth of the matter was that he was still thinking deeply of the visit of Professor Beecher to Mary Nestor, and wondering what it portended.

But if Tom's sleep was troubled that night he said nothing of it to his friends. He was up early the next morning, for they were to leave that day, and there was still considerable to be done in seeing that their baggage and supplies were safely loaded, and in attending to the last details of some business matters.

While at the hotel they had several glimpses of the members of the Beecher party who were awaiting the arrival of the young professor who was to lead them into the wilds of Honduras. But our friends did not seek the acquaintance of their rivals. The latter, likewise, remained by themselves, though they knew doubtless that there was likely to be a strenuous race for the possession of the idol of gold, then, it was presumed, buried deep in some forest-covered city.

Professor Bumper had made his arrangements carefully. As he explained to his friends, they would take the steamer from New York to Puerto Cortes, one of the principal seaports of Honduras. This is a town of about three thousand inhabitants, with an excellent harbor and a big pier along which vessels can tie up and discharge their cargoes directly into waiting cars.

The preparations were finally completed. The party went aboard the steamer, which was a large freight vessel, carrying a limited number of passengers, and late one afternoon swung down New York Bay.

"Off for Honduras!" cried Ned gaily, as they passed the Statue of Liberty. "I wonder what will happen before we see that little lady again."

"Who knows?" asked Tom, shrugging his shoulders, Spanish fashion. And there came before him the vision of a certain "little lady," about whom he had been thinking deeply of late.

VAL JACINTO

"Rather tame, isn't it, Tom?"

"Well, Ned, it isn't exactly like going up in an airship," and Tom Swift who was gazing over the rail down into the deep blue water of the Caribbean Sea, over which their vessel was then steaming, looked at his chum beside him.

"No, and your submarine voyage had it all over this one for excitement," went on Ned. "When I think of that—"

"Bless my sea legs!" interrupted Mr. Damon, overhearing the conversation. "Don't speak of *that* trip. My wife never forgave me for going on it. But I had a fine time," he added with a twinkle of his eyes.

"Yes, that was quite a trip," observed Tom, as his mind went back to it. "But this one isn't over yet remember. And I shouldn't be surprised if we had a little excitement very soon."

"What do you mean?" asked Ned.

Up to this time the voyage from New York down into the tropical seas had been anything but exciting. There were not many passengers besides themselves, and the weather had been fine.

At first, used as they were to the actions of unscrupulous rivals in trying to thwart their efforts, Tom and Ned had been on the alert for any signs of hidden enemies on board the steamer. But aside from a little curiosity when it became known that they were going to explore little-known portions of Honduras, the other passengers took hardly any interest in our travelers.

It was thought best to keep secret the fact that they were going to search for a wonderful idol of gold. Not even the mule and ox-cart drivers, whom they would hire to take them into the wilds of the interior would be told of the real object of the search. It would be given out that they were looking for interesting ruins of ancient cities, with a view to getting such antiquities as might be there.

"What do you mean?" asked Ned again, when Tom did not answer him immediately. "What's the excitement?"

"I think we're in for a storm," was the reply. "The barometer is falling and I see the crew going about making everything snug. So we may have a little trouble toward this end of our trip."

"Let it come!" exclaimed Mr. Damon. "We're not afraid of trouble, Tom. Swift, are we?"

"No, to be sure we're not. And yet it looks as though the storm would be a bad one."

"Then I am going to see if my books and papers are ready, so I can get them together in a hurry in case we have to take to the life-boats," said Professor Bumper, coming on deck at that moment. "It won't do to lose them. If we didn't have the map we might not be able to find—"

"Ahem!" exclaimed Tom, with unnecessary emphasis it seemed. "I'll help you go over your papers, Professor," he added, and with a wink and a motion of his hand, he enjoined silence on his friend. Ned looked around for a reason for this, and observed a man, evidently of Spanish extraction, passing them as he paced up and down the deck.

"What's the matter?" asked the scientist in a whisper, as the man went on. "Do you know him? Is he a——?"

"I don't know anything about him," said Tom; "but it is best not to speak of our trip before strangers."

"You are right, Tom," said Professor Bumper. "I'll be more careful."

A storm was brewing, that was certain. A dull, sickly yellow began to obscure the sky, and the water, from a beautiful blue, turned a slate color and ran along the sides of the vessel with a hissing sound as though the sullen waves would ask nothing better than to suck the craft down into their depths. The wind, which had been freshening, now sang in louder tones as it hummed through the rigging and the funnel stays and bowled over the receiving conductors of the wireless.

Sharp commands from the ship's officers hastened the work of the crew in making things snug, and life lines were strung along deck for the safety of such of the passengers as might venture up when the blow began.

The storm was not long in coming. The howling of the wind grew louder, flecks of foam began to separate themselves from the crests of the waves, and the vessel pitched, rolled and tossed more violently. At first Tom and his friends thought they were in for no more than an ordinary blow, but as the storm progressed, and the passengers became aware of the anxiety on the part of the officers and crew, the alarm spread among them.

It really was a violent storm, approaching a hurricane in force, and at one time it seemed as though the craft, having been heeled far over under a staggering wave that swept her decks, would not come back to an even keel.

There was a panic among some of the passengers, and a few excited men behaved in a way that caused prompt action on the part of the first officer, who drove them back to the main cabin under threat of a revolver. For the men were determined to get to the lifeboats, and a small craft would not have had a minute to live in such seas as were running.

But the vessel proved herself sturdier than the timid ones had dared to hope, and she was soon running before the blast, going out of her course, it is true, but avoiding the danger among the many cays, or small islands, that dot the Caribbean Sea.

There was nothing to do but to let the storm blow itself out, which it did in two days. Then came a period of delightful weather. The cargo had shifted somewhat, which gave the steamer a rather undignified list.

This, as well as the loss of a deckhand overboard, was the effect of the hurricane, and though the end of the trip came amid sunshine and sweet-scented tropical breezes, many could not forget the dangers through which they had passed.

In due time Tom and his party found themselves safely housed in the small hotel at Puerto Cortes, their belongings stored in a convenient warehouse and themselves, rather weary by reason of the stress of weather, ready for the start into the interior wilds of Honduras.

"How are we going to make the trip?" asked Ned, as they sat at supper, the first night after their arrival, eating of several dishes, the red-pepper condiments of which caused frequent trips to the water pitcher.

"We can go in two ways, and perhaps we shall find it to our advantage to use both means," said Professor Bumper. "To get to this city of Kurzon," he proceeded in a low voice, so that none of the others in the dining-room would hear them, "we will have to go either by mule back or boat to a point near Copan. As near as I can tell by the ancient maps, Kurzon is in the Copan valley.

"Now the Chamelecon river seems to run to within a short distance of there, but there is no telling how far up it may be navigable. If we can go by boat it will be much more comfortable. Travel by mules and ox-carts is slow and sure, but the roads are very bad, as I have heard from friends who have made explorations in Honduras.

"And, as I said, we may have to use both land and water travel to get us where we want to go. We can proceed as far as possible up the river, and then take to the mules."

"What about arranging for boats and animals?" asked Tom. "I should think—"

He suddenly ceased talking and reached for the water, taking several large swallows.

"Whew!" he exclaimed, when he could catch his breath. "That was a hot one."

"What did you do?" asked Ned.

"Bit into a nest of red pepper. Guess I'll have to tell that cook to scatter his hits. He's bunching 'em too much in my direction," and Tom wiped the tears from his eyes.

"To answer your question," said Professor Bumper, "I will say that I have made partial arrangements for men and animals, and boats if it is found feasible to use them. I've been in correspondence with one of the merchants here, and he promised to make arrangements for us."

"When do we leave?" asked Mr. Damon.

"As soon as possible. I am not going to risk anything by delay," and it was evident the professor referred to his young rival whose arrival might be expected almost any time.

As the party was about to leave the table, they were approached by a tall, dignified Spaniard who bowed low, rather exaggeratedly low, Ned thought, and addressed them in fairly good English.

"Your pardons, Senors," he began, "but if it will please you to avail yourself of the humble services of myself, I shall have great pleasure in guiding you into the interior. I have at my command both mules and boats."

"How do you know we are going into the interior?" asked Tom, a bit sharply, for he did not like the assurance of the man.

"Pardon, Senor. I saw that you are from the States. And those from the States do not come to Honduras except for two reasons. To travel and make explorations or to start trade, and professors do not usually engage in trade," and he bowed to Professor Bumper.

"I saw your name on the register," he proceeded, "and it was not difficult to guess your mission," and he flashed a smile on the party, his white teeth showing brilliantly beneath his small, black moustache.

"I make it my business to outfit traveling parties, either for business, pleasure or scientific matters. I am, at your service, Val Jacinto," and he introduced himself with another low bow.

For a moment Tom and his friends hardly knew how to accept this offer. It might be, as the man had said, that he was a professional tour conductor, like those who have charge of Egyptian donkey-boys and guides. Or might he not be a spy?

This occurred to Tom no less than to Professor Bumper. They looked at one another while Val Jacinto bowed again and murmured:

"At your service!"

"Can you provide means for taking us to the Copan valley?" asked the professor. "You are right in one respect. I am a scientist and I purpose doing some exploring near Copan. Can you get us there?"

"Most expensively—I mean, most expeditionlessly," said Val Jacinto eagerly. "Pardon my unhappy English. I forget at times. The charges will be most moderate. I can send you by boat as far as the river travel is good, and then have mules and ox-carts in waiting."

"How far is it?" asked Tom.

"A hundred miles as the vulture flies, Senor, but much farther by river and road. We shall be a week going."

"A hundred miles in a week!" groaned Ned. "Say, Tom, if you had your aeroplane we'd be there in an hour."

"Yes, but we haven't it. However, we're in no great rush."

"But we must not lose time," said Professor Bumper. "I shall consider your offer," he added to Val Jacinto.

"Very good, Senor. I am sure you will be pleased with the humble service I may offer you, and my charges will be small. Adios," and he bowed himself away.

"What do you think of him?" asked Ned, as they went up to their rooms in the hotel, or rather one large room, containing several beds.

"He's a pretty slick article," said Mr. Damon. "Bless my check-book! but he spotted us at once, in spite of our secrecy."

"I guess these guide purveyors are trained for that sort of thing," observed the scientist. "I know my friends have often spoken of having had the same experience. However, I shall ask my friend, who is in business here, about this Val Jacinto, and if I find him all right we may engage him "

Inquiries next morning brought the information, from the head of a rubber exporting firm with whom the professor was acquainted, that the Spaniard was regularly engaged in transporting parties into the interior, and was considered efficient, careful and as honest as pos-sible, considering the men he engaged as workers.

"So we have decided to engage you," Professor Bumper informed Val Jacinto the afternoon following the meeting.

"I am more than pleased, Senor. I shall take you into the wilds of Honduras. At your service!" and he bowed low.

"Humph! I don't just like the way our friend Val says that," observed Tom to Ned a little later. "I'd have been better pleased if he had said he'd guide us into the wilds and out again."

If Tom could have seen the crafty smile on the face of the Spaniard as the man left the hotel, the young inventor might have felt even less confidence in the guide.

In the Wilds

"All aboard! Step lively now! This boat makes no stops this side of Boston!" cried Ned Newton gaily, as he got into one of the several tree canoes provided for the transportation of the party up the Chamelecon river, for the first stage of their journey into the wilds of Honduras. "All aboard! This reminds me of my old camping days, Tom."

It brought those days back, in a measure, to Tom also. For there were a number of canoes filled with the goods of the party, while the members themselves occupied a larger one with their personal baggage. Strong, half-naked Indian paddlers were in charge of the canoes which were of sturdy construction and light draft, since the river, like most tropical streams, was of uncertain depths, choked here and there with sand bars or tropical growths.

Finding that Val Jacinto was regularly engaged in the business of taking explorers and mine prospectors into the interior, Professor Bumper had engaged the man. He seemed to be efficient. At the promised time he had the canoes and paddlers on hand and the goods safely stowed away while one big craft was fitted up as comfortably as possible for the men of the party.

As Ned remarked, it did look like a camping party, for in the canoes were tents, cooking utensils and, most important, mosquito canopies of heavy netting.

The insect pests of Honduras, as in all tropical countries, are annoying and dangerous. Therefore it was imperative to sleep under mosquito netting.

On the advice of Val Jacinto, who was to accompany them, the travelers were to go up the river about fifty miles. This was as far as it would be convenient to use the canoes, the guide told Tom and his friends, and from there on the trip to the Copan valley would be made on the backs of mules, which would carry most of the baggage and equipment. The heavier portions would be transported in ox-carts.

As Professor Bumper expected to do considerable excavating in order to locate the buried city, or cities, as the case might be, he had to contract for a number of Indian diggers and laborers. These could be hired in Copan, it was said.

The plan, therefore, was to travel by canoes during the less heated parts of the day, and tie up at night, making camp on shore in the net-protected tents. As for the Indians, they did not seem to mind the bites of the insects. They sometimes made a smudge fire, Val Jacinto had said, but that was all.

"Well, we haven't seen anything of Beecher and his friends," remarked the young inventor as they were about to start.

"No, he doesn't seem to have arrived," agreed Professor Bumper. "We'll get ahead of him, and so much the better."

"Well, are we all ready to start?" he continued, as he looked over the little flotilla which carried his party and his goods.

"The sooner the better!" cried Tom, and Ned fancied his chum was unusually eager.

"I guess he wants to make good before Beecher gets the chance to show Mary Nestor what he can do," thought Ned. "Tom sure is after that idol of gold."

"You may start, Senor Jacinto," said the professor, and the guide called something in Indian dialect to the rowers. Lines were cast off and the boats moved out into the stream under the influence of the sturdy paddlers.

"Well, this isn't so bad," observed Ned, as he made himself comfortable in his canoe. "How about it, Tom?"

"Oh, no. But this is only the beginning."

A canopy had been arranged over their boat to keep off the scorching rays of the sun. The boat containing the exploring party and Val Jacinto took the lead, the baggage craft following. At the place where it flowed into the bay on which Puerto Cortes was built, the stream was wide and deep.

The guide called something to the Indians, who increased their stroke.

"I tell them to pull hard and that at the end of the day's journey they will have much rest and refreshment," he translated to Professor Bumper and the others.

"Bless my ham sandwich, but they'll need plenty of some sort of refreshment," said Mr. Damon, with a sigh. "I never knew it to be so hot."

"Don't complain yet," advised Tom, with a laugh. "The worst is yet to come."

It really was not unpleasant traveling, aside from the heat. And they had expected that, coming as they had to a tropical land. But, as Tom said, what lay before them might be worse.

In a little while they had left behind them all signs of civilization. The river narrowed and flowed sluggishly between the banks which were luxuriant with tropical growth. Now and then some lonely Indian hut could be seen, and occasionally a craft propelled by a man who was trying to gain a meager living from the rubber forest which hemmed in the stream on either side.

As the canoe containing the men was paddled along, there floated down beside it what seemed to be a big, rough log.

"I wonder if that is mahogany," remarked Mr. Damon, reaching over to touch it. "Mahogany is one of the most valuable woods of Honduras, and if this is a log of that nature——

"Bless my watch chain!" he suddenly cried. It's alive!"

And the "log" was indeed so, for there was a sudden flash of white teeth, a long red opening showed, and then came a click as an immense alligator, having opened and closed his mouth, sank out of sight in a swirl of water.

Mr. Damon drew back so suddenly that he tilted the canoe, and the black paddlers looked around wonderingly.

"Alligator," explained Jacinto succinctly, in their tongue.

"Ugh!" they grunted.

"Bless my—bless my—" hesitated Mr. Damon, and for one of the very few times in his life his language failed him.

"Are there many of them hereabouts?" asked Ned, looking back at the swirl left by the saurian.

"Plenty," said the guide, with a shrug of his shoulders. He seemed to do as much talking that way, and with his hands, as he did in speech. "The river is full of them."

"Dangerous?" queried Tom.

"Don't go in swimming," was the significant advice. "Wait, I'll show you," and he called up the canoe just behind.

In this canoe was a quantity of provisions. There was a chunk of meat among other things, a gristly piece, seeing which Mr. Damon had objected to its being brought along, but the guide had said it would do for fish bait. With a quick motion of his hand, as he sat in the awning-covered stern with Tom, Ned and the others, Jacinto sent the chunk of meat out into the muddy stream.

Hardly a second later there was a rushing in the water as though a submarine were about to come up. An ugly snout was raised, two rows of keen teeth snapped shut as a scissors-like jaw opened, and the meat was gone.

"See!" was the guide's remark, and something like a cold shiver of fear passed over the white members of the party. "This water is not made in which to swim. Be careful!"

"We certainly shall," agreed Tom. "They're fierce."

"And always hungry," observed Jacinto grimly.

"And to think that I—that I nearly had my hand on it," murmured Mr. Damon. "Ugh! Bless my eyeglasses!"

"The alligator nearly had your hand," said the guide. "They can turn in the water like a flash, wherefore it is not wise to pat one on the tail lest it present its mouth instead."

They paddled on up the river, the dusky Indians now and then breaking out into a chant that seemed to give their muscles new energy. The song, if song it was, passed from one boat to the other, and as the chant boomed forth the craft shot ahead more swiftly.

They made a landing about noon, and lunch was served. Tom and his friends were hungry in spite of the heat. Moreover, they were experienced travelers and had learned not to fret over inconveniences and discomforts. the Ind-ians ate by themselves, two acting as servants to Jacinto and the professor's party.

As is usual in traveling in the tropics, a halt was made during the heated middle of the day. Then, as the afternoon shadows were waning, the party again took to the canoes and paddled on up the river.

"Do you know of a good place to stop during the night?" asked Professor Bumper of Jacinto.

"Oh, yes; a most excellent place. It is where I always bring scientific parties I am guiding. You may rely on me."

It was within an hour of dusk—none too much time to allow in which to pitch camp in the tropics, where night follows day suddenly—when a halt was called, as a turn of the river showed a little clearing on the edge of the forest-bound river.

"We stay here for the night," said Jacinto. "It is a good place."

"It looks picturesque enough," observed Mr. Damon. "But it is rather wild."

"We are a good distance from a settlement," agreed the guide. "But one can not explore— and find treasure in cities," and he shrugged his shoulders again.

"Find treasure? What do you mean?" asked Tom quickly. "Do you think that we——?"

"Pardon, Senor," replied Jacinto softly. "I meant no offense. I think that all you scientific parties will take treasure if you can find it."

"We are looking for traces of the old Honduras civilization," put in Professor Bumper.

"And doubtless you will find it," was the somewhat too courteous answer of the guide. "Make camp quickly!" he called to the Indians in their tongue. "You must soon get under the nets or you will be eaten alive!" he told Tom. "There are many mosquitoes here."

The tents were set up, smudge fires built and supper quickly prepared. Dusk fell rapidly, and as Tom and Ned walked a little way down toward the river before turning in under the mosquito canopies, the young financial man said:

"Sort of lonesome and gloomy, isn't it, Tom?"

"Yes. But you didn't expect to find a moving picture show in the wilds of Honduras, did you?"

"No, and yet— Look out! What's that?" suddenly cried Ned, as a great soft, black shadow seemed to sweep out of a clump of trees toward him. Involuntarily he clutched Tom's arm and pointed, his face showing fear in the fast-gathering darkness.

The Vampires

Tom Swift looked deliberately around. It was characteristic of him that, though by nature he was prompt in action, he never acted so hurriedly as to obscure his judgment. So, though now Ned showed a trace of strange excitement, Tom was cool.

"What is it?" asked the young inventor. "What's the matter? What did you think you saw, Ned; another alligator?"

"Alligator? Nonsense! Up on shore? I saw a black shadow, and I didn't *think* I saw it, either. I really did."

Tom laughed quietly.

"A shadow!" he exclaimed. "Since when were you afraid of shadows, Ned?"

"I'm not afraid of ordinary shadows," answered Ned, and in his voice there was an uncertain tone. "I'm not afraid of my shadow or yours, Tom, or anybody's that I can see. But this wasn't any human shadow. It was as if a great big blob of wet darkness had been waved over your head."

"That's a queer explanation," Tom said in a low voice. "A great big blob of wet darkness!"

"But that just describes it," went on Ned, looking up and around. "It was just as if you were in some dark room, and some one waved a wet velvet cloak over your head—spooky like! It didn't make a sound, but there was a smell as if a den of some wild beast was near here. I remember that odor from the time we went hunting with your electric rifle in the jungle, and got near the den in the rocks where the tigers lived."

"Well, there is a wild beast smell all around here," admitted Tom, sniffing the air. "It's the alligators in the river I guess. You know they have an odor of musk."

"Do you mean to say you didn't feel that shadow flying over us just now?" asked Ned.

"Well, I felt something sail through the air, but I took it to be a big bird. I didn't pay much attention. To tell you the truth I was thinking about Beecher—wondering when he would get here," added Tom quickly as if to forestall any question as to whether or not his thoughts had to do with Beecher in connection with Tom's affair of the heart.

"Well it wasn't a bird—at least not a regular bird," said Ned in a low voice, as once more he looked at the dark and gloomy jungle that stretched back from the river and behind the little clearing where the camp had been made.

"Come on!" cried Tom, in what he tried to make a cheerful voice. "This is getting on your nerves, Ned, and I didn't know you had any. Let's go back and turn in. I'm dog-tired and the mosquitoes are beginning to find that we're here. Let's get under the nets. Then the black shadows won't get you."

Not at all unwilling to leave so gloomy a scene, Ned, after a brief glance up and down the dark river, followed his chum. They found Professor Bumper and Mr. Damon in their tent, a separate one having been set up for the two men adjoining that of the youths.

"Bless my fountain pen!" exclaimed Mr. Damon, as he caught sight of Tom and Ned in the flickering light of the smudge fire between the two canvas shelters. "We were just wondering what had become of you."

"We were chasing shadows!" laughed Tom. "At least Ned was. But you look cozy enough in there."

It did, indeed, look cheerful in contrast to the damp and dark jungle all about. Professor Bumper, being an experienced traveler, knew how to provide for such comforts as were possible. Folding cots had been opened for himself, Mr. Damon and the guide to sleep on, others, similar, being set up in the tent where Tom and Ned were to sleep. In the middle of the tent the professor had made a table of his own and Mr. Damon's suit cases, and on this placed a small dry battery electric light. He was making some notes, doubtless for a future book. Jacinto was going about the camp, seeing that the Indians were at their duties, though most of them had gone directly to sleep after supper.

"Better get inside and under the nets," advised Professor Bumper to Tom and Ned. "The mosquitoes here are the worst I ever saw."

"We're beginning to believe that," returned Ned, who was unusually quiet. "Come on, Tom. I can't stand it any longer. I'm itching in a dozen places now from their bites."

As Tom and Ned had no wish for a light, which would be sure to attract insects, they entered their tent in the dark, and were soon stretched out in comparative comfort. Tom was just on the edge of a deep sleep when he heard Ned murmur:

"I can't understand it!"

"What's that?" asked the young inventor.

"I say I can't understand it."

"Understand what?"

"That shadow. It was real and yet—"

"Oh, go to sleep!" advised Tom, and, turning over, he was soon breathing heavily and regularly, indicating that he, at least, had taken his own advice.

Ned, too, finally succumbed to the overpowering weariness of the first day of travel, and he, too, slept, though it was an uneasy slumber, disturbed by a feeling as though some one were holding a heavy black quilt over his head, preventing him from breathing.

The feeling, sensation or dream—whatever it was—perhaps a nightmare—became at last so real to Ned that he struggled himself into wakefulness. With an effort he sat up, uttering an inarticulate cry. To his surprise he was answered. Some one asked:

"What is the matter?"

"Who—who are you?" asked Ned quickly, trying to peer through the darkness.

"This is Jacinto—your guide," was the soft answer. "I was walking about camp and, hearing you murmuring, I came to your tent. Is anything wrong?"

For a moment Ned did not answer. He listened and could tell by the continued heavy and regular breathing of his chum that Tom was still asleep.

"Are you in our tent?" asked Ned, at length:

"Yes," answered Jacinto. "I came in to see what was the matter with you. Are you ill?"

"No, of course not," said Ned, a bit shortly. "I—I had a bad dream, that was all. All right now."

"For that I am glad. Try to get all the sleep you can, for we must start early to avoid the heat of the day," and there was the sound of the guide leaving and arranging the folds of the mosquito net behind him to keep out the night-flying insects.

Once more Ned composed himself to sleep, and this time successfully, for he did not have any more unpleasant dreams. The quiet of the jungle settled down over the camp, at least the comparative quiet of the jungle, for there were always noises of some sort going on, from the fall of some rotten tree limb to the scream or growl of a wild beast, while, now and again, from the river came the pig-like grunts of the alligators.

It was about two o'clock in the morning, as they ascertained later, when the whole camp— white travelers and all—was suddenly awakened by a wild scream. It seemed to come from one of the natives, who called out a certain word ever and over again. To Tom and Ned it sounded like:

"Oshtoo! Oshtoo! Oshtoo!"

"What's the matter?" cried Professor Bumper.

"The vampires!" came the answering voice of Jacinto. "One of the Indians has been attacked by a big vampire bat! Look out, every one! It may be a raid by the dangerous creatures! Be careful!"

Notwithstanding this warning Ned stuck his head out of the tent. The same instant he was aware of a dark enfolding shadow passing over him, and, with a shudder of fear, he jumped back.

A FALSE FRIEND

"What is it? What's the matter?" cried Tom springing from his cot and hastening to the side of his chum in the tent. "What has happened, Ned?"

"I don't know, but Jacinto is yelling something about vampires!"

"Vampires?"

"Yes. Big bats. And he's warning us to be careful. I stuck my head out just now and I felt that same sort of shadow I felt this evening when we were down near the river."

"Nonsense!"

"I tell you I did!"

At that instant Tom flashed a pocket electric lamp he had taken from beneath his pillow and in the gleam of it he and Ned saw fluttering about the tent some dark, shadow-like form, at the sight of which Tom's chum cried:

"There it is! That's the shadow! Look out!" and he held up his hands instinctively to shield his face.

"Shadow!" yelled Tom, unconsciously adding to the din that seemed to pervade every part of the camp. "That isn't a shadow. It's substance. It's a monster bat, and here goes for a strike at it!"

He caught up his camera tripod which was near his cot, and made a swing with it at the creature that had flown into the tent through an opening it had made for itself.

"Look out!" yelled Ned. "If it's a vampire it'll—"

"It won't do anything to me!" shouted Tom, as he struck the creature, knocking it into the corner of the tent with a thud that told it must be completely stunned, if not killed. "But what's it all about, anyhow?" Tom asked. "What's the row?"

From without the tent came the Indian cries of:

"Oshtoo! Oshtoo!"

Mingled with them were calls of Jacinto, partly in Spanish, partly in the Indian tongue and partly in English.

"It is a raid by vampire bats!" was all Tom and Ned could distinguish. "We shall have to light fires to keep them away, if we can suc-ceed. Every one grab up a club and strike hard!"

"Come on!" cried Tom, getting on some clothes by the light of his gleaming electric light which he had set on his cot.

"You're not going out there, are you?" asked Ned.

"I certainly am! If there's a fight I want to be in it, bats or anything else. Here, you have a light like mine. Flash it on, and hang it somewhere on yourself. Then get a club and come on. The lights will blind the bats, and we can see to hit 'em!"

Tom's plan seemed to be a good one. His lamp and Ned's had small hooks on them, so they could be carried in the upper coat pocket, showing a gleam of light and leaving the hands free for use.

Out of the tents rushed the young men to find Professor Bumper and Mr. Damon before them. The two men had clubs and were striking about in the half darkness, for now the Indians had set several fires aglow. And in the gleams, constantly growing brighter as more fuel was piled on, the young inventor and his chum saw a weird sight.

Circling and wheeling about in the camp clearing were many of the black shadowy forms that had caused Ned such alarm. Great bats they were, and a dangerous species, if Jacinto was to be believed.

The uncanny creatures flew in and out among the trees and tents, now swooping low near the Indians or the travelers. At such times clubs would be used, often with the effect of killing or stunning the flying pests. For a time it seemed as if the bats would fairly overwhelm the camp, so many of them were there. But the increasing lights, and the attacks made by the Indians and the white travelers turned the tide of battle, and, with silent flappings of their soft, velvety wings, the bats flew back to the jungle whence they had emerged.

"We are safe—for the present!" exclaimed Jacinto with a sigh of relief.

"Do you think they will come back?" asked Tom.

"They may—there is no telling."

"Bless my speedometer!" cried Mr. Damon, "If those beasts or birds—whatever they are— come back I'll go and hide in the river and take my chances with the alligators!"

"The alligators aren't much worse," asserted Jacinto with a visible shiver. "These vampire bats sometimes depopulate a whole village."

"Bless my shoe laces!" cried Mr. Damon. "You don't mean to say that the creatures can eat up a whole village?"

"Not quite. Though they might if they got the chance," was the answer of the Spanish guide. "These vampire bats fly from place to place in great swarms, and they are so large and blood-thirsty that a few of them can kill a horse or an ox in a short time by sucking its blood. So when the villagers find they are visited by a colony of these vampires they get out, taking their live stock with them, and stay in caves or in densely wooded places until the bats fly on. Then the villagers come back.

"It was only a small colony that visited us tonight or we would have had more trouble. I do not think this lot will come back. We have killed too many of them," and he looked about on the ground where many of the uncanny creatures were still twitching in the death struggle.

"Come back again!" cried Mr. Damon. "Bless my skin! I hope not! I've had enough of bats— and mosquitoes," he added, as he slapped at his face and neck.

Indeed the party of whites were set upon by the night insects to such an extent that it was necessary to hurry back to the protection of the nets.

Tom and Ned kicked outside the bat the former had killed in their tent, and then both went back to their cots. But it was some little time before they fell asleep. And they did not have much time to rest, for an early start must be made to avoid the terrible heat of the middle of the day.

"Whew!" whistled Ned, as he and Tom arose in the gray dawn of the morning when Jacinto announced the breakfast which the Indian cook had prepared. "That was some night! If this is a sample of the wilds of Honduras, give me the tameness of Shopton."

"Oh, we've gone through with worse than this," laughed Tom. "It's all in the day's work. We've only got started. I guess we're a bit soft, Ned, though we had hard enough work in that tunnel-digging."

After breakfast, while the Indians were making ready the canoes, Professor Bumper, who, in a previous visit to Central America, had become interested in the subject, made a brief examination of some of the dead bats. They were exceptionally large, some almost as big as hawks. and were of the sub-family *Desmodidae*, the scientist said.

"This is a true blood-sucking bat," went on the professor. "This," and he pointed to the nose-leaves, "is the sucking apparatus. The bat makes an opening in the skin with its sharp teeth and proceeds to extract the blood. I can well believe two or three of them, attacking a steer or mule at once, could soon weaken it so the animal would die."

"And a man, too?" asked Ned.

"Well a man has hands with which to use weapons, but a helpless quadruped has not. Though if a sufficient number of these bats attacked a man at the same time, he would have small chance to escape alive. Their bites, too, may be poisonous for all I know."

The Indians seemed glad to leave the "place of the bats," as they called the camp site. Jacinto explained that the Indians believed a vampire could kill them while they slept, and they were very much afraid of the blood-sucking bats. There were many other species in the tropics, Professor Bumper explained, most of which lived on fruit or on insects they caught. The blood-sucking bats were comparatively few, and the migratory sort fewer still.

"Well, we're on our way once more," remarked Tom as again they were in the canoes being paddled up the river. "How much longer does your water trip take, Professor?"

"I hardly know," and Professor Bumper looked to Jacinto to answer.

"We go two more days in the canoes," the guide answered, "and then we shall find the mules waiting for us at a place called Hidjio. From then on we travel by land until—well until you get to the place where you are going.

"I suppose you know where it is?" he added, nodding toward the professor. "I am leaving that part to you."

"Oh, I have a map, showing where I want to begin some excavations," was the answer. "We must first go to Copan and see what arrangements we can make for laborers. After that—well, we shall trust to luck for what we shall find."

"There are said to be many curious things," went on Jacinto, speaking as though he had no interest. "You have mentioned buried cities. Have you thought what may be in them—great heathen temples, idols, perhaps?"

For a moment none of the professor's companions spoke. It was as though Jacinto had tried to get some information. Finally the scientist said:

"Oh, yes, we may find an idol. I understand the ancient people, who were here long before the Spaniards came, worshiped idols. But we shall take whatever antiquities we find."

"Huh!" grunted Jacinto, and then he called to the paddlers to increase their strokes.

The journey up the river was not very eventful. Many alligators were seen, and Tom and Ned shot several with the electric rifle. Toward the close of the third day's travel there was a cry from one of the rear boats, and an alarm of a man having fallen overboard was given.

Tom turned in time to see the poor fellow's struggles, and at the same time there was a swirl in the water and a black object shot forward.

"An alligator is after him!" yelled Ned.

"I see," observed Tom calmly. "Hand me the rifle, Ned."

Tom took quick aim and pulled the trigger. The explosive electric bullet went true to its mark, and the great animal turned over in a death struggle. But the river was filled with them, and no sooner had the one nearest the unfortunate Indian been disposed of than another made a dash for the man.

There was a wild scream of agony and then a dark arm shot up above the red foam. The waters seethed and bubbled as the alligators fought under it for possession of the paddler. Tom fired bullet after bullet from his wonderful rifle into the spot, but though he killed some of the alligators this did not save the man's life. His body was not seen again, though search was made for it.

The accident cast a little damper over the party, and there was a feeling of gloom among the Indians. Professor Bumper announced that he would see to it that the man's family did not want, and this seemed to give general satisfaction, especially to a brother who was with the party.

Aside from being caught in a drenching storm and one or two minor accidents, nothing else of moment marked the remainder of the river journey, and at the end of the third day the canoes pulled to shore and a night camp was made.

"But where are the mules we are to use in traveling to-morrow?" asked the professor of Jacinto.

"In the next village. We shall march there in the morning. No use to go there at night when all is dark."

"I suppose that is so."

The Indians made camp as usual, the goods being brought from the canoes and piled up near the tents. Then night settled down.

"Hello!" cried Tom, awakening the next morning to find the sun streaming into his tent. "We must have overslept, Ned. We were to start before old Sol got in his heavy work, but we haven't had breakfast yet."

"I didn't hear any one call us," remarked Ned.

"Nor I. Wonder if we're the only lazy birds." He looked from the tent in time to see Mr. Damon and the professor emerging. Then Tom noticed something queer. The canoes were not on the river bank. There was not an Indian in sight, and no evidence of Jacinto.

"What's the matter?" asked the young inventor. "Have the others gone on ahead?"

"I rather think they've gone back," was the professor's dry comment.

"Gone back?"

"Yes. The Indians seem to have deserted us at the ending of this stage of our journey."

"Bless my time-table!" cried Mr. Damon. "You don't say so! What does it mean? What has becomes of our friend Jacinto?"

"I'm afraid he was rather a false friend," was the professor's answer. "This is the note he left. He has gone and taken the canoes and all the Indians with him," and he held out a paper on which was some scribbled writing.

FORWARD AGAIN

"What does it all mean?" asked Tom, seeing that the note was written in Spanish, a tongue which he could speak slightly but read indifferently.

"This is some of Beecher's work," was Professor Bumper's grim comment. "It seems that Jacinto was in his pay."

"In his pay!" cried Mr. Damon. "Do you mean that Beecher deliberately hired Jacinto to betray us?"

"Well, no. Not that exactly. Here, I'll translate this note for you," and the professor proceeded to read:

"Senors: I greatly regret the step I have to take, but I am a gentleman, and, having given my word, I must keep it. No harm shall come to you, I swear it on my honor!"

"Queer idea of honor he has!" commented Tom, grimly.

Professor Bumper read on:

"Know then, that before I engaged myself to you I had been engaged by Professor Beecher through a friend to guide him into the Copan valley, where he wants to make some explorations, for what I know not, save maybe that it is for gold. I agreed, in case any rival expeditions came to lead them astray if I could.

"So, knowing from what you said that you were going to this place, I engaged myself to you, planning to do what I have done. I greatly regret it, as I have come to like you, but I had given my promise to Professor Beecher's friend, that I would first lead him to the Copan valley, and would keep others away until he had had a chance to do his exploration.

"So I have led you to this wilderness. It is far from the Copan, but you are near an Indian village, and you will be able to get help in a week or so. In the meanwhile you will not starve, as you have plenty of supplies. If you will travel northeast you will come again to Puerto Cortes in due season. As for the money I had from you, I deposit it to your credit, Professor Beecher having made me an allowance for steering rival parties on the wrong trail. So I lose nothing, and I save my honor.

"I write this note as I am leaving in the night with the Indians. I put some harmless sedative in your tea that you might sleep soundly, and not awaken until we were well on our way. Do not try to follow us, as the river will carry us swiftly away. And, let me add, there is no personal animosity on the part of Professor Beecher against you. I should have done to any rival expedition the same as I have done with you. JACINTO."

For a moment there was silence, and then Tom Swift burst out with:

"Well, of all the mean, contemptible tricks of a human skunk this is the limit!"

"Bless my hairbrush, but he is a scoundrel!" ejaculated Mr. Damon, with great warmth.

"I'd like to start after him the biggest alligator in the river," was Ned's comment.

Professor Bumper said nothing for several seconds. There was a strange look on his face, and then he laughed shortly, as though the humor of the situation appealed to him.

"Professor Beecher has more gumption than I gave him credit for," he said. "It was a clever trick!"

"Trick!" cried Tom.

"Yes. I can't exactly agree that it was the right thing to do, but he, or some friend acting for him, seems to have taken precautions that we are not to suffer or lose money. Beecher goes on the theory that all is fair in love and war, I suppose, and he may call this a sort of scientific war."

Ned wondered, as he looked at his chum, how much love there was in it. Clearly Beecher was determined to get that idol of gold.

"Well, it can't be helped, and we must make the best of it," said Tom, after a pause.

"True. But now, boys, let's have breakfast, and then we'll make what goods we can't take with us as snug as possible, until we can send the mule drivers after them," went on Professor Bumper.

"Send the mule drivers after them?" questioned Ned. "What do you mean to do?"

"Do? Why keep on, of course. You don't suppose I'm going to let a little thing like this stand between me and the discovery of Kurzon and the idol of gold, do you?"

"But," began Mr. Damon, "I don't see how—"

"Oh, we'll find a way," interrupted Tom. "It isn't the first time I've been pretty well stranded on an expedition of this kind, and sometimes from the same cause—the actions of a rival. Now we'll turn the tables on the other fellows and see how they like it. The professor's right —let's have breakfast. Jacinto seems to have told the truth. Nothing of ours is missing."

Tom and Ned got the meal, and then a consultation was held as to what was best to be done.

"We can't go on any further by water, that's sure," said Tom. "In the first place the river is too shallow, and secondly we have no canoes. So the only thing is to go on foot through the jungle."

"But how can we, and carry all this stuff?" asked Ned.

"We needn't carry it!" cried Professor Bumper. "We'll leave it here, where it will be safe enough, and tramp on to the nearest Indian village. There we'll hire bearers to take our stuff on until we can get mules. I'm not going to turn back!"

"Good!" cried Mr. Damon. "Bless my rubber boots! but that's what I say—keep on!"

"Oh, no! we'll never turn back," agreed Tom.

"But how can we manage it?" asked Ned.

"We've just got to! And when you have to do a thing, it's a whole lot easier to do than if you just feel as though you ought to. So, lively is the word!" cried Tom, in answer.

"We'll pack up what we can carry and leave the rest," added the scientist.

Being an experienced traveler Professor Bumper had arranged his baggage so that it could be carried by porters if necessary. Everything could be put into small packages, including the tents and food supply.

"There are four of us," remarked Tom, "and if we can not pack enough along with us to enable us to get to the nearest village, we had better go back to civilization. I'm not afraid to try."

"Nor I!" cried Mr. Damon.

The baggage, stores and supplies that were to be left behind were made as snug as possible, and so piled up that wild beasts could do the least harm. Then a pack was made up for each one to carry.

They would take weapons, of course, Tom Swift's electric rifle being the one he choose for himself. They expected to be able to shoot game on their way, and this would provide them food in addition to the concentrated supply they carried. Small tents, in sections, were carried, there being two, one for Tom and Ned and one for Mr. Damon and the professor.

As far as could be learned from a casual inspection, Jacinto and his deserting Indians had taken back with them only a small quantity of food. They were traveling light and down stream, and could reach the town much more quickly than they had come away from it.

"That Beecher certainly was slick," commented Professor Bumper when they were ready to start. "He must have known about what time I would arrive, and he had Jacinto waiting for us. I thought it was too good to be true, to get an experienced guide like him so easily. But it was all planned, and I was so engrossed in thinking of the ancient treasures I hope to find that I never thought of a possible trick. Well, let's start!" and he led the way into the jungle, carrying his heavy pack as lightly as did Tom.

Professor Bumper had a general idea in which direction lay a number of native villages, and it was determined to head for them, blazing a path through the wilderness, so that the Indians could follow it back to the goods left behind.

It was with rather heavy hearts that the party set off, but Tom's spirits could not long stay clouded, and the scientist was so good-natured about the affair and seemed so eager to do the utmost to render Beecher's trick void, that the others fell into a lighter mood, and went on more cheerfully, though the way was rough and the packs heavy.

They stopped at noon under a bower they made of palms, and, spreading the nets over them, got a little rest after a lunch. Then, when the sun was less hot, they started off again.

"Forward is the word!" cried Ned cheerfully. "Forward!"

They had not gone more than an hour on the second stage of their tramp when Tom, who was in the lead, following the direction laid out by the compass, suddenly stopped, and reached around for his electric rifle, which he was carrying at his back.

"What is it?" asked Ned in a whisper.

"I don't know, but it's some big animal there in the bushes," was Tom's low-voiced answer. "I'm ready for it."

The rustling increased, and a form could be seen indistinctly. Tom aimed the deadly gun and stood ready to pull the trigger.

Ned, tho had a side view into the underbrush, gave a sudden cry.

"Don't shoot, Tom!" he yelled. "It's a man!"

A NEW GUIDE

In spite of Ned Newton's cry, Tom's finger pressed the switch-trigger of the electric rifle, for previous experience had taught him that it was sometimes the best thing to awe the natives in out-of-the-way corners of the earth. But the young inventor quickly elevated the muzzle, and the deadly missile went hissing through the air over the head of a native Indian who, at that moment, stepped from the bush.

The man, startled and alarmed, shrank back and was about to run into the jungle whence he had emerged. Small wonder if he had, considering the reception he so unwittingly met with. But Tom. aware of the necessity for making inquiries of one who knew that part of the jungle, quickly called to him.

"Hold on!" he shouted. "Wait a minute. I didn't mean that. I thought at first you were a tapir or a tiger. No harm intended. I say, Professor," Tom called back to the savant, "you'd better speak to him in his lingo, I can't manage it. He may be useful in guiding us to that Indian village Jacinto told us of."

This Professor Bumper did, being able to make himself understood in the queer part-Spanish dialect used by the native Hondurians, though he could not, of course, speak it as fluently as had Jacinto.

Professor Bumper had made only a few remarks to the man who had so unexpectedly appeared out of the jungle when the scientist gave an exclamation of surprise at some of the answers made.

"Bless my moving picture!" cried Mr. Damon.

"What's the matter now? Is anything wrong? Does he refuse to help us?"

"No, it isn't that," was the answer. "In fact he came here to help us. Tom, this is the brother of the Indian who fell overboard and who was eaten by the alligators. He says you were very kind to try to save his brother with your rifle, and for that reason he has come back to help us."

"Come back?" queried Tom.

"Yes, he went off with the rest of the Indians when Jacinto deserted us, but he could not stand being a traitor, after you had tried to save his brother's life. These Indians are queer people.

They don't show much emotion, but they have deep feelings. This one says he will devote himself to your service from now on. I believe we can count on him. He is deeply grateful to you, Tom."

"I'm glad of that for all our sakes. But what does he say about Jacinto?"

The professor asked some more questions, receiving answers, and then translated them.

"This Indian, whose name is Tolpec, says Jacinto is a fraud," exclaimed Professor Bumper. "He made all the Indians leave us in the night, though many of them were willing to stay and fill the contract they had made. But Jacinto would not let them, making them desert. Tolpec went away with the others, but because of what Tom had done he planned to come back at the first chance and be our guide. Accordingly he jumped ashore from one of the canoes, and made his way to our camp. He got there, found it deserted and followed us, coming up just now."

"Well I'm glad I didn't frighten him off with my gun," remarked Tom grimly. "So he agrees with us that Jacinto is a scoundrel, does he? I guess he might as well classify Professor Beecher in the same way."

"I am not quite so sure of that," said Professor Bumper slowly. "I can not believe Beecher would play such a trick as this, though some over-zealous friend of his might."

"Oh, of course Beecher did it!" cried Tom. "He heard we were coming here, figured out that we'd start ahead of him, and he wanted to side-track us. Well, he did it all right," and Tom's voice was bitter.

"He has only side-tracked us for a while," announced Professor Bumper in cheerful tones.

"What do you mean?" asked Mr. Damon.

"I mean that this Indian comes just in the nick of time. He is well acquainted with this part of the jungle, having lived here all his life, and he offers to guide us to a place where we can get mules to transport ourselves and our baggage to Copan."

"Fine!" cried Ned. "When can we start?"

Once more the professor and the native conversed in the strange tongue, and then Professor Bumper announced:

"He says it will be better for us to go back where we left our things and camp there. He will stay with us tonight and in the morning go on to the nearest Indian town and come back with porters and helpers."

"I think that is good advice to follow," put in Tom, "for we do need our goods; and if we reached the settlement ourselves, we would have to send back for our things, with the uncertainty of getting them all."

So it was agreed that they would make a forced march back through the jungle to where they had been deserted by Jacinto. There they would make camp for the night, and until such time as Tolpec could return with a force of porters.

It was not easy, that backward tramp through the jungle, especially as night had fallen. But the new Indian guide could see like a cat, and led the party along paths they never could have found by themselves. The use of their pocket electric lights was a great help, and possibly served to ward off the attacks of jungle beasts, for as they tramped along they could hear stealthy sounds in the underbush on either side of the path, as though tigers were stalking them. For there was in the woods an animal of the leopard family, called tiger or "tigre" by the natives, that was exceedingly fierce and dangerous. But watchfulness prevented any accident, and eventually the party reached the place where they had left their goods. Nothing had been disturbed, and finally a fire was made, the tents set up and a light meal, with hot tea served.

"We'll get ahead of Beecher yet," said Tom.

"You seem as anxious as Professor Bumper," observed Mr. Damon,

"I guess I am," admitted Tom. "I want to see that idol of gold in the possession of our party."

The night passed without incident, and then, telling his new friends that he would return as soon as possible with help, Tolpec, taking a small supply of food with him, set out through the jungle again.

As the green vines and creepers closed after him, and the explorers were left alone with their possessions piled around them, Ned remarked:

"After all, I wonder if it was wise to let him go?"

"Why not?" asked Tom.

"Well, maybe he only wanted to get us back here, and then he'll desert, too. Maybe that's what he's done now, making us lose two or three days by inducing us to return, waiting for what will never happen—his return with other natives."

A silence followed Ned's intimation.

In the Coils

"Ned, do you really think Tolpec is going to desert us?" asked Tom.

"Well, I don't know," was the slowly given reply. "It's a possibility, isn't it?"

"Yes, it is," broke in Professor Bumper. "But what if it is? We might as well trust him, and if he proves true, as I believe he will, we'll be so much better off. If he proves a traitor we'll only have lost a few days, for if he doesn't come back we can go on again in the way we started."

"But that's just it!" complained Tom. "We don't want to lose any time with that Beecher chap on our trail."

"I am not so very much concerned about him," remarked Professor Bumper, dryly.

"Why not?" snapped out Mr. Damon.

"Well, because I think he'll have just about as hard work locating the hidden city, and finding the idol of gold, as we'll have. In other words it will be an even thing, unless he gets too far ahead of us, or keeps us back, and I don't believe he can do that now.

"So I thought it best to take a chance with this Indian. He would hardly have taken the trouble to come all the way back, and run the risks he did, just to delay us a few days. However, we'll soon know. Meanwhile, we'll take it easy and wait for the return of Tolpec and his friends."

Though none of them liked to admit it, Ned's words had caused his three friends some anxiety, and though they busied themselves about the camp there was an air of waiting impatiently for something to occur. And waiting is about the hardest work there is.

But there was nothing for it but to wait, and it might be at least a week, Professor Bumper said, before the Indian could return with a party of porters and mules to move their baggage.

"Yes, Tolpec has not only to locate the settlement," Tom admitted, "but he must persuade the natives to come back with him. He may have trouble in that, especially if it is known that he has left Jacinto, who, I imagine, is a power among the tribes here."

But there were only two things left to do—wait and hope. The travelers did both. Four days passed and there was no sign of Tolpec. Eager-ly, and not a little anxiously, they watched the jungle path along which he had disappeared.

"Oh, come on!" exclaimed Tom one morning, when the day seemed a bit cooler than its predecessor. "Let's go for a hunt, or something! I'm tired of sitting around camp."

"Bless my watch hands! So am I!" cried Mr. Damon. "Let's all go for a trip. It will do us good."

"And perhaps I can get some specimens of interest," added Professor Bumper, who, in addition to being an archaeologist, was something of a naturalist.

Accordingly, having made everything snug in camp, the party, Tom and Ned equipped with electric rifles, and the professor with a butterfly net and specimen boxes, set forth. Mr. Damon said he would carry a stout club as his weapon.

The jungle, as usual, was teeming with life, but as Ned and Tom did not wish to kill wantonly they refrained from shooting until later in the day. For once it was dead, game did not keep well in that hot climate, and needed to be cooked almost immediately.

"We'll try some shots on our back trip," said the young inventor.

Professor Bumper found plenty of his own particular kind of "game" which he caught in the net, transferring the specimens to the boxes he carried. There were beautiful butterflies, moths and strange bugs in the securing of which the scientist evinced great delight, though when one beetle nipped him firmly and painfully on his thumb his involuntary cry of pain was as real as that of any other person.

"But I didn't let him get away," he said in triumph when he had dropped the clawing insect into the cyanide bottle where death came painlessly. "It is well worth a sore thumb."

They wandered on through the jungle, taking care not to get too far from their camp, for they did not want to lose their way, nor did they want to be absent too long in case Tolpec and his native friends should return.

"Well, it's about time we shot something, I think," remarked Ned, when they had been out about two hours. "Let's try for some of these wild turkeys. They ought to go well roasted even if it isn't Thanksgiving."

"I'm with you," agreed Tom. "Let's see who has the best luck. But tone down the charge in your rifle and use a smaller projectile, or you'll have nothing but a bunch of feathers to show for your shot. The guns are loaded for deer."

The change was made, and once more the two young men started off, a little ahead of Professor Bumper and Mr. Damon. Tom and Ned had not gone far, however, before they heard a strange cry from Mr. Damon.

"Tom! Ned!" shouted the eccentric man, "Here's a monster after me! Come quick!"

"A tiger!" ejaculated Tom, as he began once more to change the charge in his rifle to a larger one, running back, meanwhile, in the direction of the sound of the voice.

There were really no tigers in Honduras, the jaguar being called a tiger by the natives, while the cougar is called a lion. The presence of these animals, often dangerous to man, had been indicated around camp, and it was possible that one had been bold enough to attack Mr. Damon, not through hunger, but because of being cornered.

"Come on, Ned!" cried Tom. "He's in some sort of trouble!"

But when, a moment later, the young inventor burst through a fringe of bushes and saw Mr. Damon standing in a little clearing, with upraised club, Tom could not repress a laugh.

"Kill it, Tom! Kill it!" begged the eccentric man. "Bless my insurance policy, but it's a terrible beast!"

And so it was, at first glance. For it was a giant iguana, one of the most repulsive-looking of the lizards. Not unlike an alligator in shape, with spikes on its head and tail, with a warty, squatty ridge-encrusted body, a big pouch beneath its chin, and long-toed claws, it was enough to strike terror into the heart of almost any one. Even the smaller ones look dangerous, and this one, which was about five feet long, looked capable of attacking a man and injuring him. As a matter of fact the iguanas are harmless, their shape and coloring being designed to protect them.

"Don't be afraid, Mr. Damon," called Tom, still laughing. "It won't hurt you!"

"I'm not so positive of that. It won't let me pass."

"Just take your club and poke it out of the way," the young inventor advised. "It's only waiting to be shoved."

"Then you do it, Tom. Bless my looking glass, but I don't want to go near it! If my wife could see me now she'd say it served me just right."

Mr. Damon was not a coward, but the giant iguana was not pleasant to look at. Tom, with the butt of his rifle, gave it a gentle shove, whereupon the creature scurried off through the brush as though glad to make its escape unscathed.

"I thought it was a new kind of alligator," said Mr. Damon with a sigh of relief.

"Where is it?" asked Professor Bumper, coming up at this juncture. "A new species of alligator? Let me see it!"

"It's too horrible," said Mr. Damon. "I never want to see one again. It was worse than a vampire bat!"

Notwithstanding this, when he heard that it was one of the largest sized iguanas ever seen, the professor started through the jungle after it.

"We can't take it with us if we get it," Tom called after his friend.

"We might take the skin," answered the professor. "I have a standing order for such things from one of the museums I represent. I'd like to get it. Then they are often eaten. We can have a change of diet. you see."

"We'd better follow him," said Tom to Ned. "We'll have to let the turkeys go for a while. He may get into trouble. Come on."

Off they started through the jungle, trailing after the impetuous professor who was intent on capturing the iguana. The giant lizard's progress could be traced by the disturbance of the leaves and underbrush, and the professor was following as closely as possible.

So fast did he go that Ned, Tom and Mr. Damon, following, lost sight of him several times, and Tom finally called:

"Wait a minute. We'll all be lost if you keep this up."

"I'll have him in another minute," answered the professor. "I can almost reach him now. Then—— Oh!"

His voice ended in a scream that seemed to be one of terror. So sudden was the change that Tom and Ned, who were together, ahead of Mr. Damon, looked at one another in fear.

"What has happened?" whispered Ned, pausing.

"Don't stop to ask—come on!" shouted Tom.

At that instant again came the voice of the savant.

"Tom! Ned!" he gasped, rather than cried.

"I'm caught in the coils! Quick—quick if you would save me!"

"In the coils!" repeated Ned. "What does he mean? Can the giant iguana—"

Tom Swift did not stop to answer. With his electric rifle in readiness, he leaped forward through the jungle.

A MEETING IN THE JUNGLE

Before Tom and Ned reached the place whence Professor Bumper had called, they heard strange noises, other than the imploring voice of their friend. It seemed as though some great body was threshing about in the jungle, lashing the trees, bushes and leaves about, and when the two young men, followed by Mr. Damon, reached the scene they saw that, in a measure, this really accounted for what they heard.

Something like a great whip was beating about close to two trees that grew near together. And then, when the storm of twigs, leaves and dirt, caused by the leaping, threshing thing ceased for a moment, the onlookers saw something that filled them with terror.

Between the two trees, and seemingly bound to them by a great coiled rope, spotted and banded, was the body of Professor Bumper. His arms were pinioned to his sides and there was horror and terror on his face, that looked imploringly at the youths from above the topmost coil of those encircling him.

"What is it?" cried Mr. Damon, as he ran pantingly up. "What has caught him? Is it the giant iguana?"

"It's a snake—a great boa!" gasped Tom. "It has him in its coils. But it is wound around the trees, too. That alone prevents it from crushing the professor to death.

"Ned, be ready with your rifle. Put in the heaviest charge, and watch your chance to fire!"

The great, ugly head of the boa reared itself up from the coils which it had, with the quickness of thought, thrown about the man between the two trees. This species of snake is not poisonous, and kills its prey by crushing it to death, making it into a pulpy mass, with scarcely a bone left unbroken, after which it swallows its meal. The crushing power of one of these boas, some of which reach a length of thirty feet, with a body as large around as that of a full-grown man, is enormous.

"I'm going to fire!" suddenly cried Tom. He had seen his chance and he took it. There was the faint report—the crack of the electric rifle— and the folds of the serpent seemed to relax.

"I see a good chance now," added Ned, who had taken the small charge from his weapon, replacing it with a heavier one.

His rifle was also discharged in the direction of the snake, and Tom saw that the hit was a good one, right through the ugly head of the reptile.

"One other will be enough to make him loosen his coils!" cried Tom, as he fired again, and such was the killing power of the electric bullets that the snake, though an immense one, and one that short of decapitation could have received many injuries without losing power, seemed to shrivel up.

Its folds relaxed, and the coils of the great body fell in a heap at the roots of the two trees, between which the scientist had been standing.

Professor Bumper seemed to fall backward as the grip of the serpent relaxed, but Tom, dropping his rifle, and calling to Ned to keep an eye on the snake, leaped forward and caught his friend.

"Are you hurt?" asked Tom, carrying the limp form over to a grassy place. There was no answer, the savant's eyes were closed and he breathed but faintly.

Ned Newton fired two more electric bullets into the still writhing body of the boa.

"I guess he's all in," he called to Tom.

"Bless my horseradish! And so our friend seems to be," commented Mr. Damon. "Have you anything with which to revive him, Tom?"

"Yes. Some ammonia. See if you can find a little water."

"I have some in my flask."

Tom mixed a dose of the spirits which he carried with him, and this, forced between the pallid lips of the scientist, revived him.

"What happened?" he asked faintly as he opened his eyes. "Oh, yes, I remember," he added slowly. "The boa—"

"Don't try to talk," urged Tom. "You're all right. The snake is dead, or dying. Are you much hurt?"

Professor Bumper appeared to be considering. He moved first one limb, then another. He seemed to have the power over all his muscles.

"I see how it happened," he said, as he sat up, after taking a little more of the ammonia. "I was following the iguana, and when the big lizard came to a stop, in a little hollow place in the ground, at the foot of those two trees, I leaned over to slip a noose of rope about its neck. Then I felt myself caught, as if in the hands of a giant, and bound fast between the two trees."

"It was the big boa that whipped itself around you, as you leaned over," explained Tom, as Ned came up to announce that the snake was no longer dangerous. "But when it coiled around you it also coiled around the two trees, you, fortunately slipping between them. Had it not been that their trunks took off some of the pressure of the coils you wouldn't have lasted a minute."

"Well, I was pretty badly squeezed as it was," remarked the professor. "I hardly had breath enough left to call to you. I tried to fight off the serpent, but it was of no use."

"I should say not!" cried Mr. Damon. "Bless my circus ring! one might as well try to combat an elephant! But, my dear professor, are you all right now?"

"I think so—yes. Though I shall be lame and stiff for a few days, I fear. I can hardly walk."

Professor Bumper was indeed unable to go about much for a few days after his encounter with the great serpent. He stretched out in a hammock under trees in the camp clearing, and with his friends waited for the possible return of Tolpec and the porters.

Ned and Tom made one or two short hunting trips, and on these occasions they kept a lookout in the direction the Indian had taken when he went away.

"For he's sure to come back that way—if he comes at all," declared Ned; "which I am beginning to doubt."

"Well, he may not come," agreed Tom, who was beginning to lose some of his first hope. "But he won't necessarily come from the same direction he took. He may have had to go in an entirely different way to get help. We'll hope for the best."

A week passed. Professor Bumper was able to be about, and Tom and Ned noticed that there was an anxious look on his face. Was he, too, beginning to despair?

"Well, this isn't hunting for golden idols very fast," said Mr. Damon, the morning of the eighth day after their desertion by the faithless Jacinto. "What do you say, Professor Bumper; ought we not to start off on our own account?"

"We had better if Tolpec does not return today," was the answer.

They had eaten breakfast, had put their camp in order, and were about to have a consultation on what was best to do, when Tom suddenly called to Ned, who was whistling:

"Hark!"

Through the jungle came a faint sound of singing —not a harmonious air, but the somewhat barbaric chant of the natives.

"It is Tolpec coming back!" cried Mr. Damon. "Hurray! Now our troubles are over t Bless my meal ticket! Now we can start!"

"It may be Jacinto," suggested Ned.

"Nonsense! you old cold-water pitcher!" cried Tom. "It's Tolpec! I can see him! He's a good scout all right!"

And then, walking at the head of a band of Indians who were weirdly chanting while behind them came a train of mules, was Tolpec, a cheerful grin covering his honest, if homely, dark face.

"Me come back!" he exclaimed in gutteral English, using about half of his foreign vocabulary.

"I see you did," answered Professor Bumper in the man's own tongue. "Glad to see you. Is everything all right?"

"All right," was the answer. "These Indians will take you where you want to go, and will not leave you as Jacinto did."

"We'll start in the morning!" exclaimed the savant his own cheerful self again, now that there was a prospect of going further into the interior. "Tell the men to get something to eat, Tolpec. There is plenty for all."

"Good!" grunted the new guide and soon the hungry Indians, who had come far, were satisfying their hunger.

As they ate Tolpec explained to Professor Bumper, who repeated it to the youths and Mr. Damon, that it had been necessary to go farther than he had intended to get the porters and mules. But the Indians were a friendly tribe, of which he was a member, and could be depended on.

There was a feast and a sort of celebration in camp that night. Tom and Ned shot two deer, and these formed the main part of the feast and the Indians made merry about the fire until nearly midnight. They did not seem to mind in the least the swarms of mosquitoes and other bugs that flew about, attracted by the light. As for Tom Swift and his friends, their nets protected them.

An early start was made the following morning. Such packages of goods and supplies as could not well be carried by the Indians in their head straps, were loaded on the backs of the pack-mules. Tolpec explained that on reaching the Indian village, where he had secured the porters, they could get some ox-carts which would be a convenience in traveling into the interior toward the Copan valley.

The march onward for the next two days was tiresome; but the Indians Tolpec had secured were as faithful and efficient as he had described them, and good progress was made.

There were a few accidents. One native fell into a swiftly running stream as they were fording it and lost a box containing some much-needed things. But as the man's life was saved Professor Bumper said it made up for the other loss. Another accident did not end so auspiciously. One of the bearers was bitten by a poisonous snake, and though prompt measures were taken, the poison spread so rapidly that the man died.

In due season the Indian village was reached. where, after a day spent in holding funeral services over the dead bearer, preparations were made for proceeding farther.

This time some of the bearers were left behind, and ox-carts were substituted for them, as it was possible to carry more goods this way,

"And now we're really off for Copan!" exclaimed Professor Bumper one morning, when the cavalcade, led by Tolpec in the capacity of head guide, started off. "I hope we have no more delays."

"I hope not, either," agreed Tom. "That Beecher may be there ahead of us."

Weary marches fell to their portion. There were mountains to climb, streams to ford or swim, sending the carts over on rudely made rafts. There were storms to endure, and the eternal heat to fight.

But finally the party emerged from the lowlands of the coast and went up in among the hills, where though the going was harder, the climate was better. It was not so hot and moist.

Not wishing to attract attention in Copan itself, Professor Bumper and his party made a detour, and finally, after much consultation with Tom over the ancient maps, the scientist announced that he thought they were in the vicinity of the buried city.

"We will begin test excavations in the morning," he said.

The party was in camp, and preparations were made for spending the night in the forest, when from among the trees there floated to the ears of our friends a queer Indian chant.

"Some one is coming," said Tom to Ned.

Almost as he spoke there filed into the clearing where the camp had been set up, a cavalcade of white men, followed by Indians. And at the sight of one of the white men Tom Swift uttered a cry.

"Professor Beecher!" gasped the young inventor.

THE LOST MAP

The on-marching company of white men, with their Indian attendants, came to a halt on the edge of the clearing as they caught sight of the tents already set up there. The barbaric chant of the native bearers ceased abruptly, and there was a look of surprise shown on the face of Professor Fenimore Beecher. For Professor Beecher it was, in the lead of the rival expedition.

"Bless my shoe laces!" exclaimed Mr. Damon.

"Is it really Beecher?" asked Ned, though he knew as well as Tom that it was the young archaeologist.

"It certainly is!" declared Tom. "And he has nerve to follow us so closely!"

"Maybe he thinks we have nerve to get here ahead of him," suggested Ned, smiling grimly.

"Probably," agreed Tom, with a short laugh. "Well, it evidently surprises him to find us here at all, after the mean trick he played on us to get Jacinto to lead us into the jungle and desert us."

"That's right," assented Ned. "Well, what's the next move?"

There seemed to be some doubt about this on the part of both expeditions. At the sight of Professor Beecher, Professor Bumper, who had come out of his tent, hurriedly turned to Tom and asked him what he thought it best to do.

"Do!" exclaimed the eccentric Mr. Damon, not giving Tom time to reply. "Why, stand your ground, of course! Bless my house and lot! but we're here first! For the matter of that, I suppose the jungle is free and we can no more object to his coming: here than he can to our coming. First come, first served, I suppose is the law of the forest."

Meanwhile the surprise occasioned by the unexpected meeting of their rivals seemed to have spread something like consternation among the white members of the Beecher party. As for the natives they evidently did not care one way or the other.

There was a hasty consultation among the professors accompanying Mr. Beecher, and then the latter himself advanced toward the tents of Tom and his friends and asked:

"How long have you been here?"

"I don't see that we are called upon to answer that question," replied Professor Bumper stiffly.

"Perhaps not, and yet—"

"There is no perhaps about it!" said Professor Bumper quickly. "I know what your object is, as I presume you do mine. And, after what I may term your disgraceful and unsportsmanlike conduct toward me and my friends, I prefer not to have anything further to do with you. We must meet as strangers hereafter."

"Very well," and Professor Beecher's voice was as cold and uncompromising as was his rival's. "Let it be as your wish. But I must say I don't know what you mean by unsportsmanlike conduct."

"An explanation would be wasted on you," said Professor Bumper stiffly. "But in order that you may know I fully understand what you did I will say that your efforts to thwart us through your tool Jacinto came to nothing. We are here ahead of you."

"Jacinto!" cried Professor Beecher in real or simulated surprise. "Why, he was not my `tool,' as you term it."

"Your denial is useless in the light of his confession," asserted Professor Bumper.

"Confession?"

"Now look here!" exclaimed the older professor, "I do not propose to lower myself by quarreling with you. I know certainly what you and your party tried to do to prevent us from getting here. But we got out of the trap you set for us, and we are on the ground first. I recognize your right to make explorations as well as ourselves, and I presume you have not fallen so low that you will not recognize the unwritten law in a case of this kind—the law which says the right of discovery belongs to the one who first makes it."

"I shall certainly abide by such conduct as is usual under the circumstances," said Professor Beecher more stiffly than before. "At the same time I must deny having set a trap. And as for Jacinto—"

"It will be useless to discuss it further!" broke in Professor Bumper.

"Then no more need be said," retorted the younger man. "I shall give orders to my friends, as well as to the natives, to keep away from your camp, and I shall expect you to do the same regarding mine."

"I should have suggested the same thing myself," came from Tom's friend, and the two rival scientists fairly glared at one another, the others of both parties looking on with interest.

Professor Bumper turned and walked defiantly back to his tent. Professor Beecher did the same thing. Then, after a short consultation among the white members of the latter's organization, their tents were set up in another clearing, removed and separated by a screen of trees and bushes from those of Tom Swift's friends. The natives of the Beecher party also withdrew a little way from those of Professor Bumper's organization, and then preparations for spending the night in the jungle went on in the rival headquarters.

"Well, he certainly had nerve, to deny, practically, that he had set Jacinto up to do what he did," commented Tom.

"I should say so!" agreed Ned.

"How do you imagine he got here nearly as soon as we did, when he did not start until later?" asked Mr. Damon.

"He did not have the unfortunate experience of being deserted in the jungle," replied Tom. "He probably had Jacinto, or some of that unprincipled scoundrel's friends, show him a short route to Copan and he came on from there."

"Well, I did hope we might have the ground to ourselves, at least for the preliminary explorations and excavations. But it is not to be. My rival is here," sighed Professor Bumper.

"Don't let that discourage you!" exclaimed Tom. "We can fight all the better now the foe is in the open, and we know where he is."

"Yes, Tom Swift, that is true," agreed the scientist. "I am not going to give up, but I shall have to change my plans a little. Perhaps you will come into the tent with me," and he nodded to Tom and Ned. "I want to talk over certain matters with you and Mr. Damon."

"Pleased to," assented the young inventor, and his financial secretary nodded.

A little later, supper having been eaten, the camp made shipshape and the natives settled down, Tom, Ned, Mr. Damon and Professor Bumper assembled in the tent of the scientist, where a dry battery lamp gave sufficient illumination to show a number of maps and papers scattered over an improvised table.

"Now, gentlemen," said the professor, "I have called you here to go over my plans more in detail than I have hitherto done, now we are on the ground. You know in a general way what I hope to accomplish, but the time has come when I must be specific.

"Aside from being on the spot, below which, or below the vicinity where, I believe, lies the lost city of Kurzon and, I hope, the idol of gold, a situation has arisen—an unexpected situation, I may say—which calls for different action from that I had counted on.

"I refer to the presence of my rival, Professor Beecher. I will not dwell now on what he has done. It is better to consider what he may do."

"That's right," agreed Ned. "He may get up in the night, dig up this city and skip with that golden image before we know it."

"Hardly," grinned Tom.

"No," said Professor Bumper. "Excavating buried cities in the jungle of Honduras is not as simple as that. There is much work to be done. But accidents may happen, and in case one should occur to me, and I be unable to prosecute the search, I want one of you to do it. For that reason I am going to show you the maps and ancient documents and point out to you where I believe the lost city lies. Now, if you will give me your attention, I'll proceed."

The professor went over in detail the story of how he had found the old documents relating to the lost city of Kurzon, and of how, after much labor and research, he had located the city in the Copan valley. The great idol of gold was one of the chief possessions of Kurzon, and it was often referred to in the old papers; copies and translations of which the professor had with him.

"But this is the most valuable of all," he said, as he opened an oiled-silk packet. "And before I show it to you, suppose you two young men take a look outside the tent."

"What for?" asked Mr. Damon.

"To make sure that no emissaries from the Beecher crowd are sneaking around to overhear what we say," was the somewhat bitter answer of the scientist. "I do not trust him, in spite of his attempted denial."

Tom and Ned took a quick but thorough observation outside the tent. The blackness of the jungle night was in strange contrast to the light they had just left.

"Doesn't seem to be any one around here," remarked Ned, after waiting a minute or two.

"No. All's quiet along the Potomac. Those Beecher natives are having some sort of a song-fest, though."

In the distance, and from the direction of their rivals' camp, came the weird chant.

"Well, as long as they stay there we'll be all right," said Tom. "Come on in. I'm anxious to hear what the professor has to say."

"Everything's quiet," reported Ned.

"Then give me your attention," begged the scientist.

Carefully, as though about to exhibit some, precious jewel, he loosened the oiled-silk wrappings and showed a large map, on thin but tough paper.

"This is drawn from the old charts," the professor explained. "I worked on it many months, and it is the only copy in the world. If it were to be destroyed I should have to go all the way back to New York to make another copy. I have the original there in a safe deposit vault."

"Wouldn't it have been wise to make two copies?" asked Tom.

"It would have only increased the risk. With one copy, and that constantly in my possession, I can be sure of my ground. Otherwise not. That is why I am so careful of this. Now I will show you why I believe we are about over the ancient city of Kurzon."

"Over it!" cried Mr. Damon. "Bless my gunpowder! What do you mean?" and he looked down at the earthen floor of the tent as though expecting it to open and swallow him.

"I mean that the city, like many others of Central and South America, is buried below the refuse of centuries," went on the professor. "Very soon, if we are fortunate, we shall be looking on the civilization of hundreds of years ago—how long no one knows.

"Considerable excavation has been done in Central America," went on Professor Bumper, "and certain ruins have been brought to light. Near us are those of Copan, while toward the frontier are those of Quirigua, which are even better preserved than the former. We may visit them if we have time. But I have reason to believe that in this section of Copan is a large city, the existence of which has not been made certain of by any one save myself—and, perhaps, Professor Beecher.

"Certainly no part of it has seen the light of day for many centuries. It shall be our pleasure to uncover it, if possible, and secure the idol of gold."

"How long ago do you think the city was buried?" asked Tom.

"It would be hard to say. From the carvings and hieroglyphics I have studied it would seem that the Mayan civilization lasted about five hundred years, and that it began perhaps in the year A. D. five hundred."

"That would mean," said Mr. Damon, "that the ancient cities were in ruins, buried, perhaps, long before Columbus discovered the new world."

"Yes," assented the professor. "Probably Kurzon, which we now seek, was buried deep for nearly five hundred years before Columbus landed at San Salvadore. The specimens of writing and architecture heretofore disclosed indicate that. But, as a matter of fact, it is very hard to decipher the Mayan pictographs. So far, little but the ability to read their calendars and numerical system is possessed by us, though we are gradually making headway.

"Now this is the map of the district, and by the markings you can see where I hope to find what I seek. We shall begin digging here," and he made a small mark with a pencil on the map.

"Of course," the professor explained, "I may be wrong, and it will take some time to discover the error if we make one. When a city is buried thirty or forty feet deep beneath earth and great trees have grown over it, it is not easy to dig down to it."

"How do you ever expect to find it?" asked Ned.

"Well, we will sink shafts here and there. If we find carved stones, the remains of ancient pottery and weapons, parts of buildings or building stones, we shall know we are on the right track," was the answer. "And now that I have shown you the map, and explained how valuable it is, I will put it away again. We shall begin our excavations in the morning."

"At what point?" asked Tom.

"At a point I shall indicate after a further consultation of the map. I must see the configuration of the country by daylight to decide. And now let's get some rest. We have had a hard day."

The two tents housing the four white members of the Bumper party were close together, and it was decided that the night would be divided into four watches, to guard against possible treachery on the part of the Beecher crowd.

"It seems an unkind precaution to take against a fellow scientist," said Professor Bumper, "but I can not afford to take chances after what has occurred."

The others agreed with him, and though standing guard was not pleasant it was done. However the night passed without incident, and then came morning and the excitement of getting breakfast, over which the Indians made merry. They did not like the cold and darkness, and always welcomed the sun, no matter how hot.

"And now," cried Tom, when the meal was over, "let us begin the work that has brought us here."

"Yes," agreed Professor Bumper, "I will consult the map, and start the diggers where I think the city lies, far below the surface. Now, gentlemen, if you will give me your attention—"

He was seeking through his outer coat pockets, after an ineffectual search in the inner one. A strange look came over his face.

"What's the matter?" asked Tom.

"The map—the map!" gasped the professor. "The map I was showing you last night! The map that tells where we are to dig for the idol of gold! It's gone!"

"The map gone?" gasped Mr. Damon.

"I—I'm afraid so," faltered the professor. "I put it away carefully, but now—"

He ceased speaking to make a further search in all his pockets.

"Maybe you left it in another coat," suggested Ned.

"Or maybe some of the Beecher crowd took it!" snapped Tom.

"EL TIGRE!"

The four men gazed at one another. Consternation showed on the face of Professor Bumper, and was reflected, more or less, on the countenances of his companions.

"Are you sure the map is gone?" asked Tom. "I know how easy it is to mislay anything in a camp of this sort. I couldn't at first find my safety razor this morning, and when I did locate it the hoe was in one of my shoes. I'm sure a rat or some jungle animal must have dragged it there. Now maybe they took your map, Professor. That oiled silk in which it was wrapped might have appealed to the taste of a rat or a snake."

"It is no joking matter," said Professor Bumper. "But I know you appreciate the seriousness of it as much as I do, Tom. But I had the map in the pocket of this coat, and now it is gone!"

"When did you put it there?" asked Ned.

"This morning, just before I came to breakfast."

"Oh, then you have had it since last night!" Tom ejaculated.

"Yes, I slept with it under my clothes that I rolled up for a pillow, and when it was my turn to stand guard I took it with me. Then I put it back again and went to sleep. When I awoke and dressed I put the packet in my pocket and ate breakfast. Now when I look for it—why, it's gone!"

"The map or the oiled-silk package?" asked Mr. Damon, who, once having been a businessman, was sometimes a stickler for small points.

"Both," answered the professor. "I opened the silk to tie it more smoothly, so it would not be such a lump in my pocket, and I made sure the map was inside."

"Then the whole thing has been taken—or you have lost it," suggested Ned.

"I am not in the habit of losing valuable maps," retorted the scientist. "And the pocket of my coat I had made deep, for the purpose of carrying the long map. It could not drop out."

"Well, we mustn't overlook any possible chances," suggested Tom. "Come on now, we'll search every inch of the ground over which you traveled this morning, Professor."

"It *must* be found," murmured the scientist. "Without it all our work will go for naught."

They all went into the tent where the professor and Mr. Damon had slept when they were not on guard. The camp was a busy place, with the Indians finishing their morning meal, and getting ready for the work of the day. For word had been given out that there would be no more long periods of travel.

In consequence, efforts were being directed by the head men of the bearers to making a more permanent camp in the wilderness. Shelters of palm-thatched huts were being built, a site for cooking fires made, and, at the direction of Mr. Damon, to whom this part was entrusted, some sanitary regulations were insisted on.

Leaving this busy scene, the four, with solemn faces, proceeded to the tent where it was hoped the map would be found. But though they went through everything, and traced and retraced every place the professor could remember having traversed about the canvas shelter, no signs of the important document could be found.

"I don't believe I dropped it out of my pocket," said the scientist, for perhaps the twentieth time.

"Then it was taken," declared Tom.

"That's what I say!" chimed in Ned. "And by some of Beecher's party!"

"Easy, my boy," cautioned Mr. Damon. "We don't want to make accusations we can't prove."

"That is true," agreed Professor Bumper. "But, though I am sorry to say it of a fellow archaelogist, I can not help thinking Beecher had something to do with the taking of my map."

"But how could any of them get it?" asked Mr. Damon. "You say you had the map this morning, and certainly none of them has been in our camp since dawn, though of course it is possible that some of them sneaked in during the night."

"It does seem a mystery how it could have been taken in open daylight, while we were about camp together," said Tom. "But is the loss such a grave one, Professor Bumper?"

"Very grave. In fact I may say it is impossible to proceed with the excavating without the map."

"Then what are we to do?" asked Ned.

"We must get it back!" declared Tom.

"Yes," agreed the scientist, "we can not work without it. As soon as I make a little further search, to make sure it could not have dropped in some out-of-the-way place, I shall go over to Professor Beecher's camp and demand that he give me back my property."

"Suppose he says he hasn't taken it?" asked Tom.

"Well, I'm sure he either took it personally, or one of his party did. And yet I can't understand how they could have come here without our seeing them," and the professor shook his head in puzzled despair.

A more detailed search did not reveal the missing map, and Mr. Damon and his friend the scientist were on the point of departing for the camp of their rivals, less than a mile away, when Tom had what really amounted to an inspiration.

"Look here, Professor!" he cried. "Can you remember any of the details of your map—say, for instance, where we ought to begin excavating to get at the wonders of the underground city?"

"Well, Tom, I did intend to compare my map with the configuration of the country about here. There is a certain mountain which serves as a landmark and a guide for a starting point. I think that is it over there," and the scientist pointed to a distant snow-capped peak.

The party had left the low and marshy land of the true jungle, and were among the foothills, though all about them was dense forest and underbush, which, in reality, was as much a jungle as the lower plains, but was less wet.

"The point where I believe we should start to dig," said the professor, "is near the spot where the top of the mountain casts a shadow when the sun is one hour high. At least that is the direction given in the old manuscripts. So, though we can do little without the map, we might make a start by digging there."

"No, not there!" exclaimed Tom.

"Why not?"

"Because we don't want to let Beecher's crowd know that we are on the track of the idol of gold."

"But they know anyhow, for they have the map," commented Ned, puzzled by his chum's words.

"Maybe not," said Tom slowly. "I think this is a time for a big bluff. It may work and it may not. Beecher's crowd either has the map or they have not. If they have it they will lose no time in trying to find the right place to start digging and then they'll begin excavating.

"Very good! If they do that we have a right to dig near the same place. But if they have not the map, which is possible, and if we start to dig where the professor's memory tells him is the right spot, we'll only give them the tip, and they'll dig there also."

"I'm sure they have the map," the professor said. "But I believe your plan is a good one, Tom."

"Just what do you propose doing?" asked Ned.

"Fooling 'em!" exclaimed Tom quickly. "We'll dig in some place remote from the spot where the mountain casts its shadow. They will think, if they haven't the map, that we are proceeding by it, and they'll dig, too. When they find nothing, as will also happen to us, they may go away.

"If, on the other hand, they have the map, and see us digging at a spot not indicated on it, they will be puzzled, knowing we must have some idea of where the buried city lies. They will think the map is at fault, perhaps, and not make use of it. Then we can get it back."

"Bless my hatband!" cried Mr. Damon. "I believe you're right, Tom. We'll dig in the wrong place to fool 'em."

And this was done. Search for the precious map was given up for the time being, and the professor and his friends set the natives to work digging shafts in the ground, as though sinking them down to the level of the buried city.

But though this false work was prosecuted with vigor for several days, there was a feeling of despair among the Bumper party over the loss of the map.

"If we could only get it back!" exclaimed the professor, again and again.

Meanwhile the Beecher party seemed inactive. True, some members of it did come over to look on from a respectful distance at what the diggers were doing. Some of the rival helpers, under the direction of the head of the expedition, also began sinking shafts. But they were not in the locality remembered by Professor Bumper as being correct.

"I can't imagine what they're up to," he said. "If they have my map they would act differently, I should think."

"Whatever they're up to," answered Tom, "the time has come when we can dig at the place where we can hope for results." And the following day shafts were started in the shadow of the mountain.

Until some evidence should have been obtained by digging, as to the location beneath the surface of a buried city, there was nothing for the travelers to do but wait. Turns were taken in directing the efforts of the diggers, and an occasional inspection was made of the shafts.

"What do you expect to find first?" asked Tom of Professor Bumper one day, when the latter was at the top of a shaft waiting for a bucket load of dirt to be hoisted up.

"Potsherds and artifacts," was the answer.

"What sort of bugs are they?" asked Ned with a laugh. He and Tom were about to go hunting with their electric rifles.

"Artifacts are things made by the Indians—or whatever members of the race who built the ancient cities were called—such as household articles, vases, ornaments, tools and so on. Anything made by artificial means is called an artifact."

"And potsherds are things with those Chinese laundry ticket scratches on them," added Tom.

"Exactly," said the professor, laughing. "Though some of the strange-appearing inscriptions give much valuable information. As soon as we find some of them—say a broken bit of pottery with hieroglyphics on—I will know I am on the right track."

And while the scientist and Mr. Damon kept watch at the top of the shaft, Tom and Ned went out into the jungle to hunt. They had killed some game, and were stalking a fine big deer, which would provide a feast for the natives, when suddenly the silence of the lonely forest was broken by a piercing scream, followed by an agonized cry of

"El tigre! El tigre!"

POISONED ARROWS

"Did you hear that, Tom?" asked Ned, in a hoarse whisper.

"Surely," was the cautious answer. "Keep still, and I'll try for a shot."

"Better be quick," advised Ned in a tense voice. "The chap who did that yelling seems to be in trouble!"

And as Ned's voice trailed off into a whisper, again came the cry, this time in frenzied pain.

"El tigre! El tigre!" Then there was a jumble of words.

"It's over this way!" and this time Ned shouted, seeing no need for low voices since the other was so loud.

Tom looked to where Ned had parted the bushes alongside a jungle path. Through the opening the young inventor saw, in a little glade, that which caused him to take a firmer grip on his electric rifle, and also a firmer grip on his nerves.

Directly in front of him and Ned, and not more than a hundred yards away, was a great tawny and spotted jaguar—the "tigre" or tiger of Central America. The beast, with lashing tail, stood over an Indian upon whom it seemed to have sprung from some lair, beating the unfortunate man to the ground. Nor had he fallen scatheless, for there was blood on the green leaves about him, and it was not the blood of the spotted beast.

"Oh, Tom, can you—can you—" and Ned faltered.

The young inventor understood the unspoken question.

"I think I can make a shot of it without hitting the man," he answered, never turning his head. "It's a question, though, if the beast won't claw him in the death struggle. It won't last long, however, if the electric bullet goes to the right place, and I've got to take the chance."

Cautiously Tom brought his weapon to bear. Quiet as Ned and he had been after the discovery, the jaguar seemed to feel that something was wrong. Intent on his prey, for a time he had stood over it, gloating. Now the brute glanced uneasily from side to side, its tail nervously twitching, and it seemed trying to gain, by a sniffing of the air, some information as to the direction in which danger lay, for Tom and Ned had stooped low, concealing themselves by a screen of leaves.

The Indian, after his first frenzied outburst of fear, now lay quiet, as though fearing to move, moaning in pain.

Suddenly the jaguar, attracted either by some slight movement on the part of Ned or Tom, or perhaps by having winded them, turned his head quickly and gazed with cruel eyes straight at the spot where the two young men stood behind the bushes.

"He's seen us," whispered Ned.

"Yes," assented Tom. "And it's a perfect shot. Hope I don't miss!"

It was not like Tom Swift to miss, nor did he on this occasion. There was a slight report from the electric rifle—a report not unlike the crackle of the wireless—and the powerful projectile sped true to its mark.

Straight through the throat and chest under the uplifted jaw of the jaguar it went—through heart and lungs. Then with a great coughing, sighing snarl the beast reared up, gave a convulsive leap forward toward its newly discovered enemies, and fell dead in a limp heap, just beyond the native over which it had been crouching before it delivered the death stroke, now never to fall.

"You did it, Tom! You did it!" cried Ned, springing up from where he had been kneeling to give his chum a better chance to shoot. "You did it, and saved the man's life!" And Ned would have rushed out toward the still twitching body.

"Just a minute!" interposed Tom. "Those beasts sometimes have as many lives as a cat. I'll give it one more for luck." Another electric projectile through the head of the jaguar produced no further effect than to move the body slightly, and this proved conclusively that there was no life left. It was safe to approach, which Tom and Ned did.

Their first thought, after a glance at the jaguar, was for the Indian. It needed but a brief examination to show that he was not badly hurt. The jaguar had leaped on him from a low tree as he passed under it, as the boys learned afterward, and had crushed the man to earth by the weight of the spotted body more than by a stroke of the paw.

The American jaguar is not so formidable a beast as the native name of tiger would cause one to suppose, though they are sufficiently dan-gerous, and this one had rather badly clawed the Indian. Fortunately the scratches were on the fleshy parts of the arms and shoulders, where, though painful, they were not necessarily serious.

"But if you hadn't shot just when you did, Tom, it would have been all up with him," commented Ned.

"Oh, well, I guess you'd have hit him if I hadn't," returned the young inventor. "But let's see what we can do for this chap."

The man sat up wonderingly—hardly able to believe that he had been saved from the dreaded "tigre." His wounds were bleeding rather freely, and as Tom and Ned carried with them a first-aid kit they now brought it into use. The wounds were bound up, the man was given water to drink and then, as he was able to walk, Tom and Ned offered to help him wherever he wanted to go.

"Blessed if I can tell whether he's one of our Indians or whether he belongs to the Beecher crowd," remarked Tom.

"Senor Beecher," said the Indian, adding, in Spanish, that he lived in the vicinity and had only lately been engaged by the young professor who hoped to discover the idol of gold before Tom's scientific friend could do so.

Tom and Ned knew a little Spanish, and with that, and simple but expressive signs on the part of the Indian, they learned his story. He had his palm-thatched hut not far from the Beecher camp, in a small Indian village, and he, with others, had been hired on the arrival of the Beecher party to help with the excavations. These, for some reason, were delayed.

"Delayed because they daren't use the map they stole from us," commented Ned.

"Maybe," agreed Tom.

The Indian, whose name, it developed, was Tal, as nearly as Tom and Ned could master it, had left camp to go to visit his wife and child in the jungle hut, intending to return to the Beecher camp at night. But as he passed through the forest the jaguar had dropped on him, bearing him to earth.

"But you saved my life, Senor," he said to Tom, dropping on one knee and trying to kiss Tom's hand, which our hero avoided. "And now my life is yours," added the Indian.

"Well, you'd better get home with it and take care of it," said Tom. "I'll have Professor Bumper come over and dress your scratches in a better and more careful way. The bandages we put on are only temporary."

"My wife she make a poultice of leaves—they cure me," said the Indian.

"I guess that will be the best way," observed Ned. "These natives can doctor themselves for some things, better than we can."

"Well, we'll take him home," suggested Tom. "He might keel over from loss of blood. Come on," he added to Tal, indicating his object.

It was not far to the native's hut from the place where the jaguar had been killed, and there Tom and Ned underwent another demonstration of affection as soon as those of Tal's immediate family and the other natives understood what had happened.

"I hate this business!" complained Tom, after having been knelt to by the Indian's wife and child, who called him the "preserver" and other endearing titles of the same kind. "Come on, let's hike back."

But Indian hospitality, especially after a life has been saved, is not so simple as all that.

"My life—my house—all that I own is yours," said Tal in deep gratitude. "Take everything," and he waved his hand to indicate all the possessions in his humble hut.

"Thanks," answered Tom, "but I guess you need all you have. That's a fine specimen of blow gun though," he added, seeing one hanging on the wall. "I wouldn't mind having one like that. If you get well enough to make me one, Tal, and some arrows to go with it, I'd like it for a curiosity to hang in my room at home."

"The Senor shall have a dozen," promised the Indian.

"Look, Ned," went on Tom, pointing to the native weapon. "I never saw one just like this. They use small arrows or darts, tipped with wild cotton, instead of feathers."

"These the arrows," explained Tal's wife, bringing a bundle from a corner of the one-room hut. As she held them out her husband gave a cry of fear.

"Poisoned arrows! Poisoned arrows!" he exclaimed. "One scratch and the senors are dead men. Put them away!"

In fear the Indian wife prepared to obey, but as she did so Tom Swift caught sight of the package and uttered a strange cry.

"Thundering hoptoads, Ned!" he exclaimed. "The poisoned arrows are wrapped in the piece of oiled silk that was around the professor's missing map!"

An Old Legend

Fascinated, Tom and Ned gazed at the package the Indian woman held out to them. Undoubtedly it was oiled silk on the outside, and through the almost transparent covering could be seen the small arrows, or darts, used in the blow gun.

"Where did you get that?" asked Tom, pointing to the bundle and gazing sternly at Tal.

"What is the matter, Senor?" asked the Indian in turn. "Is it that you are afraid of the poisoned arrows? Be assured they will not harm you unless you are scratched by them."

Tom and Ned found it difficult to comprehend all the rapid Spanish spoken by their host, but they managed to understand some, and his eloquent gestures made up the rest.

"We're not afraid," Tom said, noting that the oiled skin well covered the dangerous darts. "But where did you get that?"

"I picked it up, after another Indian had thrown it away. He got it in your camp, Senor. I will not lie to you. I did not steal. Valdez went to your camp to steal—he is a bad Indian— and he brought back this wrapping. It contained something he thought was gold, but it was not, so he—"

"Quick! Yes! Tell us!" demanded Tom eagerly. "What did he do with the professor's map that was in the oiled silk? Where is it?"

"Oh, Senors!" exclaimed the Indian woman, thinking perhaps her husband was about to be dealt harshly with when she heard Tom's excited voice. "Tal do no harm!"

"No, he did no harm," went on Tom, in a reassuring tone. "But he can do a whole lot of good if he tells us what became of the map that was in this oiled silk. Where is it?" he asked again.

"Valdez burn it up," answered Tal.

"What, burned the professor's map?" cried Ned.

"If that was in this yellow cloth—yes," answered the injured man. "Valdez he is bad. He say to me he is going to your camp to see what he can take. How he got this I know not, but he come back one morning with the yellow package. I see him, but he make me promise not to tell. But you save my life I tell you everything.

"Valdez open the package; but it is not gold, though he think so because it is yellow, and the man with no hair on his head keep it in his pocket close, so close," and Tal hugged himself to indicate what he meant.

"That's Professor Bumper," explained Ned.

"How did Valdez get the map out of the professor's coat?" asked Tom.

"Valdez he very much smart. When man with no hair on his head take coat off for a minute to eat breakfast Valdez take yellow thing out of pocket."

"The Indian must have sneaked into camp when we were eating," said Tom. "Those from Beecher's party and our workers look all alike to us. We wouldn't know one from the other, and one of our rival's might slip in."

"One evidently did, if this is really the piece of oiled silk that was around the professor's map," said Ned.

"It certainly is the same," declared the young inventor. "See, there is his name," and he stretched out his hand to point.

"Don't touch!" cried Tal. "Poisoned arrows snake poison—very dead-like and quick."

"Don't worry, I won't touch," said Tom grimly. "But go on. You say Valdez sneaked into our camp, took the oiled-silk package from the coat pocket of Professor Bumper and went back to his own camp with it, thinking it was gold."

"Yes," answered Tal, though it is doubtful if he understood all that Tom said, as it was half Spanish and half English. But the Indian knew a little English, too. "Valdez, when he find no gold is very mad. Only papers in the yellow silk-papers with queer marks on. Valdez think it maybe a charm to work evil, so he burn them up—all up!"

"Burned that rare map!" gasped Tom.

"All in fire," went on Tal, indicating by his hands the play of flames. "Valdez throw away yellow silk, and I take for my arrows so rain not wash off poison. I give to you, if you like, with blow gun."

"No, thank you," answered Tom, in disappointed tones. "The oiled silk is of no use without the map, and that's gone. Whew! but this is tough!" he said to his chum. "As long as it was only stolen there was a chance to get it back, but if it's burned, the jig is up."

"It looks so," agreed Ned. "We'd better get back and tell the professor. It he can't get along without the map it's time he started a movement toward getting another. So it wasn't Beecher, after all, who got it."

"Evidently not," assented Tom. "But I believe him capable of it."

"You haven't much use for him," remarked Ned.

"Huh!" was all the answer given by his chum.

"I am sorry, Senors," went on Tal, "but I could not stop Valdez, and the burning of the papers—"

"No, you could not help it," interrupted the young inventor. "But it just happens that it brings bad luck to us. You see, Tal, the papers in this yellow covering, told of an old buried city that the bald-headed professor—the-man-with-no-hair-on-his-head—is very anxious to discover. It is somewhere under the ground," and he waved to the jungle all about them, pointing earthwards.

"Paper Valdez burn tell of lost city?" asked Tal, his face lighting up.

"Yes. But now, of course, we can't tell where to dig for it."

The Indian turned to his wife and talked rapidly with her in their own dialect. She, too, seemed greatly excited, making quick gestures. Finally she ran out of the hut.

"Where is she going?" asked Tom suspiciously.

"To get her grandfather. He very old Indian. He know story of buried cities under trees. Very old story—what you call legend, maybe. But Goosal know. He tell same as his grandfather told him. You wait. Goosal come, and you listen."

"Good, Ned!" suddenly cried Tom. "Maybe, we'll get on the track of lost Kurzon after all, through some ancient Indian legend. Maybe we won't need the map!"

"It hardly seems possible," said Ned slowly. "What can these Indians know of buried cities that were out of existence before Columbus came here? Why, they haven't any written history."

"No, and that may be just the reason they are more likely to be right," returned Tom. "Legends handed down from one grandfather to another go back a good many hundred years. If they were written they might be destroyed as the professor's map was. Somehow or other, though I can't tell why, I begin to see daylight ahead of us."

"I wish I did," remarked Ned.

"Here comes Goosal I think," murmured Tom, and he pointed to an Indian, bent with the weight of years, who, led by Tal's wife, was slowly approaching the hut.

THE CAVERN

"Now Goosal can tell you," said Tal, evidently pleased that he had, in a measure, solved the problem caused by the burning of the professor's map. "Goosal very old Indian. He know old stories—legends—very old."

"Well, if he can tell us how to find the buried city of Kurzon and the—the things in it," said Tom, "he's all right!"

The aged Indian proceeded slowly toward the hut where the impatient youths awaited him.

"I know what you seek in the buried city," remarked Tal.

"Do you?" cried Tom, wondering if some one had indiscreetly spoken of the idol of gold.

"Yes you want pieces of rock, with strange writings on them, old weapons, broken pots. I know. I have helped white men before."

"Yes, those are the things we want," agreed Tom, with a glance at his chum. "That is—some of them. But does your wife's grandfather talk our language?"

"No, but I can tell you what he says."

By this time the old man, led by "Mrs. Tal"— as the young men called the wife of the Indian they had helped—entered the hut. He seemed nervous and shy, and glanced from Tom and Ned to his grandson-in-law, as the latter talked rapidly in the Indian dialect. Then Goosal made answer, but what it was all about the boys could not tell.

"Goosal say," translated Tal, "that he know a story of a very old city away down under ground."

"Tell us about it!" urged Tom eagerly.

But a difficulty very soon developed. Tal's intentions were good, but he was not equal to the task of translating. Nor was the understanding of Tom and Ned of Spanish quite up to the mark.

"Say, this is too much for me!" exclaimed Tom. "We are losing the most valuable part of this by not understanding what Goosal says, and what Tal translates."

"What can we do?" asked Ned.

"Get the professor here as soon as possible. He can manage this dialect, and he'll get the information at first hand. If Goosal can tell where to begin excavating for the city he ought to tell the professor, not us."

"That's right," agreed Ned. "We'll bring the professor here as soon as we can."

Accordingly they stopped the somewhat difficult task of listening to the translated story and told Tal, as well as they could, that they would bring the "man-with-no-hair-on-his-head" to listen to the tale.

This seemed to suit the Indians, all of whom in the small colony appeared to be very grateful to Tom and Ned for having saved the life of Tal.

"That was a good shot you made when you bowled over the jaguar," said Ned, as the two young explorers started back to their camp.

"Better than I realized, if it leads to the discovery of Kurzon and the idol of gold," remarked Tom.

"And to think we should come across the oiled-silk holding the poisoned arrows!" went on Ned. "That's the strangest part of the whole affair. If it hadn't been that you shot the jaguar this never would have come about."

That Professor Bumper was astonished, and Mr. Damon likewise, when they heard the story of Tom and Ned, is stating it mildly.

"Come on!" exclaimed the scientist, as Tom finished, "we must see this Goosal at once. If my map is destroyed, and it seems to be, this old Indian may be our only hope. Where did he say the buried city was, Tom?"

"Oh, somewhere in this vicinity, as nearly as I could make out. But you'd better talk with him yourself. We didn't say anything about the idol of gold."

"That's right. It's just as well to let the natives think we are only after ordinary relics."

"Bless my insurance policy!" gasped Mr. Damon. "It does not seem possible that we are on the right track."

"Well, I think we are, from what little information Goosal gave us," remarked Tom. "This buried city of his must be a wonderful place."

"It is, if it is what I take it to be," agreed the professor. "I told you I would bring you to a land of wonders, Tom Swift, and they have hardly begun yet. Come, I am anxious to talk to Goosal."

In order that the Indians in the Bumper camp might not hear rumors of the new plan to locate the hidden city, and, at the same time, to keep rumors from spreading to the camp of the rivals, the scientist and his friends started a new shaft, and put a shift of men at work on it.

"We'll pretend we are on the right track, and very busy," said Tom. "That will fool Beecher."

"Are you glad to know he did not take your map Professor Bumper?" asked Mr. Damon.

"Well, yes. It is hard to believe such things of a fellow scientist."

"If he didn't take it he wanted to," said Tom. "And he has done, or will do, things as unsportsmanlike."

"Oh, you are hardly fair, perhaps, Tom," commented Ned.

"Um!" was all the answer he received.

With the Indians in camp busy on the excavation work, and having ascertained that similar work was going on in the Beecher outfit, Professor Bumper, with Mr. Damon and the young men, set off to visit the Indian village and listen to Goosal's story. They passed the place where Tom had slain the jaguar, but nothing was left but the bones; the ants, vultures and jungle animals having picked them clean in the night.

On the arrival of Tom and his friends at the Indian's hut, Goosal told, in language which Professor Bumper could understand, the ancient legend of the buried city as he had had it from his grandfather.

"But is that all you know about it, Goosal?" asked the savant.

"No, Learned One. It is true most of what I have told you was told to me by my father and his father's father. But I—I myself—with these eyes, have looked upon the lost city."

"You have!" cried the professor, this time in English. "Where? When? Take us to it! How do you get here?"

"Through the cavern of the dead," was the answer when the questions were modified.

"Bless my diamond ring!" exclaimed Mr. Damon, when Professor Bumper translated the reply. "What does he mean?"

And then, after some talk, this information came out. Years before, when Goosal was a young man, he had been taken by his grandfather on a journey through the jungle. They stopped one day at the foot of a high mountain, and, clearing away the brush and stones at a certain place, an entrance to a great cavern was revealed. This, it appeared, was the Indian burial ground, and had been used for generations.

Goosal, though in fear and trembling, was lead through it, and came to another cavern, vaster than the first. And there he saw strange and wonderful sights, for it was the remains of a buried city, that had once been the home of a great and powerful tribe unlike the Indians—the ancient Mayas it would seem.

"Can you take us to this cavern?" asked the professor.

"Yes," answered Goosal. "I will lead to it those who saved the life of Tal—them and their friends. I will take you to the lost city!"

"Good!" cried Mr. Damon, when this had been translated. "Now let Beecher try to play any more tricks on us! Ho! for the cavern and the lost city of Kurzon."

"And the idol of gold," said Tom Swift to himself. "I hope we can get it ahead of Beecher. Perhaps if I can help in that—Oh, well, here's hoping, that's all!" and a little smile curved his lips.

Greatly excited by the strange news, but maintaining as calm an air outwardly as possible, so as not to excite the Indians, Tom and his friends returned to camp to prepare for their trip. Goosal had said the cavern lay distant more than a two-days' journey into the jungle.

THE STORM

"Now," remarked Tom, once they were back again in their camp, "we must go about this trip to the cavern in a way that will cause no suspicion over there as to what our object is," and he nodded in the direction of the quarters of his rival.

"Do you mean to go off quietly?" asked Ned.

"Yes. And to keep the work going on here, at these shafts," put in the scientist, "so that if any of their spies happen to come here they will think we still believe the buried city to be just below us. To that end we must keep the Indians digging, though I am convinced now that it is useless."

Accordingly preparations were made for an expedition into the jungle under the leadership of Goosal. Tal had not sufficiently recovered from the jaguar wounds to go with the party, but the old man, in spite of his years, was hale and hearty and capable of withstanding hardships.

One of the most intelligent of the Indians was put in charge of the digging gangs as foreman, and told to keep them at work, and not to let them stray. Tolpec, whose brother Tom had tried to save, proved a treasure. He agreed to remain behind and look after the interests of his friends, and see that none of their baggage or stores were taken.

"Well, I guess we're as ready as we ever shall be," remarked Tom, as the cavalcade made ready to start. Mules carried the supplies that were to be taken into the jungle, and others of the sturdy animals were to be ridden by the travelers. The trail was not an easy one, Goosal warned them.

Tom and his friends found it even worse than they had expected, for all their experience in jungle and mountain traveling. In places it was necessary to dismount and lead the mules along, sometimes pushing and dragging them. More than once the trail fairly hung on the edge of some almost bottomless gorge, and again it wound its way between great walls of rock, so poised that they appeared about to topple over and crush the travelers. But they kept on with dogged patience, through many hardships.

To add to their troubles they seemed to have entered the abode of the fiercest mosquitoes encountered since coming to Honduras. At times it was necessary to ride along with hats covered with mosquito netting, and hands encased in gloves.

They had taken plenty of condensed food with them, and they did not suffer in this respect. Game, too, was plentiful and the electric rifles of Tom and Ned added to the larder.

One night, after a somewhat sound sleep induced by hard travel on the trail that day, Tom awoke to hear some one or something moving about among their goods, which included their provisions.

"Who's there?" asked the young inventor sharply, as he reached for his electric rifle.

There was no answer, but a rattling of the pans.

"Speak, or I'll fire!" Tom warned, adding this in such Spanish as he could muster, for he thought it might be one of the Indians. No reply came, and then, seeing by the light of the stars a dark form moving in front of the tent occupied by himself and Ned, Tom fired.

There was a combined grunt and squeal of pain, then a savage growl, and Ned yelled:

"What's the matter, Tom?" for he had been awakened, and heard the crackle of the electrical discharge.

"I don't know," Tom answered. "But I shot something—or somebody!"

"Maybe some of Beecher's crowd," ventured his chum. But when they got their electric torches, and focused them on the inert, black object, it was found to be a bear which had come to nose about the camp for dainty morsels.

Bruin was quite dead, and as he was in prime condition there was a feast of bear meat at the following dinner. The white travelers found it rather too strong for their palates, but the Indians reveled in it.

It was shortly after noon the next day, when Goosal, after remarking that a storm seemed brewing, announced that they would be at the entrance to the cavern in another hour.

"Good!" cried Professor Bumper. "At last we are near the buried city."

"Don't be too sure," advised Mr. Damon, "We may be disappointed. Though I hope not for your sake, my dear Professor."

Goosal now took the lead, and the old Indian, traveling on foot, for he said he could better look for the old landmark that way than on the back of a mule, walked slowly along a rough cliff.

"Here. somewhere, is the entrance to the cav-ern," said the aged man. "It was many years ago that I was here—many years. But it seems as though yesterday. It is little changed."

Indeed little did change in that land of wonders. Only nature caused what alterations there were. The hand of man had long been absent.

Slowly Goosal walked along the rocky trail, on one side a sheer rock, towering a hundred feet or more toward the sky. On the other side a deep gash leading to a great fertile valley below.

Suddenly the old man paused, and looked about him as though uncertain. Then, more slowly still, he put out his hand and pulled at some bushes that grew on a ledge of the rock. They came away, having no depth of earth, and a small opening was disclosed.

"It is here," said Goosal quietly. "The entrance to the cavern that leads to the burial place of the dead, and the city that is dead also. It is here."

He stood aside while the others hurried forward. It took but a few minutes to prove that he was right—at least as to the existence of the cavern—for the four men were soon peering into the opening.

"Come on!" cried Tom, impetuously.

"Wait a moment," suggested the professor, "Sometimes the air in these places is foul. We must test it." But a torch one of the Indians threw in burned with a steady glow. That test was conclusive at least. They made ready to enter.

Torches of a light bark, that glowed with a steady flame and little smoke, had been provided, as well as a good supply of electric dry-battery lamps, and the way into the cavern was thus well lighted. At first the Indians were afraid to enter, but a word or two from Goosal reassured them, and they followed Professor Bumper, Tom, and the others into the cavern.

For several hundred feet there was nothing remarkable about the cave. It was like any other cavern of the mountains, though wonderful for the number of crystal formations on the root and walls—formations that sparkled like a million diamonds in the flickering lights.

"Talk about a wonderland!" cried Tom. "This is fairyland!"

A moment later, as Goosal walked on beside the professor and Tom, the aged Indian came to a pause, and, pointing ahead, murmured:

"The city of the dead!"

They saw the niches cut in the rock walls. niches that held the countless bones of those who had died many, many years before. It was a vast Indian grave.

"Doubtless a wealth of material of historic interest here," said Professor Bumper, flashing his torch on the skeletons. "But it will keep. Where is the city you spoke of, Goosal?"

"Farther on, Senor. Follow me."

Past the stone graves they went, deeper and deeper into the great cave. Their footsteps echoed and re-echoed. Suddenly Tom, who with Ned had gone a little ahead, came to a sudden halt and said:

"Well, this may be a burial place sure enough, but I think I see something alive all right—if it isn't a ghost."

He pointed ahead. Surely those were lights flickering and moving about, and, yes, there were men carrying them. The Bumper party came to a surprised halt. The other lights advanced, and then, to the great astonishment of Professor Bumper and his friends, there confronted them in the cave several scientists of Professor Beecher's party and a score or more of Indians. Professor Hylop, who was known to Professor Bumper, stepped forward and asked sharply:

"What are you doing here?"

"I might ask you the same thing," was the retort.

"You might, but you would not be answered," came sharply. "We have a right here, having discovered this cavern, and we claim it under a concession of the Honduras Government. I shall have to ask you to withdraw."

"Do you mean leave here?" asked Mr Damon.

"That is it, exactly. We first discovered this cave. We have been conducting explorations in it for several days, and we wish no outsiders."

"Are you speaking for Professor Beecher'" asked Tom.

"I am. But he is here in the cave, and will speak for himself if you desire it. But I represent him, and I order you to leave. If you do not go peaceably we will use force. We have plenty of it," and he glanced back at the Indians grouped behind him—scowling savage Indians.

"We have no wish to intrude," observed Professor Bumper, "and I fully recognize the right of prior discovery. But one member of our party (he did not say which one) was in this cave many years ago. He led us to it."

"Ours is a government concession!" exclaimed Professor Hylop harshly. "We want no intruders! Go!" and he pointed toward the direction whence Tom's party had come.

"Drive them out!" he ordered the Indians in Spanish, and with muttered threats the dark-skinned men advanced toward Tom and the others.

"You need not use force," said Professor Bumper.

He and Professor Hylop had quarreled bitterly years before on some scientific matter, and the matter was afterward found to be wrong. Perhaps this made him vindictive.

Tom stepped forward and started to protest, but Professor Bumper interposed.

"I guess there is no help for it but to go. It seems to be theirs by right of discovery and government concession," he said, in disappointed tone. "Come friends"; and dejectedly they retraced their steps.

Followed by the threatening Indians, the Bumper party made its way back to the entrance. They had hoped for great things, but if the cavern gave access to the buried city—the ancient city of Kurzon on the chief altar of which stood the golden idol, Quitzel—it looked as though they were never to enter it.

"We'll have to get our Indians and drive those fellows out!" declared Tom. "I'm not going to be beaten this way—and by Beecher!"

"It is galling," declared Professor Bumper. "Still he has right on his side, and I must give in to priority, as I would expect him to. It is the unwritten law."

"Then we've failed!" cried Tom bitterly.

"Not yet," said Professor Bumper. "If I can not unearth that buried city I may find another in this wonderland. I shall not give up."

"Hark! What's that noise?" asked Tom, as they approached the entrance to the cave.

"Sounds like a great wind blowing," commented Ned.

It was. As they stood in the entrance they looked out to find a fierce storm raging. The wind was sweeping down the rocky trail, the rain was falling in veritable bucketfuls from the overhanging cliff, and deafening thunder and blinding lightning roared and flashed.

"Surely you would not drive us out in this storm," said Professor Bumper to his former rival.

"You can not stay in the cave! You must get out!" was the answer, as a louder crash of thunder than usual seemed to shake the very mountain.

Entombed Alive

For an instant Tom and his friends paused at the entrance to the wonderful cavern, and looked at the raging storm. It seemed madness to venture out into it, yet they had been driven from the cave by those who had every right of discovery to say who, and who should not, partake of its hospitality.

"We can't go out into that blow!" cried Ned. "It's enough to loosen the very mountains!"

"Let's stay here and defy them!" murmured Tom. "If the—if what we seek—is here we have as good a right to it as they have."

"We must go out," said Professor Bumper simply. "I recognize the right of my rival to dispossess us."

"He may have the right, but it isn't human," said Mr. Damon. "Bless my overshoes! If Beecher himself were here he wouldn't have the heart to send us out in this storm."

"I would not give him the satisfaction of appealing to him," remarked Professor Bumper. "Come, we will go out. We have our ponchos, and we are not fair-weather explorers. If we can't get to the lost city one way we will another. Come my friends."

And despite the downpour, the deafening thunder and the lightning that seemed ready to sear one's eyes, he walked out of the cave entrance, followed by Tom and the others.

"Come on!" cried Tom, in a voice he tried to render confident, as they went out into the terrible storm. "We'll beat 'em yet!"

The rain fell harder than ever. Small torrents were now rushing down the trail, and it was only a question of a few minutes before the place where they stood would be a raging river, so quickly does the rain collect in the mountains and speed toward the valleys.

"We must take to the forest!" cried Tom. "There'll be some shelter there, and I don't like the way the geography of this place is behaving. There may be a landslide at any moment."

As he spoke he motioned upward through the mist of the rain to the sloping side of the mountain towering above them. Loose stones were beginning to roll down, accompanied by patches of earth loosened by the water. Some of the patches carried with them bunches of grass and small bushes.

"Yes, it will be best to move into the jungle," said the professor. "Goosal, you had better take the lead."

It was wonderful to see how well the aged Indian bore up in spite of his years, and walked on ahead. They had left their mules tethered some distance back, in a sheltering clump of trees, and they hoped the animals would be safe.

The guide found a place where they could leave the trail, though going down a dangerous slope, and take to the forest. As carefully as possible they descended this, the rain continuing to fall, the wind to blow, the lightning to sizzle all about them and the thunder to boom in their ears.

They went on until they were beneath the shelter of the thick jungle growth of trees, which kept off some of the pelting drops.

"This is better!" exclaimed Ned, shaking his poncho and getting rid of some of the water that had settled on it.

"Bless my overcoat!" cried Mr. Damon. "We seem to have gotten out of the frying pan into the fire!"

"How?" asked Tom. "We are partly sheltered here, though had we stayed in the cave in spite of—"

A deafening crash interrupted him, and following the flash one of the giant trees of the forest was seen to blaze up and then topple over.

"Struck by lightning!" yelled Ned.

"Yes; and it may happen to us!" exclaimed Mr. Damon. "We were safer from the lightning in the open. Maybe—"

Again came an interruption, but this time a different one. The very ground beneath their feet seemed to be shaking and trembling.

"What is it?" gasped Ned, while Goosal fell on his knees and began fervently to pray.

"It's an earthquake!" yelled Tom Swift.

As he spoke there came another sound—the sound of a mass of earth in motion. It came from the direction of the mountain trail they had just left. They looked toward it and their horror-stricken eyes saw the whole side of the mountain sliding down.

Slowly at first the earth slid down, but constantly gathering force and speed. In the face of this new disaster the rain seemed to have ceased and the thunder and lightning to be less severe. It was as though one force of nature gave way to the other.

"Look! Look!" gasped Ned.

In silence, which was broken now only by a low and ominous rumble, more menacing than had been the awful fury of the elements, the travelers looked.

Suddenly there was a quicker movement of seemingly one whole section of the mountain. Great rocks and trees, carried down by the appalling force of the landslide were slipping over the trail, obliterating it as though it had never existed.

"There goes the entrance to the cavern!" cried Ned, and as the others looked to where he pointed they saw the hole in the side of the mountain —the mouth of the cave that led to the lost city of Kurzon—completely covered by thousands of tons of earth and stones.

"That's the end of them!" exclaimed Tom, as the rumble of the earthquake died away.

"Of—" Ned stopped, his eyes staring.

"Of Professor Beecher's party. They're entombed alive!"

THE REVOLVING STONE

Stunned, not alone by the realization of the awfulness of the fate of their rivals, but also by the terrific storm and the effect of the earthquake and the landslide, Tom and his friends remained for a moment gazing toward the mouth of the cavern, now completely out of sight, buried by a mass of broken trees, tangled bushes, rocks and earth. Somewhere, far beyond that mass, was the Beecher party, held prisoners in the cave that formed the entrance to the buried city.

Tom was the first to come to a realization of what was needed to be done.

"We must help them!" he exclaimed, and it was characteristic of him that he harbored no enmity.

"How?" asked Ned.

"We must get a force of Indians and dig them out," was the prompt answer.

At Tom's vigorous words Professor Bumper's forces were energized into action, and he stated: "Fortunately we have plenty of excavating tools. We may be in time to save them. Come on! the storm seems to have passed as suddenly as it came up, and the earthquake, which, after all did not cover a wide area, seems to be over. We must start the work of rescue at once. We must go back to camp and get all the help we can muster."

The storm, indeed, seemed to be over, but it was no easy matter to get back over the soggy, rain-soaked ground to the trail they had left to take shelter in the forest. Fortunately the earthquake had not involved that portion where they had left their mules, but most of the frightened animals had broken loose, and it was some little time before they could all be caught.

"It is no use to try to get back to camp tonight," said Tom, when the last of the pack and saddle animals had been corralled. "It is getting late and there is no telling the condition of the trail. We must stay here until morning."

"But what about them?" and Mr. Damon nodded in the direction of the entombed ones.

"We can help them best by waiting until the beginning of a new day," said the professor. "We shall need a large force, and we could not bring it up tonight. Besides, Tom is right, and if we tried to go along the trail after dark, torn and disturbed as it is bound to be by the rain, we might get into difficulties ourselves. No, we must camp here until morning and then go for help."

They all decided finally this was best. The professor, too, pointed out that their rivals were in a large and roomy cave, not likely to suffer from lack of air nor food or water, since they must have supplies with them.

"The only danger is that the cave has been crushed in," added Tom; "but in that event we would be of no service to them anyhow."

The night seemed very long, and it was a most uncomfortable one, because of the shock and exertions through which the party had passed. Added to this was the physical discomfort caused by the storm.

But in time there was the light in the east that meant morning was at hand, and with it came action. A hasty breakfast, cups of steaming coffee forming a most welcome part, put them all in better condition, and once more they were on their way, heading back to the main camp where they had left their force of Indians.

"My!" exclaimed Tom, as they made their way slowly along, "it surely was some storm! Look at those big trees uprooted over there. They're almost as big as the giant redwoods of California, and yet they were bowled over as if they were tenpins."

"I wonder if the wind did it or the earthquake," ventured Mr. Damon.

"No wind could do that," declared Ned. "It must have been the landslide caused by the earthquake."

"The wind could do it if the ground was made soft by the rain; and that was probably what did it," suggested Tom.

"There is no harm in settling the point," commented Professor Bumper. "It is not far off our trail, and will take only a few minutes to go over to the trees. I should like to get some photographs to accompany an article that perhaps I shall write on the effects of sudden and severe tropical storms. We will go to look at the overturned trees and then we'll hurry on to camp to get the rescue party."

The uprooted trees lay on one side of the mountain trail, perhaps a mile from the mouth of the cave which had been covered over, entombing the Beecher party. Leaving the mules in charge of one of the Indians, Professor Bumper and his friends, accompanied by Goosal, approached the fallen trees. As they neared them they saw that in falling the trees had lifted with their roots a large mass of earth and imbedded rocks that had clung to the twisted and gnarled fibers. This mass was as large as a house.

"Look at the hole left when the roots pulled out!" cried Ned. "Why, it's like the crater of a small volcano!" he added. And, as they stood on the edge of it looking curiously at the hole made, the others agreed with Tom's chum.

Professor Bumper was looking about, trying to ascertain if there were any evidences of the earthquake in the vicinity, when Tom, who had cautiously gone a little way down into the excavation caused by the fallen trees, uttered a cry of surprise.

"Look!" he shouted. "Isn't that some sort of tunnel or underground passage?" and he pointed to a square opening, perhaps seven feet high and nearly as broad, which extended, no one knew where, downward and onward from the side of the hole made by the uprooting of the trees.

"It's an underground passage all right," said Professor Bumper eagerly; "and not a natural one, either. That was fashioned by the hand of man, if I am any judge. It seems to go right under the mountain, too. Friends, we must explore this! It may be of the utmost importance! Come, we have our electric torches, and we shall need them, for it's very dark in there," and he peered into the passage in front of which they all stood now. It seemed to have been tunneled through the earth, the sides being lined by either slabs of stone, or walls made by a sort of concrete.

"But what about the rescue work?" asked Mr. Damon.

"I am not forgetting Professor Beecher and his friends," answered the scientist.

"Perhaps this may be a better means of rescuing them than by digging them out, which will take a week at least," observed Tom.

"This a better way?" asked Ned, pointing to the tunnel.

"That's it," confirmed the savant. "If you will notice it extends back in the direction of the cave from which we were driven. Now if there is a buried city beneath all this jungle, this mountain of earth and stones, the accumulation of centuries, it is probably on the bottom of some vast cavern. It is my opinion that we were only in one end of that cavern, and this may be the entrance to another end of it."

"Then," asked Mr. Damon, "do you mean that we can enter here, get into the cave that contains the buried city, or part of it, and find there Beecher and his friends?"

"That's it. It is possible, and if we could it would save an immense lot of work, and probably be a surer way to save their lives than by digging a tunnel through the landslide to find the mouth of the cave where we first entered."

"It's a chance worth taking," said Mr. Damon. "Of course it is a chance. But then everything connected with this expedition is; so one is no worse than another. As you say, we may find the entombed men more easily this way than any other."

"I wonder," said Tom slowly, "if, by any chance, we shall find, through this passage, the lost city we are looking for."

"And the idol of gold," added Ned.

"Goosal, do you know anything about this?" asked Professor Bumper. "Did you ever hear of another passage leading to the cave where you saw the ancient city?"

"No, Learned One, though I have heard stories about there being many cities, or parts of a big one, beneath the mountain, and when it was above ground there were many entrances to it."

"That settles it!" cried the professor in English, having talked to Goosal in Spanish. "We'll try this and see where it leads."

They entered the stone-lined passage. In spite of the fact that it had probably been buried and concealed from light and air for centuries, as evidenced by the growth of the giant trees above it, the air was fresh.

"And this is one reason," said Tom, in commenting on this fact, "why I believe it leads to some vast cavern which is connected in some fashion with the outer air. Well, perhaps we shall soon make a discovery."

Eagerly and anxiously the little party pressed forward by the light of the pocket electric lamps. They were obsessed by two thoughts—what they might find and the necessity for aiding in the rescue of their rivals.

On and on they went, the darkness illuminated only by the torches they carried. But they noticed that the air was still fresh, and that a gentle wind blew toward them. The passage was undoubtedly artificial, a tunnel made by the hands of men now long crumbled into dust. It had a slightly upward slope, and this, Professor Bumper said, indicated that it was bored upward and perhaps into the very heart of the mountain somewhere in the interior of which was the Beecher party.

Just how far they went they did not know, but it must have been more than two miles. Yet they did not tire, for the way was smooth.

Suddenly Tom, who, with Professor Bumper, was in the lead, uttered a cry, as he held his torch above his head and flashed it about in a circle.

"We're blocked!" he exclaimed. "We're up against a stone wall!"

It was but too true. Confronting them, and extending from side to side across the passage and from roof to floor, was a great rough stone. Immense and solid it seemed when they pushed on it in vain.

"Nothing short of dynamite will move that," said Ned in despair. "This is a blind lead. We'll have to go back."

"But there must be something on the other side of that stone," cried Tom. "See, it is pierced with holes, and through them comes a current of air. If we could only move the stone!"

"I believe it is an ancient door," remarked Professor Bumper.

Eagerly and frantically they tried to move it by their combined weight. The stone did not give the fraction of the breadth of a hair.

"We'll have to go back and get some of your big tunnel blasting powder, Tom," suggested Ned.

As he spoke old Goosal glided forward. He had remained behind them in the passage while they were trying to move the rock. Now he said something in Spanish.

"What does he mean?" asked Ned.

"He asks that he be allowed to try," translated Professor Bumper. "Sometimes, he says, there is a secret way of opening stone doors in these underground caves. Let him try."

Goosal seemed to be running his fingers lightly over the outer edge of the door. He was muttering to himself in his Indian tongue.

Suddenly he uttered an exclamation, and, as he did so, there was a noise from the door itself. It was a grinding, scraping sound, a rumble as though rocks were being rolled one against the other.

Then the astonished eyes of the adventurers saw the great stone door revolve on its axis and swing to one side, leaving a passage open through which they could pass. Goosal had discovered the hidden mechanism.

What lay before them?

THE IDOL OF GOLD

"Forward! cried Tom Swift.

"Where?" asked Mr Damon, hanging back for an instant. "Bless my compass, Tom! do you know where you're going?"

"I haven't the least idea, but it must lead to something, or the ancients who made this revolving stone door wouldn't have taken such care to block the passage."

"Ask Goosal if he knows anything about it," suggested Mr. Damon to the professor.

"He says he never was here before," translated the savant, "but years ago, when he went into the hidden city by the cave we left yesterday, he saw doors like this which opened this way."

"Then we're on the right track!" cried Tom. "If this is the same kind of door, it must lead to the same place. Ho for Kurzon and the idol of gold!"

As they passed through the stone door, Tom and Professor Bumper tried to get some idea of the mechanism by which it worked. But they found this impossible, it being hidden within the stone itself or in the adjoining walls. But, in order that it might not close of itself and entomb them, the portal was blocked open with stones found in the passage.

"It's always well to have a line of retreat open," said Tom. "There's no telling what may lie beyond us."

For a time there seemed to be nothing more than the same passage along which they had come. Then the passage suddenly widened, like the large end of a square funnel. Upward and outward the stone walls swept, and they saw dimly before them, in the light of their torches, a vast cavern, seemingly formed by the falling in of mountains, which, in toppling over, had met overhead in a sort of rough arch, thus protecting, in a great measure, that which lay beneath them.

Goosal, who had brought with him some of the fiber bark torches, set a bundle of them aflame. As they flared up, a wondrous sight was revealed to Tom Swift and his friends.

Stretching out before them, as though they stood at the end of an elevated street and gazed down on it, was a city—a large city, with streets, houses, open squares, temples, statues, fountains, dry for centuries—a buried and forgotten city— a city in ruins—a city of the dead, now dry as dust, but still a city, or, rather, the strangely preserved remains of one.

"Look!" whispered Tom. A louder voice just then, would have seemed a sacrilege. "Look!"

"Is it what we are looking for?" asked Ned in a low voice.

"I believe it is," replied the professor. "It is the lost city of Kurzon, or one just like it. And now if we can find the idol of gold our search will be ended—at least the major part of it."

"Where did you expect to find the idol?" asked Tom.

"It should be in the main temple. Come, we will walk in the ancient streets—streets where no feet but ours have trod in many centuries. Come!"

In eager silence they pressed on through this newly discovered wonderland. For it was a wonderful city, or had been. Though much of it was in ruins, probably caused by an earthquake or an eruption from a volcano, the central portion, covered as it was by the overtoppling mountains that formed the arching roof, was well preserved.

There were rude but beautiful stone buildings. There were archways; temples; public squares; and images, not at all beautiful, for they seemed to be of man-monsters—doubtless ancient gods. There were smoothly paved streets; wondrously carved fountains, some in ruins, all now as dry as bone, but which must have been places of beauty where youths and maidens gathered in the ancient days.

Of the ancient population there was not a trace left. Tom and his friends penetrated some of the houses, but not so much as a bone or a heap of mouldering dust showed where the remains of the people were. Either they had fled at the approaching doom of the city and were buried elsewhere, or some strange fire or other force of nature had consumed and obliterated them.

"What a wealth of historic information I shall find here!" murmured Professor Bumper, as he caught sight of many inscriptions in strange characters on the walls and buildings. "I shall never get to the end of them."

"But what about the idol of gold?" asked Mr. Damon, "Do you think you'll find that?"

"We must hurry on to the temple over there," said the scientist, indicating a building further along.

"And then we must see about rescuing your rivals, Professor," put in Tom.

"Yes, Tom. But fortunately we are on the ground here before them," agreed the professor.

Undoubtedly it was the chief temple, or place of worship, of the long-dead race which the explorers now entered. It was a building beautiful in its barbaric style, and yet simple. There were massive walls, and a great inner court, at the end of which seemed to be some sort of altar. And then, as they lighted fresh torches, and pressed forward with them and their electric lights, they saw that which caused a cry of satisfaction to burst from all of them.

"The idol of gold!"

Yes, there it squatted, an ugly, misshapen, figure, a cross between a toad and a gila monster, half man, half beast, with big red eyes—rubies probably—that gleamed in the repulsive golden face. And the whole figure, weighing many pounds, seemed to be of *solid gold*!

Eagerly the others followed Professor Bumper up the altar steps to the very throne of the golden idol. The scientist touched it, tried to raise it and make sure of its solidity and material.

"This is it!" he cried. "It is the idol of gold! I have found We have found it, for it belongs to all of us!"

"Hurray!" cried Tom Swift, and Ned and Mr. Damon joined in the cry.

There was no need for silence or caution now; and yet, as they stood about the squat and ugly figure, which, in spite of its hideousness, was worth a fortune intrinsically and as an antique, they heard from the direction of the stone passage a noise.

"What is it?" asked Tom Swift.

There was a murmur of voices.

"Indians!" cried Professor Bumper, recognizing the language—a mixture of Spanish and Indian.

The cave was illuminated by the glare of other torches which seemed to rush forward. A moment later it was seen that they were being carried by a number of Indians.

"Friends," murmured Goosal, using the Spanish term, "Amigos."

"They are our own Indians!" cried Tom Swift. "I see Tolpec!" and he pointed to the native who had deserted from Jacinto's force to help them.

"How did they get here?" asked Professor Bumper.

This was quickly told. In their camp, where, under the leadership of Tolpec they had been left to do the excavating, the natives had heard, seen and felt the effects of the storm and the earthquake, though it did little damage in their vicinity. But they became alarmed for the safety of the professor and his party and, at Tolpec's suggestion, set off in search of them.

The Indians had seen, passing along the trail, the uprooted trees, and had noted the footsteps of the explorers going down to the stone passage. It was easy for them to determine that Tom and his friends had gone in, since the marks of their boots were plainly in evidence in the soft soil.

None of the Indians was as much wrought up over the discovery of Kurzon and the idol as were the white adventurers. The gold, of course, meant something to the natives, but they were indifferent to the wonders of the underground city. Perhaps they had heard too many legends concerning such things to be impressed.

"That statue is yours—all yours," said old Goosal when he had talked with his relatives and friends among the natives. "They all say what you find you keep, and we will help you keep it."

"That's good," murmured Professor Bumper. "There was some doubt in my mind as to our right to this, but after all, the natives who live in this land are the original owners, and if they pass title to us it is clear. That settles the last difficulty."

"Except that of getting the idol out," said Mr. Damon.

"Oh, we'll accomplish that!" cried Tom.

"I can hardly believe my good luck," declared Professor Bumper. "I shall write a whole book on this idol alone and then—"

Once more came an interruption. This time it was from another direction, but it was of the same character—an approaching band of torch-bearers. They were Indians, too, but leading them were a number of whites.

And at their head was no less personage than Professor Beecher himself.

For a moment, as the three parties stood together in the ancient temple, in the glare of many torches, no one spoke. Then Professor Bumper found his voice.

"We are glad to see you," he said to his rival. "That is glad to see you alive, for we saw the landslide bury you. And we were coming to dig you out. We thought this cave—the cave of the buried city—would lead us to you easier than by digging through the slide. We have just discovered this idol," and he put his hand on the grim golden image.

"Oh, you have discovered it, have you?" asked Professor Beecher, and his voice was bitter.

"Yes, not ten minutes ago. The natives have kindly acknowledged my right to it under the law of priority. I am sorry but—"

With a look of disgust and chagrined disappointment on his face, Professor Beecher turned to the other scientists and said:

"Let us go. We are too late. He has what I came after."

"Well, it is the fortune of war—and discovery," put in Mr. Hardy, one of the party who seemed the least ill-natured. "Your luck might have been ours, Professor Bumper. I congratulate you."

"Thank you! Are you sure your party is all right—not in need of assistance? How did you get out of the place you were buried?"

"Thank you! We do not require any help. It was good of you to think of us. But we got out the way we came in. We did not enter the tunnel as you did, but came in through another entrance which was not closed by the landslide. Then we made a turn through a gateway in a tunnel connecting with ours—a gateway which seems to have been opened by the earthquake— and we came here, just now.

"Too late, I see, to claim the discovery of the idol of gold," went on Mr. Hardy. "But I trust you will be generous, and allow us to make observations of the buildings and other relics."

"As much as you please, and with the greatest pleasure in the world," was the prompt answer of Professor Bumper. "All I lay sole claim to is the golden idol. You are at liberty to take whatever else you find in Kurzon and to make what observations you like."

"That is generous of you, and quite in contrast to—er—to the conduct of our leader. I trust he may awaken to a sense of the injustice he did you."

But Professor Beecher was not there to hear this. He had stalked away in anger.

"Humph!" grunted Tom. Then he continued: "That story about a government concession was all a fake, Professor, else he'd have put up a fight now. Contemptible sneak!"

In fact the story of Tom Swift's trip to the underground land of wonders is ended, for with the discovery of the idol of gold the main object of the expedition was accomplished. But their adventures were not over by any means, though there is not room in this volume to record them.

Suffice it to say that means were at once taken to get the golden image out of the cave of the ancient city. It was not accomplished without hard work, for the gold was heavy, and Professor Bumper would not, naturally, consent to the shaving off of so much as an ear or part of the flat nose, to say nothing of one of the half dozen extra arms and legs with which the ugly idol was furnished.

Finally it was safely taken out of the cave, and along the stone passage to the opening formed by the overthrown trees, and thence on to camp.

And at the camp a surprise awaited Tom.

Some long-delayed mail had been forwarded from the nearest place of civilization and there were letters for all, including several for our hero. One in particular he picked out first and read eagerly.

"Well, is every little thing all right, Tom?" asked Ned, as he saw a cheerful grin spread itself over his chum's face.

"I should say it is, and then some! Look here, Ned. This is a letter from—"

"I know. Mary Nestor. Go on."

"How'd you guess?"

"Oh, I'm a mind-reader."

"Huh! Well, you know she was away when I went to call to say good-bye, and I was a little afraid Beecher had got an inside edge on me."

"Had he?"

"No, but he tried hard enough. He went to see Mary in Fayetteville, just as you heard, be-fore he came on to join his party, but he didn't pay much of a visit to her."

"No?"

"No. Mary told him he'd better hurry along to Central America, or wherever it was he intended going, as she didn't care for him as much as he flattered himself she did."

"Good!" cried Ned. "Shake, old man. I'm glad!"

They shook hands.

"Well, what's the matter? Didn't you read all of her letter?" asked Ned when he saw his chum once more perusing the epistle.

"No. There's a postscript here.

"'Sorry I couldn't see you before you left. It was a mistake, but when you come back—'"

"Oh, that part isn't any of your affair!" and, blushing under his tan, Tom thrust the letter into his pocket and strode away, while Ned laughed happily.

With the idol of gold safe in their possession, Professor Bumper's party could devote their time to making other explorations in the buried city. This they did, as is testified to by a long list of books and magazine articles since turned out by the scientist, dealing strictly with archaeo-logical subjects, touching on the ancient Mayan race and its civilization, with particular reference to their system of computing time.

Professor Beecher, young and foolish, would not consent to delve into the riches of the ancient city, being too much chagrined over the loss of the idol.

It seems he had really promised to give a part of it to Mary Nestor. But he never got the chance.

His colleagues, after their first disappointment at being beaten, joined forces with Professor Bumper in exploring the old city, and made many valuable discoveries.

In one point Professor Bumper had done his rival an injustice. That was in thinking Professor Beecher was responsible for the treachery of Jacinto. That was due to the plotter's own work. It was true that Professor Beecher had tentatively engaged Jacinto, and had sent word to him to keep other explorers away from the vicinity of the ancient city if possible; but Jacinto, who did not return Professor Bumper's money, as he had promised, had acted treacherously in order to enrich himself. Professor Beecher had nothing to do with that, nor had he with the taking of the map, as has been seen, the loss of which, after all, was a blessing in disguise, for Kurzon would never have been located by following the directions given there, as it was very inaccurate.

In another point it was demonstrated that the old documents were at fault. This was in reference to the golden idol having been overthrown and another set up in its place, an act which had caused the destruction of Kurzon.

It is true that the city was destroyed, or rather, buried, but this catastrophe was probably brought about by an earthquake. And another great idol, one of clay, was found, perhaps a rival of Quitzel, but it was this clay image which was thrown down and broken, and not the golden one.

Perhaps an effort had been made, just before the burying of the city, to change idols and the system of worship, but Quitzel seemed to have held his own. The old manuscripts were not very reliable, it was found, except in general.

"Well, I guess this will hold Beecher for a while," said Tom, the night of the arrival of Mary's letter, and after he had written one in answer, which was dispatched by a runner to the nearest place whence mail could be forwarded.

"Yes, luck seems to favor you," replied Ned. "You've had a hand in the discovery of the idol of gold, and—"

"Yes. And I discovered something else I wasn't quite sure of," interrupted Tom, as he felt to make sure he had a certain letter safe in his pocket.

It was several weeks later that the explorations of Kurzon came to an end—a temporary end, for the rainy season set in, when the tropics are unsuitable for white men. Tom, Professor Bumper, Ned and Mr. Damon set sail for the United States, the valuable idol of gold safe on board.

And there, with their vessel plowing the blue waters of the Caribbean Sea, we will take leave of Tom Swift and his friends.

Tom Swift and His War Tank
Or Doing His Bit For Uncle Sam

TABLE OF CONTENTS:

Past Memories

Ceasing his restless walk up and down the room, Tom Swift strode to the window and gazed across the field toward the many buildings, where machines were turning out the products evolved from the brains of his father and himself. There was a worried look on the face of the young inventor, and he seemed preoccupied, as though thinking of something far removed from whatever it was his eyes gazed upon.

"Well, I'll do it!" suddenly exclaimed Tom. "I don't want to, but I will. It's in the line of 'doing my bit,' I suppose; but I'd rather it was something else. I wonder—"

"Ha! Up to your old tricks, I see, Tom!" exclaimed a voice, in which energy and friendliness mingled pleasingly. "Up to your old tricks!"

"Oh, hello, Mr. Damon!" cried Tom, turning to shake hands with an elderly gentleman—that is, elderly in appearance but not in action, for he crossed the room with the springing step of a lad, and there was the enthusiasm of youth on his face. "What do you mean—my old tricks?"

"Talking to yourself, Tom. And when you do that it means there is something in the wind. I hope, as a sort of side remark, it isn't rain that's in the wind, for the soldiers over at camp have had enough water to set up a rival establishment with Mr. Noah. But there's something going on, isn't there? Bless my memorandum book, but don't tell me there isn't, or I shall begin to believe I have lost all my deductive powers of reasoning! I Come in here, after knocking two or three times, to which you pay not the least attention, and find you mysteriously murmuring to yourself.

"The last time that happened, Tom, was just before you started to dig the big tunnel— No, I'm wrong. It was just before you started for the Land of Wonders, as we decided it ought to be called. You were talking to yourself then, when I walked in on you, and— Say, Tom!" suddenly exclaimed Mr. Damon eagerly, "don't tell me you're going off on another wild journey like that—don't!"

"Why?" asked Tom, smiling at the energy of his caller.

"Because if you are, I'll want to go with you, of course, and if I go it means I'll have to start in as soon as I can to bring my wife around to my way of thinking. The last time I went it took me two weeks to get her to consent, and then she didn't like it. So if—"

"No, Mr. Damon," interrupted Tom, "I don't count on going on any sort of a trip—that is, any long one. I was just getting ready to take a little spin in the Hawk, and if you'd like to come along—"

"You mean that saucy little airship of yours, Tom, that's always trying to sit down on her tail, or tickle herself with one wing?"

"That's the Hawk!" laughed Tom; "though that tickling business you speak of is when I spiral. Don't you like it?"

"Can't say I do," observed Mr. Damon dryly.

"Well, I'll promise not to try any stunts if you come along," Tom went on.

"Where are you going?" asked his friend.

"Oh, no place in particular. As you surmised, I've been doing a bit of thinking, and—"

"Serious thinking, too, Tom!" interrupted Mr. Damon. "Excuse me, but I couldn't help overhearing what you said. It was something about going to do something though you didn't want to, and that it was part of your 'bit'. That sounds like soldier talk. Are you going to enlist, Tom?"

"No."

"Um! Well, then—"

"It's something I can't talk about, Mr. Damon, even to you, as yet," Tom said, and there was a new quality in his voice, at which his friend looked up in some surprise.

"Oh, of course, Tom, if it's a secret—"

"Well, it hasn't even got that far, as yet. It's all up in the air, so to speak. I'll tell you in due season. But, speaking of the air, let's go for a spin. It may drive some of the cobwebs out of my brain. Did I hear you say you thought it would rain?"

"No, it's as clear as a bell. I said I hoped it wouldn't rain for the sake of the soldiers in camp. They've had their share of wet weather, and, goodness knows, they'll get more when they get to Flanders. It seems to do nothing but rain in France."

"It is damp," agreed Tom. "And, come to think of it, they are going to have some airship contests over at camp today— for the men who are being trained to be aviators, you know. It just occurred to me that we might fly over there and watch them."

"Fine!" cried Mr. Damon. "That's the very thing I should like. I'll take a chance in your Hawk, Tom, if you'll promise not to try any spiral stunts."

"I promise, Mr. Damon. Come on! I'll have Koku run the machine out and get her ready for a flight to Camp. It's a good day for a jaunt in the air."

"Get out the Hawk, Koku," ordered the young inventor, as he motioned to a big man—a veritable giant—who nodded to show he understood. Koku was really a giant, one of a race of strange beings, and Tom Swift had brought the big man with him when he escaped from captivity, as those will remember who have read that book.

"Going far, Tom?" asked an aged man, coming to the door of one of the many buildings of which the shed where the airship was kept formed one.

"Not very far, Father," answered the young inventor. "Mr. Damon and I are going for a little spin over to Camp Grant, to see some aircraft contests among the army birdmen."

"Oh, all right, Tom. I just wanted to tell you that I think I've gotten over that difficulty you found with the big carburetor you were working on. You didn't say what you wanted it for, except that it was for a heavy duty gasolene engine, and you couldn't get the needle valve to work as you'd like. I think I've found a way."

"Good, Dad! I'll look at it when I come back. That Carburetor did bother me, and if I can get that to work— well, maybe we'll have something soon that will—"

But Tom did not finish his sentence, for Koku was getting the aircraft in operation and Mr. Damon was already taking his place behind the pilot's seat, which would be occupied by Tom.

"All ready, are you, Koku?" asked the young inventor.

"All ready, Master," answered the giant.

There was a roar like that of a machine gun as the Hawk's engine spun the propeller, and then, after a little run across the sod, it mounted into the air, carrying Tom and Mr. Damon with it.

"Mind you, Tom, no stunts!" called the visitor to the young inventor through the speaking tube apparatus, which enabled a conversation to be carried on, even above the roar of the powerful engine. "Bless my overshoes! if you try, looping the loop with me—"

"I won't do anything like that!" promised Tom.

Away they soared, swift as a veritable hawk, and soon, after there had unrolled below their eyes a succession of fields and forest, there came into view rows and rows of small brown objects, among which beings, like ants, seemed crawling about

"There's the Camp!" exclaimed Tom.

"I see," and Mr. Damon nodded.

As they approached, they saw, starting up from a green space amid the brown tents, what appeared to be big bugs of a dirty white color splotched with green.

"The aircraft—and they have camouflage paint on," said Tom. "We can watch 'em from up here!"

Mr. Damon nodded, though Tom could not see him, sitting in front of his friend as he was.

Up and up circled the army aircraft, and they seemed to bow and nod a greeting to the Hawk, which was soon in the midst of them. Tom and Mr. Damon, flying high, though at no great speed, looked at the maneuvers of the veterans and the learners—many of whom might soon be engaging the Boches in far-off France.

"Some of 'em are pretty good!" called Tom, through the tube. "That one fellow did the loop as prettily as I've ever seen it done," and Tom Swift had a right to speak as one of authority.

Tom and his friend watched the aircraft for some time, and then started off in a long flight, attaining a high speed, which, at first, made Mr. Damon gasp, until he became used to it. He was no novice at flying, and had even operated aeroplanes himself, though at no great height.

Suddenly the Hawk seemed to falter, almost as does a bird stricken by a hunter's gun. The craft seemed to hang in the air, losing motion as though about to plunge to earth unguided.

"What's the matter?" cried Mr. Damon.

"One of the control wires broken!" was Tom's laconic answer. "I'll have to volplane down. Sit tight, there's no danger!"

Mr. Damon knew that with so competent a pilot as Tom Swift in the forward seat this was true, but, nevertheless, he was a bit nervous until he felt the smooth, gliding motion, with now and then an upward tilt, which showed that Tom was coming down from the upper regions in a series of long glides. The engine had stopped, and the cessation of the thundering noise made it possible for Tom and his passenger to talk without the use of the speaking tube.

"All right?" asked Mr. Damon.

"All right," Tom answered, and a little later the machine was rolling gently over the turf of a large field, a mile or so from the camp.

Before Tom and Mr. Damon could get out of their seats, a man, seemingly springing up from some hollow in the ground, walked toward them.

"Had an accident?" he asked, in what he evidently meant for a friendly voice.

"A little one, easily mended," Tom answered.

He was about to take off his goggles, but at sight of the man's face a change came over the countenance of Tom Swift, and he replaced the eye protectors. Then Tom turned to Mr. Damon, as if to ask a question, but the stranger came so close, evidently curious to see the aircraft at close quarters, that the young inventor could not speak without being overheard.

Tom got out his kit of tools to repair the broken control, and the man watched him curiously. As he tinkered away, something was stirring among the past memories of the inventor. A question he asked himself over and over again was:

"Where have I seen this man before? His face is familiar, but I can't place him. He is associated with something unpleasant. But where have I seen this man before?"

Tom's Indifference

"Did you make this machine yourself?" asked the stranger of Tom, as the young inventor worked at the damaged part of his craft.

Mr. Damon had also alighted, taken off his goggles, and was looking aloft, where the army aircraft were going through various evolutions, and down below, where the young soldiers were drilling under such conditions, as far as possible, as they might meet with when some of their number went "over the top." Mr. Damon was murmuring to himself such remarks as:

"Bless my fountain pen! look at that chap turning upside down! Bless my inkwell!"

"I beg your pardon," remarked Tom Swift, following the remark of the man, whose face he was trying to recall. It was not that Tom had not heard the question, but he was trying to gain time before answering.

"I asked if you made this machine yourself," went on the man, as he peered about at the Hawk. "It isn't like any I've ever seen before, and I know something about airships. It has some new wrinkles on it, and I thought you might have evolved them yourself. Not that it's an amateur affair, by any means!" he added hastily, as if fearing the young inventor might resent the implication that his machine was a home-made product

"Yes, I originated this," answered Tom, as he put a new turn-buckle in place; "but I didn't actually construct it— that is, except for some small parts. It was made in the shop—"

"Over at the army construction plant, I presume," interrupted the man quickly, as he motioned toward the big factory, not far from Shopton, where aircraft for Uncle Sam's Army were being turned out by the hundreds.

"Might as well let him think that," mused Tom; "at least until I can figure out who he is and what he wants."

"This is different from most of those up there," and the stranger pointed toward the circling craft on high. "A bit more speedy, I guess, isn't it?"

"Well, yes, in a way," agreed Tom, who was lending over his craft. He stole a side look at the man. The face was becoming more and more familiar, yet something about it puzzled Tom Swift.

"I've seen him before, and yet he didn't look like that," thought the young inventor. "It's different, somehow. Now why should my memory play me a trick like this? Who in the world can he be?"

Tom straightened up, and tossed a monkey wrench into the tool box.

"Get everything fixed?" asked the stranger.

"I think so," and the young inventor tried to make his answer pleasant. "It was only a small break, easily fixed."

"Then you'll be on your way again?"

"Yes. Are you ready?" called Tom to Mr. Damon.

"Bless my timetable, yes! I didn't think you'd start back again so soon. There's one young fellow up there who has looped the loop three times, and I expect him to fall any minute."

"Oh, I guess he knows his business," Tom said easily. "We'll be getting back now."

"One moment!" called the man. "I beg your pardon for troubling you, but you seem to be a mechanic, and that's just the sort of man I'm looking for. Are you open to an offer to do some inventive and constructive work?"

Tom was on his guard instantly.

"Well, I can't say that I am," he answered. "I am pretty busy—"

"This would pay well," went on the man eagerly. "I am a stranger around here, but I can furnish satisfactory references. I am in need of a good mechanic, an inventor as well, who can do what you seem to have done so well. I had hopes of getting some one at the army plant"

"I guess they're not letting any of their men go," said Tom, as Mr. Damon climbed to his seat in the Hawk.

"No, I soon found that out. But I thought perhaps you—"

Tom shook his head.

"I'm sorry," he answered, "but I'm otherwise engaged, and very busy."

"One moment!" called the man, as he saw Tom about to start "Is the Swift Company plant far from here?"

Tom felt something like a thrill go through him. There was an unexpected note in the man's voice. The face of the young inventor lightened, and the doubts melted away.

"No, it isn't far," Tom answered, shouting to be heard above the crackling bangs of the motor. And then, as the craft soared into the air, he cried exultingly:

"I have it! I know who he is! The scoundrel! His beard fooled me, and he probably didn't know me with these goggles on. But now I know him!"

"Bless my calendar!" cried Mr. Damon. "What are you talking about?"

But Tom did not answer, for the reason that just then the Hawk fell into an "air pocket," and needed all his attention to straighten her out and get her on a level course again.

And while Tom Swift is thus engaged in speeding his aircraft along the upper regions toward his home, it will take but a few moments to acquaint my new readers with something of the history of the young inventor. Those who have read the previous books in this series need be told nothing about our hero.

Tom Swift was an inventor of note, as was his father. Mr. Swift was now quite aged and not in robust health, but he was active at times and often aided Tom when some knotty point came up.

Tom and his father lived on the outskirts of the town of Shopton, and near their home were various buildings in which the different machines and appliances were made. Tom's mother was dead, but Mrs. Baggert, the housekeeper, was as careful in looking after Tom and his father as any woman could be.

In addition to these three, the household consisted of Eradicate Sampson, an aged colored servant, and, it might almost be added, his mule Boomerang; but Boomerang had manners that, at times, did not make him a welcome addition to any household. Then there was the giant Koku, one of two big men Tom had brought back with him from the land where the young inventor had been held captive for a time.

The first book of this series is called "Tom Swift and His Motor Cycle," and it was in acquiring possession of that machine that Tom met his friend Mr. Wakefield Damon, who lived in a neighboring town. Mr. Damon owned the motor cycle originally, but when it attempted to climb a tree with him he sold it to Tom.

Tom had many adventures on the machine, and it started him on his inventive career. From then on he had had a series of surprising adventures. He had traveled in his motor boat, in an airship, and then had taken to a submarine. In his electric runabout he showed what the speediest car on the road Could do, and when he sent his wireless message, the details of which can be found set down in the volume of that name, Tom saved the castaways of Earthquake Island.

Tom Swift had many other thrilling escapes, one from among the diamond makers, and another from the caves of ice; and he made the quickest flight on record in his sky racer.

Tom's wizard camera, his great searchlight, his giant cannon, his photo telephone, his aerial warship and the big tunnel he helped to dig, brought him credit, fame, and not a little money. He had not long been back from an expedition to Honduras, dubbed "the land of wonders," when he was again busy en some of his many ideas. And it was to get some relief from his thoughts that he had taken the flight with Mr. Damon on the day the present story opens.

"What are you so excited about, Tom?" asked his friend, as the Hawk alighted near the shed hack of the young inventor's home. "Bless my scarf pin! but any one would think you'd just discovered the true method of squaring the circle."

"Well, it's almost as good as that, and more practical," Tom said, with a smile, as he motioned to Koku to put away the aircraft "I know who that man is, now."

"What man, Tom?"

"The one who was questioning me when I was fixing the airship. I kept puzzling and puzzling as to his identity, and, all at once, it came to me. Do you know who he is, Mr. Damon?"

"No, I can't say that I do, Tom. But, as you say, there was something vaguely familiar about him. It seemed as if I must have seen him before, and yet—"

"That's just the way it struck me. What would you say if I told you that man was Blakeson, of Blakeson and Grinder, the rival tunnel contractors who made such trouble for us?"

"You mean down in Peru, Tom?"

"Yes."

Mr. Damon started in surprise, and then exclaimed:

"Bless my ear mufflers, Tom, but you're right! That was Blakeson! I didn't know him with his beard, but that was Blakeson, all right! Bless my foot-warmer! What do you suppose he is doing around here?"

"I don't know, Mr. Damon, but I'd give a good deal to know. It isn't any good, I'll wager on that. He didn't seem to know me or you, either—unless he did and didn't let on. I suppose it was because of my goggles—and you were gazing up in the air most of the time. I don't think he knew either of us."

"It didn't seem so, Tom. But what is he doing here? Do you think he is working at the army camp, or helping make Liberty Motors for the aircraft that are going to beat the Germans?"

"Hardly. He didn't seem to be connected with the camp. He wanted a mechanic, and hinted that I might do. Jove! if he really didn't know who I was, and finds out, say! won't he be surprised?"

"Rather," agreed Mr Damon. "Well, Tom, I had a nice little ride. And now I must be getting back. But if you contemplate a trip anywhere, don't forget to let me know."

"I don't count on going anywhere soon," Tom answered. "I have something on hand that will occupy all my time, though I don't just like it. However, I'm going to do my best," and he waved good-bye to Mr. Damon, who went off blessing various parts of his anatomy or clothing, an odd habit he had.

As Tom turned to go into the house, the unsettled look still on his face, some one hailed him.

"I say, Tom. Hello! Wait a minute! I've got something to show you!"

"Oh, hello, Ned Newton!" Called back the young inventor. "Well, if it's Liberty Bonds, you don't need to show me any, for dad and I will buy all we can without seeing them."

"I know that, Tom, and it was a dandy subscription you gave me. I didn't come about that, though I may be around the next time Uncle Sam wants the people to dig down in their socks. This is something different," and Ned Newton, a young banker of Shopton and a lifelong friend of Tom's, drew a paper from his pocket as he advanced across the lawn.

"There, Tom Swift!" he cried, flipping out an illustrated page, evidently from some illustrated newspaper. "There's the very latest from the other side. A London banker friend of mine sent it to me, and it got past the censor all right. It's the first authentic photograph of the newest and biggest British tank. Isn't that a wonder?"

Ned held up the paper which had in it a fullpage photograph of a monster tank—those weird machines traveling on endless steel belts of caterpillar construction, armored, riveted and plated, with machine guns bristling here and there.

"Isn't that great, Tom? Can you beat it? It's the most wonderful machine of the age, even counting some of yours. Can you beat it?"

Tom took the paper indifferently, and his manner surprised his chum.

"Well, what's the matter, Tom?" asked Ned. "Don't you think that great? Why don't you say something? You don't mean to say you've seen that picture before?"

"No, Ned."

"Then what's the matter with you? Isn't that wonderful?"

NED IS WORRIED

Tom Swift did not answer for several seconds. He stood holding the paper Ned had given him, the sun slanting on the picture of the big British tank. But the young inventor did not appear to see it. Instead, his eyes were as though contemplating something afar off.

"Well, this gets me!" cried Ned, his voice showing impatience. "Here I go and get a picture of the latest machine the British armies are smashing up the Boches with, and bring it to you fresh from the mail—I even quit my Liberty Bond business to do it, and I know some dandy prospects, too—and here you look at it like a—like a fish!" burst out Ned.

"Say, old man, I guess that's right!" admitted Tom. "I wasn't thinking about it, to tell you the truth."

"Why not?" Ned demanded. "Isn't it great, Tom? Did you ever see anything like it?"

"Yes."

"You did?" Cried Ned, in surprise. "Where? Say, Tom Swift, are you keeping something from me?"

"I mean no, Ned. I never have seen a British tank."

"Well, did you ever see a picture like this before?" Ned persisted.

"No, not exactly like that But—"

"Well, what do you think of it?" cried the young banker, who was giving much of his time to selling bonds for the Government. "Isn't it great?"

Tom considered a moment before replying. Then he said slowly:

"Well, yes, Ned, it is a pretty good machine. But—"

"But!' Howling tomcats! Say, what's the 'matter with you, anyhow, Tom? This is great! 'But!' 'But me no buts!' This is, without exception, the greatest thing out since an airship. It will win the war for us and the Allies, too, and don't you forget it! Fritz's barbed wire and dugouts and machine gun emplacements can't stand for a minute against these tanks! Why, Tom, they can crawl on their back as well as any other way, and they don't mind a shower of shrapnel or a burst of machine gun lead, any more than an alligator minds a swarm of gnats. The only thing that makes 'em hesitate a bit is a Jack Johnson or a Bertha shell, and it's got to be a pretty big one, and in the right place, to do much damage. These tanks are great, and there's nothing like 'em."

"Oh, yes there is, Ned!"

"There is!" cried Ned. "What do you mean?"

"I mean there may be something like them—soon."

"There may? Say, Tom—"

"Now don't ask me a lot of questions, Ned, for I can't answer them. When I say there may be something like them, I mean it isn't beyond the realms of possibility that some one—perhaps the Germans—may turn out even bigger and better tanks."

"Oh!" And Ned's voice showed his disappointment. "I thought maybe you were in on that game yourself, Tom. Say, couldn't you get up something almost as good as this?" and he indicated the picture in the paper. "Isn't that wonderful?"

"Oh, well, it's good, Ned, but there are others. Yes, Dad, I'm coming," he called, as he saw his father beckoning to him from a distant building.

"Well, I've got to get along," said Ned. "But I certainly am disappointed, Tom. I thought you'd go into a fit over this picture—it's one of the first allowed to get out of England, my London friend said. And instead of enthusing you're as cold as a clam;" and Ned shook his head in puzzled and disappointed fashion as he walked slowly along beside the young inventor.

They passed a new building, one of the largest in the group of the many comprising the Swift plant. Ned looked at the door which bore a notice to the effect that no one was admitted unless bearing a special permit, or accompanied by Mr. Swift or Tom.

"What's this, Tom?" asked Ned. "Some new wrinkle?"

"Yes, an invention I'm working on. It isn't in shape yet to be seen."

"It must be something big, Tom," observed Ned, as he viewed the large building.

"It is."

"And say, what a whopping big fence you've got around the back yard!" went on the young banker. "Looks like a baseball field, but it would take some scrambling on the part of a back-lots kid to get over it."

"That's what it's for—to keep people out."

"I see! Well, I've got to get along. I'm a bit back in my day's quota of selling Liberty Bonds, and I've got to hustle. I'm sorry I bothered you about that tank picture, Tom."

"Oh, it wasn't a bother—don't think that for a minute, Ned! I was glad to see it."

"Well, he didn't seem so, and his manner was certainly queer," mused Ned, as he walked away, and turned in time to see Tom enter the new building, which had such a high fence all around it "I never saw him more indifferent. I wonder if Tom isn't interested in seeing Uncle Sam help win this war? That's the way it struck me. I thought surely Tom would go up in the air, and say this was a dandy," and Ned unfolded the paper and took another look at the British tank photograph. "If there's anything can beat that I'd like to see it," he mused.

"But I suppose Tom has discovered some new kind of air stabilizer, or a different kind of carburetor that will vaporize kerosene as well as gasolene. If he has, why doesn't he offer it to Uncle Sam? I wonder if Tom is pro-German? No, of Course he can't be!" and Ned laughed at his own idea.

"At the same time, it is queer," he mused on. "There is something wrong with Tom Swift."

Once more Ned looked at the picture. It was a representation of one of the newest and largest of the British tanks. In appearance these are not unlike great tanks, though they are neither round nor square, being shaped, in fact, like two wedges with the broad ends put together, and the sharper ends sticking out, though there is no sharpness to a tank, the "noses" both being blunt.

Around each outer edge runs an endless belt of steel plates, hinged together, with ridges at the joints, and these broad belts of steel plates, like the platforms of some moving stairways used in department stores, moving around, give motion to the tank.

Inside, well protected from the fire of enemy guns by steel plates, are the engines for driving the belts, or caterpillar wheels, as they are called. There is also the steering apparatus, and the guns that fire on the enemy. There are cramped living and sleeping quarters for the tank's crew, more limited than those of a submarine.

The tank is ponderous, the smallest of them, which were those first constructed, weighing forty-two tons, or about as much as a good-sized railroad freight car. And it is this ponderosity, with its slow but resistless movement, that gives the tank its power.

The tank, by means of the endless belts of steel plates, can travel over the roughest country. It can butt into a tree, a stone wall, or a house, knock over the obstruction, mount it, crawl over it, and slide down into a hole on the other side and crawl out again, on the level, or at an angle. Even if overturned, the tanks can sometimes right themselves and keep on. At the rear are trailer wheels, partly used in steering and partly for reaching over gaps or getting out of holes. The tanks can turn in their own length, by moving one belt in one direction and the other oppositely.

Inside there is nothing much but machinery of the gasolene type, and the machine guns. The tank is closed except for small openings out of which the guns project, and slots through which the men inside look out to guide themselves or direct their fire.

Such, in brief, is a British tank, one of the most powerful and effective weapons yet loosed against the Germans. They are useful in tearing down the barbed-wire entanglements on the Boche side of No Man's Land, and they can clear the way up to and past the trenches, which they can straddle and wriggle across like some giant worm.

"And to think that Tom Swift didn't enthuse over these!" murmured Ned. "I wonder what's the matter with him!"

QUEER DOINGS

There was a subdued air of activity about the Swift plant. Subdued, owing to the fact that it was mostly confined to one building—the new, large one, about which stretched a high and strong fence, made with tongue-and-groove boards so that no prying eyes might find a crack, even, through which to peer.

In and out of the other buildings the workmen went as they pleased, though there were not many of them, for Tom and his father were devoting most of their time and energies to what was taking place in the big, new structure. But here there was an entirely different procedure.

Workmen went in and out, to be sure, but each time they emerged they were scrutinized carefully, and when they went in they had to exhibit their passes to a man on guard at the single entrance; and the passes were not scrutinized perfunctorily, either.

Near the building, about which there seemed to be an air of mystery, one day, a week after the events narrated in the opening chapters, strolled the giant Koku. Not far away, raking up a pile of refuse, was Eradicate Sampson, the aged colored man of all work. Eradicate approached nearer and nearer the entrance to the building, pursuing his task of gathering up leaves, dirt and sticks with the teeth of his rake. Then Koku, who had been lounging on a bench in the shade of a tree, Called:

"No more, Eradicate!"

"No mo' whut?" asked the negro quickly. "I didn't axt yo' fo' nuffin yit!"

"No more come here!" said the giant, pointing to the building and speaking English with an evident effort. "Master say no one come too close."

"Huh! He didn't go fo' t' mean me!" exclaimed Eradicate. "I kin go anywheres; I kin!"

"Not here!" and Koku interposed his giant frame between the old man and the first step leading into the secret building. "You no come in here."

"Who say so?"

"Me—I say so! I on guard. I what you call special policeman—detectiff—no let enemies in!"

"Huh! You's a hot deteckertiff, yo' is!" snorted Eradicate. "Anyhow, dem orders don't mean me! I kin go anywhere, I kin!"

"Not here!" said Koku firmly. "Master Tom say let nobody come near but workmen who have got writing-paper. You no got!"

"No, but I kin git one, an' I's gwine t' hab it soon! I'll see Massa Tom, dat's whut I will. I guess yo' ain't de only deteckertiff on de place. I kin go on guard, too!" and Eradicate, dropping his rake, strolled away in his temper to seek the young inventor.

"Well, Rad, what is it?" asked Tom, as he met the colored man. The young inventor was on his way to the mysterious shop. "What is troubling you?"

"It's dat dar giant. He done says as how he's on guard—a deteckertiff—an' I can't go nigh dat buildin' t' sweep up de refuse."

"Well, that's right, Rad. I'd prefer that you keep away. I'm doing some special work in there and it's—"

"Am it dangerous, Massa Tom? I ain't askeered! Anybody whut kin drive mah mule Boomerang—"

"I know, Eradicate, but this isn't so dangerous. It's just secret, and I don't want too many people about. You can go anywhere else except there. Koku is on guard."

"Den can't I be, Massa Tom?" asked the colored man eagerly. "I kin guard an' detect same as dat low-down, good-fo'-nuffin white trash Koku!"

Tom hesitated.

"I suppose I could get you a sort of officer's badge," he mused, half aloud.

"Dat's whut I want!" eagerly exclaimed Eradicate. "I ain't gwine hab dat Koku—dat cocoanut—crowin' ober me! I kin guard an' detect as good's anybody!"

And the upshot of it was that Eradicate was given a badge, and put on a special post, far enough from Koku to keep the two from quarreling, and where, even if he failed in keeping a proper lookout, the old servant could do no harm by his oversight

"It'll please him, and won't hurt us," said Tom to his father. "Koku will keep out any prying persons."

"I suppose you are doing well to keep it a secret, Tom," said Mr. Swift, "but it seems as if you might announce it soon."

"Perhaps we may, Dad, if all goes well. I've given her a partial shop-tryout, and she works well. But there is still plenty to do. Did I tell you about meeting Blakeson?"

"Yes, and I can't understand why he should be in this vicinity. Do you think he has had any intimation of what you are doing?"

"It's hard to say, and yet I would not be surprised. When Uncle Sam couldn't keep secret the fact of our first soldiers sailing for France. How can I expect to keep this secret? But they won't get any details until I'm ready, I'm sure of that."

"Koku is a good discourager," said Mr. Swift, with a chuckle. "You couldn't have a better guard, Tom."

"No, and if I can keep him and Eradicate from trying to pull off rival detective stunts, or 'deteckertiff,' as Rad calls it, I'll be all right. Now let's have another go at that carburetor. There's our weak point, for it's getting harder and harder all the while to get high-grade gasolene, and we'll have to come to alcohol of low proof, or kerosene, I'm thinking."

"I wouldn't be surprised, Tom. Well, perhaps we can get up a new style of carburetor that will do the trick. Now look at this needle valve; I've given it a new turn," and father and son went into technical details connected with their latest invention.

These were busy days at the Swift plant. Men came and went—men with queerly shaped parcels frequently—and they were admitted to the big new building after first passing Eradicate and then Koku, and it would be hard to say which guard was the more careful. Only, of course, Koku had the final decision, and more than one person was turned back after Eradicate had passed him, much to the disgust of the negro.

"Pooh! Dat giant don't know a workman when he sees 'im!" snorted Eradicate. "He so lazy his own se'f dat he don't know a workman! Ef I sees a spy, Massa Tom, or a crook, I's gwine git him, suah pop!"

"I hope you do, Rad. We can't afford to let this secret get out," said the young inventor.

It was one evening, when taking a short cut to his home, that Mr. Nestor. the father of Mary Nestor, in whom Tom was more than ordinarily interested, passed not far from the big enclosure which was guarded, on the factory side, day and night. Inside, though out of sight and hidden by the high fence, were other guards.

As Mr. Nestor passed along the fence, rather vaguely wondering why it was so high, tight and strong, he felt the ground trembling beneath his feet. It rumbled and shook as though a distant train were passing, and yet there was none due now, for Mr. Nestor had just left one, and another would not arrive for an hour.

"That's queer," mused Mary's father. "If I didn't know to the contrary, I'd say that sounded like heavy guns being fired from a distance, or else blasting. It seems to come from the Swift place," he went on. "I wonder what they're up to in there."

Suddenly the rumbling became more pronounced, and mingled with it, in the dusk of the evening, were the shouts of men.

"Look out!" some one cried. "She's going for the fence!"

A second later there was a cracking and straining of boards, and the fence near Mr. Nestor bulged out as though something big, powerful and mighty were pressing it from the inner side.

But the fence held, or else the pressure was removed, for the bulge went back into place, though some of the boards were splintered.

"Have to patch that up in the morning," called another voice, and Mr. Nestor recognized it as that of Tom Swift.

"What queer doings are going on here?" mused Mary's father. "Have they got a wild bull shut up in there, and is he trying to get out? Lucky for me he didn't," and he hurried on, the rumbling noise become fainter until it died away altogether.

That night, after his supper and while reading the paper and smoking a cigar, Mr. Nestor spoke to his daughter.

"Mary, have you seen anything of Tom Swift lately?"

"Why, yes, Father. He was over for a little while the other night, but he didn't stay long. Why do you ask?"

"Oh, nothing special. I just came past his place and I heard some queer noises, that's all. He's up to some more of his tricks, I guess. Has be enlisted yet?"

"No.

"Is he going to?"

"I don't know," and Mary seemed a bit put out by this simple question. "What do you mean by his tricks?" she asked, and a close observer might have thought she was anxious to get away from the subject of Tom's enlistment.

"Oh, like that one when he sent you something in a box labeled 'dynamite,' and gave us all a scare. You can't tell what Tom Swift is going to do next. He's up to something now, I'll wager, and I don't believe any good will come of it"

"You didn't think so after he sent his wireless message, and saved us from Earthquake Island," said Mary, smiling.

"Hum! Well, that was different," snapped Mr. Nestor. "This time I'm sure he's up to some nonsense! The idea of crashing down a fence! Why doesn't he enlist like the other chaps, or sell Liberty Bonds like Ned Newton?" and Mr. Nestor looked sharply at his daughter. "Ned gave up a big salary as the Swifts financial man—a place he had held for a year—to go back to the bank for less, just so he could help the Government in the financial end of this war. Is Tom doing as much for his country?"

"I'm sure I don't know," answered Mary; and soon after, with averted face, she left the room.

"Hum! Queer goings on," mused Mr. Nestor. "Tom Swift may be all right, but he's got an unbalanced streak in him that will bear looking out for, that's what I think!"

And having settled this matter, at least to his own satisfaction, Mr. Nestor resumed his smoking and reading.

A little later the bell rang. There was a murmur of voices in the hall, and Mr. Nestor, half listening, heard a voice he knew.

"There's Tom Swift now!" he exclaimed. "I'm going to find out why he doesn't enlist!"

"Is He a Slacker?"

Mr. Nestor, whatever else he was, proved to be a prudent father. He did not immediately go into the front room, whither Mary and Tom hastened, their voices mingling in talk and laughter.

Mr. Nestor, after leaving the young folks alone for a while, with a loud "Ahem!" and a rattling of his paper as he laid it aside, started for the parlor.

"Good-evening, Mr. Nestor!" said Tom, rising to shake hands with the father of his young and pretty hostess.

"Hello, Tom!" was the cordial greeting, in return. "What's going on up at your place?" went on Mr. Nestor, as he took a chair.

"Oh, nothing very special," Tom answered. "We're turning out different kinds of machines as usual, and dad and I are experimenting, also as usual"

"I suppose so. But what nearly broke the fence tonight?"

Tom started, and looked quickly at his host.

"Were you there?" he asked quickly.

"Well, I happened to be passing—took a short cut home— and I heard some queer goings on at your place. I was speaking to Mary about them, and wondering—"

"Father, perhaps Tom doesn't want to talk about his inventions," interrupted Mary. "You know some of them are secret—"

"Oh, I wasn't exactly asking for information!" exclaimed Mr. Nestor quickly. "I just happened to hear the fence crash, and I was wondering if something was coming out at me. Didn't know but what that giant of yours was on a rampage, Tom," and he laughed.

"No, it wasn't anything like that," and Tom's voice was more sober than the occasion seemed to warrant. "It was one of our new machines, and it didn't act just right. No great damage was done, though. How do you find business, Mr. Nestor, since the war spirit has grown stronger?" asked Tom, and it seemed to both Mary and her father that the young inventor deliberately changed the subject.

"Well, it isn't all it might be," said the other. "It's hard to get good help. A lot of our boys enlisted, and some were taken in the draft. By the way, Tom, have they called on you yet?"

"No. Not yet"

"You didn't enlist?"

"Ned Newton tried to," broke in Mary, "but the quota for this locality was filled, and they told him he'd better wait for the draft. He wouldn't do that and tried again. Then the bank people heard about it and had him exempted. They said he was too valuable to them, and he has been doing remarkably well in selling Liberty Bonds!" and Mary's eyes sparkled with her emotions.

"Yes, Ned is a crackerjack salesman!" agreed Tom, no less enthusiastically. "He's sold more bonds, in proportion, for his bank, than any other in this county. Dad and I both took some, and have promised him more. I am glad now that we let him go, although we valued his services highly. We hope to have him back later."

"He can put me down for more bonds too!" said Mr. Nestor. "I'm going to see Germany beaten if it takes every last dollar I have!"

"That's what I say!" Cried Mary. "I took out all my savings, except a little I'm keeping to buy a wedding present for Jennie Morse. Did you know she was going to get married, Tom?" she asked.

"I heard so."

"Well, all but what I want for a wedding present to her has gone into Liberty Bonds. Isn't this a history-making time, Tom?"

"Indeed it is, Mary!"

"Everybody who has a part in it—whether he fights as a soldier or only knits like the Red Cross girls—will be telling about it for years after," went on the girl, and she looked at Tom eagerly.

"Yes," he agreed. "These are queer times. We don't know exactly where we're at. A lot of our men have been called. We tried to have some of them exempted, and did manage it in a few cases."

"You did?" cried Mr. Nestor, as if in surprise. "You stopped men from going to war!"

"Only so they could work on airship motors for the Government," Tom quietly explained.

"Oh! Well, of course, that's part of the game," agreed Mary's father. "A lot more of our boys are going off next week. Doesn't it make you thrill, Tom, when you see them marching off, even if they haven't their uniforms yet? Jove, if I wasn't too old, I'd go in a minute!"

"Father!" cried Mary.

"Yes, I would!" he declared. "The German government has got to be beaten, and we've got to do our bit; everybody has—man, woman and child!"

"Yes," agreed Tom, in a low voice, "that's very true. But every one, in a sense, has to judge for himself what the 'bit' is. We can't all do the same."

There was a little silence, and then Mary went over to the piano and played. It was a rather welcome relief, under the circumstances, from the conversation.

"Mary, what do you think of Tom?" asked Mr. Nestor, when the visitor had gone.

"What do I think of him?" And she blushed.

"I mean about his not enlisting. Do you think he's a slacker?"

"A slacker? Why, Father!"

"Oh, I don't mean he's afraid. We've seen proof enough of his courage, and all that. But I mean don't you think he wants stirring up a bit?"

"He is going to Washington to-morrow, Father. He told me so tonight. And it may be—"

"Oh. well, then maybe it's all right," hastily said Mr. Nestor. "He may he going to get a commission in the engineer corps. It isn't like Tom Swift to hang back, and yet it does begin to look as though he cared more for his queer inventions—machines that butt down fences than for helping Uncle Sam. But I'll reserve judgment."

"You'd better, Father!" and Mary laughed—a little. Yet there was a worried look on her face.

During the next few nights Mr. Nestor made it a habit to take the short cut from the railroad station, coming past the big fence that enclosed one particular building of the Swift plant.

"I wonder if there's a hole where I could look through," said Mr. Nestor to himself. "Of course I don't believe in spying on what another man is doing, and yet I'm too good a friend of Tom's to want to see him make a fool of himself. He ought to be in the army, or helping Uncle Sam in some way. And yet if he spends all his time on some foolish contraption, like a new kind of traction plow, what good is that? If I could get a glimpse of it, I might drop a friendly hint in his ear."

But there were no cracks in the fence, or, if there were, it was too dark to see them, and also too dark to behold anything on the other side of the barrier. So Mr. Nestor, wondering much, kept on his way.

It was a day or so after this that Ned Newton paid a visit to the Swift home. Mr. Swift was not in the house, being out in one of the various buildings, Mrs. Baggert said.

"Where's Tom?" asked the bond salesman.

"Oh, he hasn't come back from Washington yet," answered the housekeeper.

"He is making a long stay."

"Yes, be went about a week ago on some business. But we expect him back today."

"Well, then I'll see him. I called to ask if Mr. Swift didn't want to take a few more bonds. We want to double our allotment for Shopton. and beat out some of the other towns in this section. I'll go to see Mr. Swift."

On his way to find Tom's father Ned passed the big building in front of which Eradicate and Koku were on guard. They nodded to Ned, who passed them, wondering much as to what it was Tom was so secretive about.

"It's the first time I remember when he worked on an invention without telling me something about it," mused Ned. "Well, I suppose it will all come out in good time. Anything new, Rad?"

"No, Massa Ned, nuffin much. I'm detectin' around heah; keepin' Dutchmen spies away!"

"And Koku is helping you, I suppose?"

"Whut, him? Dat big, good-fo'-nuffin white trash? No, sah! I's detectin' by mahse'f, dat's whut I is!" and Eradicate strutted proudly up and down on his allotted part of the beat, being careful not to approach the building too closely, for that was Koku's ground.

Ned smiled, and passed on. He found Mr. Swift, secured his subscription to more bonds, and was about to leave when he heard a call down the road and saw Tom coming in his small racing car, which had been taken to the depot by one of the workmen.

"Hello, old man!" cried Ned affectionately, as his chum alighted with a jump. "Where have you been?"

"Down to Washington. Had a bit of a chat with the President and gave him some of my views."

"About the war, I suppose?" laughed Ned.

"Yes."

"Did you get your commission?"

"Commission?" And there was a wondering look on Tom's face.

"Yes. Mary Nestor said she thought maybe you were going to Washington to take an examination for the engineering corps or something like that. Did you get made an officer?"

"No," answered Tom slowly. "I went to Washington to get exempted."

"Exempted?" Cried Ned, and his voice sounded strained.

SEEING THINGS

For a moment Tom Swift looked at his chum. Then something of what was passing in the mind of the young bond salesman must have been reflected to Tom, for he said

"Look here, old man; I know it may seem a bit strange to go to all that trouble to get exempted from the draft, to which I am eligible, but, believe me, there's a reason. I can't say anything now, but I'll tell you as soon as I can— tell everybody, in fact Just now it isn't in shape to talk about."

"Oh, that's all right, Tom," and Ned tried to make his voice sound natural. "I was just wondering, that's all. I wanted to go to the front the worst way, but they wouldn't let me. I was sort of hoping you could, and come back to tell me about it."

"I may yet, Ned."

"You may? Why, I thought—"

"Oh, I'm only exempted for a time. I've got certain things to do, and I couldn't do 'em if I enlisted or was drafted. So I've been excused for a time. Now I've got a pile of work to do. What are you up to Ned? Same old story?"

"Liberty Bonds—yes. Your father just took some more."

"And so will I, Ned. I can do that, anyhow, even if I don't enlist. Put me down for another two thousand dollars' worth."

"Say, Tom, that's fine! That will make my share bigger than I counted on. Shopton will beat the record."

"That's good. We ought to pull strong and hearty for our home town. How's everything else?"

"Oh, so-so. I see Koku and Eradicate trying to outdo one another in guarding that part of your plant," and Ned nodded toward the big new building.

"Yes, I had to let Rad play detective. Not that he can do anything—he's too old. But it keeps him and Koku from quarreling all the while. I've got to be pretty careful about that shop. It's got a secret in it that— Well, the less said about it the better."

"You're getting my curiosity aroused, Tom," remarked Ned.

"It'll have to go unsatisfied for a while. Wait a bit and I'll give you a ride. I've got to go over to Sackett on business, and if you're going that way I'll take you."

"What in?"

"The Hawk."

"That's me!" cried Ned. "I haven't been in an aircraft for some time."

"Tell Miles to run her out," requested Tom. "I've got to go in and say hello to dad a minute, and then I'll be with you."

"Seems like something was in the wind, Tom —big doings?" hinted Ned.

"Yes, maybe there is. It all depends on how she turns out"

"You might be speaking of the Hawk or—Mary Nestor!" said Ned, with a sidelong look at his chum.

"As it happens, it's neither one," said Tom, and then he hastened away, to return shortly and guide his fleet little airship, the Hawk, on her aerial journey.

From then on, at least for some time, neither Tom nor Ned mentioned the matters they had been discussing—Tom's failure to enlist, his exemption, and what was being built in the closely guarded shop.

Tom's business in Sackett did not take him long, and then he and Ned went for a little ride in the air.

"It's like old times!" exclaimed Ned, his eyes shining, though Tom could not see them for two reasons. One was that Ned was sitting behind him, and the other was that Ned wore heavy goggles, as did the young pilot. Also, they had to carry on their talk through the speaking tube arrangement

"Yes, it is a bit like old times," agreed Tom. "We've had some great old experiences together, Ned, haven't we?"

"We surely have! I wonder if we'll have any more? When we were in the submarine, and in your big airship Say, that big one is the one I always liked! I like big things."

"Do you?" asked Tom. "Well, maybe, when I get—"

But Tom did not finish, for the Hawk unexpectedly poked her nose into an empty pocket in the air just then, and needed a firm hand on the controls. Furthermore, Tom decided against making the confidence that was on the tip of his tongue.

At last the aircraft was straightened out and the pilot guided her on toward the army encampment

"That's the place I'd like to be," called Ned through the tube as the faint, sweet notes of a bugle floated up from the parade ground.

"Yes, it would be great," admitted Tom. "But there are other things to do for Uncle Sam besides wearing khaki."

"Tom's up to some game," mused Ned. "I mustn't judge him too hastily, or I might make a mistake. And Mary mustn't, either. I'll tell her so."

For Mary Nestor had spoken to Ned concerning Tom, and the curiously secretive air about certain of his activities. And the girl, moreover, had spoken rather coldly of her friend. Ned did not like this. It was not like Mary and Tom to be at odds.

Once more the Hawk came to the ground, this time near the airship sheds adjoining the Swift works. Just as Tom and Ned alighted, one of the workmen summoned the young inventor toward the shop, which was so closely guarded by Koku and Eradicate on the outside.

"I'll have to leave you, Ned," remarked Tom, as he turned away from his chum. "There's a conference on about a new invention."

"Oh, that's all right. Business is business, you know. I've got some bond calls to make myself. I'll see you later."

"Oh, by the way, Ned!" exclaimed Tom, turning back for a moment, "I met an old friend the other day; or rather an old enemy."

"Hum! When you spoke first, I thought you might mean Professor Swyington Bumper, that delightful scientist," remarked Ned. "But he surely was no enemy."

"No; but I meant some one I met about the same time. I met Blakeson, one of the rival contractors when I helped dig the big tunnel."

"Is that so? Where'd you meet him?"

"Right around here. It was certainly a surprise, and at first I couldn't place him. Then the memory of his face came back to me," and Tom related the incident which had taken place the day he and Mr. Damon were out in the Hawk.

"What's he doing around here?" asked Ned.

"That's more than I can say," Tom answered.

"Up to no good, I'll wager!"

"I agree with you," came from Tom. "But I'm on the watch."

"That's wise, Tom. Well, I'll see you later."

During the week which followed this talk Ned was very busy on Liberty Bond work, and, he made no doubt, his chum was engaged also. This prevented them from meeting, but finally Ned, one evening, decided to walk over to the Swift home.

"I'll pay Tom a bit of a call," he mused. "Maybe he'll feel more like talking now. Some of the boys are asking why he doesn't enlist, and maybe if I tell him that he'll make some explanation that will quiet things down a bit. It's a shame that Tom should be talked about."

With this intention in view, Ned kept on toward his chum's house, and he was about to turn in through a small grove of trees, which would lead to a path across the fields, when the young bond salesman was surprised to hear some one running toward him. He could see no one, for the path wound in and out among the trees, but the noise was plain.

"Some one in a hurry," mused Ned.

A moment later he caught sight of a small lad named Harry Telford running toward him. The boy had his hat in his hand, and was speeding through the fast-gathering darkness as though some one were after him.

"What's the rush?" asked Ned. "Playing cops and robbers?" That was a game Tom and Ned had enjoyed in their younger days.

"I—I'm runnin' away!" panted Harry. "I—I seen something!"

"You saw something?" repeated Ned. "What was it—a ghost?" and he laughed, thinking the boy would do the same.

"No, it wasn't no ghost!" declared Harry, casting a look over his shoulder. "It was a wild elephant that I saw, and it's down in a big yard with a fence around it."

"Where's that?" asked Ned. "The circus hasn't come to town this evening, has it?"

"No," answered Harry, "it wasn't no circus. I saw this elephant down in the big yard back of one of Mr. Swift's factories."

"Oh, down there, was it!" exclaimed Ned. "What was it like?"

"Well, I was walking along the top of the hill," explained Harry, "and there's one place where, if you climb a tree, you can look right down in the big fenced-in yard. I guess I'm about the only one that knows about it."

"I don't believe Tom does," mused Ned, "or he'd have had that tree cut down. He doesn't want any spying, I take it. Well, what'd you see?" he asked Harry aloud.

"Saw an elephant, I tell you!", insisted the younger boy. "I was in the tree, looking down, for a lot of us kids has tried to peek through the fence and couldn't I wanted to see what was there."

"And did you?" asked Ned.

"I sure did! And it scared me, too," admitted Harry. "All at once, when I was lookin', I saw the big doors at the back of the shed open, and the elephant waddled out."

"Are you sure you weren't 'seeing things,' like the little boy in the story?" asked Ned.

"Well, I sure did see something!" insisted Harry. "It was a great big gray thing, bigger'n any elephant I ever saw in any circus. It didn't seem to have any tail or trunk, or even legs, but it went slow, just like an elephant does, and it shook the ground, it stepped so hard!"

"Nonsense!" cried Ned.

"Sure I saw it!" cried Harry. "Anyhow," he added, after a moment's thought, "it was as big as an elephant, though not like any I ever saw."

"What did it do?" asked Ned.

"Well, it moved around and then it started for the fence nearest me, where I was up in the tree. I thought it might have seen me, even though it was gettin' dark, and it might bust through; so I ran!"

"Hum! Well, you surely were seeing things," murmured Ned, but, while he made light of what the boy told him, the young bank Clerk was thinking: "What is Tom up to now?"

Up a Tree

"Want to come and have a look?" asked Harry, as Ned paused in the patch of woods, which were in deeper darkness than the rest of the countryside, for night was fast falling.

"Have a look at what?" asked Ned, who was thinking many thoughts just then.

"At the elephant I saw back of the Swift factory. I wouldn't be skeered if you came along."

"Well, I'm going over to see Tom Swift, anyhow," answered Ned, "so I'll walk that way. You can come if you like. I don't care about spying on other people's property—"

"I wasn't spyin'!" exclaimed Harry quickly. "I just happened to look. And then I seen something."

"Well, come on," suggested Ned. "If there's anything there, we'll have a peep at it."

His idea was not to try to see what Tom was evidently endeavoring to conceal, but it was to observe whence Harry had made his observation, and be in a position to tell Tom to guard against unexpected lookers-on from that direction.

During the walk back along the course over which Harry had run so rapidly a little while before, Ned and the boy talked of what the latter had seen.

"Do you think it could be some new kind of elephant?" asked Harry. "You know Tom Swift brought back a big giant from one of his trips, and maybe he's got a bigger elephant than any one ever saw before."

"Nonsense!" laughed Ned. "In the first place, Tom hasn't been on any trip, of late, except to Washington, and the only kind of elephants there are white ones."

"Really?" asked Harry.

"No, that was a joke," explained Ned. "Anyhow, Tom hasn't any giant elephants concealed up his sleeve, I'm sure of that."

"But what could this be?" asked Harry. "It moved just like some big animal."

"Probably some piece of machinery Tom was having carted from one shop to another," went on the young bank clerk. "Most likely he had it covered with a big piece of canvas to keep off the dew, and it was that you saw."

"No, it wasn't!" insisted Harry, but he could not give any further details of what he had seen so that Ned could recognize it. They kept on until they reached the hill, at the bottom of which was the Swift home and the grounds on which the various shops were erected.

"Here's the place where you can look down right into the yard with the high fence around it," explained Harry, as he indicated the spot.

"I can't see anything."

"You have to climb up the tree," Harry went on. "Here, this is the one, and he indicated a stunted and gnarled pine, the green branches of which would effectually screen any one who once got in it a few feet above the ground.

"Well, I may as well have a look," decided Ned. "It can't do Tom any harm, and it may be of some service to him. Here goes!"

Up into the tree he scrambled, not without some difficulty, for the branches were close together and stiff, and Ned tore his coat in the effort. But he finally got a position where, to his surprise, he could look down into the very enclosure from which Tom was so particular to keep prying eyes.

"You can see right down in it!" Ned exclaimed.

"I told you so," returned Harry. "But do you see—it?"

Ned looked long and carefully. It was lighter, now that they were out of the clump of woods, and he had the advantage of having the last glow of the sunset at his back. Even with that it was difficult to make out objects on the surface of the enclosed field some hundred or more feet below.

"Do you see anything?" asked Harry again.

"No, I can't say I do," Ned answered. "The place seems to be deserted."

"Well, there was something there," insisted Harry. "Maybe you aren't lookin' at the right place."

"Have a look yourself, then," suggested Ned, as he got down, a task no more to his liking than the climb upward had been.

Harry made easier work of it, being smaller and more used to climbing trees, a luxury Ned had, perforce, denied himself since going to work in the bank.

Harry peered about, and then, with a sigh that had in it somewhat of disappointment, said:

"No; there's nothing there now. But I did see something."

"Are you sure?" asked Ned.

"Positive!" asserted the other.

"Well, whatever it was—some bit of machinery he was moving, I fancy—Tom has taken it in now," remarked Ned. "Better not say anything about this, Harry. Tom mightn't like it known."

"No, I won't."

"And don't come here again to look. I know you like to see strange things, but if you'll wait I'll ask Tom, as soon as it's ready, to let you have a closer view of whatever it was you saw. Better keep away from this tree."

"I will," promised the younger lad. "But I'd like to know what it was—if it really was a giant elephant Say! if a fellow had a troop of them he could have a lot of fun with 'em, couldn't he?"

"How?" asked Ned, hardly conscious of what his companion was saying.

"Why, he could dress 'em up in coats of mail, like the old knights used to wear, and turn 'em loose against the Germans. Think of a regiment of elephants, wearin' armor plates like a battleship, carryin' on their backs a lot of soldiers with machine guns and chargin' against Fritz! Cracky, that would be a sight!"

"I should say so!" agreed Ned, with a laugh. "There's nothing the matter with your imagination, Harry, my boy!"

"And maybe that's what Tom's doin'!"

"What do you mean?"

"I mean maybe he is trainin' elephants to fight in the war. You know he made an aerial warship, so why couldn't he have a lot of armor plated elephants?"

"Oh, I suppose he could if he wanted to," admitted Ned. "But I guess he isn't doing that. Don't get to going too fast in high speed, Harry, or you may have nightmare. Well, I'm going down to see Tom."

"And you won't tell him I was peekin'?"

"Not if you don't do it again. I'll advise him to have that tree cut down, though. It's too good a vantage spot."

Harry turned and went in the direction of his home, while Ned kept on down the hill toward the house of his chum. The young bond salesman was thinking of many things as he tramped, along, and among them was the information Harry had just given.

But Ned did not pay a visit to his chum that evening. When he reached the house he found that Tom had gone out, leaving no word as to when he would be back.

"Oh, well, I can tell him to-morrow," thought Ned.

It was not, however, until two days later that Ned found the time to visit Tom again. On this occasion, as before, he took the road through the clump of woods where he had seen Harry running.

"And while I'm about it," mused Ned, "I may as well go on to the place where the tree stands and make sure, by daylight, what I only partially surmised in the evening— that Tom's place can be looked down on from that vantage point."

Sauntering slowly along, for he was in no special hurry, having the remainder of the day to himself, Ned approached the hill where the tree stood from which Harry had said he had seen what he took to be a giant elephant, perhaps in armor.

"It's a good clear day," observed Ned, "and fine for seeing. I wonder if I'll be able to see anything."

It was necessary first to ascend the hill to a point where it overhung, in a measure, the Swift property, though the holdings of Tom and his father were some distance beyond the eminence. The tree from which Ned and Harry had made their observations was on a knob of the hill, the stunted pine standing out from among others like it

"Well, here goes for another torn coat," grimly observed Ned, as he prepared to climb. "But I'll be more careful. First, though, let's see if I can see anything without getting up."

He paused a little way from the pine, and peered down the hill. Nothing could be seen of the big enclosed field back of the building about which Tom Was so careful.

"You have to be up to see anything," mused Ned. "It's up a tree for me! Well, here goes!"

As Ned started to work his way up among the thick, green branches, he became aware, suddenly and somewhat to his surprise, that he was not the only person who knew about the observation spot. For Ned saw, a yard above his head, as he started to climb, two feet, encased in well-made boots, standing on a limb near the trunk of the tree.

"Oh, ho!" mused Ned. "Some one here before me! Where there are feet there must be legs, and where there are legs, most likely a body. And it isn't Harry, either! The feet are too big for that. I wonder—"

But Ned's musings were suddenly cut short, for the person up the tree ahead of him moved quickly and stepped on Ned's fingers, with no light tread.

"Ouch!" exclaimed the young bank clerk involuntarily, and, letting go his hold of the limb, he dropped to the ground, while there came a startled exclamation from the screen of pine branches above him.

DETECTIVE RAD

"Who's there?" came the demand from the unseen person in the tree.

"I might ask you the same thing," was Ned's sharp retort, as he nursed his skinned and bruised fingers. "What are you doing up there?"

There was no answer, but a sound among the branches indicated that the person up the tree was coming down. In another moment a man leaped to the ground lightly and stood beside Ned. The lad observed that the stranger was clean shaven, except for a small moustache which curled up at the ends slightly.

"For all the world like a small edition of the Kaiser's," Ned described it afterward.

"What are you doing here?" demanded the man, and his voice had in it the ring of authority. It was this very quality that made Ned bristle up and "get on his ear," as he said later. The young clerk did not object to being spoken to authoritatively by those who had the right, but from a stranger it was different

"I might ask you the same thing," retorted Ned. "I have as much right here as you, I fancy, and I can climb trees, too, but I don't care to have my fingers stepped on," and he looked at the scarified members of his left hand.

"I beg your pardon. I'm sorry if I hurt you. I didn't mean to. And of course this is a public place, in a way, and you have a right here. I was just climbing the tree to—er—to get a fishing pole!"

Ned had all he could do to keep from laughing. The idea of getting a fishing pole from a gnarled and stunted pine struck him as being altogether novel and absurd. Yet it was not time to make fun of the man. The latter looked too serious for that.

"Rather a good view to be had from up where you were, eh?" asked Ned suggestively.

"A good view?" exclaimed the other. "I don't know what you mean!"

"Oh, then you didn't see anything," Ned went on. "Perhaps it's just as well. Are you fond of fishing?"

"Very. I have— But I forget, I do not know you nor you me. Allow me to introduce myself. I am Mr. Walter Simpson, and I am here on a visit I just happened to walk out this way, and, seeing a small stream, thought I should like to fish. I usually carry lines and hooks, and all I needed was the pole. I was looking for it when I heard you, and—"

"I felt you!" interrupted Ned, with a short laugh. He told his own name, but that was all, and seemed about to pass on.

"Are there any locomotive shops around here?" asked Mr. Simpson.

"Locomotive shops?" queried Ned. "None that I know of. Why?"

"Well, I heard heavy machinery being used down there;" and he waved his hand toward Tom's shops, "and I thought—"

"Oh, you mean Shopton!" exclaimed Ned. "That's the Swift plant. No, they don't make locomotives, though they could if they wanted to, for they turn out airships, submarines, tunnel diggers, and I don't know what."

"Do they make munitions there—for the Allies?" asked Mr. Simpson, and there was an eager look on his face.

"No, I don't believe so," Ned answered; "though, in fact, I don't know enough of the place to be in a position to give you any information about it," he told the man, not deeming it wise to go into particulars.

Perhaps the man felt this, as he did not press for an answer.

The two stood looking at one another for some little time, and then the man, with a bow that had in it something of insolence, as well as politeness, turned and went down the path up which Ned had come.

The young bank clerk waited a little while, and then turned his attention to the tree which seemed to have suddenly assumed an importance altogether out of proportion to its size.

"Well, since I'm here I'll have a look up that tree," decided Ned.

Favoring his bruised hand, Ned essayed the ascent of the tree more successfully this time. As he rose up among the branches he found he could look down directly into the yard with the high fence about it. He could see only a portion, good as his vantage point was, and that portion had in it a few workmen—nothing else.

"No elephants there," said Ned, with a smile, as he remembered Harry's excitement. "Still it's just as well for Tom to know that his place can be looked down on. I'll go and tell him."

As Ned descended the tree he caught a glimpse, off to one side among some bushes, of something moving.

"I wonder if that's my Simp friend, playing I spy?" mused Ned. "Guess I'd better have a look."

He worked his way carefully close to the spot where he had seen the movement. Proceeding then with more caution, watching each step and parting the bushes with a careful hand, Ned beheld what he expected.

There was the late occupant of the pine tree the man who had stepped on Ned's fingers, applying a small telescope to his eye and gazing in the direction of Tom Swift's home.

The man stood concealed in a screen of bushes with his back toward Ned, and seemed oblivious to his surroundings. He moved the glass to and fro, and seemed eagerly intent on discovering something.

"Though what he can see of Tom's place from there isn't much," mused Ned. "I've tried it myself, and I know; you have to be on an elevation to look down. Still it shows he's after something, all right. Guess I'll throw a little scare into him."

As yet, Ned believed himself unobserved, and that his presence was not suspected was proved a moment later when he shouted:

"Hey! What are you doing there?"

He had his eye on the partially concealed man, and the latter. as Ned said afterward, jumped fully two feet in the air, dropping his telescope as he did so, and turning to face the lad.

"Oh, it's you, is it?" he faltered.

"No one else;" and Ned grinned. "Looking for a good place to fish, I presume?"

Then, at least for once, the man's suave manner dropped from him as if it had been a mask. He bared his teeth in a snarl as he answered:

"Mind your own business!"

"Something I'd advise you also to do," replied Ned smoothly. "You can't see anything from there," he went on. "Better go back to the tree and—cut a fishing pole!"

With this parting shot Ned sauntered down the hill, and swung around to make his way toward Tom's home. He paid no further attention to the man, save to determine, by listening, that the fellow was searching among the bushes for the dropped telescope.

The young inventor was at home, taking a hasty lunch which Mrs. Baggert had set out for him, the while he poured over some blueprint drawings that, to Ned's unaccustomed eyes, looked like the mazes of some intricate puzzle.

"Well, where have you been keeping yourself, old man?" asked Tom Swift, after he had greeted his friend.

"I might ask the same of you," retorted Ned, with a smile. "I've been trying to find you to give you some important information, and I made up my mind, after what happened today, to write it and leave it for you if I didn't see you."

"What happened today?" asked Tom, and there was a serious look on his face.

"You are being spied upon—at least, that part of your works enclosed in the new fence is," replied Ned.

"You don't mean it!" Cried Tom. "This accounts for some of it, then."

"For some of what?" asked Ned.

"For some of the actions of that Blakeson, He's been hanging around here, I understand, asking too many questions about things that I'm trying to keep secret—even from my best friends," and as Tom said this Ned fancied there was a note of regret in his voice.

"Yes, you are keeping some things secret, Tom," said Ned, determined "to take the bull by the horns," as it were.

"I'm sorry, but it has to be," went on Tom. "In a little while

"Oh, don't think that I'm at all anxious to know things!" broke in Ned. "I was thinking of some one else, Tom—another of your friends."

"Do you mean Mary?"

Ned nodded.

"She feels rather keenly your lack of explanations," went on the young bank clerk. "If you could only give her a hint

"I'm sorry, but it can't be done," and Tom spoke firmly. "But you haven't told me all that happened. You say I am being spied upon."

"Yes," and Ned related what had taken place in the tree.

"Whew!" whistled Tom. "That's going some with a vengeance! I must have that tree down in a jiffy. I didn't imagine there was a spot where the yard could be overlooked. But I evidently skipped that tree. Fortunately it's on land owned by a concern with which I have some connection, and I can have it chopped down without any trouble. Much obliged to you, Ned. I shan't forget this in a hurry. I'll go right away and—"

Tom's further remark was interrupted by the hurried entrance of Eradicate Sampson. The old man was smiling in pleased anticipation, evidently, at the same time, trying hard not to give way to too much emotion.

"I's done it, Massa Tom!" he cried exultingly.

"Done what?" asked the young inventor. "I hope you and Koku haven't had another row."

"No, sah! I don't want nuffin t' do wif dat ornery, low-down white trash! But I's gone an' done whut I said I'd do!"

"What's that, Rad? Come on, tell us! Don't keep us in suspense."

"I's done some deteckertiff wuk, lest laik I said I'd do, an' I's cotched him! By golly, Massa Tom! I's cotched him black-handed, as it says!"

"Caught him? Whom have you caught, Rad?" cried Tom. "Do you suppose he means he's caught the man you saw up the tree, Ned? The man you think is a German spy?"

"It couldn't be. I left him only a little while ago hunting for his telescope."

"Then whom have you caught, Rad?" cried Tom. "Come on, I'll give you credit for it. Tell us!"

"I's cotched dat Dutch Sauerkrauter, dat's who I's cotched, Massa Tom! By golly, I's cotched him!"

"But who, Rad? Who is he?"

"I don't know his name, Massa Tom, but he's a Sauerkrauter, all right. Dat's whut he eats for lunch, an' dat's why I calls him dat. I's cotched him, an' he's locked up in de stable wif mah mule Boomerang. An' ef he tries t' git out Boomerang'll jest natchully kick him into little pieces—dat's whut Boomerang will do, by golly!"

A NIGHT TEST

"Come on, Ned," said Tom, after a moment or two of silent contemplation of Eradicate. "I don't know what this cheerful camouflager of mine is talking about, but we'll have to go to see, I suppose. You say you have shut some one up in Boomerang's stable, Rad?"

"Yes, sah, Massa Tom, dat's whut I's gone an done."

"And you say he's a German?"

"I don't know as to dat, Massa Tom, but he suah done eat sauerkraut 'mostest ebery meal. Dat's whut I call him—a Sauerkrauter! An' he suah was spyin'."

"How do you know that, Rad?"

"'Cause he done went from his own shop on annuder man's ticket into de secret shop, dat's whut he went an' done!"

"Do you mean to tell me, Rad," went on Tom, "that one of the workmen from another shop entered Number Thirteen on the pass issued in the name of one of the men regularly employed in my new shop?"

"Dat's whut he done, Massa Tom."

"How do you know?"

"'Cause I detected him doin' it. Yo'-all done made me a deteckertiff, an' I detected."

"Go on, Rad."

"Well, sah, Massa Tom, I seen dish yeah Dutchman git a ticket-pass offen one ob de reg'lar men. Den he went in de unlucky place an' stayed fo' a long time. When he come out I jest natchully nabbed him, dat's whut I done, an' I took him to Boomerang's stable."

"How'd you get him to go with you?" asked Ned, for the old colored man was feeble, and most of the men employed at Tom's plant were of a robust type.

"I done fooled him. I said as how I'd lest brought from town in mah mule cart some new sauerkraut, an' he could sample it if he liked. So he went wif me, an' when I got him to de stable I pushed him in and locked de door!"

"Come on!" cried Tom to his chum. "Rad may be right, after all, and one of my workmen may be a German spy, though I've tried to weed them all out.

"However, no matter about that, if he was employed in another shop, he had no right to go into Number Thirteen. That's a violation of rules. But if he's in Rad's ramshackle stable he can easily get out."

"No, sah, dat's whut he can't do!" insisted the colored man.

"Why not?" asked Tom.

"'Cause Boomerang's on guard, an' yo'-all knows how dat mule of mine can use his heels!"

"I know, Rad," went on Tom; "but this fellow will find a way of keeping out of their way. We must hurry."

"Oh, he's safe enough," declared the colored man. "I done tole Koku to stan' guard, too! Dat low-down white trash ob a giant is all right fo' guardin', but he ain't wuff shucks at detectin'!" said Eradicate, with pardonable pride. "By golly, maybe I's too old t' put on guard, but I kin detect, all right!"

"If this proves true, I'll begin to believe you can," replied Tom. "Hop along, Ned!"

Followed by the shuffling and chuckling negro, Tom and Ned went to the rather insecure stable where the mule Boomerang was kept. That is, the stable was insecure from the standpoint of a jail. But the sight of the giant Koku marching up and down in front of the place, armed with a big club, reassured Tom.

"Is he in there, Koku?" asked the young inventor.

"Yes, Master! He try once come out, but he approach his head very close my defense weapon and he go back again."

"I should think he would," laughed Ned, as he noted the giant's club.

"Well, Rad, let's have a look at your prisoner. Open the door, Koku," commanded Tom.

"Better look out," advised Ned. "He may be armed."

"We'll have to take a chance. Besides, I don't believe he is, or he'd have fired at Koku. There isn't much to fear with the giant ready for emergencies. Now we'll see who he is. I can't imagine one of my men turning traitor."

The door was opened and a rather miserable-looking man shuffled out. There was a bloody rag on his head, and he seemed to have made more of an effort to escape than Koku described, for he appeared to have suffered in the ensuing fight.

"Carl Schwen!" exclaimed Tom. "So it was you, was it?"

The German, for such he was, did not answer for a moment He appeared downcast, and as if suffering. Then a change came over him. He straightened up, saluted as a soldier might have done, and a sneering look came into his face. It was succeeded by one of pride as the man exclaimed:

"Yes, it is I! And I tried to do what I tried to do for the Fatherland! I have failed. Now you will have me shot as a spy, I suppose!" he added bitterly.

Tom did not answer directly. He looked keenly at the man, and at last said:

"I am sorry to see this. I knew you were a German, Schwen, but I kept you employed at work that could not, by any possibility, be considered as used against your country. You are a good machinist, and I needed you. But if what I hear about you is true, it is the end."

"It is the end," said the man simply. "I tried and failed. If it had not been for Eradicate—Well, he's smarter than I gave him credit for, that's all!"

The man spoke very good English, with hardly a trace of German accent, but there was no doubt as to his character.

"What will you do with him, Tom?" asked Ned.

"I don't know. I'll have to do a little investigating first. But he must be locked up. Schwen," went on the young inventor, "I'm sorry about this, but I shall have to give you into the custody of a United States marshal. You are not a naturalized citizen, are you?"

The man muttered something in German to the effect that he was not naturalized and was glad of it.

"Then you come under the head of an enemy alien," decided Tom, who understood what was said, "and will have to be interned. I had hoped to avoid this, but it seems it cannot be. I am sorry to lose you, but there are more important matters. Now let's get at the bottom of this."

Schwen was, after a little delay, taken in charge by the proper officer, and then a search was made of his room, for, in common with some of the other workmen, he lived in a boarding house not far from the plant

There, by a perusal of his papers, enough was revealed to show Tom the danger he had escaped.

"And yet I don't know that I have altogether escaped it," he said to Ned, as they talked it over. "There's no telling how long this spy work may have been going on. If he has discovered all the secrets of Shop Thirteen it may be a bad thing for the Allies and—"

"Look out!" warned Ned, with a laugh. "You'll be saying things you don't want to, Tom and not at all in keeping with your former silence."

"That's so," agreed the young inventor, with a sigh. "But if things go right I'll not have to keep silent much longer. I may be able to tell you everything."

"Don't tell me—tell Mary," advised his chum. "She feels your silence more than I do. I know how such things are."

"Well, I'll be able to tell her, too," decided Tom. "That is, if Schwen hasn't spoiled everything. Look here, Ned, these papers show he's been in correspondence with Blakeson and Grinder."

"What about, Tom?"

"I can't tell. The letters are evidently written in code, and I can't translate it offhand. But I'll make another attempt at it. And here's one from a person who signs himself Walter Simpson, but the writing is in German."

"Walter Simpson!" cried Ned. "That's my friend of the tree!"

"It is?" cried Tom. "Then things begin to fit themselves together. Simpson is a spy, and he was probably trying to communicate with Schwen. But the latter didn't get the information he wanted, or, if he did get it, he wasn't able to pass it on to the man in the tree. Eradicate nipped him just in time."

And, so it seemed, the colored man had done. by accident he had discovered that Schwen had prevailed on one of the workmen in Shop 13 to change passes with him. This enabled the German spy to gain admittance to the secret place, which Tom thought was so well guarded. The man who let Schwen take the pass was in the game, too, it appeared, and he was also placed under arrest. But he was a mere tool in the pay of the others, and had no chance to gain valuable information.

A hasty search of Shop 13 did not reveal anything missing, and it was surmised (for Schwen would not talk) that he had not found time to go about and get all that he was after.

Soon after Schwen's arrest the "Spy Tree," as Tom called it, was cut down.

"Eradicate certainly did better than I ever expected he would," declared Tom. "Well, if all goes well, there won't be so much need for secrecy after a day or so. We're going to give her a test, and then—"

"Give who a test?" asked Ned, with a smile.

"You'll soon see," answered Tom, with an answering grin. "I hereby invite you and Mr. Damon to come over to Shop Thirteen day after to-morrow night and then— Well, you'll see what you'll see."

With this Ned had to be content, and he waited anxiously for the appointed time to come.

"I surely will be glad when Tom is more like himself," he mused, as he left his chum. "And i guess Mary will be, too. I wonder if he's going to ask her to the exhibition?"

It developed that Tom had done so, a fact which Ned learned on the morning of the day set for the test.

"Come over about nine o'clock," Tom said to his chum. "I guess it will be dark enough then."

Meanwhile Schwen and Otto Kuhn, the other man involved, had been locked up, and all their papers given into the charge of the United States authorities. A closer guard than ever was kept over No. 13 shop, and some of the workmen, against whom there was a slight suspicion, were transferred.

"Well, we'll see what we shall see," mused Ned on the appointed evening, when a telephone message from Mr. Damon informed the young bank clerk that the eccentric man was coming to call for him before going on to the Swift place.

A RUNAWAY GIANT

"What do you think it's all about, Mr. Damon?"

"I'm sure I don't know, Ned."

The two were at the home of the young bank clerk, preparing to start for the Swift place, it being nearly nine o'clock on the evening named by the youthful inventor.

"Bless my hat-rack!" went on the eccentric man, "but Tom isn't at all like himself of late. He's working on some invention, I know that, but it's all I do know. He hasn't given me a hint of it."

"Nor me, nor any of his friends," added Ned. "And he acts so oddly about enlisting—doesn't want even to speak of it. How he got exempted I don't know, but I do know one thing, and that is Tom Swift is for Uncle Sam first, last and always!"

"Oh, of course!" agreed Mr. Damon. "Well, we'll soon know, I guess. We'd better start, Ned."

"It's useless to try to guess what it is Tom is up to. He has kept his secret well. The nearest any one has come to it was when Harry figured out that Tom had a band of giant elephants which he was fitting with coats of steel armor to go against the Germans," observed Ned, when be and Mr. Damon were on their way.

"Well, that mightn't be so bad," agreed Mr. Damon. "But—um—elephants—and wild giant ones, too! Bless my circus ticket, Ned! do you think we'd better go in that case?"

"Oh, Tom hasn't anything like that!" laughed Ned. "That was only Harry's crazy notion after he saw something big and ungainly careening about the enclosed yard of Shop Thirteen. Hello, there go Mary Nestor and her father!" and Ned pointed to the opposite side of the street where the girl and Mr. Nestor could be seen in the light of a street lamp.

"They're going out to see Tom's secret," said Mr. Damon. "There's plenty of room in my car. Let's ask them to go with us."

"Surely," agreed Ned, and a moment later he and Mary were in the rear seat while Mr. Damon and Mr. Nestor were in the front, Mr. Damon at the wheel, and they were soon speeding down the road.

"I do hope everything will go all right," observed Mary.

"What do you mean?" asked Ned.

"I mean Tom is a little bit anxious about this test."

"Did he tell you what it was to be?"

"No; but when he called to invite father and me to be present he seemed worried. I guess it's a big thing, for he never has acted this way before—not talking about his work."

"That's right," assented Ned. "But the secret will soon be disclosed, I fancy. But how is it you aren't going to the dance with Lieutenant Martin? He told me you had half accepted for tonight."

"I had." And if it had been light enough Ned would have seen Mary blushing. "I was going with him. It's a dance for the benefit of the Red Cross to get money for comfort kits for the soldiers. But when Tom sent word that he'd like to have me present tonight, why—"

"Oh, I see!" broke in Ned, with a little laugh. "'Nough said!"

Mary's blushes were deeper, but the kindly night hid them.

Then they conversed on matters connected with the big war—the selling of Liberty Bonds, the Red Cross work and the Surgical Dressings Committee, in which Mary was the head of a junior league.

"Everybody in Shopton seems to be doing something to help win the war," said Mary, and as there was just then a lull in the talk between her father and Mr. Damon her words sounded clearly.

"Yes, everybody—that is, all but a few," said Mr. Nestor, "and they ought to get busy. There are some young fellows in this town that ought to be wearing khaki, and I don't mean you, Ned Newton. You're doing your bit, all right."

"And so is Tom Swift!" exclaimed Mr. Damon, as if there had been an implied accusation against the young inventor. "I heard, only today, that one of his inventions—a gas helmet that he planned—is in use on the Western front in Europe. Tom gave his patents to the government, and even made a lot of the helmets free to show other factories how to turn them out to advantage."

"He did?" cried Mr. Nestor.

"That's what he did. Talk about doing your bit—"

"I didn't know that," observed Mary's father slowly. "Do you suppose it's a test of another gas helmet that Tom has asked us out to see tonight?"

"I hardly think so," said Ned. "He wouldn't wait until after dark for that This is something big, and Tom must intend to have it out in the open. He probably waited until after sunset so the neighbors wouldn't come out in flocks. There's been a lot of talk about what is going on in Shop Thirteen, especially since the arrest of the German spies, and the least hint that a test is under way would bring out a big crowd."

"I suppose so," agreed Mr. Nestor. "Well, I'm glad to know that Tom is doing something for Uncle Sam, even if it's only helping with gas helmets. Those Germans are barbarians, if ever there were any, and we've got to fight them the same way they fight us! That's the only way to end the war! Now if I had my way, I'd take every German I could lay my hands on—"

"Father, pretzels!" exclaimed Mary.

"Eh? What's that, my dear?"

"I said pretzels!"

"Oh!" and Mr. Nestor's voice lost its sharpness.

"That's my way of quieting father down when he gets too strenuous in his talk about the war," explained Mary. "We agreed that whenever he got excited I was to say 'pretzels' to him, and that would make him remember. We made up our little scheme after he got into an argument with a man on the train and was carried past his station."

"That's right," admitted Mr. Nestor, with a laugh. "But that fellow was the most obstinate, pig-headed Dutchman that ever tackled a plate of pig's knuckles and sauerkraut, and if he had the least grain of common sense he'd—"

"Pretzels!" cried Mary.

"Eh? Oh, yes, my dear. I was forgetting again."

There was a moment of merriment, and then, after the talk had run for a while in other and safer channels, Mr. Damon made the announcement:

"I think we're about there. We'll be at Tom's place when we make the turn and—"

He was interrupted by a low, heavy rumbling.

"What's that?" asked Mr. Nestor.

"It's getting louder—the noise," remarked Mary. "It sounds as if some big body were approaching down the road— the tramp of many feet. Can it be that troops are marching away?"

"Bless my spark plug!" suddenly cried Mr. Damon. "Look!"

They gazed ahead, and there, seen in the glare of the automobile headlights, was an immense, dark body approaching them from across a level field. The rumble and roar became more pronounced and the ground shook as though from an earthquake.

A glaring light shone out from the ponderous moving body, and above the roar and rattle a voice called:

"Out out of the way! We've lost control! Look out!"

"Bless my steering wheel!" gasped Mr. Damon, "that was Tom Swift's voice! But what is he doing in that—thing?"

"It must be his new invention!" exclaimed Ned.

"What is it?" asked Mr. Nestor.

"A giant," ventured Ned. "It's a giant machine of some sort and —"

"And it's running away!" cried Mr. Damon, as he quickly steered his car to one side—and not a moment too soon! An instant later in a cloud of dust, and with a rumble and a roar as of a dozen express trains fused into one, the runaway giant—of what nature they could only guess—flashed and lumbered by, Tom Swift leaning from an opening in the thick' steel side, and shouting something to his friends.

Tom's Tank

"What was it?" gasped Mary, and, to her surprise, she found herself close to Ned, clutching his arm.

"I have an idea, but I'd rather let Tom tell you," he answered.

"But where's it going?" asked Mr. Nestor. "What in the world does Tom Swift mean by inviting us out here to witness a test, and then nearly running us down under a Juggernaut?"

"Oh, there must be some mistake, I'm sure," returned his daughter. "Tom didn't intend this."

"But, bless my insurance policy, look at that thing go! What in the world is it?" cried Mr. Damon.

The "thing" was certainly going. It had careened from the road, tilted itself down into a ditch and gone on across the fields, lights shooting from it in eccentric fashion.

"Maybe we'd better take after it," suggested Mr. Nestor. "If Tom is—"

"There, it's stopping!" cried Ned. "Come on!"

He sprang from the automobile, helped Mary to get out, and then the two, followed by Mr. Damon and Mr. Nestor, made their way across the fields toward the big object where it had come to a stop, the rumbling and roaring ceasing.

Before the little party reached the strange machine—the "runaway giant," as they dubbed it in their excitement—a bright light flashed from it, a light that illuminated their path right up to the monster. And in the glare of this light they saw Tom Swift stepping out through a steel door in the side of the affair.

"Are you all right?" he called to his friends, as they approached.

"All right, as nearly as we can be when we've been almost scared to death, Tom," said Mr. Nestor.

"I'm surely sorry for what happened," Tom answered, with a relieved laugh. "Part of the steering gear broke and I had to guide it by operating the two motors alternately. It can be worked that way, but it takes a little practice to become expert."

"I should say so!" cried Mr. Damon. "But what in the world does it all mean, Tom Swift? You invite us out to see something—"

"And there she is!" interrupted the young inventor. "You saw her a little before I meant you to, and not under exactly the circumstances I had planned. But there she is!" And he turned as though introducing the metallic monster to his friends.

"What is she, Tom?" asked Ned. "Name it!"

"My latest invention, or rather the invention of my father and myself," answered Tom, and his voice showed the love and reverence he felt for his parent. "Perhaps I should say adaptation instead of invention," Tom went on, "since that is what it is. But, at any rate, it's my latest—dad's and mine—and it's the newest, biggest, most improved and powerful fighting tank that's been turned out of any shop, as far as I can learn.

"Ladies—I mean lady and gentlemen—allow me to present to you War Tank A, and may she rumble till the pride of the Boche is brought low and humble!" cried Tom.

"Hurray! That's what I say!" cheered Ned.

"That's what I have been at work on lately. I'll give you a little history of it, and then you may come inside and have a ride home."

"In that?" cried Mr. Damon.

"Yes. I can't promise to move as speedily as your car, but I can make better time than the British tanks. They go about six miles an hour, I understand, and I've got mine geared to ten. That's one improvement dad and I have made."

"Ride in that!" cried Mr. Nestor. "Tom, I like you, and I'm glad to see I've been mistaken about you. You have been doing your bit, after all; but—"

"Oh, I've only begun!" laughed Tom Swift.

"Well, no matter about that. However much I like you," went on Mr. Nestor, "I'd as soon ride on the wings of a thunderbolt as in Tank A, Tom Swift."

"Oh, it isn't as bad as that!" laughed the young scientist. "But neither is it a limousine. However, come inside, anyhow, and I'll tell you something about it. Then I guess we can guide it back. The men are repairing the break."

The visitors entered the great craft through the door by which Tom had emerged. At first all they saw was a small compartment, with walls of heavy steel, some shelves of the same and a seat which folded up against the wall made of like powerful material.

"This is supposed to be the captain's room, where he stays when he directs matters." Tom explained. "The machinery is below and beyond here."

"How'd you come to evolve this?" asked Ned. "I haven't seen half enough of the outside, to say nothing of the inside."

"You'll have time enough," Tom said. "This is my first completed tank. There are some improvements to be made before we send it to the other side to be copied.

"Then they'll make them in England as well as here, and from here we'll ship them in sections."

"I don't see how you ever thought of it!" exclaimed the girl, in wonder.

"Well, I didn't all at once," Tom answered, with a laugh. "It came by degrees. I first got the idea when I heard of the British tanks.

"When I had read how they went into action and what they accomplished against the barbed wire entanglements, and how they crossed the trenches, I concluded that a bigger tank, one capable of more speed, say ten or twelve miles an hour, and one that could cross bigger excavations—the English tanks up to this time can cross a ditch of twelve feet—I thought that, with one made on such specifications, more effective work could be done against the Germans."

"And will yours do that?" asked Ned. "I mean will it do ten miles an hour, and straddle over a wider ditch than twelve feet?"

"It'll do both," promptly answered Tom. "We did a little better than eleven miles an hour a while ago when I yelled to you to get out of the way just now. It's true we weren't under good control, but the speed had nothing to do with that. And as for going over a big ditch, I think we straddled one about fourteen feet across back there, and we can do better when I get my grippers to working."

"Grippers!" exclaimed Mary.

"What kind of trench slang is that, Tom Swift?" asked Mr. Damon.

"Well, that's a new idea I'm going to try out It's something like this," and while from a distant part of the interior of Tank A came the sound of hammering, the young inventor rapidly drew a rough pencil sketch.

It showed the tank in outline, much as appear the pictures of tanks already in service—the former simile of two wedge-shaped pieces of metal put together broad end to broad end, still holding good. From one end of the tank, as Tom drew it, there extended two long arms of latticed steel construction.

"The idea is," said Tom, "to lay these down in front of the tank, by means of cams and levers operated from inside. If we get to a ditch which we can't climb down into and out again, or bridge with the belt caterpillar wheels, we'll use the grippers. They'll be laid down, taking a grip on the far side of the trench, and we'll slide across on them."

"And leave them there?" asked Mr. Damon.

"No, we won't leave them. We'll pick them up after we have passed over them and use them in front again as we need them. A couple of extra pairs of grippers may be carried for emergencies, but I plan to use the same ones over and over again."

"But what makes it go?" asked Mary. "I don't want all the details, Tom," she said, with a smile, "but I'd like to know what makes your tank move."

"I'll be able to show you in a little while," he answered. "But it may be enough now if I tell you that the main power consists of two big gasolene engines, one on either side. They can be geared to operate together or separately. And these engines turn the endless belts made of broad, steel plates, on which the tank travels. The belts pass along the outer edges of the tank longitudinally, and go around cogged wheels at either end of the blunt noses.

"When both belts travel at the same rate of speed the tank goes in a straight line, though it can be steered from side to side by means of a trailer wheel in the rear. Making one belt—one set of caterpillar wheels, you know—go faster than the other will make the tank travel to one side or the other, the turn being in the direction of the slowest moving belt. In this way we can steer when the trailer wheels are broken."

"And what does your tank do except travel along, not minding a hail of bullets?" asked Mr. Nestor.

"Well," answered Tom, "it can do anything any other tank can do, and then some more. It can demolish a good-sized house or heavy wall, break down big trees, and chew up barbed-wire fences as if they were toothpicks. I'll show you all that in due time. Just now, if the repairs are finished, we can get back on the road—"

At that moment a door leading into the compartment where Tom and his friends were talking opened, and one of the workmen said:

"A man outside asking to see you, Mr. Swift."

"Pardon me, but I won't keep you a moment," interrupted a suave voice. "I happened to observe your tank, and I took the liberty of entering to see

"Simpson!" cried Ned Newton, as he recognized the man who had been up the tree. "It's that spy, Simpson, Tom!"

BRIDGING A GAP

Such surprise showed both on the face of Ned Newton and that of the man who called himself Walter Simpson that it would be hard to say which was in the greater degree. For a moment the newcomer stood as if he had received all electric shock, and was incapable of motion. Then, as the echoes of Ned's voice died away and the young bank clerk, being the first to recover from the shock, made a motion toward the unwelcome and uninvited intruder, Simpson exclaimed.

"I will not bother now. Some other time will do as well."

Then, with a haste that could be called nothing less than precipitate, he made a turn and fairly shot out of the door by which he had entered the tank.

"There he goes!" cried Mr. Damon. "Bless my speedometer, but there he goes!"

"I'll stop him!" cried Ned. "We've got to find out more about him! I'll get him, Tom!"

Tom Swift was not one to let a friend rush alone into what might be danger. He realized immediately what his chum meant when he called out the identity of the intruder, and, wishing to clear up some of the mystery of which he became aware when Schwen was arrested and the paper showing a correspondence with this Simpson were found, Tom darted out to try to assist in the capture.

"He went this way!" cried Ned, who was visible in the glare of the searchlight that still played its powerful beams over the stern of the tank, if such an ungainly machine can be said to have a bow and stern. "Over this way!"

"I'm with you!" cried Tom. "See if you can pick up that man who just ran out of here!" he cried to the operator of the searchlight in the elevated observation section of what corresponded to the conning tower of a submarine. This was a sort of lookout box on top of the tank, containing, among other machines, the searchlight. "Pick him up!" cried Tom.

The operator flashed the intense white beam, like a finger of light, around in eccentric circles. but though this brought into vivid relief the configuration of the field and road near which the tank was stalled, it showed no running fugitive. Tom and Ned were observed—shadows of black in the glare—by Mary and her friends in the tank, but there was no one else.

"Come on!" cried Ned. "We can find him, Tom!"

But this was easier said than done. Even though they were aided by the bright light, they caught no glimpse of the man who called himself Simpson.

"Guess he got away," said Tom, when he and Ned had circled about and investigated many clumps of bushes, trees, stumps and other barriers that might conceal the fugitive.

"I guess so," agreed Ned. "Unless he's hiding in what we might call a shell crater."

"Hardly that," and Tom smiled. "Though if all goes well the men who operate this tank later may be searching for men in real shell holes."

"Is this one going to the other side?" asked Ned, as the two walked back toward the tank.

"I hope it will be the first of my new machines on the Western front," Tom answered. "But I've still got to perfect it in some details and then take it apart. After that, if it comes up to expectations, we'll begin making them in quantities."

"Did you get him?" asked Mr. Damon eagerly, as the two young men came back to join Mary and her friends.

"No, he got away," Tom answered.

"Did he try to blow up the tank?" asked Mr. Nestor, who had an abnormal fear of explosives. "Was he a German spy?"

"I think he's that, all right," said Ned grimly. "As to his endeavoring to blow up Tom's tank, I believe him capable of it, though he didn't try it tonight—unless he's planted a time bomb somewhere about, Tom."

"Hardly, I guess," answered the young inventor. "He didn't have a chance to do that. Anyhow we won't remain here long. Now, Ned, what about this chap? Is he really the one you saw up in the tree?"

"I not only saw him but I felt him," answered Ned, with a rueful look at his fingers. "He stepped right on me. And when he came inside the tank tonight I knew him at once. I guess he was as surprised to see me as I was to see him."

"But what was his object?" asked Mr. Nestor.

"He must have some connection with my old enemy, Blakeson," answered Tom, "and we know he's mixed up with Schwen. From the looks of him I should say that this Simpson, as he calls himself, is the directing head of the whole business. He looks to be the moneyed man, and the brains of the plotters. Blakeson is smart, in a mechanical way, and Schwen is one of the best machinists I've ever employed. But this Simpson strikes me as being the slick one of the trio."

"But what made him come here, and what did he want?" asked Mary. "Dear me! it's like one of those moving picture plots, only I never saw one with a tank in it before—I mean a tank like yours, Tom."

"Yes, it is a bit like moving picture—especially chasing Simpson by searchlight," agreed the young inventor. "As to what he wanted, I suppose he came to spy out some of my secret inventions—dad's and mine. He's probably been hiding and sneaking around the works ever since we arrested Schwen. Some of my men have reported seeing strangers about, but I have kept Shop Thirteen well guarded.

"However, this fellow may have been waiting outside, and he may have followed the tank when we started off a little while ago for the night test. Then, when he saw our mishap and noticed that we were stalled, he came in, boldly enough, thinking, I suppose, that, as I had never seen him, he would take a chance on getting as much information as he could in a hurry."

"But he didn't count on Ned's being here!" chuckled Mr. Damon.

"No; that's where he slipped a cog," remarked Mr. Nestor. "Well, Tom, I like your tank, what I've seen of her, but it's getting late and I think Mary and I had better be getting back home."

"We'll be ready to start in a little while," Tom said, after a brief consultation with one of his men. "Still, perhaps it would be just as well if you didn't ride back with me. She may go all right, and then, again, she may not. And as it's dark, and we're in a rough part of the field, you might be a bit shaken up. Not that the tank minds it!" the young inventor hastened to add "She's got to do her bit over worse places than this—much worse—but I want to get her in a little better working shape first. So if you don't mind, Mary, I'll postpone your initial trip."

"Oh, I don't mind, Tom! I'm so glad you've made this! I want to see the war ended, and I think machines like this will help."

"I'll ride back with you, Tom, if you don't mind," put in Ned. "I guess a little shaking up won't hurt me."

"All right—stick. We're going to start very soon."

"Well, I'm coming over to-morrow to have a look at it by daylight," said Mr. Damon, as he started toward his car.

"So am I," added Mary. "Please call for me, Mr. Damon."

"I will," he promised.

Mr. Nestor, his daughter, and Mr. Damon went back to the automobile, while Ned remained with Tom. In a little while those in the car heard once more the rumbling and roaring sound and felt the earth tremble. Then, with a flashing of lights, the big, ungainly shape of the tank lifted herself out of the little ditch in which she had come to a halt, and began to climb back to the road.

Ned Newton stood beside Tom in the control tower of the great tank as she started on her homeward way.

"Isn't it wonderful!" murmured Mary, as she saw Tank A lumbering along toward the road. "Oh, and to think that human beings made that To think that Tom should know how to build such a wonderful machine!"

"And run it, too, Mary! That's the point! Make it run!" cried her father. "I tell you, that Tom Swift is a wonder!"

"Bless my dictionary, he sure is!" agreed Mr. Damon.

Along the road, back toward the shop whence it had emerged, rumbled the tank. The noise brought to their doors inhabitants along the country thoroughfare, and some of them were frightened when they saw Tom Swift's latest war machine, the details of which they could only guess at in the darkness.

"She'll butt over a house if it gets in her path, knock down trees, chew up barbed-wire, and climb down into ravines and out again, and go over a good-sized stream without a whimper," said Tom, as he steered the great machine.

There was little chance then for Ned to see much of the inside mechanism of the tank. He observed that Tom, standing in the forward tower, steered it very easily by a small wheel or by a lever, alternately, and that he communicated with the engine room by means of electric signals.

"And she steers by electricity, too," Tom told his friend. "That was one difficulty with the first tanks. They had to be steered by brute force, so to speak, and it was a terrific strain on the man in the tower. Now I can guide this in two ways: by the electric mechanism which swings the trailer wheels to either side, or by varying the speed of the two motors that work the caterpillar belts. So if one breaks down, I have the other."

"Got any guns aboard her—I mean machine guns?" asked Ned.

"Not yet. But I'm going to install some. I wanted to get the tank in proper working order first. The guns are only incidental, though of course they're vitally necessary when she goes into action. I've got 'em all ready to put in. But first I'm going to try the grippers."

"Oh, you mean the gap-bridgers?" asked Ned.

"That's it," answered Tom. "Look out, we're going over a rough spot now."

And they did. Ned was greatly shaken up, and fairly tossed from side to side of the steering tower. For the tank contained no springs, except such as were installed around the most delicate machinery, and it was like riding in a dump cart over a very rough road.

"However, that's part of the game," Tom observed.

Tank A reached her "harbor" safely—in other words, the machine shop enclosed by the high fence, inside of which she had been built.

Tom and Ned made some inquiries of Koku and Eradicate as to whether or not there had been any unusual sights or sounds about the place. They feared Simpson might have come to the shop to try to get possession of important drawings or data.

But all had been quiet, Koku reported Nor had Eradicate seen or heard anything out of the ordinary.

"Then I guess we'll lock up and turn in," decided Tom. "Come over to-morrow, Ned."

"I will," promised the young bank clerk. "I want to see more of what makes the wheels go round." And he laughed at his own ingenuousness.

The next day Tom showed his friends as much as they cared to see about the workings of the tank. They inspected the powerful gasolene engines, saw how they worked the endless belts made of plates of jointed steel, which, running over sprocket wheels, really gave the tank its power by providing great tractive force.

Any self-propelled vehicle depends for its power, either to move itself or to push or to pull, on its tractive force—that is, the grip it can get on the ground.

In the case of a bicycle little tractive power is needed, and this is provided by the rubber tires, which grip the ground. A locomotive depends for its tractive power on its weight pressing on its driving wheels, and the more driving wheels there are and the heavier the locomotive, the more it can pull, though in that case speed is lost. This is why freight locomotives are so heavy and have so many large driving wheels. They pull the engine along, and the cars also, by their weight pressing on the rails.

The endless steel belts of a tank are, the same as the wheels of a locomotive. And the belts, being very broad, which gives them a large surface with which to press on the ground, and the tank being very heavy, great power to advance is thus obtained, though at the sacrifice of speed. However, Tom Swift had made his tank so that it would do about ten miles and more an hour, nearly double the progress obtained up to that time by the British machines.

His visitors saw the great motors, they inspected the compact but not very attractive living quarters of the crew, for provision had to be made for the men to stay in the tank if, perchance, it became stalled in No Man's Land, surrounded by the enemy.

The tank was powerfully armored and would be armed. There were a number of machine guns to be installed, quick-firers of various types, and in addition the tank could carry a number of riflemen.

It was upon the crushing power of the tank, though, that most reliance was placed. Thus it could lead the way for an infantry advance through the enemy's lines, making nothing of barbed wire that would take an artillery fire of several days to cut to pieces.

"And now, Ned," said Tom, about a week after the night test of the tank, "I'm going to try what she'll do in bridging a gap."

"Have you got her in shape again?"

"Yes, everything is all right. I've taken out the weak part in the steering gear that nearly caused us to run you down, and we're safe in that respect now. And I've got the grippers made. It only remains to see whether they're strong enough to bear the weight of my little baby," and Tom affectionately patted the steel sides of Tank A.

While his men were getting the machine ready for a test out on the road, and for a journey across a small stream not far away, Torn told his chum about conceiving the idea for the tank and carrying it out secretly with the aid of his father and certain workmen.

"That's the reason the government exempted me from enlisting," Tom said. "They wanted me to finish this tank. I didn't exactly want to, but I considered it my 'bit.' After this I'm going into the army, Ned."

"Glad to hear it, old man. Maybe by that time I'll have this Liberty Bond work finished, and I'll go with you. We'll have great times together! Have you heard anything more of Simpson, Blakeson and Scoundrels?" And Ned laughed as he named this "firm."

"No," answered Tom. "I guess we scared off that slick German spy."

Once more the tank lumbered out along the road. It was a mighty engine of war, and inside her rode Tom and Ned. Mary and her father had been invited, but the girl could not quite get her courage to the point of accepting, nor did Mr. Nestor care to go. Mr. Damon, however, as might be guessed, was there.

"Bless my monkey wrench, Tom!" cried the eccentric man, as he noted their advance over some rough ground, "are you really going to make this machine cross Tinkle Creek on a bridge of steel you carry with you?"

"I'm going to try, Mr. Damon."

A little later, after a successful test up and down a small gully, Tank A arrived at the edge of Tinkle Creek, a small stream about twenty feet wide, not far from Tom's home. At the point selected for the test the banks were high and steep.

"If she bridges that gap she'll do anything," murmured Ned, as the tank came to a stop on the edge.

Into a Trench

Tom cast a hasty glance over the mechanism of the machine before he started to cross the stream by the additional aid of the grippers, or spanners, as he sometimes called this latest device.

Along each side, in a row of sockets, were two long girders of steel, latticed like the main supports of a bridge. They were of peculiar triangular construction, designed to support heavy weights, and each end was broadly flanged to prevent its sinking too deeply into the earth on either side of a gully or a stream.

The grippers also had a sort of clawlike arrangement on either end, working on the principle of an "orange-peel" shovel, and these claws were designed to grip the earth to prevent slipping.

The spanners would be pulled out from their sockets on the side of the tank by means of steel cables, which were operated from within. They would be run out across the gap and fastened in place. The tank was designed to travel along them to the other side of the gap, and, once there. to pick tip the girders, slip them back into place on the sides, and the engine of war would travel on.

"You are mightily excited, Tom."

"I admit it, Ned. You see, I have not tried the grippers out except on a small model. They worked there, but whether they will work in practice remains to be seen. Of course, at this stage, I'm willing to stake my all on the results. but there is always a half-question until the final try-out under practical conditions."

"Well, we'll soon see," said one of the workmen. "Are you ready, Mr. Swift?"

"All ready," answered Tom.

Tank A, as she was officially known, had come to a stop, as has been said, on the very edge of Tinkle Creek. The banks were fairly solid here, and descended precipitously to the water ten feet below. The shores were about twenty feet apart.

"Suppose the spanners break when you're halfway over, Tom?" asked his chum.

"I don't like to suppose anything of the sort. But if they do, we're going down!"

"Can you get up again?"

"That remains to be seen," was the non-committal reply. "Well, here goes, anyhow!"

Going up into the observation tower, which was only slightly raised above the roof of the highest part of the tank, Tom gave the signal for the motors to start. There was a trembling throughout the whole of the vast structure. Tom threw back a lever and Ned, peering from a side observation slot, beheld a strange sight.

Like the main arm of some great steam shovel, two long, latticed girders of steel shot out from the sides of the tank. They gave a half turn, as they were pulled forward by the steel ropes, so that they lay with their broader surfaces uppermost.

Straight across the stream they were pulled, their clawlike ends coming to a rest on the opposite bank. Then they were tightened into place by a backward pull on the operating cables, and Tom, with a sigh of relief, announced:

"Well, so far so good!"

"Do we go over now?" inquired Ned.

"Over the top—yes, I hope," answered Tom, with a laugh. "How about you down there?" he called to the engine room through a telephone which could only be used when the machinery was not in action, there being too much noise to permit the use of any but visual signals after that.

"All right," came back the answer. "We're ready when you are."

"Then here we go!" said Tom. "Hold fast, Ned! Of course there's no real telling what will happen, though I believe we'll come out of it alive."

"Cheerful prospect," murmured Ned.

The grippers were now in place. It only remained for the tank to propel herself over them, pick them up on the other side of Tinkle Creek, and proceed on her course.

Tom Swift hesitated a moment, one hand on the starting lever and the other on the steering wheel. Then, with a glance at Ned, half whimsical and half resolute, Tom started Tank A on what might prove to be her last journey.

Slowly the ponderous caterpillar belts moved around on the sprocket wheels. They ground with a clash of steel on the surface of the spanners. So long was the tank that the forward end, or the "nose," was halfway across the stream before the bottom part of the endless belts gripped the latticed bridge.

"If we fall, we'll span the creek, not fall into it," murmured Ned, as he looked from the observation slot.

"That's what I counted on," Tom said. "We'll get out, even if we do fall."

But Tank A was not destined to fall. In another moment her entire weight rested on the novel and transportable bridge Tom Swift had evolved. Then, as the gripping ends of the girders sank farther into the soil, the tank went on her way.

Slowly, at half speed, she crawled over the steel beams, making progress over the creek and as safely above the water as though on a regularly constructed bridge.

On and on she went. Now her entire weight was over the middle of the temporary structures. If they were going to give way at all, it would be at this point But they did not give. The latticed and triangular steel, than which there is no stronger form of construction, held up the immense weight of Tank A, and on this novel bridge she propelled herself across Tinkle Creek.

"Well, the worst is over," remarked Ned, as he saw the nose of the tank project beyond the farthermost bank.

"Yes, even if they collapse now nothing much can happen," Tom answered. "It won't be any worse than wallowing down into a trench and out again. But I think the spanners will hold."

And hold they did! They held, giving way not a fraction of an inch, until the tank was safely across, and then, after a little delay, due to a jamming of one of the recovery cables, the spanners were picked up, slid into the receiving sockets, and the great war engine was ready to proceed again.

"Hurrah!" cried Ned. "She did it, Tom, old man!" and he clapped his chum resoundingly on the back.

"She certainly did!" was the answer. "But you needn't knock me apart telling me that. Go easy!"

"Bless my apple pie!" cried Mr. Damon, who was as much pleased as either of the boys, "this is what I call great!"

"Yes, she did all that I could have hoped for," said Tom. "Now for the next test."

"Bless my collar button! is there another?"

"Just down into a trench and out again." Tom said. "This is comparatively simple. It's only what she'll have to do every day in Flanders."

The tank waddled on. A duck's sidewise walk is about the only kind of motion that can be compared to it. The going was easier now, for it was across a big field, and Tom told his friends that at the other end was a deep, steep and rocky ravine in which he had decided to give the tank another test.

"We'll imagine that ravine is a trench," he said, "and that we've got to get on the other side of it. Of course, we won't be under fire, as the tanks will be at the front, but aside from that the test will be just as severe."

A little later Tank A brought her occupants to the edge of the "trench."

"Now, little girl," cried Tom exultingly, patting the rough steel side of his tank, "show them what you can do!"

"Bless my plum pudding!" cried Mr. Damon, "are you really going down there, Tom Swift?"

"I am," answered the young inventor. "It won't be dangerous. We'll crawl down and crawl out. Hold fast!"

He steered the machine straight for the edge of the ravine, and as the nose slipped over and the broad steel belts bit into the earth the tank tilted downward at a sickening angle.

She appeared to be making the descent safely, when there was a sudden change. The earth seemed to slip out from under the broad caterpillar belts, and then the tank moved more rapidly.

"Tom, we're turning over!" shouted Ned. "We're capsizing!"

THE RUINED FACTORY

Only too true were the words Ned Newton shouted to his chum. Tank A was really capsizing. She had advanced to the edge of the gully and started down it, moving slowly on the caterpillar bands of steel. Then had come a sudden lurch, caused, as they learned afterward, by the slipping off of a great quantity of shale from an underlying shelf of rock.

This made unstable footing for the tank. One side sank lower than the other, and before Tom could neutralize this by speeding up one motor and slowing down the other the tank slowly turned over on its side.

"But she isn't going to stop here!" cried Ned, as he found himself thrown about like a pill in a box. "We're going all the way over!"

"Let her go over!" cried Tom, not that he could stop the tank now. "It won't hurt her. She's built for lust this sort of thing!"

And over Tank A did go. Over and over she rolled, sidewise, tumbling and sliding down the shale sides of the great gully.

"Hold fast! Grab the rings!" cried Tom to his two companions in the tower with him. "That's what they're for!"

Ned and Mr. Damon understood. In fact, the latter had already done as Tom suggested. The young inventor had read that the British tanks frequently turned turtle, and he had this in mind when he made provision in his own for the safety of passengers and crew.

As soon as he felt the tank careening, Tom had pressed the signal ordering the motors stopped, and now only the force of gravity was operating. But that was sufficient to carry the big machine to the bottom of the gulch, whither she slid with a great cloud of sand, shale and dust.

"Bless my—bless my—" Mr. Damon was murmuring, but he was so flopped about, tossed from one side to the other, and it took so much of his attention and strength to hold on to the safety ring, that he could not properly give vent; to one of his favorite expressions.

But there comes an end to all things, even to the descent of a tank, and Tom's big machine soon stopped rolling, sliding, and turning improvised somersaults, and rested in a pile of soft shale at the bottom of the gully. And the tank was resting on her back!

"We've turned turtle!" cried Ned, as he noted that he was standing on what, before, had been the ceiling of the observation tower. But as everything was of steel, and as there was no movable furniture, no great harm was done. In fact, one could as well walk on the ceiling of the tank as on the floor.

"But how are you going to get her right side up?" asked Mr. Damon.

"Oh, turning upside down is only one of the stunts of the game. I can right her," was the answer.

"How?" asked Ned.

"Well, she'll right herself if there's ground enough for the steel belts to get a grip on.

"But can the motors work upside down?"

"They surely can!" responded Tom. "I made 'em that way on purpose. The gasolene feeds by air pressure, and that works standing on its head, as well as any other way. It's going to be a bit awkward for the men to operate the controls, but we won't be this way long. Before I start to right her. though, I want to make sure nothing is broken."

Tom signaled to the engine room, and, as the power was off and the speaking tube could be used, he called through it:

"How are you down there?"

"Right-o!" came back the answer from a little Englishman Tom had hired because he knew something about the British tanks. "'Twas a bit of nastiness for a while, but it won't take us long to get up ag'in."

"That's good!" commented Tom. "I'll come down and have a look at you."

It was no easy matter, with the tank capsized, to get to the main engine room, but Tom Swift managed it. To his delight, aside from a small break in one of the minor machines, which would not interfere with the operation or motive force of the monster war engine, everything was in good shape. There was no leak from the gasolene tanks, which was one of the contingencies Tom feared, and, as he had said, the motors would work upside down as well as right side up, a fact he had proved more than once in his Hawk.

"Well, we'll make a start," he told his chief engineer. "Stand by when I give the signal, and we'll try to crawl out of this right side up."

"How are you going to do it?" asked Ned, as his chum crawled back into the observation tower.

"Well, I'm going to run her part way up the very steepest part of the ravine I can find—the side of a house would do as well if it could stand the strain. I'm going to stand the tank right up on her nose, so to speak, and tip her over so she'll come right again."

Slowly the tank started off, while Tom and his friends in the observation tower anxiously awaited the result of the novel progress. Ned and Mr. Damon clung to the safety rings. Tom put his arm through one and hung on grimly, while he used both hands on the steering apparatus and the controls.

Of course the trailer wheels were useless in a case of this kind, and the tank had to be guided by the two belts run at varying speeds.

"Here we go!" cried Tom, and the tank started. It was a queer sensation to be moving upside down, but it did not last very long. Tom steered the tank straight at the opposite wail of the ravine, where it rose steeply. One of the broad belts ran up on that side. The other was revolved in the opposite direction. Up and up, at a sickening angle, went Tank A.

Slowly the tank careened, turning completely over on her longer axis, until, as Tom shut off the power, he and his friends once more found themselves standing where they belonged—on the floor of the observation tower.

"Right side up with care!" quoted Ned, with a laugh. "Well, that was some stunt—believe me!"

"Bless my corn plaster, I should say so!" cried Mr. Damon.

"Well, I'm glad it happened," commented Tom. "It showed what she can do when she's put to it. Now we'll get out of this ditch."

Slowly the tank lumbered along, proper side up now, the men in the motor room reporting that everything was all right, and that with the exception of a slight unimportant break, no damage had been done.

Straight for the opposite steep side of the gully Tom directed his strange craft, and at a point where the wall of the gulch gave a good footing for the steel belts, Tank A pulled herself out and up to level ground.

"Well, I'm glad that's over," remarked Ned, with a sigh of relief, as the tank waddled along a straight stretch. "And to think of having to do that same thing under heavy fire !"

"That's part of the game," remarked Tom. "And don't forget that we can fire, too—or we'll be able to when I get the guns in place. They'll help to balance the machine better, too, and render her less likely to overturn."

Tom considered the test a satisfactory one and, a little later, guided his tank back to the shop, where men were set to work repairing the little damage done and making some adjustments.

"What's next on the program?" asked Ned of his chum one day about a week later. "Any more tests in view?"

"Yes," answered Tom. "I've got the machine guns in place now. We are going to try them out and also endeavor to demolish a building and some barbed wire. Like to come along?"

"I would!" cried Ned.

A little later the tank was making her way over a field. Tom pointed toward a deserted factory, which had long been partly in ruins, but some of the walls of which still stood.

"I'm going to bombard that," he announced, and then try to batter it down and roll over it like a Juggernaut. Are you game?"

"Do your worst!" laughed Ned. "Let me man one of the machine guns!"

"All right," agreed Tom. "Concentrate your fire. Make believe you're going against the Germans!"

Slowly, but with resistless energy, the tank approached the ruined factory.

"Are you sure there's no one in it, Tom?"

"Sure! Blaze away!"

Across Country

Ned Newton sighted his machine gun. Tom had showed him how to work it, and indeed the young bank clerk had had some practice with a weapon like this, erected on a stationary tripod. But this was the first time Ned had attempted to fire from the tank while it was moving, and he found it an altogether different matter.

"Say, it sure is hard to aim where you want to!" he shouted across to Tom, it being necessary, even in the conning tower, where this one gun was mounted, to speak loudly to make one's self heard above the hum, the roar and rattle of the machinery in the interior of Tank A, and below and to the rear of the two young men.

"Well, that's part of the game," Tom answered. "I'm sending her along over as smooth ground as I can pick out, but it's rough at best. Still this is nothing to what you'll get in Flanders."

"If I get there!" exclaimed Ned grimly. "Well, here goes!" and once more he tried to aim the machine gun at the middle of the brick wall of the ruined factory.

A moment later there was a rattle and a roar as the quick-firing mechanism started, and a veritable hail of bullets swept out at the masonry. Tom and Ned could see where they struck, knocking off bits of stone, brick and cement

"Sweep it, Ned! Sweep it!" cried Tom. "Imagine a crowd of Germans are charging out at you, and sweep 'em out of the way!"

Obeying this command, the young man moved the barrel of the machine gun from side to side and slightly up and down. The effect was at once apparent. The wall showed spatter-marks of the bullets over a wider area, and had a body of Teutons been before the factory, or even inside it, many of them would have been accounted for, since there were several holes in the wall through which Ned's bullets sped, carrying potential death with them.

"That's better!" shouted Tom. "That'll do the business! Now I'm going to open her up, Ned!"

"Open her up?" cried the young bank clerk, as he ceased firing.

"Yes; crack the wall of that factory as I would a nut! Watch me take it on high—that is, if the old tank doesn't go back on me!"

"You mean you're going to ride right over that building, Tom?"

"I mean I'm going to try! If Tank A does as I expect her to, she'll butt into that wall, crush it down by force and weight, and then waddle over the ruins. Watch!"

Tom sent some signals to the motor room. At once there was noticed an increase in the vibrations of the ponderous machine.

"They're giving her more speed," said Tom. "And I guess we'll need it."

Straight for the old factory went Tank A. In spite of its ruined condition, some of the walls were still firm, and seemed to offer a big obstacle to even so powerful an engine of war as this monstrous tank.

"Get ready now, Ned," Tom advised. "And when I crack her open for you cut loose with the machine gun again. This gun is supposed to fire straight ahead and a little to either side. There are other guns at left and right, amidships, as I might say, and there's also one in the stern, to take care of any attack from that direction.

"The men in charge of them will fire at the same time you do, and it will be as near like a real attack as we can make it—with the exception of not being fired back at. And I wouldn't mind if such were the case, for I don't believe anything, outside of heavy artillery, will have any effect on this tank."

Tank A was now almost at her maximum speed as she approached closer to the deserted factory. Ned and Tom, in the conning tower, saw the largest of the remaining walls looming before them. Straight at it rushed the ponderous machine, and the next moment there came a shock which almost threw Ned away from his gun and back against the steel wall behind him.

"Hold fast!" cried Tom. "Here we go! Fire. Ned! Fire!"

There was a crash as the blunt nose of the great war tank hit the wall and crumpled it up.

A great hole was made in the masonry, and what was not crushed under the caterpillar belts of the tank fell in a shower of bricks, stone and cement on top of the machine.

Like a great hail storm the broken masonry pelted the steel sides and top of the tank. But she felt them no more than does an alligator the attacks of a colony of ants. Right on through the dust the tank crushed her way. Added to the noise of the falling walls was that of the machine guns, which were barking away like a kennel of angry hounds eager to be unleashed at the quarry.

Ned kept his gun going until the heat of it warned him to stop and let the barrel cool, or he knew he would jam some of the mechanism. The other guns were firing, too, and the bullets sent up little spatter points of dust as they hit.

"Great jumping hoptoads!" yelled Ned above the riot of racket outside and inside. "Feel her go, Tom!"

"Yes, she's just chewing it up, all right!" cried the young inventor, his eyes shining with delight.

The tank had actually burst her way through the solid wall of the old factory, permission to complete the demolition of which Tom had secured from the owners. Then the great machine kept right on. She fairly "walked" over the piles of masonry, dipped down into what had been a basement, now partly filled with debris, and kept on toward another wall.

"I'm going through that, too!" cried Tom.

And he did, knocking it down and sending his tank over the piled-up ruins, while the machine guns barked, coughed and spluttered, as Ned and the others inside the tank held back the firing levers.

Right through the opposite wall, as through the one she had already demolished, the tank careened on her way, to emerge, rather battered and dust-covered, on the other side of what was left of the factory. And there was not much of it left. Tank A had well-nigh completed its demolition.

"If there'd been a nest of Germans in there," said Tom, as he brought the machine to a stop in a field beyond the factory, "they'd have gotten out in a hurry."

"Or taken the consequences," added Ned, as he wiped the sweat from his powder-blackened and oil-smeared face. "I certainly kept my gun going."

"Yes, and so did the others," reported one of the mechanics, as he emerged from the "cubby hole," where the great motors had now ceased their hum and roar.

"How'd she stand it?" asked Tom.

"All right inside," answered the man. "I was wondering how she looks from the outside."

"Oh, it would take more than that to damage her," said Tom, with pardonable pride. "That was pie for her! Solid concrete, which she may have to chew up on the Western front, may present another kind of problem, but I guess she'll be able to master that too. Well, let's have a look."

He and Ned, with some of the crew and gunners, went outside the tank. She was a sorry-looking sight, very different from the trim appearance she had presented when she first left the shop. Bricks, bits of stone, and piles of broken cement in chunks and dust lay thick on her broad back. But no real damage had been done, as a hasty examination showed.

"Well, are you satisfied, Tom?" asked his chum.

"Yes, and more," was the answer. "Of course this wasn't the hardest test to which she could have been submitted, but it will do to show what punishment she can stand. Being shot at from big guns is another matter. I'll have to wait until she gets to Flanders to see what effect that will have. But I know the kind of armor skin she has, and that doesn't worry me. There's one thing more I want to do while I have her out now."

"What's that?" asked Ned.

"Take her for a long trip cross country, and then shove her through some extra heavy barbed wire. I'm certain she'll chew that up, but I want to see it actually done. So now, if you want to come along, Ned, we'll go cross country."

"I'm with you!"

"Get inside then. We'll let the dust and masonry blow and rattle off as we go along."

The tank started off across the fields, which stretched for many miles on either side of the deserted factory, when suddenly Ned, who was again at his post in the observation tower, called:

"Look, Tom!"

"What at?"

"That corner of the factory which is still standing. Look at those men coming out and running away!"

Ned pointed, and his chum, leaning over from the steering wheel and controls, gave a start of surprise as he saw three figures clambering down over the broken debris and making their way out of what had once been a doorway.

"Did they come out of the factory, Ned?"

"They surely did! And unless I miss my guess they were in it, or around it, when we went through like a fellow carrying the football over the line for a touchdown."

"In there when the tank broke open things?"

"I think so. I didn't see them before, but they certainly ran out as we started away."

"This has got to be looked into!" decided Tom. "Come on, Ned! It may be more of that spy business !"

Tom Swift stopped the tank and prepared to get out.

THE OLD BARN

"There's no use chasing after 'em, Tom," observed Ned, as the two chums stood side by side outside the tank and gazed after the three men running off across the fields as fast as they could go. "They've got too much a start of us."

"I guess you're right, Ned," agreed Tom. "And we can't very well pursue them in the tank. She goes a bit faster than anything of her build, but a running man is more than a match for her in a short distance. If I had the Hawk here, there'd be a different story to tell."

"Well, seeing that you haven't," replied Ned, suppose we let them go—which we'll have to, whether we want to or not—and see where they, were hiding and if they left any traces behind."

"That's a good idea," returned Tom.

The place whence the men had emerged was a portion of the old factory farthest removed from the walls the tank had crunched its way through. Consequently, that part was the least damaged.

Tom and Ned came to what seemed to have been the office of the building when the factory was in operation. A door, from which most of the glass had been broken, hung on one hinge, and, pushing this open, the two chums found themselves in a room that bore evidences of having been the bookkeeper's department. There were the remains of cabinet files, and a broken letter press, while in one corner stood a safe.

"Maybe they were cracking that," said Ned.

"They were wasting their time if they were," observed Tom, "for the combination is broken—any one can open it," and he demonstrated this by swinging back one of the heavy doors.

A quantity of papers fell out, or what had been papers, for they were now torn and the edges charred, as if by some recent fire.

"They were burning these!" cried Ned. "You can smell the smoke yet. They came here to destroy some papers, and we surprised them!"

"I believe you're right," agreed Tom. "The ashes are still warm." And he tested them with his hand. "They wanted to destroy something, and when they found we were here they clapped the blazing stuff into the safe, thinking it would burn there.

"But the closing of the doors cut off the supply of air and the fire smouldered and went out. It burned enough so that it didn't leave us very much in the way of evidence, though," went on Tom ruefully, as he poked among the charred scraps.

"Maybe you can read some of 'em," suggested Ned.

"Part of the writing is in German," Tom said, as he looked over the mass. "I don't believe it would be worth while to try it. Still, I can save it. Here, I'll sweep the stuff into a box, and if we get a chance we can try to patch it together," and finding a broken box in what had been the factory office the young inventor managed to get into it the charred remains of the papers.

A further search failed to reveal anything that would be useful in the way of evidence to determine what object the three men could have had in hiding in the ruins, and Tom and Ned returned to the tank.

"What do you think about them, Tom?" asked Ned, as they were about to start off once more for the cross-country test.

"Well, it seems like a silly thing to say—as if I imagined my tank was all there was in this part of the country to make trouble—but I believe those men had some connection with Simpson and with that spy Schwen!"

"I agree with you!" exclaimed Ned. "And I think if we could get head or tail of those burned papers we'd find that there was some correspondence there between the man I saw up the tree and the workman you had arrested."

"Too bad we weren't a bit quicker," commented Tom. "They must have been in the factory when we charged it—probably came there to be in seclusion while they talked, plotted and planned. They must have been afraid to go out when the tank was walking through the walls."

"I guess that's it," agreed Ned. "Did you recognize any of the men, Tom?"

"No, I didn't see 'em as soon as you did, and when they were running they had their backs toward me. Was Simpson one?"

"I can't be sure. If one was, I guess he'll think we are keeping pretty closely after him, and he may give this part of the country a wide berth."

"I hope he does," returned Tom. "Do you know, Ned, I have an idea that these fellows—Schwen Simpson, and those back of them, including Blakeson—are trying to get hold of the secret of my tank for the Germans."

"I shouldn't be surprised. But you've got it finished now, haven't you? They can't get your patents away from you."

"No, it isn't that," said Tom. "There are certain secrets about the mechanism of the tank—the way I've increased the speed and power, the use of the spanners, and things like that—which would be useful for the Germans to know. I wouldn't want them to find out these secrets, and they could do that if they were in the tank a while, or had her in their possession."

"They couldn't do that, Tom—get possession of her—could they?"

"There's no telling. I'm going to be doubly on the watch. That fellow Blakeson is in the pay of the plotters, I believe. He has a big machine shop, and he might try to duplicate my tank if he knew how she was made inside."

"I see! That's why he was inquiring about a good machinist, I suppose, though he'll be mightily surprised when he learns it was you he was talking to the time your Hawk met with the little mishap."

"Yes, I guess maybe he will be a bit startled," agreed Tom. "But I haven't seen him around lately, and maybe he has given up."

"Don't trust to that!" warned Ned.

The tank was now progressing easily along over fields, hesitating not at small or big ditches, flow going uphill and now down, across a stretch of country thinly settled, where even fences were a rarity. When they came to wooden ones Tom had the workmen get out and take down the bars. Of course the tank could have crushed them like toothpicks, but Tom was mindful of the rights of farmers, and a broken fence might mean strayed cows, or the letting of cattle into a field of grain or corn, to the damage of both cattle and fodder.

"There's a barbed-wire fence," observed Ned, as he pointed to one off some distance across the field. "Why don't you try demolishing that?"

"Oh, it would be too easy! Besides, I don't want the bother of putting it up again. When I make the barbed-wire test I want some set up on heavy posts, and with many strands, as it is in Flanders. Even that won't stop the tank, but I'm anxious to see how she breaks up the wire and supports—just what sort of a breach she makes. But I have a different plan in mind now.

"I'm going to try to find a wooden building we can charge as we did the masonry factory. I want to smash up a barn, and I'll have to pick out an old one for choice, for in these war days we must conserve all we can, even old barns."

"What's the idea of using a barn, Tom?"

"Well, I want to test the tank under all sorts of conditions—the same conditions she'll meet with on the Western front. We've proved that a brick and stone factory is no obstacle."

"Then how could a flimsy wooden barn be?"

"Well, that's just it. I don't think that it will, but it may be that a barn when smashed will get tangled up in the endless steel belts, and clog them so they'll jam. That's the reason I want to try a wooden structure next."

"Do you know where to find one?"

"Yes; about a mile from here is one I've had my eyes on ever since I began constructing the tank. I don't know who owns it, but it's such a ramshackle affair that he can't object to having it knocked into kindling wood for him. If he does holler, I can pay him for the damage done. So now for a barn, Ned, unless you're getting tired and want to go back?"

"I should say not! Speaking of barns, I'm with you till the cows come home! Want any more machine gun work?"

"No, I guess not. This barn isn't particularly isolated, and the shooting might scare horses and cattle. We can smash things up without the guns."

The tank was going on smoothly when suddenly there was a lurch to one side, and the great machine quickly swung about in a circle.

"Hello!" cried Ned. "What's up now? Some new stunt?"

"Must be something wrong," answered the young inventor. "One of the belts has stopped working. That's why we're going in a circle."

He shut off the power and hastened down to the motor room. There he found his men gathered about one of the machines.

"What's wrong?" asked Tom quickly.

"Just a little accident," replied the head machinist. "One of the boys dropped his monkey wrench and it smashed some spark plugs. That caused a short circuit and the left hand motor went out of business. We'll have her fixed in a jiffy."

Tom looked relieved, and the machinist was as good as his word. In a few minutes the tank was moving forward again. It crossed out to the road, to the great astonishment of some farmers, and the fright of their horses, and then Tom once more swung her into the fields.

"There's the old barn I spoke of," he remarked to Ned. "It's almost as bad a ruin as the factory was. But we'll have a go at it."

"Going to smash it?" asked Ned.

"I'm going right through it!" Tom cried

VEILED THREATS

Like some prehistoric monster about to charge down upon another of its kind, Tank A, under the guidance of Tom Swift, reeled and bumped her way over the uneven fields toward the old barn. Within the monster of steel and iron were raucous noises: the clang and clatter of the powerful gasolene motors; the rattle of the wheels and gears; all making so much noise that, in the engine room proper, not a word could be heard. Every order had to be given by signs, and Tom sent his electric signals from the conning tower in the same way. When running at full speed, it was almost impossible, even in the tower, which was some distance removed from the engine room, to hear voices unless the words were shouted.

"Why don't you go at it?" cried Ned to his "friend, who was peering through the observation slot in the tower."

"I'm getting in good position," Tom answered. "Or rather, the worst position I can find. I want to give the tank a good try-out, and I'm going at the barn on the assumption that this is in enemy country and that I can't pick and choose my advance.

"So I want to come up through that gully, and go at the barn from the long way. That will be the worst possible way I could do it, and if old Tank A stands the gaff I'll know she's a little bit nearer all right."

"I think she's all right as she is!" asserted Ned in a yell, for just then Tom signaled for more speed, and the consequent increase in the rattling and banging noises made it correspondingly difficult for talk to be heard.

The big machine now tipped into the little gully spoken of by Tom. This meant a dip downward, and then a climb out again and an attack on the barn going uphill and at an angle. But, as the young inventor had said, it would make a severe test and that was what he wanted to give his ponderous machine.

Ned grasped one of the safety rings, as, with a reel to one side, almost as if it were going to capsize, the tank rumbled on. Tom cast a half-amused smile at his chum, and then threw over the guiding lever.

The tank rolled down into the gully. It was rough and filled with stones and boulders, some of considerable size. But Tank A made less than nothing even of the largest rocks. Some she crushed beneath her steel belts. Others she simply "walked" over, smashing them down into the soil.

Now the big machine reached the bottom of the gulch and started up the sides, which, though not as steep as the trench in which she had capsized, still were not easy going.

"Now for it!" cried Tom, as he signaled for full speed.

Up climbed the tank. Now she was half-way. A moment later, and she was at the top, and then a forward careening motion told that she had passed over the summit and was ready for the attack proper.

Ned gave a quick glance through the slot nearest him. He had a glimpse of the barn, and then he saw something else. This was the sight of a man running away from the dilapidated structure—a man who glanced toward the tank with a face that showed great fright.

"Stop! Stop!" yelled Ned. "There may be folks in there, Tom! I just saw a man run out!"

"All right!" Tom cried, though Ned could hardly hear him. "Tell me when we get on the other side! We're going through now!"

"But," shouted Ned, "don't you understand? I saw a man come out of there! Maybe there's more inside! Wait, Tom, and—"

But it was too late. The next instant there was a smashing, grinding, splintering crash, a noise as of a thunder-clap, and Tank A fairly ate her way through the old barn as a rat might eat his way into a soft cheese, only infinitely more quickly.

On and on and through and through went the tank, knocking beams, boards, rafters and timbers hither and thither. Minding not at all the weight of great beams on her back, caring nothing for those that got in the way of her steel belts, heeding not the wall of wood that reared itself before her in a barrier of splinters and slivers, Tank A went on and on until finally, with another grinding crash, as she smashed her way through the farthermost wall, the great engine of war emerged on the other side and came panting into the field, dragging with her a part of the structure clinging to her steel sides.

"Well," cried Tom, with a laugh, as he signaled for the power to be shut off, thereby making it possible for ordinary conversation to be heard, "I guess we didn't do a thing to that barn!"

"Not much left of it, for a fact, Tom," agreed Ned, as he looked through the after observation slots at the ruin in the rear. "But didn't you hear what I was saying?"

"I heard you yelling something to me, but I was too anxious to go at it as fast as I could. I didn't want to stop then. What was the trouble?"

"That's what I'm afraid of, Tom—there may be trouble. Just before you tackled the barn for a knockdown, instead of a touchdown, as we might say, I saw a man running out of it. I thought if there was one there, perhaps there might be more. That's why I yelled to you."

"A man running from the old barn!" cried Tom. "Whew!" he whistled. "I wish I had seen him. But, Ned, if one ran out of harm's way, any others who might possibly be in there would do the same thing, wouldn't they?"

"I hope so," returned Ned doubtfully.

"Great Scott!" cried Tom, as the possibility was borne home to him. "If anything has happened—"

He sprang for the door of the tower and threw over the catch, springing out, followed by Ned. From the engine room of the armored tank the men came, smiles of gratification on their faces.

"We certainly busted her wide open, Mr. Swift!" called the chief mechanician.

"Yes," assented the young inventor; but there was not as much gratification in his voice as there should have been. "There isn't much of a barn left, but Ned thinks he saw some one run out, and if there was one man there may have been more. We'd better have a look around, I guess."

The engineering force exchanged glances. Then Hank Baldwin, who was in charge of the motors, said:

"Well, if there was anybody in that barn when we chewed her up I wouldn't give much for his hide, German or not."

"Let us hope no one was in there," murmured Tom.

They turned to go back to the demolished structure, fear and worry in their hearts. No more complete ruin could be imagined. If a cyclone had swept over the barn it could not have more certainly leveled it. And, not only was it leveled, crushed down in the center by the great weight of the tank, but the boards and beams were broken into small pieces. Parts of them clung in long, grotesque splinters to the endless steel belts.

"I don't see how we're going to find anybody if he's in there," remarked Hank.

"We'll have to," insisted Tom. "We can look about and call. If any one is there he may have been off to one side or to one end, and be protected under the debris. I wish I had heard you call, Ned."

"I wish you had, Tom. I yelled for all I was worth."

"I know you did. I was too eager to go on, and, at the same time, I really couldn't stop well on that hill. I had to keep on going. Well, now to learn the worst!"

They walked back toward the demolished barn. But they had not reached it when from around the corner swung a big automobile. In it were several men, but chief, in vision at least, among them, was a burly farmer who had a long, old-fashioned gun in his hands. On his bearded face was a grim look as he leaped out before the machine had fairly stopped, and called:

"Hold on, there! I guess you've done damage enough! Now you can pay for it or take the consequences!" And he motioned to Tom, Ned, and the others to halt.

READY FOR FRANCE

Such was the reaction following the crashing through of the barn, coupled with the sudden appearance of the men in the automobile and the threat of the farmer, that, for the moment, Tom, Ned, or their companions from the tank could say nothing. They just stood staring at the farmer with the gun, while he grimly regarded them. It was Tom who spoke first.

"What's the idea?" asked the young inventor. "Why don't you want us to look through the ruins?"

"You'll learn soon enough!" was the grim answer.

But Tom was not to be put off with undecided talk.

"If there's been an accident," he said, "we're sorry for it. But delay may be dangerous. If some one is hurt—"

"You'll be hurt, if I have my way about it!" snapped the farmer, "and hurt in a place where it always tells. I mean your pocketbook! That's the kind of a man I am—practical."

"He means if we've killed or injured any one we'll have to pay damages," whispered Ned to Tom. "But don't agree to anything until you see your lawyer. That's a hot one, though, trying to claim damages before he knows who's hurt!"

"I've got to find out more about this," Tom answered. He started to walk on.

"No you don't!" cried the farmer, with a snarl. "As I said, you folks has done damage enough with your threshing machine, or whatever you call it. Now you've got to pay!"

"We are willing to," said Tom, as courteously as he could. "But first we want to know who has been hurt, or possibly killed. Don't you think it best to get them to a doctor. and then talk about money damages later?"

"Doctor? Hurt?" cried the farmer, the other men in the auto saying nothing. "Who said anything about that?"

"I thought," began Tom, "that you—"

"I'm talkin' about damages to my barn!" cried the farmer. "You had no right to go smashing it up this way, and you've got to pay for it, or my name ain't Amos Kanker!"

"Oh!" and there was great relief in Tom's voice. "Then we haven't killed any one?"

"I don't know what you've done," answered the farmer, and his voice was not a pleasant one. "I'm sure I can't keep track of all your ructions. All I know is that you've ruined my barn, and you've got to pay for it, and pay good, too!"

"For that old ramshackle?" cried Ned.

"Hush!" begged Tom, in a low voice. "I'm willing to pay, Ned, for the sake of having proved what my tank could do. I'm only too glad to learn no one was hurt. Was there?" he asked, turning to the farmer.

"Was there what?"

"Was there anybody in your barn?"

"Not as I knows on," was the grouchy answer. "A man who saw your machine coming thought she was headed for my building, and he run and told me. Then some friends of mine brought me here in their machine. I tell you I've got all the evidence I need ag'in you, an' I'm going to have damages! That barn was worth three thousand dollars if it was worth a cent, and—"

"This matter can easily be settled," said Tom, trying to keep his temper. "My name is Swift, and—"

"Don't get swift with me, that's all I ask!" and the farmer laughed grimly at his clumsy joke.

"I'll do whatever is right," Tom said, with dignity. "I live over near Shopton, and if you want to send your lawyer to see mine, why—"

"I don't believe in lawyers!" broke in the farmer. "All they think of is to get what they can for theirselves. And I can do that myself. I'll get it out of you before you leave, or, anyhow, before you take your contraption away," and he glanced at the tank.

The same suspicion came at once to Tom and Ned, and the latter gave voice to it when he murmured in a low voice to his chum:

"This is a frame-up—a scheme, Tom. He doesn't care a rap for the barn. It's some of that Blakeson's doing, to make trouble for you."

"I believe you!" agreed Tom. "Now I know what to do."

He looked toward the collapsed barn, as if making a mental computation of its value, and then turned toward the farmer.

"I'm very sorry," said Tom, "if I have caused any trouble. I wanted to test my machine out on a wooden structure, and I picked your barn. I suppose I should have come to you first, but I did not want to waste time. I saw the barn was of practically no value

"No value!" broke in the farmer. "Well, I'll show you, young man, that you can't play fast and loose with other people's property and not settle!"

"I'm perfectly willing to, Mr. Kanker. I could see that the barn was almost ready to fall, and I had already determined, before sending my tank through it, to pay the owner any reasonable sum. I am willing to do that now."

"Well, of course if you're so ready to do that," replied the farmer, and Ned thought he caught a glance pass between him and one of the men in the auto, "if you're ready to do that, just hand over three thousand dollars, and we'll call it a day's work. It's really worth more, but I'll say three thousand for a quick settlement."

"Why, this barn," cried Ned, "isn't worth half that! I know something about real estate values, for our bank makes loans on farms around here—"

"Your bank ain't made me no loans, young man!" snapped Mr. Kanker. "I don't need none. My place is free and clear! And three thousand dollars is the price of my barn you've knocked to smithereens. If you don't want to pay, I'll find a way to make you. And I'll hold you, or your tank, as you call it, security for my damages! You can take your choice about that."

"You can't hold us!" cried Tom. "Such things aren't done here!"

"Well, then, I'll hold your tank!" cried the farmer. "I guess it'll sell for pretty nigh onto what you owe me, though what it's good for I can't see. So you pay me three thousand dollars or leave your machine here as security."

"That's the game!" whispered Ned. "There's some plot here. They want to get possession of your tank, Tom, and they've seized on this chance to do it."

"I believe you," agreed the young inventor. "Well, they'll find that two can play at that game. Mr. Kanker," he went on, "it is out of the question to claim your barn is worth three thousand dollars."

"Oh, is it?" sneered the farmer. "Well, I didn't ask you to come here and make kindling wood of it! That was your doings, and you've had your fun out of it. Now you can pay the piper, and I'm here to make you pay!" And he brought the gun around in a menacing manner.

"He's right, in a way," said Ned to his chum. "We should have secured his permission first. He's got us in a corner, and almost any jury of farmers around here, after they heard the story of the smashed barn, would give him heavy damages. It isn't so much that the barn is worth that as it is his property rights that we've violated. A farmer's barn is his castle, so to speak."

"I guess you're right," agreed Tom, with a rather rueful face. "But I'm not going to hand him over three thousand dollars. In fact, I haven't that much with me."

"Oh, well, I don't suppose he'd want it all in cash."

But, it appeared, that was just what the farmer wanted. He went over all his arguments again, and it could not be denied that he had the law on his side. As he rightly said, Tom could not expect to go about the country, "smashing up barns and such like," without being willing to pay.

"Well, what you going to do?" asked the farmer at last. "I can't stay here all day. I've got work to do. I can't go around smashing barns. I want three thousand dollars, or I'll hold your contraption for security."

This last he announced with more conviction after he had had a talk with one of the men in the automobile. And it was this consultation that confirmed Tom and Ned in their belief that the whole thing was a plot, growing out of Tom's rather reckless destruction of the barn; a plot on the part of Blakeson and his gang. That they had so speedily taken advantage of this situation carelessly given them was only another evidence of how closely they were on Tom's trail.

"That man who ran out of the barn must have been the same one who was in the factory," whispered Ned to his chum. "He probably saw us coming this way and ran on ahead to have the farmer all primed in readiness. Maybe he knew you had planned to ram the barn."

"Maybe he did. I've had it in mind for some time, and spoken to some of my men about it."

"More traitors in camp, then, I'm afraid, Tom. We'll have to do some more detective work. But let's get this thing settled. He only wants to hold your tank, and that will give the man, into whose hands he's playing, a chance to inspect her."

"I believe you. But if I have to leave her here I'll leave some men on guard inside. It won't be any worse than being stalled in No Man's Land. In fact, it won't be so bad. But I'll do that rather than be gouged."

"No, Tom, you won't. If you did leave some one on guard, there'd be too much chance of their getting the best of him. You must take your tank away with you."

"But how can I? I can't put up three thousand dollars in cash, and he says he won't take a check for fear I'll stop payment. I see his game, but I don't see how to block it."

"But I do!" cried Ned.

"What!" exclaimed Tom. "You don't mean to say, even if you do work in a bank, that you've got three thousand in cash concealed about your person, do you?"

"Pretty nearly, Tom, or what is just as good. I have that amount in Liberty Bonds. I was going to deliver them to a customer who has ordered them but not paid for them. They are charged up against me at the bank, but I'm good for that, I guess. Now I'll loan you these bonds, and you can give them to this cranky old farmer as security for damages. Mind, don't make them as a payment. They're simply security—the same as when an autoist leaves his car as bail. Only we don't want to leave our car, we'd rather have it with us," and he looked over at the tank, bristling with splinters from the demolished barn.

"Well, I guess that's the only way out," said Tom. "Lucky you had those bonds with you. I'll take them, and give you a receipt for them. In fact, I'll buy them from you and let the farmer hold them as security."

And this, eventually, was done. After much hemming and hawing and consultation with the men in the automobile, Mr. Kanker said he would accept the bonds. It was made clear that they were not in payment of any damages, though Tom admitted he was liable for some, but that Uncle Sam's war securities were only a sort of bail, given to indicate that, some time later, when a jury had passed on the matter, the young inventor would pay Mr. Kanker whatever sum was agreed upon as just.

"And now," said Tom, as politely as he could under the circumstances, "I suppose we will be allowed to depart."

"Yes, take your old shebang offen my property!" ordered Mr. Kanker, with no very good grace. "And if you go knocking down any more barns, I'll double the price on you!"

"I guess he's a bit roiled because he couldn't hold the tank," observed Ned to Tom, as they walked together to the big machine. "His friends —our enemies—evidently hoped that was what could be done. They want to get at some of the secrets."

"I suppose so," conceded Tom. "Well, we're out of that, and I've proved all I want to."

"But I haven't—quite," said Ned.

"What's missing?" asked his chum, as they got back in the tank.

"Well, I'd like to make sure that the fellow who ran from the factory was the same one I saw sneaking out of the barn. I believe he was, and I believe that Simpson's crowd engineered this whole thing."

"I believe so, too," Tom agreed. "The next thing is to prove it. But that will keep until later. The main thing is we've got our tank, and now I'm going to get her ready for France."

"Will she be in shape to ship soon?" asked Ned.

"Yes, if nothing more happens. I've got a few little changes and adjustments to make, and then she'll be ready for the last test—one of long distance endurance mainly. After that, apart she comes to go to the front, and we'll begin making 'em in quantities here and on the other side."

"Good!" cried Ned. "Down with the Huns!"

Without further incident of moment they went back to the headquarters of the tank, and soon the great machine was safe in the shop where she had been made.

The next two weeks were busy ones for Tom, and in them he put the finishing touches on his machine, gave it a long test over fields and through woods, until finally he announced:

"She's as complete as I can make her! She's ready for France!"

TOM IS MISSING

With Tom Swift's announcement, that his tank was at last ready for real action, came the end of the long nights and days given over on the part of his father, himself, and his men to the development and refinement of the machine, to getting plans and specifications ready so that the tanks could be made quickly and in large numbers in this country and abroad and to the actual building of Tank A. Now all this was done at last, and the first completed tank was ready to be shipped.

Meanwhile the matter of the demolished barn had been left for legal action. Tom and Ned, it developed, had done the proper thing under the circumstances, and they were sure they had foiled at least one plan of the plotters.

"But they won't stop there," declared Ned, who had constituted himself a sort of detective. "They're lying back and waiting for another chance, Tom."

"Well, they won't get it at my tank!" declared the young inventor, with a smile. "I've finished testing her on the road. All I need do now is to run her around this place if I have to; and there won't be much need of that before she's taken apart for shipment. Did you get any trace of Simpson or the men who are with him—Blakeson and the others?"

"No," Ned answered. "I've been nosing around about that farmer, Kanker, but I can't get anything out of him. For all that, I'm sure he was egged on to his hold-up game by some of your enemies. Everything points that way."

"I think you're right," agreed Tom. "Well, we won't bother any more about him. When the trial comes on, I'll pay what the jury says is right. It'll be worth it, for I proved that Tank A can eat up brick, stone or wooden buildings and not get indigestion. That's what I set out to do. So don't worry any more about it, Ned."

"I'm not worrying, but I'd like to get the best of those fellows. The idea of asking three thousand dollars for a shell of a barn!"

"Never mind," replied Tom. "We'll come out all right."

Now that the Liberty Loan drive had somewhat slackened, Ned had more leisure time, and he spent parts of his days and not a few of his evenings at Tom Swift's. Mr. Damon was also a frequent visitor, and he never tired of viewing the tank. Every chance he got, when they tested the big machine in the large field, so well fenced in, the eccentric man was on hand, with his. "bless my—!" whatever happened to come most readily to his mind.

Tom, now that his invention was well-nigh perfected, was not so worried about not having the tank seen, even at close range, and the enclosure was not so strictly guarded.

This in a measure was disappointing to Eradicate, who liked the importance of strutting about with a nickel shield pinned to his coat, to show that he was a member of the Swift & Company plant. As for the giant Koku, he really cared little what he did, so long as he pleased Tom, for whom be had an affection that never changed. Koku would as soon sit under a shady tree doing nothing as watch for spies or traitors, of whose identity he was never sure.

So it came that there was not so strict a guard about the place, and Tom and Ned had more time to themselves. Not that the young inventor was not busy, for the details of shipping Tank A to France came to him, as did also the arrangements for making others in this country and planning for the manufacture abroad.

It was one evening, after a particularly hard day's work, when Tom had been making a test in turning the tank in a small space in the enclosed yard, that the two young men were sitting in the machine shop, discussing various matters.

The telephone bell rang, and Ned, being nearest, answered.

"It's for you, Tom," he said, and there was a smile on the face of the young bank clerk.

"Um!" murmured Tom, and he smiled also.

Ned could not repress more smiles as Tom took up the conversation over the wire, and it did not take long for the chum of the youthful inventor to verify his guess that Mary Nestor was at the other end of the instrument.

"Yes, yes," Tom was heard to say. "Why, of course, I'll be glad to come over. Yes, he's here. What? Bring him along? I will if he'll come. Oh, tell him Helen is there! 'Nough said! He'll come, all right!"

And Tom, without troubling to consult his friend, hung up the receiver.

"What's that you're committing me to?" asked Ned.

"Oh, Mary wants us to come over and spend the evening. Helen Sever is there, and they say we can take them downtown if we like."

"I guess we like," laughed Ned. "Come along! We've had enough of musty old problems," for he had been helping Tom in some calculations regarding strength of materials and the weight-bearing power of triangularly constructed girders as compared to the arched variety.

"Yes, I guess it will do us good to get out," and the two friends were soon on their way.

"What's this?" asked Mary, with a laugh, as Tom held out a package tied with pink string. "More dynamite?" she added, referring to an incident which had once greatly perturbed the excitable Mr. Nestor.

"If she doesn't want it, perhaps Helen will take it," suggested Ned, with a twinkle in his eyes. "Halloran said they were just in fresh—"

"Oh, you delightful boy!" cried Helen. "I'm just dying for some chocolates! Let me open them, Mary, if you're afraid of dynamite."

"The only powder in them," said Tom, "is the powdered sugar. That can't blow you up."

And then the young people made merry, Tom, for the time being, forgetting all about his tank.

It was rather late when the two young men strolled back toward the Swift home, Ned walking that way with his chum. Tom started out in the direction of the building where the tank was housed,

"Going to have a good-night look at her?" asked Ned.

"Well, I want to make sure the watchman is on guard. We'll begin taking her apart in a few days, and I don't want anything to happen between now and then."

They walked on toward the big structure, and, as they approached from the side, they were both startled to see a dark shadow—at least so it seemed to the youths—dart away from one of the windows.

"Look!" gasped Ned.

"Hello, there!" cried Tom sharply. "Who's that? Who are you?"

There was no answer, and then the fleeing shadow was merged in the other blackness of the night.

"Maybe it was the watchman making his rounds," suggested Ned.

"No," answered Tom, as he broke into a run. "If it was, he'd have answered. There's something wrong here!"

But he could find nothing when he reached the window from which he and Ned had seen the shadow dart. An examination by means of a pocket electric light betrayed nothing wrong with the sash, and if there were footprints beneath the casement they indicated nothing, for that side of the factory was one frequently used by the workmen.

Tom went into the building, and, for a time, could not find the watchman. When he did come upon the man, he found him rubbing his eyes sleepily, and acting as though he had just awakened from a nap.

"This isn't any way to be on duty!" said Tom sharply. "You're not paid for sleeping!"

"I know it, Mr. Swift," was the apologetic answer. "I don't know what's come over me tonight. I never felt so sleepy in all my life. I had my usual sleep this afternoon, too, and I've drunk strong coffee to keep awake."

"Are you sure you didn't drink anything else?"

"You know I'm a strict temperance man."

"I know you are," said Tom; "but I thought maybe you might have a cold, or something like that."

"No, I haven't taken a thing. I did have a drink of soda water before I came on duty, but that's all."

"Where'd you get it?" asked Tom.

"Well, a man treated me."

"Who?"

"I don't know his name. He met me on the street and asked me how to get to Plowden's hardware store. I showed him— walked part of the way, in fact—and when I left he said he was going to have some soda, and asked me to have some. I did, and it tasted good."

"Well, don't go to sleep again," suggested Tom good-naturedly. "Did you hear anything at the side window a while ago?"

"Not a thing, Mr. Swift. I'll be all right now. I'll take a turn outside in the air."

"All right," assented the young inventor.

Then, as he turned to go into the house and was bidding Ned good-night, Tom said:

"I don't like this."

"What?" asked his chum.

"My sleepy watchman and the figure at the window. I more than half suspect that one of Blakeson's tools followed Kent for the purpose of buying him soda, only I think they might have put a drop or two of chloral in it before he got it. That would make him sleep."

"What are you going to do, Tom?"

"Put another man on guard. If they think they can get into the factory at night, and steal my plans, or get ideas from my tank, I'll fool 'em. I'll have another man on guard."

This Tom did, also telling Koku to sleep in the place, to be ready if called. But there was no disturbance that night, and the next day the work of completing the tank went on with a rush,

It was a day or so after this, and Tom had fixed on it as the time for taking the big machine apart for shipment, that Ned received a telephone message at the bank from Mr. Damon.

"Is Tom Swift over with you?" inquired the eccentric man.

"No. Why?" Ned answered.

"Well, I'm at his shop, and he isn't here. His father says he received a message from you a little while ago, saying to come over in a hurry, and he went. Says you told him to meet you out at that farmer Kanker's place. I thought maybe—"

"At Kanker's place!" cried Ned. "Say, something's wrong, Mr. Damon! Isn't Tom there?"

"No; I'm at his home, and he's been gone for some time. His father supposed he was with you. I thought I would telephone to make sure."

"Whew!" whistled Ned. "There's something doing here, all right, and something wrong! I'll be right over!" he added, as he hung up the receiver.

The Search

"Haven't you seen anything of him?" asked Mr. Damon, as Ned jumped out of his small runabout at the Swift home as soon as possible after receiving the telephone message that seemed to presage something wrong.

"Seen him? No, certainly not!" answered the young bank clerk. "I'm as much surprised as you are over it. What happened, anyhow?"

"Bless my memorandum pad, but I hardly know!" answered the eccentric man. "I arrived here a little while ago, stopping in merely to pay Tom a visit, as I often do, and he wasn't here. His father was anxiously waiting for him, too, wishing to consult him about some shop matters. Mr. Swift said Tom had gone out with you, or over to your house—I wasn't quite sure which at first—and was expected back any minute.

"Then I called you up," went on Mr. Damon, "and I was surprised to learn you hadn't seen Tom. There must be something wrong, I think."

"I'm sure of it!" exclaimed Ned. "Let's find Mr. Swift. And what's this about his going to meet me over at the place of that farmer, Mr. Kanker, where we had the trouble about the barn Tom demolished?"

"I hardly know, myself. Perhaps Mr. Swift can tell us."

But Mr. Swift was able to throw but little light on Tom's disappearance—whether a natural or forced disappearance remained to be seen.

"No matter where he is, we'll get him," declared Ned. "He hasn't been away a great while, and it may turn out that his absence is perfectly natural."

"And if it's due to the plots of any of his rivals," said Mr. Damon, "I'll denounce them all as traitors, bless my insurance policy, if I don't! And that's what they are! They're playing into the hands of the enemy!"

"All right," said Ned. "But the thing to do now is to get Tom. Perhaps Mrs. Baggert can help us."

It developed that the housekeeper was of more assistance in giving information than was Mr. Swift.

"It was several hours ago," she said, "that the telephone rang and some one asked for Tom. The operator shifted the call to the phone out in the tank shop where he was, and Tom began to talk. The operator, as Tom had instructed her, listened in, as Tom wants always a witness to most matters that go on over his wires of late."

"What did she hear?" asked Ned eagerly.

"She heard what she thought was your voice, I believe," the housekeeper said.

"Me!" cried the young bank clerk. "I haven't talked to Tom today, over the phone or any other way. But what next?"

"Well, the operator didn't listen much after that, knowing that any talk between Tom and you was of a nature not to need a witness. Tom hung up and then he came in here, quite excited, and began to get ready to go out."

"What was he excited about?" asked Mr. Damon. "Bless my unlucky stars, but a person ought to keep calm under such circumstances! That's the only way to do! Keep calm! Great Scott! But if I had my way, all those German spies would be — Oh, pshaw! Nothing is too bad for them! It makes my blood boil when I think of what they've done! Tom should have kept cool!"

"Go on. What was Tom excited about?" Ned turned to the housekeeper.

"Well, he said you had called him to tell him to meet you over at that farmer's place," went on Mrs. Baggert. "He said you had some news for him about the men who had tried to get hold of some of his tank secrets, and he was quite worked up over the chance of catching the rascals."

"Whew!" whistled Ned. "This is getting more complicated every minute. There's something deep here, Mr. Damon."

"I agree with you, Ned. And the sooner we find Tom Swift the better. What next, Mrs. Baggert?"

"Well, Tom got ready and went away in his small automobile. He said he'd be back as soon as he could after meeting you."

"And I never said a word to him!" cried Ned. "It's all a plot—a scheme of that Blakeson gang to get him into their power. Oh, how could Tom be so fooled? He knows my voice, over the phone as well as otherwise. I don't see how he could be taken in."

"Let's ask the telephone operator," suggested Mr. Damon. "She knows your voice, too. Perhaps she can give us a clue."

A talk with the young woman at the telephone switchboard in the Swift plant brought out a new point. This was that the speaker, in response to whose information Tom Swift had left home, had not said he was Ned Newton.

"He said," reported Miss Blair, "that he was speaking for you, Mr. Newton, as you were busy in the bank. Whoever it was, said you wanted Tom to meet you at the Kanker farm. I heard that much over the wire, and naturally supposed the message came from you."

"Well, that puts a little different face on it," said Mr. Damon. "Tom wasn't deceived by the voice, then, for he must have thought it was some one speaking for you, Ned."

"But the situation is serious, just the same," declared Ned. "Tom has gone to keep an appointment I never made, and the question is with whom will he keep it?"

"That's it!" cried the eccentric man. "Probably some of those scoundrels were waiting at the farm for him, and they've got him no one knows where by this time!"

"Oh, hardly as bad as that," suggested Ned. "Tom is able to look out for himself. He'd put up a big fight before he'd permit himself to be carried off."

"Well, what do you think did happen?" asked Mr. Damon.

"I think they wanted to get him out to the farm to see if they couldn't squeeze some more money out of him," was the answer. "Tom was pretty easy in that barn business, and I guess Kanker was sore because he haven't asked a larger sum. They knew Tom wouldn't come out on their own invitation, so they forged my name, so to speak."

"Can you get Tom back?" asked Mrs. Baggert anxiously.

"Of course!" declared Ned, though it must be admitted he spoke with more confidence than he really felt. "We'll begin the search right away."

"And if I can get my hands on any of those villains—" spluttered Mr. Damon, dancing around, as Mrs. Baggert said, "like a hen on a hot griddle," which seemed to describe him very well, "if I can get hold of any of those scoundrels, I'll—I'll— Bless my collar button, I don't know what I will do! Come on, Ned!"

"Yes, I guess we'd better get busy," agreed the young bank clerk. "Tom has gone somewhere, that's certain, and under a misapprehension. It may be that we are needlessly alarmed, or they may mean bad business. At any rate, it's up to us to find Tom."

In Ned's runabout, which was a speedier car than that of the eccentric man, the two set off for Kanker's farm. On the way they stopped at various places in town, where Tom was in the habit of doing business, to inquire if he had been seen.

But there was no trace of him. The next thing to do was to learn if he had really started for the Kanker farm.

"For if he didn't go there," suggested Ned, "it will look funny for us to go out there making inquiries about him. And it may be that after he got that message Tom decided not to go."

Accordingly they made enough inquiries to establish the fact that Tom had started for the farm of the rascally Kanker, who had been so insistent in the matter of his almost worthless barn.

A number of people who knew Tom well had seen him pass in the direction of Kanker's place, and some had spoken to him, for the young inventor was well known in the vicinity of Shopton and the neighboring towns.

"Well, out to Kanker's we'll go!" decided Ned. "And if anything has happened to Tom there—well, we'll make whoever is responsible wish it hadn't!"

"Bless my fountain pen, but that's what we will!" chimed in Mr. Damon.

And so the two began the search for the missing youth.

A Prisoner

Amos Kanker came to the door of his farmhouse as Ned and Mr. Damon drove up in the runabout. There was an unpleasant grin on the not very prepossessing face of the farmer, and what Ned thought was a cunning look, as he slouched out and asked:

"Well, what do you want? Come to smash up any more of my barns at three thousand dollars a smash?"

"Hardly," answered Ned shortly. "Your prices are too high for such ramshackle barns as you have. Where's Tom Swift?" he asked sharply.

"Huh! Do you mean that young whipper-snapper with his big traction engine?" demanded Mr. Kanker.

"Look here!" blustered Mr. Damon, "Tom Swift is neither a whippersnapper nor is his machine a traction engine. It's a war tank."

"That doesn't matter much to me," said the farmer, with a grating laugh. "It looks like a traction engine, though it smashes things up more'n any one I ever saw."

"That isn't the point," broke in Ned. "Where is my friend, Tom Swift? That's what we want to know."

"Huh! What makes you think I can tell you?" demanded Kanker.

"Didn't he come out here?" asked Mr. Damon.

"Not as I knows of," was the surly answer.

"Look here!" exclaimed Ned, and his tones were firm, with no bluster nor bluff in them, "we came out here to find Tom Swift, and were going to find him! We have reason to believe he's here—at least, he started for here," he substituted, as he wished to make no statement he could not prove. "Now we don't claim we have any right to be on your property, and we don't intend to stay here any longer than we can help. But we do claim the right, in common decency, to ask if you have seen anything of Tom. There may have been an accident; there may have been foul play; and there may be international complications in this business. If there are, those involved won't get off as easily as they think. I'd advise you to keep a civil tongue in your head and answer our questions. If we have to get the police and detectives out here, as well as the governmental department of justice, you may have to answer their questions, and they won't be as decent to you as we are!"

"Hurray!" whispered Mr Damon to Ned. "That's the way to talk!"

And indeed the forceful remarks of the young bank clerk did appear to have a salutary effect on the surly farmer. His manner changed at once and his grin faded.

"I don't know nothing about Tom Swift or any of your friends," he said. "I've got my farm work to do, and I do it. It's hard enough to earn a living these war times without taking part in plots. I haven't seen Tom Swift since the trouble he made about my barn."

"Then he hasn't been here today?" asked Ned.

"No; and not for a good many days."

Ned looked at Mr. Damon, and the two exchanged uneasy glances. Tom had certainly started for the Kanker farm, and indeed had come to within a few miles of it. That much was certain, as testified to by a number of residents along the route from Shopton, who had seen the young inventor passing in his car.

Now it appeared he had not arrived. The changed air of the farmer seemed to indicate that he was speaking the truth. Mr. Damon and Ned were inclined to believe him. If they had any last, lingering doubts in the matter, they were dispelled when Mr. Kanker said:

"You can search the place if you like. I haven't any reason to feel friendly toward you, but I certainly don't want to get into trouble with the Government. Look around all you like."

"No, we'll take your word for it," said Ned, quickly concluding that now they had got the farmer where they wanted him, they could gain more by an appearance of friendliness than by threats or harsh words. "Then you haven't seen him, either?"

"Not a sign of him."

"One thing more," went on Tom's chum, "and then we'll look farther. Weren't you induced by a man named Simpson, or one named Blakeson, to make the demand of three thousand dollars' damage for your barn?"

"No, it wasn't anybody of either of those names," admitted Mr. Kanker, evidently a bit put out by the question.

"It was some one, though, wasn't it?" insisted Ned.

"Waal, a man did come to me the day the barn was smashed, and just afore it happened, and said an all-fired big traction engine was headed this way, and that a young feller who was half crazy was running it. This man—I don't know who he was, being a stranger to me—said if the engine ran into any of my property and did damages I should collect for it on the spot, or hold the machine.

"Sure enough, that's what happened, and I did it. That man had an auto, and he brought me and some of my men out to the smashed barn. That's all I know about it."

"I thought some one put you up to it," commented Ned. "This was some of the gang's work," he went on to Mr. Damon. "They hoped to get possession of Tom's tank long enough to find out some of the secrets. By having the Liberty Bonds, I fooled 'em."

"That's what you did!" said Mr. Damon. "But what can we do now?"

"I don't know," Ned was forced to admit. "But I should think we'd better go back to the last place where he was seen to pass in his auto, and try to get on his trail."

Mr. Damon agreed that this was a wise plan, and, after a casual look around the farmhouse and other buildings on Kanker's place and finding nothing to arouse their suspicions, the two left in Ned's speedy little machine.

"It is mighty queer!" remarked the young bank clerk, as they shot along the country road. "It isn't like Tom to get caught this way."

"Maybe he isn't caught," suggested the other. "Tom has been in many a tight place and gotten out, as you and I well know. Maybe it will be the same now, though it does look suspicious, that fake message coming from you."

"Not coming from me, you mean," corrected Ned. "Well, we'll do the best we can."

They proceeded back to where they had last had a trace of Tom in his machine, and there could only confirm what they had learned at first, namely, that the young inventor had departed in the direction of the Kanker farm, after having filled his radiator with water, and chatting with a farmer he knew.

"Then this is where the trail divides," said Ned, as they went back over the road, coming to a point where the highway branched off. "If he went this way, he went to Kanker's place, or he would be in the way of going. He isn't there, it seems, and didn't go there."

"If he took the other road, where would he go?" asked Mr. Damon.

"Any one of a dozen places. I guess we'll have to follow the trail and make all the inquiries we can."

But from the point where the two roads branched, all trace of Tom Swift was lost. No one had seen him in his machine, though he was known to more than one resident along the high way.

"Well, what are we going to do?" asked Mr. Damon, after they had traveled some distance and had obtained no dews.

"Suppose we call up his home," suggested Ned, as they came to a country store where there was a telephone. "It may be he has returned. In that case, all our worry has gone for nothing."

"I don't believe it has," said Mr. Damon. "But if we call up and ask if Tom is back it will show we haven't found him, and his father will be more worried than ever."

"We can ask the telephone girl, and tell her to keep quiet about it," decided Ned; and this they did.

But the answer that came back over the wire was discouraging. For Tom had not returned, and there was no word from him. There was an urgent message for him, too, from government officials regarding the tank, the girl reported.

"Well, we've just got to find him—that's all!" declared Ned. "I guess we'll have to make a regular search of it. I did hope we'd find him out at the Kanker farm. But since he isn't there, nor anywhere about, as far as we can tell, we've got to try some other plan."

"You mean notify the authorities?" — asked Mr. Damon.

"Hardly that—yet. But I'll get some of Tom's friends who have machines, and we'll start them out on the trail. In that way we can cover a lot of ground."

Late that afternoon, and far into the night, a number of the friends of Tom and Ned went about the country in automobiles, seeking news of the young inventor. Mr. Swift became very anxious over the non-return of his son, and felt the authorities should be notified; but as all agreed that the local police could not handle the matter and that it would have to be put into the hands of the United States Secret Service, he consented to wait for a while before doing this.

All the next day the search was kept up, and Ned and Mr. Damon were getting discouraged, not to say alarmed, when, most unexpectedly, they received a clue.

They had been traveling around the country on little-frequented roads in the hope that perhaps Tom might have taken one and disabled his machine so that he was unable to proceed.

"Though in that case he could, and would, have sent word," said Ned.

"Unless he's hurt," suggested Mr. Damon.

"Well, maybe that is what's happened," Ned was saying, when they noticed coming toward them a very much dilapidated automobile, driven by a farmer, and on the seat beside him was a small, barefoot boy.

"Which is the nearest road to Shopton?" asked the man, bringing his wheezing machine to a stop.

"Who are you looking for in Shopton?" asked Ned, while a strange feeling came over him that, somehow or other, Tom was concerned in the question.

"I'm looking for friends of a Tom Swift," was the answer.

"Tom Swift? Where is he? What's happened to him?" cried Ned.

"Bless my dyspepsia tablets!" exclaimed Mr. Damon. "Do you know where he is?"

"Not exactly," answered the farmer; "but here's a note from some one that signs himself 'Tom Swift,' and it says he's a prisoner!"

Rescued

For a moment Ned and Mr. Damon gazed at the farmer in his rattletrap of an auto, and then they looked at the fluttering piece of paper in his hand. Thence their gaze traveled to the ragged and barefoot lad sitting beside the farmer.

"I found it!" announced the boy.

"Found what?" asked Ned.

"That there note!"

Without asking any more questions, reserving them until they knew more about the matter, Mr. Damon and Ned each reached out a hand for the paper the farmer held. The latter handed it to Ned, being nearest him, and at a sight of the handwriting the young bank clerk exclaimed:

"It's from Tom, all right!"

"What happened to him?" cried Mr. Damon. "Where is he? Is he a prisoner?"

"So it seems," answered Ned. "Wait, I'll read It to you," and he read:

"'Whoever picks this up please send word at once to Mr. Swift or to Ned Newton in Shopton, or to Mr. Damon of Waterfield. I am a prisoner, locked in the old factory. Tom Swift'"

"Bless my quinine pills!" cried Mr Damon. "What in the world does it mean? What factory?"

"That's just what we've got to find out," decided Ned. "Where did you get this?" he asked the farmer's boy.

"Way off over there," and he pointed across miles of fields. "I was lookin' for a lost cow, and I went past an old factory. There wasn't nobody in the place, as far as I knowed, but all at once I heard some one yell, and then I seen something white, like a bird, sail out of a high window. I was scared for a minute, thinkin' it might be tramps after me."

"And what did you do, Sonny?" asked Mr. Damon, as the boy paused.

"Well, after a while I went to where the white thing lay, and I picked it up. I seen it was a piece of paper, with writin' on it, and it was wrapped around part of a brick."

"And did you go near the factory to find out who called or who threw the paper out?" Ned queried.

"I didn't," the boy answered, "I was scared. I went home, and didn't even start to find the lost cow.

"No more he did," chimed in the farmer. "He come runnin' in like a whitehead, and as soon as I saw the paper and heard what Bub had to say, I thought maybe I'd better do somethin'."

"Did you go to the factory?" asked Ned eagerly.

"No. I thought the best thing to do would be to find this Mr. Swift, or the other folks mentioned in this letter. I knowed, in a general way, where

Shopton was, but I'd never been there, doing my tradin' in the other direction, and so I had to stop and ask the road. If you can tell me—"

"We're two of the persons spoken of in that note," said Mr. Damon, as he mentioned his name and introduced Ned. "We have been looking for our friend Tom Swift for two days now. We must find him at once, as there is no telling what he may be suffering."

"Where is this old factory you speak of," continued Mr. Damon, "and how can we get there? It's too bad one of you didn't go back, after finding the note, to tell Tom he was soon to be rescued."

"Waal, maybe it is," said the farmer, a bit put out by the criticism. "But I figgered it would be better to look up this young man's friends and let them do the rescuin', and not lose no time, 'specially as it's about as far from my place to the factory as it is to Shopton."

"Well, I suppose that's so," agreed Ned. "But what is this factory?"

"It's an old one where they started to make beet sugar, but it didn't pan out," the farmer said. "The place is in ruins, and I did hear, not long ago, that somebody run a threshin' machine through it, an' busted it up worse than before."

"Great horned toads!" cried Ned. "That must be the very factory Tom ran his tank through. And to think he should be a prisoner there!"

"Held by whom, do you suppose?" asked Mr. Damon.

"By that Blakeson gang, I imagine," Ned answered. "There's no time to lose. We must go to his rescue!"

"Of course!" agreed Mr. Damon. "We're much obliged to you for bringing this note," he went on to the farmer. "And here is something to repay you for your trouble," and he took out his wallet

"Shucks! I didn't do this for pay!" objected the farmer. "It's a pity I wouldn't help anybody what's in trouble! If I'd a-knowed what it meant, me and Bub here would have gone to the factory ourselves, maybe, and done the work quicker. But I didn't know—what with war times and such-like—but that it would be better to deliver the note."

"It turns out as well, perhaps," agreed Ned. "We'll look after Tom now."

"And I'll come along and help," said the farmer. "If there's a gang of tramps in that factory, you may need some reinforcements. I've got a couple of new axe handles in my machine, and they'll come in mighty handy as clubs."

"That's so," said Mr. Damon. "But I fancy Tom is simply locked in the deserted factory office, with no one on guard. We can get him out once we get there, and we'll be glad to have you come with us. So if you won't take any reward, maybe your boy will, as he found the note," and Mr. Damon pressed some bills into the hands of the boy, who, it is needless to say, was glad to get them.

It was a run of several miles back to the deserted factory, and though they passed houses on the way, it was decided that no addition to their force was necessary, though they did stop at a blacksmith shop, where they borrowed a heavy sledge to batter down a door if such action should be needed.

The farmer's rattletrap of a car, in spite of its appearance, was not far behind Ned's runabout, and in a comparatively short time all were within sight of the ruined place—a ruin made more complete by the passage through it of Tom Swift's war tank.

"And to think of his being there all this while!" exclaimed Mr. Damon, as he and Ned leaped from their machine.

"If he only is there!" murmured the young bank clerk.

"What do you mean? Didn't the note he threw out say he was there?"

"Yes, but something may have happened in the meanwhile. Those plotters, if they'd do a thing like this, are capable of anything. They may have kidnapped Tom again."

"Anyway, we'll soon find out," murmured Ned, as they advanced toward the ruin, Mr. Damon and the farmer each armed with an axe helve, while Ned carried the blacksmith's sledge.

They went into the end of the factory that was less ruined than the central part, where the tank had crashed through, and made their way into what had been the office—the place where they had found the burned scraps of paper.

"Hark!" exclaimed Ned, as they climbed up the broken steps. "I heard a noise."

"It's him yellin'—like he did afore he threw out the note," said the boy. Then, as they listened, they heard a distant voice calling:

"Hello! Hello, there! If that is any friend of mine, let me out, or send word to Mr. Damon or Ned Newton! Hello!"

"Hello yourself, Tom Swift!" yelled Ned, too delighted to wait for any other confirmation that it was his friend who was shouting. "We've come to rescue you, Tom!"

There was a moment of silence, and then a voice asked:

"Who is there?"

"Ned Newton, Mr. Damon, and some other friends of yours!" answered the young bank clerk, for surely the farmer and his son could be called Tom's friends.

An indistinguishable answer came back, and then Ned cried:

"Where are you, Tom? Tell us, so we can get you out!"

They all listened, and faintly heard:

"I'm in some sort of an old vault, partly underground. It's below what used to be the office. There's a flight of steps, but be careful, as they're rotten."

Eagerly they looked around Mr. Damon saw a door in one corner of the office, and tried to open it. It was locked, but a few blows from the sledge smashed it, and then some steps were revealed.

Down these, using due caution, went Ned and the others, and at the bottom they came upon another door. This was of sheet iron and was fastened on the outside by a big padlock.

"Stand back!" cried Ned, as he swung the sledge, and with a few blows broke the lock to pieces.

Then they pulled open the door, and into the light staggered Tom Swift, a most woe-begone figure, and showing the effects of his imprisonment. But he was safe and unharmed, though much disheveled from his attempts to escape.

"Thank Heaven, you've come!" he murmured, as he clasped Ned's hand. "Is the tank all right?"

"All right!" cried Ned. "And now tell us about yourself. How in the world did you get here?"

"It's quite a yarn," answered Tom. "I've got to pull myself together before I answer," and he sank wearily down on a step, looking very haggard and worn.

GONE

"Here, eat some of this," and Ned held something out to his chum. "It'll bring you up quicker than anything else, except a cup of hot tea, and we'll get that as soon as you can get away from here," went on the young bank clerk.

"What is it?" Tom asked, and his voice was very weary.

"It's a mixture of chocolate and nuts," replied Ned. "It's a new form of emergency ration issued to soldiers before they go over the top. Our Y.M.C.A. is sending a lot to the boys from around here who are in France. I was helping pack the boxes ready for shipment, and I kept out some to show you. Lucky I had it with me. Eat it, and you'll feel a lot better in a few minutes. You haven't had much to eat, have you?"

"Very little," answered Tom, as he nibbled half-heartedly at the confection Ned gave him. while Mr. Damon went out to the automobile and came back with a thermos bottle filled with cool water. He always provided himself with this on taking an automobile trip.

Tom managed to eat some of the chocolate, and then took a drink of the cool water. In a little while he declared that he felt better.

"Then come out of here!" exclaimed Ned. "You can tell tis how it all happened and what they did to you. But I can see that last—they treated you like a dog, didn't they?"

"Pretty nearly," answered Tom; "but they didn't have things all their own way. I think I made one or two of them remember me," and he glanced at his swollen and bruised hands. Indeed, he bore the marks of having been in a fierce fight.

"Are you sure the tank's all right?" he asked Ned again. "That has been worrying me more than my own condition. I could think of only one reason why they got me here and held me prisoner, and that was to get me out of the way while they captured my tank. Then they haven't got her?" he asked eagerly.

"Not a look at her," Ned answered. "She was safe in the shop when we set out this morning."

"And now it's late afternoon," murmured Tom. "Well, I hope nothing has happened since," and there was vague alarm in his voice, an alarm at which Ned and Mr. Damon wondered.

"Couldn't you stop at some farmhouse and get fixed up a little?" asked Mr. Kimball, the farmer who had brought the note to Ned and Mr. Damon.

"I need to get fixed up somewhere," replied Tom, with a rueful look at himself—his hands, his torn clothes, and his general dilapidated appearance. "But I don't want to lose any time. I'm afraid something has happened at home, Ned."

"Nonsense! How could there, with Koka on guard, to say nothing of Eradicate!"

"Well, maybe you're right," agreed Tom; "but I'll feel better when I see my tank in her shed. Let's have some more of that concentrated porterhouse steak of yours, Ned. It is good, and it fills out my stomach, which was getting more intimate with my backbone than I liked to feel."

More of the really good confection and another drink of refreshing water made Tom feel better, and he was soon able to walk along without staggering from weakness.

"And now let's get out of here," advised Ned, "unless you've left something back in that vault you want, Tom," and he motioned to his chum's late prison.

"Nothing there but bad memories," was the reply, with a rueful smile. "I'm as ready to go as you are, Ned. It was good of you and Mr. Damon to come for me, and you" — and he looked questioningly at Mr. Kimball.

"If it hadn't been for Mr. Kimball and his boy, we wouldn't have found you—at least so soon," said Ned, and he told of the finding of the note and what had followed.

"That's the only way I could think of for getting help," said Tom. "They took every scrap of paper from me, but I found some in the lining of my hat—some I'd stuffed in after I had a hair cut and my hat was too large. For a pencil I used burnt matches. Oh, but I'm glad to be out!" and he breathed deep of the fresh air.

"How did you get in there?" asked Ned wonderingly.

"Those fellows—of course. The German plotters, I'm going to call them, for I believe that Blakeson and his gang— though I didn't see him—are really working in the interests of Germany to get the secret of my tank."

"Well, they haven't got her yet," said Ned. "and they're not likely to now. Go on, Tom, if you feel able tell us in a few words what happened. We've been trying to think, but can't."

"Well, it all happened because I didn't think enough," said Tom, who was rapidly recovering his strength and nerve. "When I got that message that seemed to come from you, Ned, I should have known better than to take a chance. But it seemed genuine, and as I had no reason to suspect a trap, I started off at once. I thought maybe Kanker had repented and was going to make amends for all the trouble he caused.

"Anyhow, I started off in my machine, and I hadn't got more than to the crossroads when I saw a fellow out tinkering with his auto. Of course I stopped to ask if I could help, for I can't bear to see any machinery out of order, and as I was stooping over the engine to see what was wrong I was pounced on from behind, bound and tied, and before I could do a thing I was bundled into the car—a big limousine, and taken away.

"The crossroads was as far as we could trace you," remarked Ned.

"Well, it wasn't as far as they took me, by any means," Tom said. "They brought me here, took me out of the machine—and I noticed that they'd brought mine along—and then they carted me into the vault.

"But they didn't have it all their own way," said Tom grimly. "I managed to get the ropes loose, and I had a regular knock down and drag out with them for a while. But they were too many for me, and locked me up in that place after taking away everything I had in my pockets."

"Were they highwaymen?" asked Mr. Kimtall.

"No, for they tossed back my money, watch and some trifles like that," Tom answered. "I didn't recognize any of the men, though one of them must have known me, for when they had me tied I heard one of them ask if I was the right party, and another said I was. I know they must belong to the same gang that Simpson, Blakeson, and Schwen are members of—the German spies."

"But what was their object?" asked Ned. "Did they try to force you to tell them the secrets of the tank?"

"No; and that's the funny part which makes me so suspicious," Tom answered. "If they'd tried to force something out of me, I would understand it better. But they just kept me a prisoner after taking away what papers I had."

"Were they of any value?" asked Mr. Damon.

"Not as regards the tank. That is, there was nothing of my plans of construction, control or anything like that, though there was some foreign correspondence that I am sorry fell into their hands. However, that can't he helped."

"And did they just keep you locked up?" asked Ned.

"That's about all they did. After the fight—and it was some fight!" declared Tom, as he recalled it with a shake of his head—" they left me here with the door shut. There must have been some one on guard, for I could faintly hear somebody moving about.

"I tried to get out, of course, but I couldn't. That vault must have been made to hold something very valuable, for it was almost as strong and solid as one in your bank, Ned. The only window was placed so high that I couldn't reach it, and it was barred at that.

"They opened the door a little, several times, to toss in once some old bags that I made into a bed, and next they gave me a little water and some sandwiches—German bologna sausage sandwiches, Ned! What do you think of that—adding insult to injury?"

"That was tough!" Ned admitted.

"Well, I had to put up with it, for I was half starved, and as sore as a boil from the fight. I didn't know what to do. I knew that you'd miss me sooner or later, and set out to find me, but I hardly thought you'd think of this place. They couldn't have picked out a much better prison to hold me, for, naturally, you wouldn't suppose enough of it was left standing, after my tank had walked through it, to make a hiding place.

"However, there was, and here I've been kept. At last I thought of the plan of sending out a message on the scrap of paper I could tear out of my hat. So I wrote it, and after several trials I managed to toss it out of the window. Then I just had to wait, and that was the hardest of all. The last twelve hours I've been without food, and I haven't heard any one around, so I guess they've skipped out and don't intend to come back."

"We didn't see any one," Ned reported. "Maybe they became frightened, Tom."

"I wish I could think that," was the answer. "What is more likely to be the case is that they're up to some new tricks. I must get back home quickly."

And after a stop had been made at a farmhouse belonging to a business acquaintance of Ned's, where Tom was able to wash and get a cup of hot tea, which added to his recuperative powers, the young inventor, with Ned and Mr. Damon, set out for Shopton.

Before Mr. Kimball started for his home, renewed thanks had been made to the farmer and his son for the part they had played in the rescue, and the young inventor, learning that the boy had a liking for things mechanical, promised to aid him in his intention to become a machinist

"But first get a good education," Tom advised. "Keep on with your school work, and when the time comes I'll take you into my shop."

"And maybe he'll make a tank that will rival yours, Tom," said Ned.

"Maybe he will! I hope he does. If he comes along fast enough, he can help with something else I'm going to start soon."

"Whats that?" asked Mr. Damon.

"Oh, it's something on the same order, designed to help batter down the German lines," Tom answered. "I haven't quite made up my mind what to call it yet. But let's get home. I want to see that my tank Is safe. The absence of the plotters from the factory makes me suspicious."

On the way back Tom told more of the details of the attack.

"But we'll forget about it all, now you're out," remarked Ned.

"And the sooner we get home, the better," added Tom. "Can't you get a little more speed out of this machine?" he asked.

"Well, it isn't the Hawk," replied Ned, "but we'll see what we can do," and he made the runabout fairly fly.

Mrs. Baggert was the first to greet Tom as they arrived at his home. She did not seem as surprised as either Tom, Ned or Mr. Damon expected her to be.

"Well, I'm glad you're all right," she said. "And it's a good thing you sent that note, for your father was so excited and worried I was getting apprehensive about him."

"What note?" asked Tom, while a queer look came into his face.

"Why, the one you sent saying you were detained on business and would probably not be home for a week, and to have Koku and the men bring the tank to you."

"Bring the tank! A note from me!" exclaimed Tom. "The plotters again! And they've got the tank!"

He ran to the big shop followed by the others. Throwing open the doors, they went inside. A glance sufficed to disclose the worst.

The place where the great tank had stood was empty.

"Gone!" gasped Tom.

Camouflaged

Two utterances Tom Swift made when the fact of the disappearance of the tank became known to him were characteristic of the young inventor. The first was:

"How did they get it away?"

And the second was:

"Come on, let's get after 'em!"

Then, for a few moments, no one said anything. Tom, Ned, and Mr. Damon, with Mrs. Baggert in the background, stood looking at the great empty machine shop.

"Well, they got her," went on Tom, with a sigh. "I was afraid of this as soon as they left me alone at the factory."

"Is anything wrong?" faltered the housekeeper. "Didn't you send for the tank, Tom?"

"No, Mrs. Baggert, I didn't," Tom answered.

"But I don't understand," the housekeeper said. "A man came with a note from you, Tom, and in it you said to have him take the tank, with Koku and the men who know how to run it. We were so glad to hear from you, and know that you were all right, that we didn't think of anything else, your father and I. So he went out and saw that the tank got off all right. Koku was glad, for it's the first chance he'd had to ride in it."

"Who was the man who brought the note?" asked Tom, and he was striving to be calm. "To think of poor old dad playing right into the hands of the plotters!" he added, in an aside to Ned.

"Well, I don't know who the man was," said Mrs. Baggert. "He seemed all right, and of course having a note from you—"

"Who has that note now?" asked Tom quickly.

"Your father."

"Come on," and Tom led the way back to the house. "I'll have a look at that document, which of course I never wrote, and then we'll get after the plotters and the tank."

"She ought to be easy to trace," observed Mr. Damon. "Bless my fountain pen, but she ought to be easy to trace! She will leave a track like a giant boa constrictor crawling along."

"Yes, I guess we can trace her, all right," assented Tom Swift; "but the point is, will there be anything left of her? What's what I'm afraid of now."

Mr. Swift was still excited, but his worry had subsided as soon as he knew Tom was safe.

"The whole thing is a forgery, but fairly well done," Tom said, as he looked at the paper his father gave him—a brief note stating that Tom was well, but detained on business, and that the tank was to be brought to him, just where the bearer of the note would indicate. Koku, the giant, and several of the machinists, who knew how to operate the big machine, were to go with it, the note said.

"That made me sure everything was all right," said Mr. Swift. "I knew, of course, Tom, that plotters might try to get hold of your war secret, but I didn't see how they could if Koku and some of your own men were in possession."

"They couldn't—as long as they remained in possession," Tom said. "But that's the trouble. I'm afraid they haven't. What has probably happened is that under the direction of this man, who brought the forged note from me, Koku and the others took the tank where he directed them, thinking to meet me. Then, reaching the place where the rest of the plotters were concealed, they overpowered Koku and the others and took possession of the machine."

"They'd have trouble with Koku," suggested Ned.

"Yes, but even a giant can't fight too big a crowd, especially if he is taken by surprise, and that's probably what happened," remarked Tom. "Now the question is where is the tank, and how can we get her back? Every minute counts. If those German spies and their helpers remain in possession long, they'll find out enough of my secrets to enable them to duplicate the machine, and especially some of the most exclusive features. We've got to get after 'em!"

"They imitated your writing pretty well, Tom," Observed Ned, as he looked at the forged note.

"Yes; that's why they took all my papers away from me—to get specimens of my handwriting. I half suspected that, but I didn't quite figure out what their game was. Well, we know the worst now, and that's better than working in the dark. Now I'm going to have a bath and get into some decent clothes, and we'll see what we can do."

"Count on me, Tom!" exclaimed Ned. "I'll go the limit with you!"

"I knew you would, old man!"

"And me, too!" cried Mr. Damon. "Bless my open fireplace, but I'll send word to my wife that I'm not coming home tonight, and we can start the first thing in the morning, Tom."

"Yes; there isn't much use in going now, as it will soon be dark."

"How are you going to trace the tank, Tom?" asked Ned, when his chum had bathed and gotten into fresh clothes.

"I'm going to tour the country around here in an auto. The tank can make ten miles an hour, but that's nothing to what an auto can do. And we oughtn't to have much trouble in tracing her. No one whose house she passed would forget her in a hurry."

"That's so," agreed Ned. "But if they took her across country—"

"A different story," agreed Tom. "Come to think of it, maybe we'd better start tonight, Ned. We can make inquiries after dark as well as by daylight and get ready for an early morning hunt"

"Let's do it, then!" suggested his chum. "I'm ready. I'll send word that I'll not be home tonight."

"Good!" cried the young inventor. "We'll have an old-fashioned hunt after our enemies, Ned!"

"And don't leave me out!" begged Mr. Damon. Hurried preparations were made for the night trip. Tom ordered out one of his speediest, though not largest, automobiles, and told his helper to get the Hawk ready, to have her so she could start at a moment's notice if needed.

"You're not going in her, are you, Tom?" asked Ned.

"I may need her to-morrow for daylight hunting. If the tank's hidden somewhere, I can spot her from above more easily than from the ground. So if we get any trace of my machine, I can phone in and have the aeroplane brought to me."

"That's a good idea!"

Inquiry at the shop where the tank had been built and kept disclosed the fact that, in addition to Koku, three of Tom's men had gone in her to help manage the machine under the direction of the man who bore the forged note. That he was one of the plotters not hitherto observed by either Ned or Tom seemed certain.

"And they took Koku and some of the men merely to make it look natural and as if it were all right," Tom said. "Naturally that deceived my father, who thought, of course, that I was waiting for the machine. Well, it was a slick trick, Ned, but we may fool them yet."

"I hope so, Tom."

Night had fully fallen when Tom, Ned, and Mr. Damon started away in the touring car.

Out onto the road rolled the automobile. During the little daylight that had remained after his arrival at home and following the discovery of the loss of the tank Tom and Ned had traced it, by the marks of the big steel caterpillar belts, to the main road. It had gone along that some distance, just how far could not be said.

"But by using the searchlight of the auto we can trace her as long as they keep her on the road," said Tom. "After that we'll have to trust to luck, and to what inquiries we can make."

The touring car carried a powerful lamp, and by its gleams it was easy to trace for a time the progress of the ponderous tank. There was no need to make inquiries of persons living along the way, though once or twice Tom did get out to ask, confirming the fact that the big machine had rumbled past in a direction away from the Swift home.

"I had an idea they might have doubled on their tracks for a time, and backed her up just to fool us," Tom said. "They might do that, keeping her in the same tracks."

But this, evidently, had not been done, and the tank was making good speed away from the Swift Louse. They kept up the search until about midnight, and then a heavy rain began just before they reached a point where several roads branched.

"Luck's with them!" exclaimed Tom. "This will wash away the marks, and we'll have to go it blind. Might as well put up here for the night," he added, as they came to a village hotel.

It was evident that little more could be done in the rain and darkness, and there was danger of over-running the trail of the tank if they kept on. So they turned in at the hotel and got what little rest they could in their anxious state of minds.

Tom tried to be cheerful and to look for the best, but it was hard work. The tank was his pet invention, and, moreover, that her secrets should fall into the hands of the enemy and be used for Germany and against the United States eventually, made the young inventor feel that everything was going wrong.

The rain kept up all night, and this would make it correspondingly hard for them to pick up the trail in the morning.

"The only thing we can do is to make inquiries," decided Tom. "Fortunately, the tank can't easily be hidden."

They started off after an early breakfast. The roads were so muddy and wet that traveling was difficult and dangerous for the automobile, and they were disappointed in finding no one who had seen or heard the tank pass up to a point not far from the hotel where they had stayed overnight. From then on the big machine seemed to have disappeared.

"I know what they've done," Tom said, when noon came and they had found no trace of the ponderous war machine. "They've left the road and taken her cross country, and we can't find the spot where they did this because the rain has washed out the marks. Well, there's only one thing left to do."

"What's that?" asked Ned.

"Get the Hawk! In that we can look down and over a big extent of country. That's what I'll do—I'll phone for the airship. The rain is stopping, I think."

The rain did cease by the time one of Tom's men brought the speedy aircraft to the place named by the young inventor in his telephone message. There were still several hours of daylight left, and Tom counted on them to allow him to rise in the air and look down on the tanks possible hiding place.

"One thing's sure," he told Ned: "I know the limit of her speed, and she can't be farther off than at some place within a circle of about one hundred and twenty-five miles from my house. And it's in the direction we're in. So if I circle around up above, I may spot her."

"I hope so," murmured Ned.

It was arranged that Mr. Damon should take the automobile back, with Tom's mechanician in it, and Tom and Ned would scout around in the aircraft, which carried only two.

"You ought to have a machine gun with you, Tom, if you plan to attack those fellows to get back the tank," Ned said.

"Oh, I don't imagine I'll need it," he said. "Anyhow, a machine gun wouldn't be of much effect against the tank. And they can't fire on us, for there wasn't any ammunition for the guns in Tank A, unless they got some of their own, and I hardly believe they'd do that. I'll take a chance, anyhow."

And so the search from the air began. It was disappointing at first. Around and around circled Tom and Ned, their eyes peering eagerly down from the heights for a sight of the tank, possibly hidden in some little-known ravine or gully.

Back and forth, like a speck in the sky, Tom guided the Hawk, while Ned took observation after observation with the binoculars.

At last, when the low-sinking sun gave warning that night would soon be upon them, Ned's glasses picked up something on the ground far below that made him sit suddenly straighter in his seat.

"What is it?" asked Tom through the speaking apparatus, feeling the movement on the part of his chum.

"I see something down there, Tom," was the answer. "It doesn't look like the tank, and yet it doesn't look as a clump of trees and bushes ought to look. Have a peep yourself. It's just beyond that river, against the side of the hill—a lonesome place, too."

Tom took the glasses while Ned assumed control of the Hawk, there being a dual system for operating and steering her.

No sooner had the young inventor got the focus on what Ned had indicated than he gave a cry.

"What is it?" asked the young bank clerk.

"Camouflaged!" cried Tom, and without stopping to explain what he meant, he handed the binoculars back to Ned and began to guide the Hawk down toward the earth at high speed.

FOILED

"Is it really Tank A, Tom?" cried Ned, through the tube, as soon as he became aware of his companion's intention. "Are you sure?"

"That's the girl, and just where you spotted her with the glasses—in that clump of bushes. But they've daubed her with green and brown paint—camouflaged her, so to speak— until she looks like part of the landscape. What made you suspicious of that particular place?"

"The green was such a bright one in contrast to the rest of the foliage around it.',

"That's what struck me," Tom answered, as he continued to drive the Hawk earthward. "They thought they were doing a smart trick—imitating the tactics of the Allies with their tanks—but they must be color blind."

Ned took another observation through the glasses. He could see the tank more easily now. There she was, fairly well hidden in a clump of bushes and small trees on the banks of a river, about a hundred miles away from Shopton. It was in a wild and desolate country, and only with the airship could the trail have thus been followed.

Ned saw that the tank had been daubed with green, yellow, and brown paint, in fantastic blotches, to make the big machine blend with the foliage; and, to a certain extent, this had been accomplished.

But, as Ned had remarked, the green used was of too vivid a hue. No natural tree put forth leaves like that, and the glass had further revealed the error.

"Look, Tom!" suddenly cried Ned. "She's moving!"

"You're right!" answered the young inventor. "They've seen us and are trying to get away."

"But they can't beat your airship, Tom."

"I know that. But their game—Oh, Ned, they're going to wreck her!" cried Tom, and there was anguish in his voice.

As the two looked down from their seats In the Hawk they saw the tank, in its fantastic dress of splotchy paint, leave her lair amid the bushes and trees, and head toward the river. Like some ponderous prehistoric monster about to take a drink, she careened her way toward the stream, which, at this point, ran between high banks.

"What's the game?" cried Ned.

"They're going to send her to smash!" cried Tom. "She's pretty tough, Tom, but she'll never stand a tumble down into the river without breaking a lot of machinery inside her."

"But if they demolish the tank they'll kill themselves, won't they? And Koku and your men, too, who must be prisoners in her!"

"They won't risk their own worthless hides, you may be sure of that!" exclaimed Tom.

"There they go, but they must have left Koku and the others to their fate!"

"Oh, if they could only get loose and take control now, Tom, they'd save your tank for you!" shouted Ned.

"Yes; but they can't, I'm afraid. They may be killed, or so securely bound that they can't get loose!"

"Can't you get the Hawk there in time to stop her?"

"I'm afraid not. By that time she'll have attained top speed and it would be taking our lives in our bands to try to make a flying jump, get inside, and shut off the motors."

"Then the tank's got to smash!" said Ned gloomily.

Tom did not answer for a moment. He and his chum watched the fleeing figures running away from the war engine. What the plotters had done, as soon as they saw the aircraft and realized that Tom had discovered them, was to start the motors and leap from the tank, closing the doors after them. Whether or not they had left Koku and the others prisoners inside remained to be seen.

But the tank was plunging her way toward the steep bank of the river, doomed, it seemed, to great damage, if not to destruction.

"Oh, if we could only halt her!" murmured Ned.

Tom Swift was busy with some apparatus on the Hawk. Ned heard the hum of an electric motor which was connected with the engine, and there soon sounded the crackle of the wireless.

"What are you doing? Signaling for help from those inside the tank?" asked Ned, for the big machine was fitted to receive and send messages of this sort

"I'm trying something more desperate than that," Tom answered.

Again the wireless crackled, Tom working it with one hand while, with the other, he guided the aircraft. Ned looked downward with wondering eyes.

The tank was still plunging her way toward the steep bank of the river. If she tumbled down this, there would be little left of the expensive and complicated machinery inside.

"The rascals did their work well," mused Ned. "They've probably gotten all the secrets they want and now they're going to spoil all Tom's hard work. It's a shame! If only—"

Ned ceased his musing. Something was taking place down below that he could not explain. The tank seemed to be slackening her progress. More and more slowly she approached the edge of the cliff.

"Tom! Tom!" yelled Ned. "You must have waked some of them up inside and they've thrown the motors out of gear! Hurrah! She's stopping!"

"I believe she is!" yelled Tom. "Oh, if it only works!"

The tank was still moving, though more slowly. Still the crackle of the wireless was heard.

And then, just as Tom shut off his own motor and let the Hawk glide on her downward way in a volplane to earth, the great, ponderous tank came to a stop, on the very edge of the precipice at the foot of which rolled the river.

"Whew!" whistled Ned, as the aircraft rolled along the ground near the war machine. "That was touch and go, Tom! They stopped her just in time."

"You mean the wireless stopped her," said Tom quietly. "I'm very much afraid that if Koku and the others are alive they're still prisoners in the craft."

"The wireless!" gasped Ned, as he and his chum got out of the Hawk. "Do you mean that you stopped her by wireless, Tom?"

"That's what I did. It was a desperate chance, but I took it. I had just installed in the tank a system of wireless control, so she could be guided as some torpedos and submarines are, by wireless impulses from the shore.

"Only I'd never given the tank system a tryout. It was all installed, and had worked perfectly on the small model I constructed. And when I saw her running away, out of control as she was, I realized the wireless was the only thing that would stop her, if that would. It might operate just opposite to what I wanted, though, and increase her speed."

"But I took the chance. I set the airship wireless current to working, and tuned it in to coincide with the control of the tank. Then, by means of the wireless impulse I shut off the motors, which can he stopped or started by hand or by electricity. I shut 'em off."

"And only just in time!" cried Ned. "Whew, Tom Swift, but that was a close call!"

"I realize that myself!" said the young inventor. "This is a new idea and has to be worked out further for our newer tanks."

"Gee!" ejaculated Ned. "Out of date before got into use! Now let's see about our friends!"

It was the work of but a moment to enter the tank, and, after making sure that the machinery was all right, Tom and Ned made their way to the interior. In one of the smallest rooms they found Koku and the others bound with ropes, and in a bad way. Koku was so tied with cords and hemp as to resemble a bale of Manilla cable.

"Cut 'em loose, Ned!" cried Tom, and the bonds were soon severed. Then came explanations.

As has been told, one of the plotters, whose identity was not learned until later, came with the forged note. The giant and Tom's men set out in the tank, and the machine was stopped at a certain place where the plotter, who gave the name of Crossleigh, told them Tom was to meet his men.

Out of ambush leaped Simpson and others, who overpowered the mechanics, even subduing Koku after a fierce fight, and then they took possession of the tank, making the others prisoners.

What happened after that could only be conjectured by Tom's men, for they were shut up in an inner room. It seemed certain, though, that the tank was taken to some secret place and there painted to resemble the verdure. Then she went on again, coming to rest where Tom and Ned saw hen

Meanwhile the plotters were gradually getting at the secrets of construction, and they were in the midst of this work when one of them saw the aeroplane. Rightly guessing what it portended, they left hurriedly, still leaving the hapless men bound, and started the tank on what they thought would be her last trip.

"But you saved her, Tom!" cried Ned. "You saved her with the wireless."

And word was sent back to Shopton by the same means to tell Mr. Swift, Mr. Damon, and the others that Tom and his tank were safe. And then, a little later, when the bound men had recovered the use of their cramped limbs, the tank was backed away from the ledge and started on her homeward way, Tom and Ned preceding her in the Hawk.

Without further incident, save a slight break which was soon repaired, Tank A soon reached her harbor again, and a double guard was posted about the shop.

"And they won't get much more chance to steal her secrets," said Tom that night, when the stories had been told.

"Why?" asked Ned.

"We start to dismantle her at once," Tom answered, "and she goes to England to be reproduced for France."

"If only those plotters haven't stolen the secrets," mused Ned.

But if they had they got little good of them. For shortly afterward government secret service agents rounded up the chief members of the gang, including Simpson and Blakeson. They, with Schwen, were sent to an internment camp for the period of the war, and enough information was obtained from them to disclose all the workings of the plot.

"It was just like lots of other stunts the German spies tried to put over on the good old U.S.A.," said Tom to Ned, the day after the dismantled tank was shipped to Great Britain. "In some way the spies found out what I was making, and then they got hold of Blakeson and Grinder. Those fellows, who so nearly queered me in the big tunnel game promised to make a tank that would beat those the British at first put out, and they took some German money in advance for doing it.

"When they found they couldn't make good, the German spies agreed to help them get possession of my secrets. They worked hard enough at it, too, but, thanks to you, Ned, and to Eradicate, who gave us the tip on Schwen, we beat 'em out"

"And so it's all over, Tom?"

"Yes, practically all over. I've given all my interests in the tank to Uncle Sam. It was the only way I could do my bit, at this time. But I've something else up my sleeve."

And those of you who care to learn what the young inventor next did may do so by reading the next volume of this series.

It was about a week after Tank A, as she was still officially called, had been shipped in sections that Ned Newton called at Tom's home. He found his chum, with a flower in his buttonhole, about to leave in his small runabout

"Oh, excuse me!" exclaimed Ned. "This is Wednesday night. I might have known. Give Mary my regards."

"I will," promised Tom, with a smile.